MOOD INDIGO

**Center Point
Large Print**

ॐ श्री गणेशाय नमः

MOOD INDIGO

A NOVEL BY

CHARLOTTE VALE ALLEN

CENTER POINT PUBLISHING
THORNDIKE, MAINE
USA

COMPASS PRESS
AUSTRALIA AND NEW ZEALAND

This Center Point Large Print edition
is published in the year 2000 by arrangement with
Charlotte Vale Allen.

This Compass Press edition is published in the year 2000
by Bolinda Publishing Pty Ltd., Tullamarine, Victoria,
Australia, by arrangement with Island Nation LLC.

The text of this Large Print edition is unabridged.
In other aspects, this book may vary from the original
edition. Printed in Thailand. Set in 16-point Plantin type
by Bill Coskrey.

US ISBN 1-58547-038-4
ANZ ISBN 1-74030-213-3

Library of Congress Cataloging-in-Publication Data

Allen, Charlotte Vale, 1941-
  Mood indigo / Charlotte Vale Allen.
    p. (large print) cm.
  ISBN 1-58547-038-4 (lib. bdg. : alk. paper)
    1. Women screenwriters--Fiction. 2. New York (N.Y.)--Fiction. 3. Large type
books. I. Title.

PS3551.L392 M66 2000
813'.54--dc21
                                                                00-038409

Australian Cataloging-in-Publication Data is available from the
National Library of Australia.

for Lynn Crosbie and Ziggy Lorenc
for reasons too numerous . . .

ACKNOWLEDGMENTS

Matthew Malowany did some much-appreciated work on the period research for this book, and Rita Vine's splendid library skills provided the medical information; Dina Watson and Lorraine Stanton offered valuable feedback during the writing of the manuscript; Beverley Endersby gave graciously of her time and her considerable editorial expertise; and a lot of people have been wonderfully supportive. Some of them are: Richard Saxl, Marc Silverman, Frank O'Meara, Virginia Valliere, Philomena Plunkett, Brooke Forbes, Judy Kern, Dianne Moggy, Pat Pelly, Susan Baldaro, Jocelyn O'Brien, Bob Cannon, Jay Davis, Angelo Rizacos, Rita Vine and Henry Mandelbaum, Nancy Phillips, and Cynthia and Michael Waldin. As always, I am indebted to my long-time companion, Walter Allen, and to our daughter, Kimberly, whose combined tolerance, caring, and encouragement are the mainstay that keeps my small ship afloat.

PROLOGUE

NOVEMBER 29TH 1934

SCENE:
Exterior Apartment Building—Night;
medium shot

DeeDee Carlson cannot believe this is happening to her. She is toppling backwards over the balcony railing of her fifteenth-floor apartment in the Ansonia, the skirt of her brand-new Mainbocher gown billowing around her. She reaches to grab hold of something, anything, but can't. There's nothing, nothing. And then she is falling, the air cold as she descends, a scream of anger and disbelief tearing from her throat as her body turns, then turns again.

Everything below comes into ever-sharper definition as she plummets closer and closer to the street: the shiny wet pavement, the hazy glow of streetlights; the automobiles and people moving below. Her arms flail frantically, attempting to alter the course of her flight. But to no effect. She is plunging, can't stop.

Directly below, near the corner of 73rd Street, is parked a Packard two-passenger convertible. If she doesn't manage to shift direction, she's going to land on it.

Close-up
This can't be happening, she keeps telling herself. Can't be. But it is. She's falling, faster and faster.

The street's rushing upward to meet her, and no matter how she twists about, she can do nothing to stop her descent.

She tells herself the soft top of the convertible will save her. She'll land as if onto a trampoline. It's canvas, after all. It'll be okay. The convertible roof's going to save her. She's not going to die. Luck's on her side.

Wide shot

But the impact is monstrous, unbelievable; a collision of terrific finality that drives all the air from her lungs so that she can't make a sound. Nor can she move. Her bones have turned to liquid. Her flesh is a soft, full bag of disconnected parts. And she hurts completely--no part of her body is exempt from it. She would never have believed you could feel such a totality of pain. But you can. She knows it now; feels it.

Close-up

Wearied, she blinks slowly once, twice, knowing she's going to die after all. Okay, okay, she thinks. Let's get it over with. Because it'll be better being dead than hurting this way. Humpty Dumpty, she thinks. That's rich!

And then her eyes close.

Cut.

December 5th. 1934

It was a Wednesday evening and, true to form, Mikhail came into the office where Honoria was just finishing work with Maybelle, to announce a desperate craving for lobster. "We go to eat!" he declared.

"We're in the middle of a snowstorm, Mick," Honoria said, with the merest hint of irritation, looking up from her notes and over to the window, where fat white flakes seemed to be flying past horizontally.

The unflappable Maybelle recrossed her legs and tapped her teeth with the eraser end of her pencil, following the exchange with interest. Ever since Honoria had gone off to Paris for a month's holiday two years earlier and returned home with not only a load of swell French clothes but a husband to boot, she and Mikhail had been, to Maybelle's mind, a lot like a movie show. You could walk in in the middle of the feature and get caught right up in the goings-on of the mysterious Russian and his clever, one-of-a-kind, New York-born wife.

From the get-go Maybelle could see how Honoria would find Mikhail attractive. He was a big, barrel-chested man, with dark hair, deep-set bedroom eyes, and a determined thrust to his chin. He positively radiated intent. Of course, if anyone knew

11

how to deal with intent, it was Honoria Barlow. Men had been giving her the glad eye, pursuing her nonstop, the entire five years Maybelle had been Honoria's girl-Friday, before Mikhail came along. Up to that point, Honoria had always been the type of woman who could take 'em or leave 'em. But go figure it. She fell for the massive Russian, and they were, to say the least, an odd match.

For one thing, Honoria had never been one to go drinking at the speaks. That wasn't her idea of a good time. Her passion was music and she'd get her dates to take her to the jazz clubs on Swing Street or maybe one of the Harlem hangouts like the Cotton Club. Maybelle had been checking coats at Small's Paradise uptown on Seventh Avenue when Honoria struck up a conversation with her one night while her date stood impatiently waiting, pointedly looking at his watch.

"I've got a hunch you'd rather be doing something else," Honoria had said, her eyes assessing. "Am I right?"

Afraid she was about to get dropped in the soup by a friendly-seeming rich white woman, Maybelle had replied with polite caution, "What makes you think that?"

"You're a bright girl and you're bored silly."

"It shows?" Maybelle asked anxiously.

"Only if somebody happens to take note of that kind of thing. And I do." Honoria winked, then smiled.

Seeing that devilish smile for the first time, Maybelle decided to take a chance and be honest.

"As a matter of fact, there's a whole lot of things I'd rather be doing," she'd confided quietly, offering a smile of her own. "Haven't had too much luck getting hired since I graduated last June."

"What's your name, dear?"

"Maybelle Robinson."

"And where did you graduate from?"

"Secretarial college."

Honoria smiled again, looking positively delighted for some reason. "Are you good, Maybelle?"

"You bet," Maybelle answered, not afraid to blow her own trumpet. "My last test, I typed eighty-eight words a minute; dictation was one-thirty."

"That's better than good. Have you got something to write with, dear?"

"Sure." Maybelle reached under the counter and came up with a pencil and a scrap of paper.

"My name's Honoria Barlow and this is my number. I'm at the Kenilworth, on Central Park West. It just so happens my girl quit a week ago and I need to replace her in the worst way."

"I'm not looking for domestic work." Maybelle was immediately, deeply disappointed, wondering when she was going to wise up and stop leaving herself open to getting hurt this way.

"Oh, I'm not looking for a maid. I thought I'd made that clear," Honoria said. "What I need very badly is a crack new secretary."

"What kind of business you in?" Maybelle asked suspiciously.

"Well, you could say I'm a medical practitioner of sorts." Again, that appealingly devilish smile, as if the woman was actually enjoying the conversation.

"You're a *doctor?*"

Honoria laughed—a big hearty sound. "Yup. A *script* doctor. Call me, Maybelle, and let's talk about the job."

"Okay. I will. Thank you, Miss Barlow."

"I mean it now. Call me!"

"I will. First thing tomorrow." Maybelle looked down at the phone number on the piece of paper, then watched the woman walk over to join her date, who was about to blow his stack. In no time flat, with a few whispered words, Honoria had the man calmed right down. Quite a lady! Maybelle had thought admiringly. Maybe she'd actually be willing to hire a colored secretary.

The next morning Maybelle phoned, halfway convinced the woman would claim no memory of their conversation the previous night. It had happened to Maybelle plenty of times before. But Honoria said, "Am I ever glad you called! I was afraid you might not. Come see me, Maybelle. I need help here and I don't mean maybe."

Beginning to believe in happy endings, Maybelle put on her best dress, the new cloche her best friend Alfreda had talked her into buying the week before, clean white gloves, and set off for her interview.

She stood outside for a good ten minutes getting her nerve up to walk into the fancy apartment building on Central Park West, and when she finally did, before she could say a word, the man on the desk was ordering her to go to the servants' entrance.

"Miss Barlow's expecting me," she interrupted him.

"You people use the other entrance," he insisted.

"Call her, please," she insisted right back, "and say Maybelle Robinson is here."

Muttering angrily under his breath, he picked up the phone. "There's a colored girl here to see you. Want I should send her to the servants' entrance?"

Gratifyingly, Maybelle heard Honoria begin barking, her voice audible even from several feet away. The man had turned very red in the face, said, "Yes, ma'am," and, after putting the receiver down, pointed Maybelle over to the elevator, where the young operator—a freckle-faced, red-haired kid of sixteen or so—had been waiting to see how it was going to go.

"You must be one important girl," he said with a kind of quiet excitement, once he'd closed the doors.

"That what it takes to ride in this elevator—importance?"

"Sure does. You're the first. That man won't let anyone colored in the front way. Which is why everybody working in this building hates Reilly. Treats people like dirt."

"But you don't, huh?"

"No, ma'am. I got enough trouble with Reilly myself, being Irish and a Catholic, and him being Irish

15

and a Protestant."

"You don't say." In the twenty years of her life, this was her first encounter with a white person who'd been on the receiving end of racism. "What's your name?" she asked, taking a liking to the kid.

"Cully. What's yours?"

"Maybelle. And, Cully, you're going to be riding me up and down in this elevator every day from now on."

"Well, if that don't beat all! How'd you swing that?"

"I'm going to be Miss Honoria Barlow's new secretary."

"I should've known," Cully said, slapping the heel of his hand to his forehead. "Miss Honey always gets her way."

"That what you call her?"

"Not to her face," the boy said, blushing, as he brought the cage to a stop and opened the door. "I wouldn't have the nerve. But she sure is one swell lady. And you're not so bad yourself, if you don't mind my saying. Bye for now, Maybelle," he said, with a grin and a two-fingered boy scout salute.

"You're a pistol, kid," Maybelle had said in parting, returning the salute.

Honoria had come to the door herself, offering her hand and apologizing for the treatment Maybelle had received downstairs. "The man's an idiot!" she'd fumed. "He won't make that mistake again, I promise you. Come on in, dear. We'll talk in the office. Ruth!" she'd called out, and a pleasant-looking, middle-aged woman poked her head out of the kitchen.

"What's up, dearie?" the woman asked. "I've got a pot on the boil here needs watching."

"This is Maybelle. We'll be in the office. Bring us some coffee, will you, please?"

"Right you are," Ruth said, and disappeared.

Honoria led the way to a good-sized room to the right of the reception hall that was, sure enough, fitted out as an office, with two desks, a row of filing cabinets against the far wall, and a pair of armchairs separated by a polished round table positioned in front of a window overlooking the street.

Honoria waved Maybelle into one of the armchairs and sank into the other, saying, "I hope you're a girl of your word, Maybelle. I'm up to my neck in scripts waiting to be typed. The fellas in Hollywood are screaming blue murder."

"Hollywood, really? And why would I lie about what I can and cannot do?" Maybelle said, looking around and wondering who paid for this swanky place. "You'd find out soon enough and then I'd look like one dumb Dora, wouldn't I?"

"Hollywood," Honoria had confirmed. "And I don't lie either. I take scripts with big problems and make them do-able. I work as hard as it takes and as long as it takes, and when I've got the thing licked, I dictate the changes. When those're typed up, I see how they play. You and I get to act out all the parts, see if the thing hangs together. If I think it does, we ship the rewrite back to California on

17

the next plane out."

"Sounds like fun. This your place?" Maybelle asked, and at once felt she'd crossed the line. She never had been able to keep her curiosity in check. Her grandma was always saying it would do her in one of these days.

"I pay the rent here, sweetheart." Honoria gave her another of those devilish smiles. "Not a single sugar daddy to my name. I think a girl ought to pay her own way."

"Me, too," Maybelle agreed. "I get the feeling," she ventured, "you're what my grandma calls a bleeding-heart liberal."

"Tell your grandma I am and I've got the scars on my chest to prove it."

Maybelle laughed hard.

"So, what's your dream, Maybelle?" Honoria had next asked.

"To put my education to good use and pay my own way. Not that the club doesn't pay. The money's pretty good. But you don't need a brain to put coats on hangers five or six hours a night."

"You sure don't," Honoria agreed emphatically as Ruth brought in the coffee. "I know how it is."

"You worked a coat-check?"

"Worse. I started out as a script girl for the Famous Players Film Company back in 1913. When it became the Famous Players-Lasky Corporation, I worked for them at the old Astoria Studio in Queens, eventually becoming one of their top screenwriters. They closed the studio temporarily in

18

1927 and started begging me to relocate to Hollywood. I'm a reasonable gal. I went out to take a look. There was no holly and nothing I consider wood."

Maybelle laughed again, and Honoria continued, "I decided it was time to stay put and take my chances freelancing. I needn't have worried. When sound came in, scripts suddenly became a whole lot more important and I had more work than I could handle. I've usually got two or three rewrites going simultaneously, which is why I need someone sharp to help me get them tightened up and back to the studios in time for the start of principal photography. You like movies, Maybelle?"

"Love them, except for westerns."

Honoria gave her an approving smile. "I think you and I are going to get along, dear."

They agreed in short order upon a month's trial, and Maybelle had started work that very afternoon.

Watching Maybelle's fingers dancing over the keyboard, Honoria had sighed with relief, and said, "Thank God."

"Amen to that," Maybelle had said without taking her eyes from the perfect Pittman she was transcribing from her steno pad.

At the beginning there were a few problems—like getting past Reilly, who harbored a grudge because of getting chewed out by Honoria that first afternoon and who went out of his way to be unpleasant—but from the start they were a good team. Maybelle had enormous respect for the way the woman's mind worked and, determined to do a good job, learned in no time at all to anticipate Honoria's needs.

At the end of the month's trial, Honoria had said, "I want you happy, Maybelle. I don't want you coming in one day to say you're leaving for more money somewhere else, so I'll give you top dollar right now, and regular raises. If there's anything wrong, or something you need, let me know. We're in this together, and I'd like it to be for the long haul."

"You can count on me, Honoria."

"I already do."

Eventually, Reilly was let go when he refused to allow a black man access to the building because, according to Reilly, "He talked funny. He wasn't dressed right and had no business here." As it happened, the oddly-dressed gentleman was a diplomat from Ethiopia who'd come to have dinner with his British counterpart who lived on the fourth floor. Within a matter of hours Reilly was gone, and Cully begged for a chance to take over Reilly's shift. Word got out and a majority of the tenants insisted he have that chance. Young Cully got a new uniform and took up his post behind the desk. At once the atmosphere downstairs improved dramatically. Cully was, as Honoria once put it, one of nature's noblemen. Now, more than six years later, most folks in the building said good day and even smiled at Maybelle as she crossed the lobby or rode the elevators. She loved getting up in the morning to come to work.

And for Honoria work was the joy and focus of her life. There was rarely a day without a phone call from some producer or director with a script scheduled to start shooting in five days, or a week. They always called at the last minute, frantic. Could Honoria please play doctor, put some of her special polish on the ailing thing in a big hurry, and save the project before it got scrapped. Oh, and by the way, there ought to be a kid at your door about now with the script in his hand.

Being a woman who couldn't resist a challenge, she'd drop what she was doing to read it right away and, unless the material was so bad there was no hope for it, she'd take it on—on top of the ones she already had going. She would put in eighteen or twenty hours at a stretch for three or four days, switching back and forth between scripts if she happened to get stalled, then dictated the rewrites to Maybelle, who'd type up the changes. Arrangements were made to ship off what was now a solid shooting script—for which some overpaid hack in Hollywood would get the screenwriting credit. And a week or two later, a very nice chunk of change would get wired to Honoria's bank account.

At first, Maybelle couldn't help asking, "Don't you mind not getting credit for your work?" And Honoria, with that smile that showed her nice healthy teeth, had replied, "I've got all the credit I need right there in those accounts you're balancing, dear. Fame is a mug's game. I'll take the do-re-mi any old time."

Every few months, she'd close up shop for a couple of weeks and refuse to answer the phone. "Time to recharge the old batteries," she'd announce, and go off bright and early one morning down to Book Row on Fourth Avenue to browse through the second-hand bookstores, particularly her favorites, the Arcadia Bookshop and the Strand. On the way home she'd stop at the Gotham Book Mart on West 47th Street to load up on the latest novels. Then, the newly acquired books stacked on the floor by the sofa, she'd curl up and read for eight or ten hours at a stretch, eating lunch from a tray and shifting only for fresh coffee or—since the burly Russian had come along—to dress for dinner.

Mikhail, though, didn't work at all—which wasn't so unusual nowadays with former big-wigs standing shamefaced in breadlines—yet he seemed to have a limitless supply of dough. There was a tailor Mikhail kept very happy; a shirtmaker and a custom shoemaker too. Everything the man put on his back was the best of the best. And Maybelle knew he wasn't freeloading off Honoria, because Maybelle kept the books and she'd have known. So the question was: Where did he get his money?

Big Mick had a lot of meetings—usually with theatrical types and usually at places like the Players or "21" or the Friar's Club—but about what was anyone's guess. With an acceptance that was remarkably atypical of the woman Maybelle had come to know very well over the years, Honoria seemed

22

content to go along with most of what her husband did. Oh, now and then, she put the kibosh on getting all dolled up to go out to hit the high spots, insisting they spend a quiet night at home. But for the most part, she seemed to think the man could do no wrong.

Maybelle had her suspicions. She actually liked Mikhail—it was hard not to; he had a playful side and was unfailingly polite to her and Ruth; to everyone, in fact—but something about him just wasn't right. She was convinced the whole thing with him and Honoria was about sex, and Maybelle was quietly, patiently, watching; waiting to kill the man if he hurt her employer in any way, or for Honoria to get back into her right mind. And it seemed likely she was bound to do the latter some time soon now. Honoria might complain when a delivery boy showed up with another script in desperate need of her doctoring skills, but she didn't mean it. She could hardly wait to get started, and once she had she hated interruptions. But for two years now Mikhail had been barging into the office, without so much as a by-your-leave, to demand that she drop everything and go out with him. And Honoria's tolerance was plainly beginning to wear thin.

"Is nothing," Mikhail said now, with a dismissing wave of one large hand. "A little snow. Nothing."

Before he could begin to tell them about *real* snow—familiar tales of Siberian blizzards and temperatures so low that one's exhalations froze solid and fell to the ground in tiny, tinkling fragments—

23

Honoria sighed and said, "Okay, okay. It's *nothing*. And I'm hungry, so we'll go. Want to come with us, May?"

"I'll pass, thanks." Knowing full well she and Honoria would put in extra hours tomorrow to make up for the time they'd be losing this evening, Maybelle closed her pad, tucked the pencil behind her ear, and went to put the cover on the Underwood.

"Okay. We'll drop you off at the subway on our way."

"I'd appreciate that," Maybelle said, offering Big Mick a smile as she went to get her things.

Grumbling under her breath, wondering why she kept on letting herself be persuaded to do things she categorically didn't want to do, Honoria marked her place in the rewrites and put aside her notes. Not bothering to change clothes, she popped into the kitchen to let Ruth know they were going out, then she bundled up in her old raccoon coat and pulled on galoshes, a hat, a muffler and gloves, while Mikhail's concession to the weather consisted of swapping his silk scarf for a woolen one and pulling on a pair of hand-stitched, cashmere-lined leather gloves. At last they made their way down to the garage.

Mikhail was a good driver and, knowing how edgy it made Honoria to be out in conditions like this, he piloted the Cadillac along the slippery streets at a cautious speed. They dropped Maybelle at the west-side IRT station at 59th Street before making their way downtown and over the bridge to Gage & Tollner in Brooklyn—one of Mikhail's favorite restaurants.

The trip took far longer than usual, and leaving the car parked half-on half-off the sidewalk—"Easier to drive away when we are coming back," he explained with typically illogical logic—they pushed inside to see that, despite the weather, the vast dining room with its mirrored walls and gaslit cut-glass chandeliers was almost full. Close to two hundred people sat indulging in the seafood concoctions for which the place was renowned. Mikhail was positively swollen with anticipation, appreciatively inhaling the fragrant air as the maître d' hurried to greet them. But his first words were not the usual, "So good to see you," but, "Your housekeeper wants you to call home right away, Mrs. Beliakof. If you'll come with me, the telephone is just over here."

The pair exchanged a bemused look, then followed the man to the telephone.

"What's happened, Ruth?" Honoria asked anxiously when the housekeeper answered.

"Chip Stevenson phoned must be an hour ago and said I was to get in touch with you at once."

"Chip?"

"That's right, dearie. He said to tell you he's been arrested and would you come, please, to bail him out."

"*Arrested?*" Honoria couldn't imagine Chip doing anything worse than leaving his rattletrap DeSoto in a no-parking zone. "What on earth for?"

Ruth's voice dropped a notch lower. "Murder," she said with an almost audible shudder.

Honoria shook her head, unable to fathom this. "That's crazy! Chip wouldn't hurt a fly. It's got to be a mistake. Where is he?" she asked, looking at Mikhail, who was watching her intently as she listened to the housekeeper. "All right. Let me think a minute. Okay. Call Leonard Rosen please, Ruth. His number's in my book on the desk. Tell him what you've just told me, and ask him to meet us downtown. We'll leave right away, but warn him it may take us a while to get back into the city."

"Okay, Miss Honor. I'll do that."

"Who is arrested?" Mikhail asked the instant she cradled the receiver.

"Chip Stevenson." *Murder? Chip? Impossible.* Yet she felt a cold clutch low in her belly.

The burly man scoffed. "Chip? What does he do, cross street on red light?"

"I'll tell you in the car." She signaled to the maître d', who came over at once. "There's a family emergency. I'm afraid we have to leave."

Mikhail's eyes fixed on a waiter going past with a laden tray. So much lovely food and he wasn't going to get any.

"I don't suppose you've got something ready we could take with us?" Honoria asked the maître d', taking pity on poor Mick, who was never without an appetite—of one sort or another.

"Five minutes," the man said, also aware of Beliakof's prodigious appetite, not to mention the size

26

of his tips. "I'll find something."

"Such a smart woman," Mikhail congratulated her. "I would never think of this."

"Ah," she said affectionately, "but you think of other, such interesting, things."

"This is true," he agreed after a moment—possibly spent translating.

She put her arm through his and leaned against him, worried about Chip. The poor kid was probably scared to death.

Ten minutes later they were in the car again, inching their way back toward Manhattan through rapidly accumulating snow while Honoria passed large peeled shrimp to Mikhail, now and then taking one for herself.

"Keep your eyes on the road, Mick," she warned, "or we'll spend the night in a snow bank."

"He gives us bread at least?" he asked rather plaintively, a man whose hunger couldn't begin to be sated by a couple of dozen boiled shrimp without even any cocktail sauce.

"He did." She broke a crusty roll, reached across, and popped a piece into his mouth, then sat back, saying, "Chip wouldn't hurt a flea. He's the all-American Joe College." And why would he use his one call to phone her instead of his father? Well, she knew the answer to that. Charles Senior would immediately assume Chip was somehow in the wrong.

"Is probably mistake," Mikhail agreed. "What more is in bag?"

Keeping her eyes on what little she could see of

the road, she felt around, coming up with another roll. "This is it," she said, passing it to him. "Sorry, Mick."

"Is not your fault," he said magnanimously. But she didn't hear him, worried by the very idea of Chip in the lock-up.

TWO

Exhausted, scared, and profoundly sad, Chip sat on a hard bench, waiting. There was a temporary lull. The detectives who'd arrested him had been summoned to their lieutenant's office and they were in there now, with the door closed. Having been assured that there was nothing he could do, Mick had gone to wait outside in the car. And Aunt Honey, after giving Chip a reassuring hug, had promised to be "Back in a tick," and was standing a short way down the hall, talking in undertones to the lawyer who had arrived nearly an hour earlier. A well-dressed, soft-spoken man whose rather sorrowful eyes seemed to miss nothing and whose aura was one of wisdom with a slow-simmering anger beneath, Mr. Rosen had had a quick chat with Chip before informing the detectives that his client would answer no further questions. Insisting that the young man be permitted to leave the smoky interrogation room, the lawyer had moved Chip out to the bench in the hallway, telling him the charges were groundless and that he'd be free to go shortly. "Sit tight, Charles, and don't say another word to

28

anyone unless I'm with you. From now on, leave everything to me."

Gratefully, Chip had said, "Yes, sir. Thank you very much." And he'd done precisely what the lawyer had requested: He had remained silent, waiting.

At twenty Charles Stevenson Junior looked perhaps sixteen or seventeen, with thick, side-parted dark hair; very clear, wide-set blue eyes; and features so well formed and symmetrical that he had an almost angelic aspect. At that moment he was pale, with smudges of fatigue discoloring the flesh beneath his eyes. He was slight and slim, and had a sensitivity that could not be concealed. He was someone who fretted about the possible meaning of chance remarks, of stray glances, of the way people stood or held their heads, of whether a direct gaze was a challenge or an insult. He was alert to innuendo, prepared to be hurt for reasons he knew he wouldn't comprehend. Experience thus far had taught him caution, and he exercised it vigilantly with the majority of people he met because often the nicest-seeming souls turned out to be anything but nice.

When he lay down to sleep at night, no matter how tired he might be, his mind seemed to click on instead of off, to begin reviewing the highs and lows of the day, the whys of the often mystifying behavior he encountered. As a result, it took him ages to get to sleep at night, so it was difficult to get up in the morning, and even more difficult to assimilate what was being taught in his classes. He didn't really come awake until mid-morning, with the result that his grades in the afternoon's courses were higher than those in the morning's. It was only the difference between As and B-pluses—nothing that would prevent him from graduating at the end of the next semester—but those two B-plus grades worried him too. They could conceivably hold him back when it came to competing for what few jobs were available. Not that he really would have to work once he graduated, but he wanted to.

After he turned twenty-one next August, if he chose to he could spend the rest of his life reading, going to movies, or listening to music; he could while away the summer watching baseball games and tennis matches, traveling to warm places for the winter months, or taking extended trips to exotic places. His mother had left the bulk of her estate to him—which had not pleased the rest of the family, particularly his father, who during the past five years had periodically predicted that Chip would fall for some clinging vine who'd take him for every last cent of his inheritance before leaving him high and dry. Then, when he learned that Chip was seeing DeeDee, instead of being glad that his prediction was unlikely to come to pass—given that she had a substantial inheritance of her own—his father had started wondering aloud how long it would take her to give Chip the gate. "No girl's going to stick around for long with a young man who has so little to recommend him."

DeeDee had been great, though. "Don't let him get you down, Chip darling," she'd told him upon hearing what Charles Senior had said. "We've got each other and that's what counts. Besides, it's not as if we're going to have to live with your father or anything."

Chip had been nuts about DeeDee, and didn't know how he'd managed to function in the week since she'd died. But somehow he had. Probably because he still couldn't believe she was gone forever, that he was never going to hear her voice on the telephone, never going to see or touch her again. It was an unbearable prospect. He'd lost the girl he loved. And just when he'd thought things couldn't get worse, two policemen had arrested him for her murder as he'd climbed from his car outside the funeral parlor late that afternoon. So he'd missed the funeral and the opportunity to say good-bye, in any fashion, to DeeDee.

From the arrest until now had been a bizarre period, along the lines of the alarming German-language novels by Franz Kafka that his philosophy professor had loaned him from his personal collection. Chip had read three of them that semester with the help of a German–English dictionary, fascinated and repelled by the incomprehensibility of the nightmarish worlds populated by persistent, absurdly hopeful heroes. And now he was living out what could well have been another Kafka novel, or maybe one of the truly terrible photoplays the Hollywood people sent Aunt Honey from time to time.

31

In would come one so godawful that she'd gather together whoever was around, saying, "You've *got* to hear this!" and then she'd read it aloud, hamming it up and sending everyone into fits.

Nothing the two detectives had accused him of made any sense. And when he'd finally remembered that he had the right to make a phone call, the older detective wasn't going to allow it. But, Johnson, the younger one, had said, "Better let the kid make his call, Spinoza." There ensued a brief argument between the two, and Chip knew from years of hearing Aunt Honey read aloud from bad scripts that the two men were acting out an unconvincing good guy-bad guy routine. But the performance ended when Spinoza abruptly went silent in mid-sentence. His face contorting, he'd pressed a hand into his sternum (Chip couldn't help wondering apprehensively if the man was about to keel over dead of a heart attack, and later could only wish that he had) before simultaneously emitting a noisy belch and and an even noisier fart.

The script, Chip thought, had taken a disgusting but interesting turn. He'd never read of any cop routine remotely like this one, and, breathing through his mouth, he watched, fascinated as Spinoza next lit several wooden matches one after another, dropping them, still burning, into the ashtray. The detective then stomped out, saying, "Gotta see a man about a dog, JJ. Take over, willya. I'll be back in five."

The instant he was gone, Johnson grabbed a newspaper from the table and began frantically fanning the air, saying, as if to himself, "Seven months being the guy's partner and I'm *never* gonna get used to this. It's all that dago red and garlic he eats." Abandoning his effort to clear the air, he said, "C'mon, kid. Let's get outta here. Pay phone's outside."

"Why are you doing this to me?" Chip quietly asked the reasonable-seeming Johnson as they stepped out into the considerably fresher air of the corridor.

Matter-of-factly, Johnson said, "Because Spinoza's got the idea you sent your girlfriend to the boneyard."

"But I loved DeeDee. I'd never have hurt her."

Johnson merely shrugged, as if the matter was of no consequence to him, one way or another. "There's the phone. Make your call. I'll be right here, waiting." He leaned against the far wall, pulled a dime novel with a lurid cover from his pocket and began reading as Chip found a nickel and tried, with trembling fingers, to fit it into the phone's slot.

Now, his stomach in knots and his mind reeling at the absurdity of the situation, he watched Honoria—his touchstone of sanity—as she and the lawyer conversed.

Chip had always considered her beautiful—not movie-star glamorous, all artful polish and unattainability, but something better, more real. She was a startling woman, even though she was getting on for forty. At five-six or so, she had a classic hourglass figure: generous breasts, a small waist,

33

and rounded hips. Her glossy black hair was cut precisely to her jawline, with bangs that fell to the tops of her eyebrows, framing gold-brown eyes that sometimes emitted a warm glow and other times seem to shoot off sparks. She had a squarish jaw and cleft chin, a strong straight nose, and a wide mouth. Her eyes were kohl-darkened; her eyebrows meticulously plucked into thin arches; mascara made her eyelashes look long and thick, and to emphasize the purity of her complexion she wore pale, almost white, face powder with vivid red lipstick; never even a hint of rouge.

Her clothes were invariably black or dark gray, simple but very smart; her legs were absolutely sensational; and when she walked into a room (even a police station) people sat up and took notice. There was something about her, a kind of fizzing energy that drew attention and also intimidated, even sometimes alienated, a lot of people, particularly his father, who for reasons not explained disliked her and had never made a secret of it. Of course, Charles Stevenson also disliked his son, and had made no secret of that, either. It only served to deepen Chip's devotion to Honoria, to make him feel more related to her than to his own father.

She had been his mother's best friend, and for most of his life Chip had wondered if his father's enmity hadn't perhaps grown out of jealousy, because no one was ever closer to his mother than Honoria. They'd met as young girls, although Chip couldn't quite remember how or where that meeting took place, or if he ever knew. What he did know was that Honoria was the one person in the world his mother was always happy to see, no matter the circumstances. "I hope you have a friend like that someday, Charlie," his mother had said often through the years. "Someone you can call at three in the morning and say, 'I've got a bad case of the blues,' and without skipping a beat he or she will say, 'Sit tight, dear. I'm on my way.' "

One of his strongest memories was of being perhaps four years old, having lunch at Schrafft's with his mother and her friend. He remembered very clearly their warmth, and the sound of their laughter. Watching them that day he understood for the first time how dearly the two women loved each other, and he was glad of it, because he also understood that, regardless of how busy she was with the family and with entertaining his father's clients, regardless of how readily she smiled to hide it, his mother was lonely. Never before had it occurred to him that grown-ups could feel the same things small children did, but that afternoon he knew that he and his mother shared similar feelings—about all kinds of things, the first being their love of Honoria, and the second their loneliness. When they saw Honoria she brought them the revitalizing gift of her caring and enthusiasm.

By the age of eight, when he was able to travel around town on his own, he'd call on the telephone and ask if he could come visit. Aunt Honey would set a day and time and he'd take the bus uptown to her cozy old apartment on East 73rd Street. When he arrived, she'd throw open the door and greet him all smiles, towing him inside, saying, "Charlie, my darling! Guess what we're going to do today!"

She dreamed up something new for every visit. They'd go skating at the Iceland Rink, or for a day-long excursion up the Hudson River on the *Alexander Hamilton,* or to see a movie at the Roxy, or Loew's State, or the Paramount. She took him to Chinatown for lunch and taught him how to use chopsticks; she introduced him to baseball and every summer took him at least half a dozen times to the Bronx to eat hot dogs and peanuts while rooting for the Yankees. Honoria had introduced him to almost everything he loved most about the city of his birth. And in the process she became inextricably a part of all of them in his mind. For a time when he was twelve, he actually wanted to marry her. It was, however, a brief phase. Yet she was, in many ways, the epitome of everything female that he admired.

When his mother got so terribly, suddenly sick and died five years ago—less than six weeks from start to finish; the most horrific experience of his life until last week—his two sisters and brother stuck like glue to their father, turning to him for answers to all their questions. But the then fifteen-and-a-half-year-old Chip had automatically sought out Honoria, and she was there to the very end to give whatever he or his mother needed. Aside from his mother, Aunt Honey was the only adult he knew who couldn't be bulldozed by Charles Stevenson.

So when they arrested Chip and carted him to the station house, he used his one phone call to get in touch with Honoria. She would, he knew, get the whole mess sorted out.

"This stinks to high heaven and they know it," a disgusted Leonard Rosen was telling Honoria. "They've haven't got a thing on the boy that'd get them anywhere near a grand jury. The charge'll be dismissed and we'll have him out of here as soon as O'Herlihy finishes reading the riot act to those two prime examples of the species Boobus Americanus."

"Why bring Chip in if they have nothing on him?" a bemused Honoria asked her old friend and one-time lover.

"The only explanation I can think of is that someone higher up is putting pressure on the commissioner and, according to nature's law, it's trickling down. For some reason, they want this case closed, and fast. Chip's prints were all over the apartment, and he's got no alibi for the night in question. Ergo: he's a murderer. Except that Chip had no motive to kill the girl. And fingerprints alone don't make a case. He admits he visited the Carlson girl the previous weekend. So, naturally, his prints turned up—along with several dozen other people's, most of whom they haven't identified. Of course, Mutt and Jeff in there are claiming they've got a witness who saw somebody on the balcony with the girl shortly before she went over. But it turns out their so-called witness can't say whether it was a male or female, or even if it was the right apartment. It was raining and foggy that night. Hard to imagine how their 'witness' could see anything at all, let alone two people—from beneath yet—fifteen stories up. Oh, yes indeed. That'll hold lots of water. Believe me, Honoria. O'Herlihy will straighten out his boys, and that'll be the end of it."

"Was the girl murdered, Leonard?" she asked, wondering why Chip had never mentioned his involvement with DeeDee Carlson. It was unlike him to be secretive. "The *Herald-Tribune* reported it as a suicide."

"So did the *Post* and the *Daily News*. But you and I both know what's published in the daily papers isn't necessarily the full story, or even an accurate one. It's just what the hack on the scene was told, or surmised. The fact is there's no way to tell whether the girl was pushed or if she jumped—unless Norris or one of his examiners found something in the autopsy we don't know about."

"Is that possible?"

"Oh, sure. The medical examiner's office could be sitting on a damning piece of physical evidence. But if that were the case, those two cretins would've used it to keep our boy in the lock-up." He shook his head. "They haven't got a thing," he repeated, lifting his cuff to check the time. "Any minute now we'll be calling it a day and heading home."

Honoria put a hand on his arm, saying, "I can always count on you to pull the fat out of the fire,

Leonard. You're a treasure and I love you dearly."

"I love you, too, you know." Leonard's gaze was suddenly melancholy.

Seeing this, Honoria was stricken to realize that the long-term affair she'd assumed to be mutually casual had been anything but. Leonard had actually been serious about her. Why hadn't he ever let her know the true extent of his feelings? Things might have been very, very different. Still, it was too late now. "Leonard," she began, wishing they could go somewhere and have a quiet talk over a drink or two. "I don't know what to say."

Recovering himself, he smiled and took hold of her hand. "Unfortunately," he said good-naturedly, "while I was sitting back, complacently considering you a sure thing, the meshuggenah Russki beat my time. The last thing in the world I expected was you coming back from a few weeks' holiday with a husband in tow."

"You don't have a complacent bone in your body. And are you calling my better half crazy, Leonard?" she asked, following his lead and keep things light.

"Never. Anyway, how could I compete with a guy twice my size and half my age?"

"You haven't been lying to me all these years about your age, have you, Len?" She feigned shock—they'd kibitzed their way through more than ten years and it seemed unlikely, even somehow impossible, that they would stop now. She wasn't sure she'd be able to handle it if matters were to turn serious between them at this particular juncture.

"Okay, so he's a couple of years younger," Leonard allowed. "That doesn't mean I wouldn't have given him a run for his money, if I'd known . . . But hey, never mind."

"You're a confirmed bachelor, and you know it."

"Confirmed has such a Catholic ring to it, don't you think? How can something Catholic possibly apply to a nice forty-one-year-old Jewish guy who grew up down on Hester Street?"

She laughed and kissed his cheek.

"Just remember," he whispered. "Things ever change with the Russki, I'll be around."

Touched, she started to reply when O'Herlihy threw open his office door and stood to one side as the two disgruntled detectives hurried past him and made their way out of the station house. Then the beleaguered-looking lieutenant stepped into the doorway saying, "The kid can go, Rosen. The charge against him's dropped. But advise him not to leave town. This isn't over yet."

"Oh, come on, Dan. Don't play games. Chip's got to drive back to New Haven first thing in the morning. Admit you've got nothing and let's be done with this, please."

"Okay, okay. The kid can go back to college."

At this, Honoria gave Leonard's hand a squeeze and turned to smile over at Chip, who was sitting, his head down, and failed to see.

"Just between us," Leonard said quietly, "why'd your boys pull him in? You knew you had nothing on him."

The harried cop rubbed his eyes with his fists, then sighed and said, "Look what I've got to work with here—a couple of clowns, for chrissake. We're so short on manpower it's laughable. All the best guys are in the breadlines, Len. I'm stuck with either softies like Jackson who gets sick at the sight of a body, or guys like Spinoza who're just putting in time till retirement and do everything by rote." He sighed again and said, "Tell the kid I'm sorry."

"Do me a favor, Dan, and tell him yourself. He missed his girlfriend's funeral because of this nonsense."

O'Herlihy thought about it for a moment, then shrugged and said, "Yeah, sure. Why not?"

The baggy-eyed, balding officer walked over to the bench to talk to Chip. He spoke a few words, gave Chip's shoulder a fatherly pat, then turned and came back. He nodded soberly at Honoria as he said, "Sorry about the whole thing, ma'am." Finally, he shook Leonard's hand and headed back into his office, saying to no one in particular, "No wonder I got bleedin' goddam ulcers."

THREE

"You'll spend the night with us, Chip," Honoria told him before he could ask.

Very relieved, he thanked her. "I was dreading the thought of going home, and I'm not up to trying to drive back to New Haven tonight."

"Does your father know about your arrest?"

41

"No, and I don't intend to tell him. Unless I have to."

"I doubt you'll have to at this point," Leonard said. "It's highly unlikely they'll charge you again."

"I still can't figure out why they hauled me in in the first place."

"That makes two of us," Len said.

"Oh, cripes!" Chip remembered. "My car's still parked uptown, outside the funeral parlor."

"You and I will go get it," Honoria said, slipping one arm through his, the other through Leonard's. "Could I talk you into coming back with us for something to eat, Len?"

"I think I'll take a rain check, grab a cab and head home. It's been a long day and I'm in court first thing in the morning."

"Let's talk tomorrow and make a definite date to get together," she said. "It's been too long and I've missed you."

"Ditto, and you're on. Well, so much for hailing a cab," he said as they stepped outside into a white, muffled world where nothing seemed to be moving except the steadily falling snow.

"Mick will give you a lift home, Len. He loves driving in this weather, the worse the better. He claims it reminds him of his childhood. Personally, I think he just likes having the roads all to himself. Come on."

"It's out of his way," said the lawyer, for some reason reluctant to find himself alone with the man she'd married. He scarcely knew Mikhail, had met him only a couple of times, but there was something about him that rubbed Len the wrong way. Aside from the obvious sexual attraction, he couldn't figure out what Honoria saw in the big lummox.

Honoria smiled and shook her head. "Bad argument. Matter of fact, it's a bad line altogether, coming from one of the best defense attorneys around." She opened the passenger door of the Cadillac and bent in to say, "You don't mind giving Len a ride home while Chip and I go get his car, do you, Mick?"

"Come, Len," the big man beckoned. "I am happy to take you."

"There you go," Honoria said, standing aside so that Leonard could climb into the car. "Oh, and don't worry, Mick. I phoned Ruth and told her to whip up some dinner."

"You are a genius woman!" Grinning, and in a hurry after spending more than an hour waiting in the car, Mikhail was already pulling away from the curb before Leonard had managed to get the door fully closed. Leonard looked as if he'd just been conned into stepping into one of those tilted rooms at a funhouse as he pulled the door shut and gave an uncertain good-bye wave.

Honoria said, "Better him than me," again slipping her arm through Chip's as they set off for the subway station. "Isn't this beautiful!" she said, looking up into the dizzying swirl of falling snow. "I love the city best when a snowstorm shuts everything down and only a few intrepid souls venture out of doors to marvel at the transformation."

"It is beautiful," Chip agreed with automatic politeness, his brain like a dried pea rattling around in an empty enamel basin. The events of the past week had drained his vital juices, leaving him feeling aged and enervated.

Once on the subway platform, where only two other people were waiting some distance away, she affected a neutral tone, asking, "Was there some reason you didn't tell me you were seeing the girl, Chip?"

"I don't know," he said tiredly, gazing off into the tunnel; a bare-headed, handsome young man in a navy Brooks Brothers topcoat with a blue and white Yale scarf wound around his neck, who shouldn't have had a care in the world. "Are you sore at me that I didn't?"

"Of course not. I'm a bit surprised and maybe the tiniest bit hurt, because you and I have never kept secrets from each other. But then, I guess it's time I accepted the fact you're not a kid anymore, and there's no reason for you to tell me every last thing you do."

"I was planning to tell you," he said guiltily because in fact this was the first time he'd ever withheld anything from her. Usually, good news or bad, he made a beeline to her door or to the nearest phone to tell her. All his life, she'd been the mirror up to which he'd held his successes and failures, his joys and woes, his never-distant worries. And she'd responded with accurate images and just the right measures of approval or advice. The things he'd never been able to discuss with his mother he'd taken to Honoria's doorstep. And upon his being invited over the threshold, she had examined his concerns as if they actually were of consequence. "But I guess I was scared I might jinx a good thing by talking about it."

"And was it a good thing?" she asked, reading the depth of misery in his eyes and wishing she had the power to make things okay again for him. Of everyone in the world, she loved this young man most. He was sweet and decent, and blessed with a rare and wonderful strain of natural enthusiasm, meeting almost every situation with an open mind. He was kind, and intrinsically gentle, but with a solid streak of pragmatism he'd inherited from his mother that saved him from being a pushover. When Chip took a stand he was immovable.

Eyes brimming, unable to speak, he nodded.

"Poor baby," she sympathized. Judging from appearances, the two kids had been lovers. And whatever it might have been for DeeDee Carlson, it was definitely an initiation for Chip into the down-in-the-dumps one day, on-top-of-the-world the next, rigged game of chance called love. Putting an arm around his shoulders, she drew him close. "You fell hard for her, huh?"

He nodded again, the tears spilling over, and let his head rest on her shoulder. He'd never in his life been so utterly miserable.

"I'm so sorry, sweetheart," she said, giving him

her handkerchief. "What a lousy break."

They rode in silence, from long habit holding hands, each looking at nothing in particular in the near-empty carriage as the train raced uptown. They didn't speak again until they were back on the street, making their way up Lexington Avenue through the thick snow.

"I was getting ready to ask DeeDee to marry me," he confessed in a rush. "I'd even picked out the ring at Tiffany's. I was going to propose to her on Christmas eve."

"Wasn't that kind of fast, Chip? How long had you known her anyway?"

"We met at a Halloween party, and we'd been dating almost two months. And what was so fast about it? You married Mikhail after only a couple of *weeks*."

"Ouch! That's kind of a low blow, kiddo."

"I'm sorry," he said a little angrily. "It's the truth, though, isn't it?"

"Baldly put, but yes. I met and married the man inside three weeks. But I wasn't twenty years old, and I'd been around the block a time or two. How many girls've you dated?"

"Not a lot," he admitted. "I know I'm young, but I'm no dope. It was the real thing, Honoria."

"I'm not debating that, *Charles*. I'm merely trying to put the pieces together."

"Look, I don't want to fight—especially not with you. I really was planning to tell you. I was just waiting for the right moment."

"And when was that going to be, d'you think?" she asked, her tone curious and non-accusing.

"I intended to tell you last week. But then . . ." His statement trailed off and they walked on saying nothing further for another minute or so. "There's the car." He pointed out the old DeSoto which was hidden beneath a good ten inches of snow.

"Hope you've got a shovel," she said wryly. "Can you drive in this stuff? Or are you a holy terror like Mick?"

"I've got a broom *and* a shovel, and this old girl and I can drive through just about anything." He held open the door for her, then ran around to slide behind the wheel. "Here goes nothing," he said, and turned the key in the ignition. The engine gave a dry cough. "Come on now, Clementine," he coaxed. "Don't let me down now. That'd be the last straw." He gave it some gas and the engine caught, turning over noisily. "Thatta girl!" He gave the dashboard a pat, then turned to Honoria, saying, "You sit tight and stay warm, while I get the snow cleared off. It'll only take a minute. Then we'll be on our way."

To his credit, he didn't misrepresent his ability. He kept both hands on the wheel, drove at a sedate fifteen miles an hour, and seemed in complete control of the car.

"What did you love about DeeDee, Chip?" she asked after a minute or two. "Tell me about the girl."

"She was loads of fun, had tons of energy, and was always on the go. Don't get me wrong, though. She was no featherhead. She was smart, and she'd paid

47

some dues." He glanced over, then returned his eyes to the road. "Her dad got clobbered on Black Tuesday, and killed himself a couple of weeks later. DeeDee and her mother had a tough time of it."

"An awful lot of people did and still are."

"Yeah, I know. What about you, Aunt Honey? Did you take a beating, too? Or am I out of line, asking something so personal?"

"Not at all. I didn't get hurt because I didn't catch the fever. The market scared me. I've always believed you shouldn't play unless you're prepared to lose, and I wasn't willing to risk what I've worked so hard to get. And the more everyone I knew invested, telling their brokers to buy buy buy, the more of a hunch I had that something was going to go wrong. Too many people buying on margin, getting rich on paper, spending like there was going to be no tomorrow. It was a house of straw, and one good wind was going to blow it away. Not me, said the third little pig. I had everything carefully socked away in my sturdy little house of brick."

"You were smart."

"Cautious," she corrected him. "I'm simply not greedy. Tell me more about DeeDee," she prompted.

"She was small and blonde," he said, starting to choke up again. "Remind me later and I'll show you some photos I've got in my overnighter. She was no cover girl, but she was special. Now she's dead and buried. And I wasn't at the funeral, didn't even have a chance to say good-bye . . . I just don't *get* it! I

48

mean, how can all this be happening? First they said it was suicide—which I knew was out of the question. Then they come along and arrest me for killing her. As if I'd *do* such a thing to the girl I loved. None of it makes any *sense*."

"You're sure she wouldn't have taken her own life?"

"Not a chance!" he insisted. "She'd just got that swell new apartment at the Ansonia, and she was busy with the decorators; she was running here and there, getting paint and fabric samples, visiting furniture showrooms and antiques shops. Plus we had plans for Christmas. She was *happy*, Aunt Honey. *Happy* people *don't* jump off *balconies*." He wiped his face on his sleeve, the movement causing the car to lurch, but he quickly righted it.

"No, they don't," she agreed as they pulled up in front of the Kenilworth. "They certainly don't."

"I need to know what really happened," he said, putting the shift into neutral. "Maybe you could help me find out."

"I don't see how."

"You know everybody. You could ask around."

"Sweetheart, if the police can't figure out the circumstances of DeeDee's death, what makes you think I could?"

"You saw those two guys. They couldn't find water if they were on a raft in the middle of Long Island Sound."

She emitted a low laugh and said, "That's a good one. I might steal it."

49

"Feel free. Could we at least talk some more about it?" he begged.

"No harm in talking."

"When?" he persisted.

"Sometime before you head back to school. Okay?"

"Okay. And thanks for coming through for me."

She leaned across the seat and kissed his cheek. "I'll always come through for you, Charlie. No matter what."

It was after eleven. Chip was in bed, in the pajamas he kept, along with several changes of clothes, in the guest room. When he was in the city, more often than not he stayed here rather than at home. Since his mother's death he hadn't felt welcome in the apartment with his father. And his sisters and brother seemed indifferent. Hands folded under his head, he lay staring at the ceiling, trying not to think of DeeDee in a coffin, when Honoria knocked at the guest-room door and came in to say good night.

"How are you doing, sweetheart?" she asked, perching on the side of the bed. He'd scarcely spoken during dinner and had eaten very little. She knew he'd probably be awake half the night, worrying.

"Worn out. But as usual, I can't drop off."

With one long, cool hand she smoothed the hair back from his forehead. "Your poor brain's running overtime again. Want warm milk or something?"

He made a face, and she laughed. "I know. I'd like

to meet whoever decided milk—hot or cold—was a good idea."

"Who named you Honoria, your mother or your father?" he asked out of the blue. "I've always wondered about that. It's such an unusual name."

"Actually, it was Sister Anne, at the Foundling Asylum."

"The Foundling Asylum? You're an *orphan?*" He sat up, eyes wide.

"Unh-hunh."

"I never knew that," he said, shocked and queasy with sudden guilt—the feeling that he should have known and should, somehow, have been able to make amends.

"I assumed you did, that your mother told you long, long ago," she said, wondering why Vanessa had neglected to tell him. Perhaps she hadn't considered it important—which would've been typical of Van. Origins had never been as important to her as character.

"I had no idea."

"About the name," she said, taking his hand and holding it between both her own. "I was left on the proverbial doorstep with a piece of paper pinned to my blanket that said 'What is left when honor is lost?' When I was five or six Sister Anne explained that it was a translation from a Latin maxim of Publilius Syrus, and it proved to her satisfaction that I'd had at least one well-educated parent. She was a romantic soul, Sister Anne, and she decided to name me Honoria the very day I was abandoned.

'You'll never be lost, my girl,' she said. 'Not with such a fine name to live up to.' And she was absolutely right. With a moniker like mine, you either wear it proudly or you give up the fight and become 'Honey' to all and sundry forever." With a smile, she said, "While I've never minded being your Aunt Honey, I'm pretty proud of the name the good sisters gave me."

Sitting up against the headboard, he said, "Now I'm very confused. I thought you and my mother met when you were little girls."

"We did—at the Church of St. Vincent Ferrer, which is just two blocks from the Sisters of Charity at Lexington and 68th. There were only a handful of us who weren't boarded out for one reason or another, and the Sisters took a group of us to Mass every Sunday. Your grandmother was there each week with your mother and her two brothers."

"But none of you were Catholic." He scratched his forehead and sat back against the headboard.

"I was for the first dozen years of my life, and your grandmother was, too, although she took the children to Mass strictly against her husband's wishes. For my part, I just liked the church, and the break in routine, the chance once a week to look at people other than orphans or nurses and nuns. And there's a statue of the Fatima Madonna I've always loved. I still go to Mass there now and then, although not too often lately. Ritual can be very reassuring, you know, sweetheart, and there's something about the specifics of ecclesial architecture that helps me put things into perspective."

"That's interesting," he said thoughtfully. "I'll have to go have another look at that church. Mother used to take me sometimes, back before Lizzy and the others were born. But, wait a minute. If Sister Anne named you, where did your surname come from?"

"The note on the blanket was signed 'R. Barlow.' "

"That's all, nothing else?"

"Nope."

"You saw it?"

"I've still got it."

"Gosh! What a sad story."

"No, it isn't, Chip. Life—as the cliché goes—really is what you make of it. Better than a third of the babies left at the Asylum died. I was one of the lucky, healthy, babies. And a family is whatever you've got, growing up. You accept the status quo until you're old enough to recognize that other people don't live the way you do. The Sisters were caring and kind, and they taught me to be independent and strong. They made me appreciate by example the results of hard work. They fed and sheltered me, saw that I got an education—which is a lot more than so many other kids got. When I was eleven I started going to the Children's Aid Society to learn typing and bookkeeping. By the time I was thirteen, I had a full-time job and was living on my own in a boarding house in the Village. I've paid my own way ever since."

"That's remarkable. I'm very proud of you."

"Thank you. I'm proud of you."

"So, my timing's crummy and I know it's a heck of a lot to ask, but will you do it for me?"

"Do what, sweetheart?"

"See if you can find out what really happened to DeeDee."

"Chip, I'm not a detective. If you're determined to get answers, maybe you should think about hiring one."

"But you could ask around, maybe talk to her maid, to her girlfriends, and some of her neighbors in the Ansonia. Find out if anyone saw or heard anything."

"Let me think about it," she hedged, very reluctant to agree to this.

He reached over, picked up two photographs from the bedside table, and handed them to her. "That's DeeDee," he said thickly, tears clotting his long eyelashes.

The first was a candid snapshot of an attractive little blonde in a very stylish, very expensive day dress. The second was a professionally done headshot, and Honoria sat for some time studying it, trying to pin down the reason for her instant and thoroughly negative reaction to the face on the glossy stock. DeeDee Carlson offered the camera the face of a smiling young woman with good skin and pretty features. But the eyes were oddly colorless and as relentlessly cold as the outside air buffeting the bedroom window. "How old did you say she was, sweetheart?"

"Twenty-four."

"Naughty boy," Honoria teased, still studying the photograph, "dating an older woman."

"Only three and a half years older."

More like three and a half decades, she thought, bothered all at once by a number of things, primarily the question of what possible attraction Chip could have had for a young woman with ice-water eyes. He was the sort of innocent fellow she'd have eaten up in one sitting; then she'd have made a show of using his bones to pick her teeth while laughing about him with her friends.

Returning the candid snapshot to the bedside table, she kept the other, saying, "Tell you what. No guarantees, but I'll go on a little fishing expedition. So if you don't mind, I'll hang on to this photo."

Immediately grateful, he quickly said, "I don't mind a bit. I've got others, if you want them."

"This'll do. No guarantees," she repeated. "Got that?"

"Got it."

"Good. Maybe before you go you could give me the names and numbers of some of her friends."

"Sure. And I've got a set of keys to the apartment."

"They're not going to let me in just because I've got your keys."

"Use my name, and they will."

"Why is that?"

He flushed but didn't look away. "I was staying there over Thanksgiving. And my umh, my name's

55

on the lease."

"Were you paying her rent?"

"Only half."

"Did you co-sign the lease?"

"No. It was in DeeDee's name."

That was a relief, she thought. "All right. I'll take the keys and have a look around, although I doubt there'll be anything to see. Now you try to get some sleep. Okay?"

He slid down in the bed and, from long-standing habit, she settled the blankets over him, then kissed him goodnight.

"Charlie is my darling," she whispered.

"I love you, too, Aunt Honey."

"Just, please, don't expect any miracles. Okay? I may come up empty-handed."

"I know. But thanks for trying."

"Only for you, sweetheart. Only for you."

FOUR

Honoria stood in the darkened living room and looked out the window at the snow that seemed to be flying in all directions at once—the world transformed into the microcosmic interior of an old paperweight—and for the first time in years she took a recollective trip through the Asylum: the ground floor of the original building with its offices, reception rooms and parlors for visitors, the community room, and an apartment for the resident physician; the second story with the apartments for the Sisters, and the sewing and linen rooms; the third, fourth, and fifth floors of dormitories for the children; and the infirmary on the top floor. On either side of the main structure were the ward buildings, each three stories high above the basement, with corridors that connected all the buildings. On 69th Street was the two-story structure that housed the laundry, a steam drying room, an ironry, and the large kitchen. In the basement of this building was an ice-vault, storerooms, engineer's rooms, and coal-bins. The west side of the second story contained the sleeping apartments for the laundresses and servants, and the entire eastern side was the quarantine wing. Under the north end of the chapel building was the mortuary. She knew every inch of the entire complex by the time she was ten, and was secretly drawn time and again to the nurseries, each with its sixteen iron cribs and sixteen iron bedsteads—each crib accommodating two infants, each bed a nurse; and to the mortuary, where sometimes as many as eighty small corpses lay still and blue in the cool depths.

She knew the bathing rooms with the French tubs that, instead of having faucets, let the water flow in under a lip; she knew the location of the drop for soiled clothing, and that of the dumb-waiter from the kitchen; she pictured the play-room with its organ; the kitchen with the two large copper boilers, one holding twenty-five gallons of milk, the other containing thirty gallons of bread and milk; the school room with its piano; the sections of Quarantine: six braying toddlers with whooping cough in one room; nine ghostly children in the Syphilitic Ward; sick and dying children grouped according to ailment.

She could still, so clearly, remember the baggy flannel drawers she'd worn under starch-stiff plaid pinafores and check blouses, the colored sashes tied around her waist; the tight, ribbon-bound braids into which her hair was briskly bound each morning by the red, roughened hands of a Sister or one of the nurses. Bread and butter for breakfast, roast beef for dinner, bread and milk for supper.

Since the city contributed a daily sum for the maintenance of every child, each infant was registered upon arrival and, if it was put out to nurse, the name of the nurse, along with other particulars, was entered in the register. Special accounts were kept for the children who were placed out to nurse (thereby giving employment to nearly a thousand poor women), and the accounts and records were meticulously kept by Sister Maria. The Asylum rule was that they would never take more than one child from the same mother, and they tried to encourage mothers to remain at the Asylum with their babies. Failing that, the Sisters made an effort to return as many children as possible to their parents, claiming that there was no child that could not, from its first arrival, be traced. With a few exceptions. R. Barlow was never located. And Sister Anne had a special fondness for the child, so the little girl was permitted to stay—a rare, slightly older child among so many helpless babies and toddlers.

There were several dozen rather unhappy women in residence with their babies—some years the number rose to over a hundred. The little girl watched them with great interest, deciding very early that, much as she loved the Sisters and many of the nurses, she would never be one of those unhappy women who brought their babies to such a place. Sister Maria once told an inquisitive Honoria that in 1896, the year when she was left there, the Asylum dealt with eight hundred and ninety-eight children, roughly fifty-five percent of whom were female. Twenty-five were placed out for adoption, one hundred and eighty-one were returned to their parents or guardians, four were transferred to other institutions, three were otherwise discharged, and four hundred and six died—of diphtheria, syphilis, marasmus (wasting away), pulmonary disorders, prematurity, convulsions, tuberculosis, tubercular meningitis, spasm of the glottis, catarrhal laryngitis, and general struma (goiters or swelling of organs). Score upon score of dead children; two hundred and seventy-nine surviving new residents.

But into the middle of her preoccupation with *infant mortality*—words the Sisters spoke often and with great concern—there appeared Vanessa. An inordinately healthy, grinning imp of a pampered child smiling across the pews each Sunday, eventually hanging back to have whispered conversations with the ever-curious child of the nuns while the Sisters shepherded their charges from the church and while the redoubtable Grandmother paused to talk to her equally redoubtable friends.

"What's your name? How old are you? I'm nine. Do you live with the Sisters? Do you like it there? I'm Vanessa. I live at 220 East 71st. Can you come visit me sometime?"

"My name is Honoria and I'm seven. I love the Sisters—not all of them, but mostly. I'll ask Sister Anne. When should I come, if I get permission?"

Twenty-six years later, her dearest friend lay in a hospital bed with the flesh almost visibly evaporating from her bones by the hour—marasmus, that wicked wasting sickness not easily forgotten—an almost unrecognizable skeletal creature clutching Honoria's hand with a final surge of strength, pleading, "Look after Charlie, Honor. Don't let Charles destroy him."

I will, you know I will. Rest now, rest.

A pair of well-muscled arms slid around her waist and she was enveloped in the overpowering warmth that was Mikhail.

"What do you do in the dark?" he murmured, lips beside her ear.

"Just reminiscing."

"About what?"

"This and that, ancient history." She continued to gaze out into the mesmerizing swirl of snow.

"Come to bed." From behind, his body fitted itself to hers, large hands rising up over her breasts as his mouth dropped to the side of her neck—taking immediate physical possession. He was a wall of solid flesh in a silk dressing gown.

He'd done precisely this that first night in Paris when he'd escorted her back to her hotel room: swarmed over her like a conquering army staking claim to another kingdom's treasures. The breath had leaked from her lungs, her brain had short-circuited, and every joint in her body had turned to liquid.

"Come to bed," he repeated, one hand smoothing her breast, the other stroking down her belly, creating a tremor that rippled outward from beneath the traveling pressure.

She wondered now, as she had two years ago in Paris, if it was a matter of age, if the resistance she'd spend a lifetime perfecting had begun to deteriorate; if she was weakening, losing her nerve after so many years of taking pleasure where she would but never, ever, putting her freedom at risk. What was this lusty foreigner of vague independent means doing here in her home, in her bed, taking up such a lot of space and attention? How the *hell* had this happened? Who was this man who every few weeks gave her an envelope stuffed with cash—sometimes four or five hundred, sometimes as much as a thousand—saying, as he did, "For the house. You take." And, bemused, yet satisfied by his insistence on contributing his more than fair share, she accepted the envelopes and placed them intact in the steel lock box that lived on the floor in a dark corner of her closet.

An involuntary twitch of pleasure as his two hands began pressing, probing, and her body heat started to soar. Dangerous to be so readily victim-

61

ized by desire. And what on earth had happened to her sense of propriety? Standing spread-legged and gasping in front of the window, pinioned by a level of appetite that was positively unseemly. Ruth could walk in. Or Chip. But she didn't want to alter the pitch by moving to the bedroom, didn't want to lose the accelerating beat that was as insistent as that of the young drummer she'd seen in a club a couple of weeks earlier who had thrashed and battered an unrelentingly demented rhythm through a thirty-two-bar solo that had left her sweating.

Blinded now by the swirling snow and the hands working their way under her clothes, she succumbed, accommodating, bracing herself against the window ledge. Her breath created a frosty circle on the glass that expanded and contracted as the air huffed from her lungs. At last she closed her eyes, out of control, her hands gripping the cold ledge while the Russian applied himself like a skilled surgeon to the examination of her body and groaned strange endearments, breathless words of affectionate praise, perhaps even love. Who could say? There were so many kinds of love, after all, so many degrees. Lust, too, contained moments of appreciation that were closely akin to love.

Early the next morning, after Chip had gone and Mikhail was finishing his usual gigantic breakfast—three eggs, six strips of bacon, a heap of home fries, four pieces of toast with jam, and half a dozen cups of coffee—Honoria ate a piece of toast and drank a cup of black coffee. His table manners were European, and it was actually pleasant to watch the fastidious fashion with which he used his knife and fork.

"I must be away again for a day or two," he said, finally aligning his utensils in the center of his clean plate.

"Oh?" she responded, accustomed now to these irregular absences. Every six or eight weeks, he would announce that he was going and, with no more than half an hour's or an hour's notice, he would depart, carrying a small leather valise. "Are you leaving after breakfast?"

He looked at his wristwatch and said, "Yes. Are you angry at this?"

"No," she answered truthfully, actually appreciative of these brief separations. "I promised Chip I'd ask around, see if I can learn anything about the girl's death."

Mikhail frowned. "Is not good idea," he said. "Why do you say you will do this?"

"There's no harm in asking," she disagreed.

"Could be a lot of harm. Why do you do this?" he asked again.

"Because Chip asked me to and I said I would."

"Be careful for me," he said softly. "Okay?"

She gave him one of her most devilish smiles and said, "Will you worry about me, Mick?"

To her surprise, he said soberly, "I will worry."

A short while later, when he was leaving, he kissed her good-bye, then held her close, again saying, "Be careful."

"You too, Mick."

She stood in the doorway and waited until he stepped into the elevator. She waved; he blew her a kiss, and the doors slid closed. Glad to have the apartment to herself for a day or two, and guilty at being glad, she took a deep breath and shut the apartment door.

"The plan is we'll wrap up these two and turn down anything new for, say, two weeks." Honoria drank some coffee, put the cup down, and returned to the newspaper.

"And you're single-handedly going to play detective?" Maybelle asked with slightly narrowed, disbelieving eyes.

As she paged through the *Times*, Honoria said, "I promised Chip I'd nose around a little, talk to the maid, some of the girl's friends and neighbors. He left me some names and numbers and a set of keys, so I'll take a look at the apartment, although I very much doubt I'll find anything there. I don't think Hauptmann's guilty, do you? I think it's the same thing as this business with Chip, but on a grander scale. They wanted to hang the baby's kidnapping on someone, and fast, so they landed on this guy. It smells bad to me."

"I don't know. He had a criminal record in Germany."

"But for small-time stuff—receiving stolen goods and petty larceny. Well, how about this? Harlow's filed for divorce again. She charges that Mr. Rossen sat up late reading in her room, thereby preventing her from 'obtaining sufficient sleep to enable her to do her best at the studios.' Poor kid has rotten taste in men. This is her third husband and she's, what, twenty-three?"

"It's pathetic. The maid's not going to talk to you, Honoria. Leastwise, she's not going to tell you anything."

"But she'll talk to you, is that it?"

"I guarantee it."

"You're proposing to join me in this? Oh, now, here's a shocker. The new van Druten play bombed in London. Ran less than two weeks. It must be a real stinker. Surprising. *The Distaff Side* was damned good."

"Let's put it this way," Maybelle went on doggedly. "There's no way on God's green earth I'm letting you play lady flatfoot alone. If that girl was murdered, there's a killer out there doesn't want anyone nosing around. So, let's get these two scripts finished, and then the *two of us* will start asking questions."

"You're thinking this'll be the all-female version of *The Thin Man*." Honoria's mouthed curved into one of her wicked smiles.

"Might could be." Maybelle tapped the eraser end of her pencil against her thumbnail, silently daring Honoria to refuse. "So, now, how're you going to get people to talk to you?"

Honoria stared at her for a long moment, the newspaper forgotten. "I hadn't even thought about that," she said. "How *am* I? *Who* am I?"

Maybelle chewed on her pencil, thinking, then asked, "You still got that press pass your sports writer buddy at the *Daily News* got you so you and Chip could go to the World Series two years back?"

"Somewhere," Honoria answered, as she started to search through her desk, smiling to herself at the memory of the great Babe pointing out the spot, then homering right to it off the Cubs' Charlie Root; Lou Gehrig hitting four homers in one game—she and Chip were hoarse from screaming. The best World Series ever.

"People *love* to talk to the press."

"That's true. They do. Here it is!" Honoria pulled the pass out from under a stack of miscellaneous programs.

"Good. So all you've got to do now is get another one of your buddies on another of the dailies to vouch for you if anybody decides to check. Then we're set to go out asking questions." She gazed meaningfully at her employer.

"Okay. We'll do it together," Honoria gave in, with the feeling that she was borrowing trouble, that she should've insisted on Chip's hiring a real detective.

Maybelle gave her boss a smile, then flipped open her steno pad, saying, "Let's get cracking on these rewrites, if we're going to get them out of here the day after tomorrow."

"I thought I might call on some of the people on Chip's list this evening."

"Fine. I'll just phone and let my grandma know I won't be over for supper."

"Are you sure about this?"

"Positive," Maybelle declared. "Sooner we get finished with this work, the sooner we can go calling on people."

"Okay, okay. Let me just find my notes."

"You're a sweetheart, Pete," Honoria was saying, wrapping up the call to one of her friends on the *Daily Mirror*. "If there's a story in it, I'll see to it the *Mirror* gets the scoop. I promise." She cradled the receiver and gave Maybelle a thumbs-up. "We're covered."

"Great. So where should we start?" Maybelle asked, coming to look over Honoria's shoulder at the list Chip had made.

"At the top, I suppose. Taffy MacDougall, best friend of the late DeeDee. What kind of name is Taffy, I ask you?"

"Sticky. Why don't I phone up, see if she'll give an interview to my boss?"

"Be my guest." Honoria propped her feet on the desk as Maybelle carried the telephone over to her desk, unhooked the receiver, dialed the number, then asked to speak to Miss MacDougall. She listened a moment, then said, "It's Miss Barlow's secretary . . . Thank you." Covering the mouthpiece with her hand, she said, "The maid. She's gone to get her."

"Coffee?" Honoria asked, lowering her feet to the floor.

"Love some, thanks. Ah, Miss MacDougall, I'm calling on behalf of Honoria Barlow . . . "

Honoria went to the kitchen, where Ruth was sitting at the table with a cup of tea, a just-lit Lucky, and the Amusements listings from that morning's *Times*. "Get you something, dearie?" the housekeeper asked.

"I'll help myself, thanks, Ruth," Honoria replied, opening the cupboard.

"If no one's eating in tonight, I thought I might take in *Flirtation Walk* at the Strand. I do love Dick Powell."

"Go right ahead. Maybelle and I will be heading out in a while ourselves."

"On the other hand, I could go to the Roxy to see Claudette Colbert in *Imitation of Life*. Or there's Fred and Ginger in *The Gay Divorcee* at the Palace."

With a laugh, Honoria said, "Time it right and you could probably see all three."

"There's a thought," Ruth said, checking the starting times.

"Enjoy yourself, dear," Honoria said, carrying the coffee back to the office.

"We're all set," Maybelle announced. "Miss Taffy MacDougall will see us at seven." She checked her watch, saying, "Want to try for two?"

"Sure." Honoria set the secretary's coffee on her desk, then moved to the window to look down at the slushy brown street below as she drank some of Ruth's powerful brew. "Who's next on the list?"

"Bunny Applegate."

"D'you suppose any of these girls have *real* names?"

"There's Fluff Connors and Bitsy Sayers. The last one's Minnie Morgan."

"Minnie's a real-enough name. What did Taffy sound like?"

"A rich white girl with a voice like a razor blade."

"Oh, dear." Honoria sighed.

"Wishing you'd said no to Chip?" Maybelle asked.

"In spades."

"It's not too late to beg off. You could call him in New Haven and say you've thought it over and it's just not a good idea. Which it isn't."

"What harm can come of it, really?" Honoria turned and leaned against the window ledge.

"Plenty," Maybelle said darkly. "Chip's off the hook. I say leave it alone."

"I gave him my word, May. I can't go back on that."

"You can, but you won't. I respect that, but it's not the smartest move you've ever made, Honoria."

"Might as well try Bunny. With luck, we can see all these girls in the next couple of days."

"And *then* you can call Chip and beg off."

"Maybe."

"You're the boss." Maybelle gulped down some of her coffee before reaching for the telephone.

FIVE

"Take a look at this and tell me what you think." Honoria passed over the studio head-shot of

69

DeeDee Carlson, then waited, struck, as always, by Maybelle's beauty. At twenty-seven, she had finally, firmly, grown into the finished version of herself. Tall and lean, with a splendid long neck supporting a well-shaped head, Maybelle carried herself with natural grace, and looked out at the world through a pair of enormous, very alert, liquid brown eyes. She had prominent, slanting cheekbones; a long, broad nose; exquisite full lips that concealed a mouthful of startlingly white, even teeth; and a firm pointed chin. Honoria liked to think of her as a princess of some innately aristocratic African tribe, and could readily picture Maybelle clad in a fabric wrap, necklaces of bone encircling her neck, with her hair—released from the prison of setting lotions and irons—a great curling black cloud framing her heart-shaped face.

"You're doing that thing again," Maybelle accused. "Staring at me."

"I enjoy staring at you," Honoria said matter-of-factly. "You're a knockout."

"Too bad you're the only one who thinks so."

"Oh, pooh! Let's not get into this argument again. You're wrong and I'm right, and that's that. So tell me what your first impression is of DeeDee." Honoria indicated the photograph.

"She *looks* okay at first glance, but the longer you look, the less okay she gets. Let's put it this way: I wouldn't have wanted to run into her at night in a dark alley. The woman had very scary eyes."

"My sentiments exactly. So the sixty-four-dollar

question is: What was she doing with Chip?"

"Beats hell out of me," Maybelle said. "One thing for sure, though. This little lady was in love with one person only—herself."

"Right again. So now we try to find out who did humanity a favor and tossed her off a balcony."

"This is going to be all kinds of fun, I don't think," Maybelle said with a laugh, returning the photograph.

The exterior of 635 Park Avenue had an unprepossessing air that gave no hint of the well-designed lavish interior. They were announced at the desk and then directed to the elevator, which ferried the two women to the fourth floor. There, they found themselves in the vestibule of an apartment that occupied the entire floor.

The door was opened by a butler—an increasingly rare sight these days—who, after taking their coats, said, with a pleasantly modulated English accent, "If you'd be kind enough to wait in the foyer, Miss MacDougall will be with you in a few moments."

The foyer was circular, and off it, ahead to the left, was the entry to a sizable formal dining room with a long table laid for dinner. An impressive drawing room was situated next to it, with a healthy fire crackling behind an ornate brass screen. And a cozy salon perhaps fourteen by eighteen lay directly to the right. Honoria guessed that the kitchen and pantry were located behind the right-hand wall of

71

the charming foyer. Both women stood taking in the elegant proportions of the rooms they could see, and the exquisite furnishings. Clearly the Mac-Dougall family had not suffered any serious set-backs as a result of the Crash.

"Quiet, isn't it?" Maybelle observed, looking first at the round antique oriental carpet with a pale blue background, then at the highly polished round mahogany table centered upon it and supporting an immense arrangement of fresh flowers.

"Like a tomb," Honoria replied. What she could see of the apartment looked like a spread in *House and Garden*, unlived in and too perfect. The only sign of human habitation was an umbrella that had been jammed wrong-side-up in a stand to one side of the closet door.

"Like a museum," Maybelle whispered, leaning forward to smell the flowers, disappointed to discover they gave off no perfume but only a damp, earthy scent.

"Sorry to keep you waiting," a high shrill voice called from the distance.

Honoria and Maybelle turned to watch the owner of the voice come down the hallway and cross the vestibule.

Taffy MacDougall was maybe an inch over five feet and dripping wet couldn't have weighed more than ninety pounds. Her small, thin body was clad in a long-sleeved, belted evening dress of rose crêpe that was skin-tight from the midriff to the knees, where it flared to the floor. It had a generous spray of silk flowers at the bodice, and over top was a sheer chiffon jacket whose flare of fabric matched that of the skirt bottom. No one older, or even five pounds heavier, could have worn the outfit. But she was young and pretty and it suited her perfectly.

"Swell dress," Honoria said, noting the engagement ring gracing the girl's delicate hand: three brilliant diamonds of better than a carat each, in a hefty platinum setting. She also wore what looked to be a pair of genuine ruby earrings, rimmed with small diamonds. Every last thing about the girl bespoke wealth.

"Isn't it just too-too divine?" Taffy agreed happily, performing a little pirouette that made the skirt fly away from trim ankles and tiny feet in high-heeled silk shoes dyed deep pink to match the dress. "It cost three months of my allowance, and Mummy hit the roof, but I just *had* to have it." Her turn completed, she offered her small limp hand to Honoria, in her grating voice saying, "Hi, I'm Laurette, but everyone calls me Taffy. Your maid can wait in the servants' hall while we talk. I'll get Norton to show her through," she said, ready to ring for the butler.

Instantly angry, Honoria contained it and said pleasantly, "I'm afraid you've got it backwards, Miss MacDougall. I'm Maybelle Robinson, Miss Barlow's assistant. We spoke on the phone, remember?" Turning to Maybelle, she asked, "Would you like me to wait in the servants' hall, Miss Barlow?"

"That won't be necessary," Maybelle said, falling

in with her employer's astounding but irresistible swap of identities. "I don't think we'll be staying." Maybelle looked down at the girl unforgivingly—a rare opportunity to allow her disdain to show. "Have Norton bring our coats, please."

"Oh, gosh! I'm sorry . . . I just assumed . . ." Taffy looked at Honoria, then back to Maybelle. "I had no idea . . . I mean . . . Oh, brother! I really put my foot into it, didn't I?"

"The problem with the world," Maybelle said evenly, in the manner of a teacher with limited patience, "is the vast number of people who make such assumptions. Our coats, if you don't mind."

"I really am sorry," Taffy insisted in her singularly irritating voice, rather admirably holding her ground and growing red in the face as she began to apologize in earnest to Maybelle. "Please don't go. I'm not . . . I didn't mean to be offensive. Honestly! Look, your assistant said"—a glance at Honoria for confirmation, then her eyes returned to Maybelle— "you wanted to talk about DeeDee's death for a newspaper piece, and I'd like to do that, because I absolutely do not believe she killed herself. It's not something DeeDee would *ever* have done!"

Maybelle looked pointedly at her watch, knowing that Honoria would abide by whatever decision she made, then said, "I suppose I can spare ten minutes."

"Please come into the drawing room," Taffy said, leading the way. "Could I have Norton get you or Miss Robinson a drink?"

"Not for me, thank you. My dear, would you care for anything?" Maybelle asked Honoria, who declined with a smile and a shake of her head, proud of the way her assistant was handling the situation. One thing about Maybelle, she was quick on the uptake.

"Please do sit down." Taffy waited until Honoria and Maybelle had seated themselves side by side on a white-on-white damask-covered settee. Then she perched carefully—the dress did not allow for easy movement—on the edge of a Queen Anne chair and watched with interest as Honoria dug around in her handbag for a notebook and her pen, asking, "Where do we start?"

"How well did you know DeeDee?" Maybelle asked, drawing the girl's rather ingenuous blue eyes over to her.

"Oh, intimately," Taffy said, touching one hand to the back of her shortish, finger-waved, caramel-colored hair—obviously the inspiration for her nickname. "We went to Miss Chapin's together. Our gang's been friends right from the first grade." Counting them off on her fingers, she said, "There was DeeDee and me, Bunny Applegate, Fluff Connors, Bitsy Sayers, and Minnie Morgan. Although Minnie didn't *really* fit with our crowd, her father being only an accountant and not even an executive, but DeeDee wanted her in so, naturally, the rest of us went along."

"DeeDee was the leader of your 'gang,' was she?" Maybelle asked with a hint of distaste.

"Oh, definitely," Taffy answered, oblivious to nuance. "She was *so* clever, and such fun. Everyone *adored* her. I just can't *believe* she's dead. It was such a terrible shock—for all of us. When I heard the news I fainted dead away. Mummy had to send for the doctor, I was so upset."

"Did she have any enemies?" Maybelle asked, following where the girl, and her own past reading of dime detective stories, led.

Taffy chewed on her upper lip, thinking, her eyes on the fire. "People were always *jealous* of her," she said, looking again at Maybelle. "But I wouldn't say she had *enemies*."

"What about boyfriends?"

"Oh, scads," Taffy said. "Scads and scads. She was terrifically popular. Boys were forever chasing after DeeDee, right from the fifth grade."

"Anybody in particular lately?"

"Well, she had been seeing a lot of this one boy, but the last time I saw her—which was only two days before she died; we were supposed to have lunch the next day but I had to cancel—anyway, she said she was thinking about breaking up with him."

"Do you happen to know his name?" Maybelle asked.

"Dick something. Whiting or Whitman. Something like that. She kept him very much to herself, didn't double and triple up, the way we usually do. So I only met him once, and that was by accident when the two of them were on their way out of El Morocco, and Doc—that's my beau—and I were on

76

our way in." Upon speaking her fiancé's name, she touched her engagement ring as if to make sure it was still there. "She seemed kind of miffed about running into us that way, to tell you the truth."

"It wasn't Chip Stevenson?"

"Chip?" Taffy smiled. "Oh, never. Chipper's an absolute pet and we all love him to death, but he's a tad on the young side for our gang."

"So you'd be surprised to learn then that DeeDee and Chip were planning to become engaged at Christmas?"

Taffy laughed loudly—the sound of a herniated Pekinese barking. "Who*ever* told you a ridiculous thing like *that?*"

"Chip did, as a matter of fact," Maybelle said.

"That's just absurd, for crying out loud. Sure, DeeDee was fond of him. We all are, as I told you. He was around a lot the past little while. But they weren't an item. We'd have known. DeeDee told the gang *everything.*"

"Perhaps she didn't, and you only *thought* she did," Honoria put in.

"She *could* keep a secret," Taffy allowed, her brow furrowing. "But something like this . . . Well, you could just knock me over with a feather. I had no idea."

"So you don't doubt it?" Maybelle asked.

"Not if Chipper says so. He's *such* a straight arrow. He'd never make a thing like that up. Gee, they're the last two people on earth I'd've *ever* thought would team up."

"Why?" Honoria and Maybelle asked simultaneously.

"Well, I guess because he's so much younger. DeeDee always went for older, more savvy men. Dick Whiting or Whitman or whatever his name is, for one, and fellas like Jonathan Stuart, Cubby Cooke, Roger Benton, and Teddy Hodges. They were all at least twenty-five. Chip's still in school, for heaven's sake, hasn't even graduated yet. He's just a *kid. But . . .*" She paused and sat turning the engagement ring around and around on her finger. After a good thirty seconds, she said, "If he says they were getting engaged, it must be true." She clapped a hand to her cheek, looking for a moment like Betty Boop: all big eyes and open mouth. "Wait till the girls hear *this!* They'll be as bowled over as I am. I just can't *imagine* why DeeDee didn't tell us."

I can, Honoria thought. *Telling you would be like taking a half-page ad in the* Times, *and for some reason she didn't want anyone to know about her and Chip.*

"Let's get back to the people who were jealous of DeeDee," Maybelle redirected the girl. "Tell us about them."

"There really hasn't been anyone since we were at Miss Chapin's," Taffy said, lacing her fingers together in her lap. "I'll admit she ruffled the feathers of a lot of salesgirls and waitresses. She tended to be a bit—well, impatient. But once you knew DeeDee, you just accepted that as part of how she was."

"Rude to people in stores and restaurants," Maybelle said.

"I suppose you could put it that way. She liked good, fast service, and when she didn't get it, she could become, as I said, impatient. You know, now that I think of it, she *was* on the outs lately with Minnie, but it was only a silly tiff."

"What about?" Honoria asked.

"I don't know all the details. But I do know it was about some boy Minnie insisted DeeDee had stolen away from her. Minnie's not exactly a beauty queen and, to be honest, I've always thought she was the teeny-weeniest bit mean about DeeDee. I mean, sometimes she said pretty awful things about her to the rest of us. Which wasn't exactly nice, considering the fact that she'd *never* have been part of our gang if it hadn't been for DeeDee. Minnie can be very ex-*asp*-erating."

"What about Mrs. Carlson? How did she and DeeDee get on?"

"Oh, they were very, very close. Mrs. C. was our favorite of all the gang's mothers. She was like one of *us*. She loved to get together and dish the dirt, look through the new magazines, try different hairdos, new shades of lipstick and nail polish. Our gang spent hours and *hours* at the Carlson place when we were teenagers. If one of us got in a pickle, we went to Mrs. C. If we were in the dumps, or just needed to let off steam, it was Mrs. C. we'd go to. And now her only child's dead. She's just *shattered*, as you can imagine." The engagement ring was turning, turning on her finger.

"And there's no one you can think of who might

have wanted DeeDee out of the way?" Honoria asked.

If Taffy noticed that Honoria had taken over the questioning, she gave no sign of it as she lowered her eyes and shook her head like a child, in her strident voice saying, "No, no one who'd actually want to *hurt* her."

"Do you happen to have phone numbers or addresses for any of these boys?" Honoria referred to her notes. "Dick Whiting or Whitman, Jonathan Stuart, Cubby Cooke, Roger Benton, Teddy Hodges."

"I've got some of them. Hang on a tick and I'll go get my address book." Taffy stood up and smoothed the taut skirt of her gown.

"While you're at it," Maybelle said, "you might ask Norton to get our coats."

"Oh! Okay," Taffy said, obviously crestfallen to learn that the interview was over.

"Well," Maybelle said as they left the building, "you sure set that little wretch on her ear."

"I thought you handled the interview exceedingly well," Honoria complimented her.

"What would you've done if she'd decided to throw Miss Barlow out on her black behind?"

"That girl's not capable of something like that," Honoria said confidently. "She's basically a decent kid who automatically thinks all people of color are servants because those are the only colored people she's ever known."

"Hmn." Maybelle sniffed. "Somebody should've taught her a long time ago to think before she opens her mouth."

"I agree completely. Who do we see next?"

"Bunny Applegate, just down the way, at 563 Park."

"Close enough for Taffy to run over and borrow a cup of sugar," Honoria said as they started southbound on Park Avenue. "Well, let's visit Bunny, then head over to West 48th and have some spaghetti at Mamma Leone's."

"Sounds good. I'm getting hungry."

"Don't go turning into Mick on me," Honoria warned jokingly. "Forever starving."

"Can I ask you something? Where does he go when he takes off on these jaunts?"

"No idea," Honoria said, pulling her cloche down as far over her ears as it would go. The wind was so fierce it was making her ears ache.

"Aren't you curious?"

"Some. But if he wanted me to know, he'd tell me."

"You're not that complacent." Maybelle couldn't believe this was the same woman who took such a strong stand on so many things.

"No, I'm not. It's not like me at all," Honoria conceded. "It could be the truth is I don't *want* to know. So I don't ask about his trips, in the same way I don't ask about where he gets his money."

"So he actually does have money of his own?"

"You betcha, sweetheart. Tons of it. And, yes, he

does pay his way."

"I wasn't going to ask," Maybelle defended herself.

Honoria's mouth reshaped itself into a knowing smile and she said, "Yes, you were. You don't trust him."

"And you do?"

Honoria thought about that before replying, "I suppose I do. God knows, I've let him farther into my life than I ever thought I'd let anybody get."

"Do you love him, Honoria?"

"That's a real poser. I don't know. What *is* love, anyway?"

"Oh, you know, all right. Why are you making out like you don't?"

"Maybe I don't want to know about that, either," Honoria said. "Sometimes, May, it's best not to question things. It's up there alongside not making assumptions."

"This doesn't sound like you," Maybelle declared, disconcerted.

"Sure it does. We stop showing ourselves completely after the age of seven or so. And that includes you and me and Ruth and Mick, and everybody we know. It's too dangerous. So we keep bits hidden, hold a few things back, just in case."

"In case of what?"

"In case," Honoria said, "things get ugly or incomprehensible and the need arises, literally or metaphorically, for us to pack up and move on. And I'm always ready for that, have been for as far back as I remember. Ah, here we are—563. A little better-looking from the outside, at least."

"Probably means it's not as ritzy inside."

"Don't bet on it, sweetheart. These are very rich girls whose daddies were smart enough to sock a bunch away for a rainy day. If it's not another full-floor apartment, it'll be a duplex at least. Didn't you notice the different window heights outside and the alternate belts of white stone around every other floor? This ain't no Hooverville, my dear. We're about to see yet another of the venues where the elite meet."

SIX

A maid hung Honoria's and Maybelle's coats in the closet in the entry hall, then started up a handsome curving staircase immediately to their left. To their right was the arched doorway opening into a spacious drawing room with well-worn, comfortable furniture and reassuring signs of casual clutter. Directly ahead they could see the near end of the dining room. The furnishings were old and elegant; the walls had dark, polished wood paneling; the paintings were modern and appealing. In contrast to Taffy MacDougall's place, this was a home that was lived in.

Hearing a baby crying, they turned back to see a frazzled, tearful young woman clad in a silk wrapper descending the staircase with a squalling infant in her arms. Still a little plump from her recent pregnancy, she none the less looked lush, lovely. She had fine features, green eyes that were red-rimmed from weeping, and a sprinkling of freckles on a whole-some, appealingly girlish face framed by shoulder-length brown hair.

Roberta Applegate had had jittery nerves since the baby was born five weeks earlier. She felt as if she'd been cheated or duped somehow. Nothing about married life and motherhood was as she'd ex-pected it to be, even though she adored Brian and they'd both very much wanted the baby. But too many of the experiences she'd had in the sixteen months of marriage had been physically or psycho-logically painful—the wedding night, and certain things Brian liked to do in bed that—despite his as-surances to the contrary and her own guilty respon-siveness—she was convinced were acts of depravity; the hours and hours of labor before the birth of Lu-cinda; the terrible inadequacy she felt at being un-able to soothe her baby.

She couldn't help thinking it might have been all right if Lucinda hadn't turned out to be a baby who could cry, for no apparent reason, for hours at a stretch unless either she or the nanny walked her up and down. And even then there was no guarantee Lucy would settle. As a result, Roberta had been getting precious little sleep, she couldn't eat, and her nerves seemed to have become raw and exposed so that the slightest thing could turn her tearful. Just then she was actually eager to talk to the reporter about DeeDee—about anything at all, in fact. The only people she'd seen in the past few weeks were her father and Minnie Morgan; everyone else seemed to be avoiding her and she was desperate for a break in what had evolved into an exhausting and frustrating routine. But it was the nanny's night off, the baby had been howling for almost an hour, and nothing would calm her.

"I'm sorry," she apologized frantically to the two women waiting below, wiping her face with the back of one hand. "Lucy's colicky. I can't get her to nurse, and she won't stop crying."

Feeling sorry for the girl, who was clearly in a wretched state, Honoria said, "Give the baby to me," and held out her arms.

Roberta hesitated, taking in the tall, oddly compelling, dark-haired woman with the dramatic makeup and enviable figure.

"It's all right," Honoria said softly, coaxingly, as if addressing a frightened child. "Give her to me."

Not knowing why, Roberta instinctively trusted her, and surrendered Lucinda into the woman's arms. Honoria held Lucy upright against her shoulder and began rhythmically stroking the infant's back. The other two watched her minister to Lucy, who cried on for a few more moments, then appeared to begin listening to whatever it was that Honoria was whispering into her ear and grew quiet.

"That's better," Honoria said and smiled. "Is there somewhere we could talk?"

"How did you *do* that?" Roberta asked, astonished, drying her face on the sleeve of her wrapper.

"Let's sit down, shall we, and I'll tell you my trade secrets."

Roberta took in the woman's wonderful smile, and all at once felt better. "The drawing room," she said, and stood aside to allow the others to precede her into the room. "I'm going to have a cup of tea and a nibble," she said, suddenly hungry. "Would either of you care to join me?"

"I'd love it," Honoria said.

"That'd just hit the spot," said Maybelle, finding the girl touching and kind of sweet.

"Oh, good. Let me just tell Cook. Please makes yourselves comfortable. I'll be right back."

More than thirty years had passed since Honoria was first permitted to help the Sisters care for the infants at the Asylum, but the love she'd always had for them was fully resurrected the instant she got close to a baby. Closing her eyes, for a few seconds a chasm of grief opened within her and she might—so easily—have gone spiraling down into its depths. But she refused to go, couldn't, wouldn't ever go back into that pit. Instead she focused, breathing in the fragrance of talcum powder and milk, the particular, almost edible, scent of infant flesh. It had an incomparable freshness—the newness of a body scarcely used. Savoring the warmth of Lucy's tiny compact body nestled to her breast, she marveled anew at what a miracle of containment a newborn was. Everything Lucy would one day be was already in place within her. Day by day, for the next decade and

86

a half or so, her character traits and personality would start to show themselves, until all the seeds inside had at last flowered. It was nothing less than miraculous. When Honoria opened her eyes, she saw Maybelle regarding her with a puzzled expression.

"This is a side of you I haven't seen before," Maybelle said. "I don't know why, but I've always assumed you didn't care much for children."

"I adore babies," Honoria told her, as Lucy's hand firmly latched on to the finger she'd offered her. "And I'm very fond of children."

It was on the tip of Maybelle's tongue to ask why she'd never had any of her own when Roberta returned, saying, "Cook will bring the tea shortly."

Awed at Lucy's contented snuffling against Honoria's breast, Roberta asked again, "*How* did you do that? She never wants to settle when I try to hold her. She just cries and cries."

"She feels your tension," Honoria explained, placing a kiss on Lucy's downy crown. "She's attuned to you, to your body, so, when you're anxious, she senses it in the way you hold her. Try to be calm when you pick her up. Put on some music, then sit with her and tell her how much you love her, how extraordinary she is. Let the rest of the world go to hell, and just enjoy your daughter."

"She doesn't want to nurse," Roberta confessed, deriving unanticipated comfort, even absolution, from this conversation. No one had said much of anything to her about how to handle the baby. At the hospital the nurses had been impatient and wouldn't take the time to help her. And the nanny seemed to think they were competing, and was trying to prove she was far more qualified to be a mother.

"Does it embarrass you?" Honoria asked.

"I want to, but actually it does," the young mother admitted, flushing. "I try. But every time I'm about to nurse Lucy, the nanny comes in and starts criticizing the way I'm doing it."

"I'd get rid of the nanny, if I were you. She's obviously more of a hindrance than a help. And this baby's not colicky, my dear. She's hungry." Getting up, Honoria carried the baby over to her mother, saying, "Why don't you go ahead and feed her?"

"*Now?*"

"Sure. Why not?"

"Oh, I *couldn't.*" The flush had now deepened and spread down her neck and upper chest.

"You could, you know. Maybelle and I won't mind, and there's no reason why you should. It's the most natural thing in the world. Does your husband mind?"

Lowering her eyes, Roberta said, "He's always asking why I get up and go to the nursery instead of staying in the bedroom and letting him watch."

Honoria gave the young woman her best smile, the one that created a dimple in her left cheek. "Sounds like you've got yourself quite a guy."

"You don't think it's—I don't know—peculiar that he'd want to watch?"

"I think it's divine. Obviously, he finds you very

attractive. And you are."

"Oh no," she disagreed demurely.

"Oh yes," Honoria insisted.

The baby was puckering its lips, sucking at the air, growing agitated. "It makes me laugh when she does that," Roberta said. "It makes her look as if she belongs in an aquarium."

All three women smiled at this, and Honoria said, "Go ahead and feed her, Bunny."

"My name is Roberta. No one calls me Bunny anymore. This is so strange."

"It isn't, you know," Maybelle interjected.

"You're both being awfully decent," Roberta said, as if accustomed to people behaving badly. "If you're sure it's all right." She opened her gown and, turning slightly away, managed after a few tries to fit the baby to her nipple. There followed a short silence, then she relaxed into the armchair and smiled at her two guests. "You know," she said, "all of a sudden I feel better than I have in ages. I'm going to ask Brian to give the nanny her notice. Oh good. Here's Cook with the tea."

A round, jolly-looking older woman in a white uniform came in carrying a tray of tea things and a plate of crustless sandwiches. Seeing Roberta nursing the baby, she broke into an approving grin, left the tray on the coffee table, and paused to place an affectionate pat on Roberta's arm. "That's the way, Miss Robin."

"Thank you, Mary."

The cook went back to the kitchen, wearing an

expression of great satisfaction. Honoria found the woman's fondness for her employer reassuring.

"Why don't I pour?" Maybelle offered.

"Thank you," Roberta said, gazing at Honoria in wonderment. "You're a very unusual woman. I've never met anyone like you."

"Nobody has," Maybelle quipped, hefting the china teapot. "They made one of her, then broke the mold."

"Well, I have to say you've made me feel better than I have in such a long time."

"Didn't your mother warn you what to expect once the baby came?" Maybelle asked.

"She died when I was nine. And I don't have any female relatives. Well, one aunt. But she's ancient, and lives in Arizona. I don't think my father's seen her in decades. And Brian's only got two brothers. His parents are divorced and his mother lives in Italy."

"What about your friends? Surely some of them have had babies," Honoria said.

"You know, it's the funniest thing. I was the first one of our crowd to get married, and I'm the first who's had a baby. I mean, we're all in our twenties now, yet I'm the only one. Isn't that odd?"

Finding this the perfect lead-in, Honoria asked, "What about DeeDee?"

"Oh, she was planning to get engaged at Christmas."

"Really? To whom, do you know?"

"To Chip Stevenson."

"Do you know him?"

"I've met him once or twice. He's a darling boy, a bit on the shy side but awfully nice. Have you interviewed him yet?"

"I have spoken to him," Honoria said. "What I find curious is that, when I mentioned it to her, Taffy claimed she hadn't heard a thing about the two of them, and was flabbergasted to hear they were planning to get engaged. She said DeeDee told the gang everything, but she hadn't said a word about Chip."

"DeeDee told everybody *but* Taffy. She was keeping it under her hat. Taffy's a terrible blabbermouth, you see. The entire *city* would've known about it inside three days if DeeDee had told her."

"Why was she keeping it under her hat?" Honoria asked.

"Haven't the foggiest," Roberta said, playing with the baby's foot as Lucy—with a tiny proprietary hand on her mother's breast—nursed vigorously. Watching her daughter for a few seconds, Roberta seemed both proud and amazed. Then, raising her head, she stared at Honoria for several seconds as if coming to a decision, then said, "DeeDee was the clever one in our gang. Taffy was the prettiest, Fluff was the brainiest, Bitsy had the best taste, and Minnie was the most ambitious. Nobody ever came right out and said it, but they considered me the most harmless and the dumbest one. I always wished I had the moxie to tell them all to go to hell, but I didn't. I was a coward. I thought none of the other girls at school would want to be friends with me, and it was better to be with the gang than all alone. DeeDee was the ringleader. There were times when I was convinced she was the kindest girl in the world, and other times I was shocked at how cruel she could be.

"When Brian and I started dating, the other girls were envious and made little cracks. But DeeDee said things that were positively vicious—as if she thought I was too stupid to understand what she was saying. We all used to talk on the phone almost every day," she explained. "Can you imagine that? We spent hours calling back and forth. When I think of it now it seems so ridiculous, such a colossal waste of time. But it was what we did, as if none of us wanted to give up the fun of having our own little clique. Some fun." She shook her head in mild dismay. "I was trying to back away from them, break out of the whole thing because it seemed so childish. Anyway, one afternoon DeeDee called up as usual. We talked about this and that for a while. Then in an obviously fake tone of concern, she started saying she was worried about how I was going to handle it when Brian gave me the gate. Because, of course, sorry as she was to be the one to have to say it, it was inevitable that he'd ditch me the minute some smarter, prettier girl came along. I was tempted to tell her that we'd become engaged the night before, but she was being such a terrible bitch that I didn't say a word. I told her I had to fly, I had a doctor's appointment. And that's when I started pulling away from the gang for real, because all of them, except for darling Minnie, who was my maid of honor, made me feel as if I didn't deserve someone as good as Brian, as if he was only dating me out of pity.

"The past few months I've hardly spoken to any of the others. I was sick of being called Bunny. Would you like to know how I got that awful nickname?" she asked angrily, then, without waiting for an answer, proceeded to tell them. "I had ugly buck teeth when I was little. Bitsy started calling me Roberta Rabbit, which I just hated. But I never let on, because as soon as those girls knew something bothered you, they'd do it even more. They were like that. Eventually it got shortened to Rabbit. Then, in the sixth grade, just before my father arranged for me to get braces on my teeth, DeeDee decided out of the blue one day to start calling me Bunny. And for the next six years I had to answer to that—even after the braces came off and my teeth were perfectly straight. If you want to know the truth, I loathed DeeDee Carlson and her 'gang.' I wasn't at all sorry to hear that she died. And if someone actually did kill her, it doesn't really surprise me." Suddenly, she remembered what Honoria had told her about the baby sensing her tension, and she calmed herself by taking several slow, deep breaths, watching for any indication that Lucy had responded to her short outburst. But Lucy only wanted to be switched to the other breast and, her former embarrassment completely forgotten now,

93

Roberta shifted the baby. She recrossed her legs, again took hold of the infant's foot, and was about to speak, when they heard the front door open.

There was the murmur of the maid's voice, then Brian Applegate stepped into view and stopped in amazement at the sight of his wife, unashamedly breast-feeding their baby in the presence of two unknown women. Transfixed, the dapper and handsome Mr. Applegate was made positively jubilant by what he saw and stood for several seconds beaming at his wife and child.

Roberta smiled and said, "Hi, Bri. Guess what! I'm giving an interview."

"You don't say." Chuckling, Brian crossed the room to kiss his wife, then moved to shake hands with both Maybelle and Honoria, saying with a crisp English accent, "Hello, good to meet you."

Names were exchanged, then Brian went to sit on the arm of his wife's chair, so elated he couldn't stop smiling.

"What's this interview about?" he asked finally, looking with interest from Honoria to Maybelle, then back to his wife.

"Miss Barlow's a journalist and she's doing a piece on DeeDee's death."

At this, Brian lost his smile. "I don't mind telling you I didn't like that girl even the slightest bit. She was always upsetting my Robin. She was a nasty piece of work and I say good riddance."

"Roberta," Honoria said, "do you know of anyone who might have wanted to harm DeeDee?"

"Gosh—"

"Probably everyone who ever met her," Brian interrupted, then said, "Sorry, darling. Didn't mean to cut you off that way."

"I can't really think of anyone," Roberta said. She thought for a few seconds. "Dick Whiting was awfully mad when DeeDee gave him the brush-off. But I can't imagine him hurting her."

"Dick Whiting," Honoria repeated. "I don't suppose you know how we could get in touch with him?"

"I'm afraid I don't."

"Actually," Brian said, "I do. He's a men's-wear buyer at Sak's. We had a bit of a chat one evening when a group of us were out to dinner. Nice chap."

"That's very helpful. Thank you." Honoria looked over at Maybelle. "I think we should be on our way now."

"Oh, Bri," Roberta said, "Miss Barlow has been so kind, such a help. Lucy doesn't have colic at all. She's just been picking up on my moods, and not getting to nurse enough. And Nanny hasn't made things any better. Please, will you fire her, Bri? I don't like her and I really don't need her. Lucy and I can manage perfectly well on our own."

"I'll take care of it first thing in the morning," he assured her with admirable immediacy. He was plainly very much in love with his wife.

"Take the baby, will you, Bri," Roberta said passing Lucy over, and then closing her wrapper. "I'd like to see my guests out."

Brian eagerly accepted his daughter, bending his face close to hers and cooing happily to her, before looking up to say, "Good to meet you both."

Both women responded in kind, then Maybelle and Honoria followed Roberta out of the room to the entry hall, where the maid—as if summoned by magic—was waiting with their coats.

Maybelle offered her hand to Roberta, saying, "Thank you for the tea. I enjoyed meeting you. And your baby's beautiful."

Clasping Maybelle's hand, Roberta said, "I liked meeting you." Then, turning to Honoria, on impulse, she embraced the older woman.

"Perhaps you'd come visit me again sometime," Roberta said rather shyly as they disengaged.

"I'd like that very much. Call me any time. I'm in the book, on Central Park West."

"Oh, I will."

Honoria put her hand on Roberta's cheek. "You," she said firmly, "are *not* dumb. And you've got a good heart. I'll bet you were far and away the nicest one of the gang."

Unaccustomed to compliments from the women she'd known, Roberta was moved almost to tears by this statement. "Thank you for today," she said. "You'll never know what it's meant to me."

"I think I do know," Honoria said gently. "Enjoy your husband and your baby, Roberta. You deserve them, and they're very lucky to have you."

SEVEN

After pressing money for the fare into Maybelle's hand, Honoria kissed her goodnight and climbed out of the cab in front of the Kenilworth. She stood on the sidewalk and waved to her assistant as the cab moved off, headed uptown. Then she turned and went inside, greeting the ever-cheerful Cully on her way to the elevator.

Knowing Honoria disliked coming home to a dark apartment, Ruth had left a few lights on. Honoria went through the rooms turning them off, then walked down the long hall to the bedroom to get undressed. She was suffering from sensory overload—too many impressions bombarding her mind. It would be hours before she'd be able to sleep, but she went through the motions anyway. As she stood creaming off her makeup before the bathroom mirror, she saw the reflection of Mikhail's silk robe hanging on the back of the door and felt a pang of something—loneliness possibly, or another quick bite of the guilt that inevitably seemed to accompany her thoughts of him. After brushing her teeth, she gave in to a peculiarly potent need and gathered the robe into her arms, holding it to her face to breathe in his scent—of tobacco and Lilac Vegetal and shaving soap. She inhaled it deep into her lungs until she felt slightly dizzy. Then she let the fabric slip from her hands, pulled on her dressing gown, belting it tightly, and switched off the light.

For a time she stood and stared at the bed, which Ruth had turned down, thinking she ought to be pleased at having it entirely to herself for a night or two. But she wasn't. She missed Mick. This was one of the occasions when she'd have aggressively sought his embrace, initiating their lovemaking— something she wasn't shy about doing. Aside from the fulminating pleasure she derived from the act, it also helped to shut down her brain. His body, his ministrations, did that for her as no one else's ever could—effectively removing her from the often chaotic attic-like repository of her thoughts and placing her instead squarely within the no less chaotic but more manageable realm of her senses.

In another day or so he'd return and she'd go back to harboring the small gritty irritation she so often felt at having him reduce the available air and space in the apartment. How, she wondered, could she long for him, on the one hand, like a giddy teenager, weak-kneed and breathless at the very thought of his touch, and, on the other, harbor this secret antipathy toward him? Duplicitous, she thought. I am that. A little selfish, a little vain, a little dishonest. But never unkind, never deceitful, never ungenerous. It was a balance, of sorts. Tallying these mental ledgers was a holdover from the teachings of the good Sisters; debits on one side, credits on the other. She made regular entries, took frequent inventory. She had to in order to justify some of her more glaring sins of omission: for example, her failure to ask what the source of Mikhail's income was, or where he went on these mysterious trips. Quite possibly she was living in a fool's paradise, and any time, without warning, it could all come crashing down around her. She didn't even know, for God's sake, how old Mick was, but suspected he was at least five years her junior. Never in her life had she accepted anyone or anything on such intentionally blind faith.

Backing away from this psychological equivalent to a dark alley, she walked barefoot to the office and stood in the doorway, looking in, considering doing some work on one or both of the current scripts. But she wasn't in the mood, didn't have the right kind of energy for it. The overload produced an internal dynamism, like sparks leaping across spaces to set small fires, one after another, in her mind. One heated impression led to another, then another, and another, on and on and on: Tiny Taffy glued into that improbable evening gown, miffed at not being let in on the big news about her old chum's planned engagement but not evidently grief-stricken at DeeDee's death; Dear Roberta, Robin, motherless mother, so in need of a few kind words, but with nothing good to say about the late leader of the gang.

The outlines were beginning to take shape, an image of DeeDee Carlson forming. Very like the way she developed a character in the course of reworking a script—revealing physical and psychological traits and tics; habits, attitudes, and history knitting together to create a character who'd have credibility and depth on screen. The picture developing of

DeeDee was not attractive, but then she hadn't expected it to be, not after seeing that so-revealing head-shot.

Obviously Chip hadn't had any idea what he was getting himself into. A pretty, slightly older girl invited him into her bed and he went gladly, believing it had to be love. Why else would she give herself to him? The poor boy's skills at self-preservation needed some refining, a bit of sharpening. But it was such a costly business, honing those skills. One did it at great personal expense, paying in doses of heartache and disillusionment. And she'd never wanted to think about her beloved boy having to suffer—as everyone had to ultimately—in order to grow up, to grow wise. Inevitable, but painful, both to experience and to see.

Wrapping her arms around herself, she continued to stand gazing into the office, noting the shifting shadows cast on the walls and ceiling from the passing vehicles on the street below, wishing again, as she had as a child, for the power to make things different, to effect minor miracles. Back then the little girl had wanted to possess a healing touch, to save sickly infants who'd been left on the Asylum doorstep to die. Now she wished she had the wherewithal to spare from pain those she loved. But it couldn't be done. You couldn't step in and take the bullet meant for them. You had to stand back and watch, too often playing silent witness while your loved ones took the blows. All you could do was offer comfort after the fact. Or, in the case of Mick, you could give him your body and a privileged view of your unfeigned reactions to his adroit and tender skills as you surrendered control for a time. You couldn't get inside anyone else's head—unless you created the characters from scratch and they subsequently got translated onto celluloid. Nothing on the screen was real, but it was the closest you could come to complete comprehension.

Physically tired, but mentally wide awake, she padded along the hall to the kitchen to put on the kettle for a cup of tea. Sinking into a chair at the table, she sat with her head propped on her hand, running down the list of primary questions she had about the late DeeDee Carlson.

Why had she broken off with Dick Whiting to take up with Chip?

Why had she wanted to keep their relationship hush-hush?

What had her purpose been in confiding the news of her impending engagement to Roberta, who was no longer a part of her inner circle? Had she merely been gloating? Or had she had some other reason?

On a subsidiary list, she wondered why, according to Maybelle, no one had answered Mrs. Carlson's telephone. It was possible that she'd closed up her apartment and gone off somewhere to mourn her daughter's death in solitude. If she had gone away, it was going to be tricky finding her. Then there was the mounting list of former friends and lovers still to be interviewed, not to mention the maid and the neighbors. Overload could well become a full-time condition. This thought was disagreeable in the extreme because, while she liked an evening out now and then, she'd never been a particularly social person. She preferred to take people in small intermittent doses, not as a daily diet. Time to herself was important not only for her work but also for her state of mind. In the past she'd often spent three or four days at a stretch working on a script, without setting foot outside the apartment. Until Mikhail came along. He thought nothing of interrupting, couldn't seem to comprehend that the bulk of the reconstructing on a script was done inside her head. So if he noticed her sitting, apparently idle, he saw no reason not to let his tremendous energy loose on her—like a big, sloppily affectionate puppy being set free of its leash.

God, that was unkind! Unfair, too. Mick was anything but sloppy. In truth he was meticulous in the extreme—except when it came to lovemaking; then he was a ravening predator, unconcerned with anything but the cause and effect of specific contact. He was a powerfully attractive man. She'd seen the way women looked at him when they were out for an evening—as if he was steak and they were starving. He didn't give them so much as a glance, which should have been reassuring but wasn't, because men *always* knew it when women found them attractive. And that being a given, the only conclusion she could draw was that he had such a serious agenda in being with her that he couldn't allow himself to be diverted from it even for a moment.

But that was unfair as well. Not once in their time together had he been less than completely attentive. And when she pointed out—not always gently, either—that he was interrupting her work, he never took exception, never took it as a personal rejection. Nine times out of ten he apologized to her, and to May, too, and with admirable good humor left them to get on with it. The times when he persisted, interrupting as he had during the previous day's snowstorm, she later had to concede he'd been right. Because either she'd been spinning her wheels, or too drained to get more of any value done just then. He seemed to understand her on a level at which she failed to understand herself. And with uncharacteristic concern, he'd come as close this morning to behaving like a husband as he had ever dared before, when in his roundabout fashion he'd asked her not to undertake this fishing expedition.

May was against it, too. She wasn't wild about it herself. So why, why, had she agreed? To satisfy Chip, of course. Bad reason. Had this been a script, she'd have rewritten the scenario to provide more substantial motivation. But she'd never been able to refuse Chip anything. Being a constitutionally decent boy with a healthy sense of proportions, he had asked for very little over the years, and often she'd found herself wishing he wanted more of her. This was the one time, though, she knew in her bones she should have said no. Doctoring the occasional mystery or suspense script didn't qualify her for the job. Besides, her natural curiosity was getting in the way.

In the course of the evening's two interviews, she'd found herself far more interested in the lives of the two, very different, young women she'd met than in gaining information about the dead girl. It was a good thing Maybelle had insisted on coming along. With her splendid sense of continuity, May invariably managed to keep her on track. And in this matter she was going to need May more than ever.

The wall clock showed it was after midnight. Time for bed, in the normal course of events. But the habits of a lifetime lost out hands down to sensory overload. The kettle boiled and she got up to turn off the gas. She carried her cup of tea to the living room, where she curled up on the sofa, reaching for *Miss Lonelyhearts*. She'd bought West's new one, *A Cool Million*, but had been putting off reading it, afraid of being disappointed. So she was rereading Lonelyhearts and *The Dream Life of Balso Snell*. Too often when she discovered a new author whose work stirred her, the next book failed to live up to the promise of the first. So she regularly put off reading new novels until she'd had a chance to linger a second, or even a third time over the earlier ones.

After a sip of tea, she opened the book, found her place, and in a matter of moments had joined the lonely and tormented population of Nathaniel West's newspaper world.

Ruth walked into the kitchen at seven-fifteen the next morning to find Honoria sitting at the table with the morning *Times* and a cup of coffee. Well able to read the woman after ten years in her employ, Ruth said, "Morning, luv. Get any sleep at all?" and opened the cabinet above the sink for a cup.

"About two hours' worth."

"Oh, dear. Hungry, I'll wager."

"Famished."

Adding cream to her coffee, Ruth said, "We'll soon set you to rights," and began assembling the ingredients for what Honoria always craved after one of her bad nights: pancakes with butter and warm maple syrup, and crisp bacon. After a swallow of coffee, she started preparing the pancake batter, asking, "Anything interesting?"

"Always," Honoria answered. "On the serious front, a Serbian contingent of the Yugoslav army crossed the frontier into Hungary yesterday. The Hungarian officers had great difficulty restraining their men from responding to the threats and imprecations of the Yugoslav soldiers, while thousands of Hungarians expelled from Yugoslavia continue to pour across the border. Ugly situation shaping up there, I'd say."

"Nasty buggers," Ruth said feelingly.

"Scary stuff that's looking more and more like war. Let's find something less depressing," Honoria said, turning to the Amusements section. "Okay. What've we got here?" She scanned the News Of The Stage column, then laughed loudly.

"What?" Ruth asked, looking over.

"Listen to this: 'Charles Winninger last evening

played *Revenge With Music* with two crutches, a plaster cast, and a broken leg,' " Honoria read aloud.

"Go *on!*" Ruth exclaimed. "He never."

"Oh, yes, he did." She read on. "'It appears that at Wednesday's matinee he fell and, as he thought, twisted his ankle. That evening he went through his somewhat strenuous part with the use of a cane. Yesterday it developed that a bone had been broken. Rather than see the show called off he insisted on taking part; and when activity was obviously out of order he paused and told the audience what he was supposed to do in the script. The house accepted the will for the deed.' I *guess* so!" Honoria laughed merrily, then continued. "'The management last evening was undecided how to proceed; Mr. Winninger and his crutches will be on hand at least through the rest of the week.' *On hand!* It's priceless."

"It's that, all right," Ruth agreed, smiling away and shaking her head over the antics of theatrical folk.

Chuckling, Honoria scanned the next item.

"What else?" Ruth prompted, briskly beating the batter.

"Here we have the day's dose of hyperbole," she said. "A review, penned by Mr. Andre Sennwald, of Garbo in *The Painted Veil.* I quote. 'Pettish folk, out of an evident spirit of wish-fulfillment, are forever discovering that Greta Garbo has outlived her fame. They are knaves and blackguards and they should be pilloried in the middle of Times Square. She continues handsomely to be the world's

106

greatest cinema actress in the Oriental triangle drama, *The Painted Veil*, which begins an engagement at the Capital this morning.' Pettish, knaves and blackguards, *pilloried*. My, my, my."

"All very nice," Ruth said drolly. "But did he like the movie?"

With another howl of laughter, Honoria scanned the rest of the substantial review. "Evidently not," she answered. "After waxing poetic about La Garbo's charms for many paragraphs, he concludes that 'the narrative carries little conviction or suggestion of depth, despite the facility with which it is told.' Love is not entirely blind, after all.

"So, let's see what's opening today. *The President Vanishes* at the Paramount, *War Is A Racket* at the Gaiety, a slew of foreign goodies. Held over are *Broadway Bill* at Radio City, *The Battle* at the Criterion, *The Gay Divorcee* at the RKO Palace, *Gambling* at the Mayfair, and yours truly's uncredited *Girl Of My Dreams*, otherwise known as a stinker for our times, at the Rialto."

"Oh, now. You don't do stinkers, dearie."

"Ruth, my darling, sometimes it can't be helped. I told them this was a lead balloon, but they never listen. Even the pontificating and never-pettish Mr. Sennwald could find not a single redeeming feature to praise. Everyone knows that next to La Garbo he loves Miriam Hopkins best, and the kindest thing he could say about her was that, regardless of the mess of pottage in which the poor dear found herself, she would always be the girl of *his* dreams. But never mind. It's all money in the bank. So what did you end up going to see last night?"

Ruth sighed. "*Imitation Of Life,*" she answered. "Ever so sad. I should've gone to see Fred and Ginger, but I changed my mind at the last minute."

"You didn't like it?"

"Oh, I *loved* it. Wept buckets."

Honoria got up and went over to plant a kiss on the top of the housekeeper's head. "Nothing like a good cry at the movies, is there? How long have I got before all that wet goo turns into food?"

"Time enough. You go ahead and have your shower. By the bye, when's Mr. Mick getting home?"

"No idea," Honoria said. "Maybe today, maybe tomorrow."

"Least he could do is tell you," Ruth said. "How's anyone supposed to make plans if she doesn't know when people are coming and going?"

"I think you should tell him that," Honoria teased, well aware of how partial Ruth was to Mikhail. She treated him like a pet elephant, forever feeding him tasty tidbits on the sly, while trying, without success, to pretend he was no bigger than a bread box.

"I just might do that little thing," Ruth said, laying strips of bacon on the griddle. "You in for dinner tonight, dearie?"

"Nope. You can go see Fred and Ginger while May and I interview a few more obscenely rich young men and women."

"If this is going to continue for a while, maybe I should cut back the grocery order. It's a sin to waste good food with so many poor souls going hungry."

Honoria paused in the doorway, thinking, then said, "Let's play it by ear. I don't think this'll take longer than a week, but I did promise Chip."

"All right, luv. Whatever you say."

"Ten minutes," Honoria said, and started down the hall, absurdly, unreasonably let down by the fact that the woman she sometimes pretended was her slightly daffy mother hadn't put her foot down, insisting Honoria abandon her efforts at amateur sleuthing. *You wanna watch out for those fantasies, kiddo,* she cautioned herself. *One of these days you might starting believing they're true.*

EIGHT

The telephone rang a few minutes past eight, just as Honoria was about to start her breakfast. Ruth said, "Go ahead and eat, dearie," and went to answer it. She came bustling right back saying, "It's Chip, wanting to talk to you."

"All right. Thanks, Ruth." Honoria walked into the living room and lifted the ear piece from the table where Ruth had set it down. "Hello, my dear. How's it going?"

"I'm getting by. What about you, Aunt Honey?"

"Just peachy." *Where is Mick?* The thought popped into her mind out of nowhere, like the first drop of rain signaling the onset of a storm.

"Making any headway?" he asked—somewhat obliquely referring to the task he'd begged her to undertake—trying but failing to sound offhanded.

"Not a lot, to be honest. It's very slow-going. So far I've only managed to talk to two of DeeDee's girlfriends. One was a big fan of hers. One wasn't. And we're having trouble reaching Mrs. Carlson. May tried three or four times yesterday, but no one was answering her line."

"That's funny," he said, baffled. "When we last talked she didn't mention anything about going away. Look, I'll phone around and try to track her down. If we do manage to connect, I'll ask her to call you."

"Good." Why suddenly did not knowing Mick's whereabouts during these mysterious absences seem to bother her? "When d'you finish up there, Chip?"

"I've got one last paper to hand in before the break and I'm better than halfway through it. It's dead as a doornail here, with maybe a couple of dozen chronic donkey's tails like me still around. The place shuts down completely by Tuesday afternoon, so I'm working nonstop to finish and get out of here by Monday."

"Where are you planning to spend the holidays, sweetheart?"

"I don't know," he said wearily. "I hate to belly-ache, but Dad's made it crystal clear he doesn't want me coming home. I got this letter he actually dictated to his secretary, all typed up, very formal, as if I was one of his clients. All this guff about how I should take stock of myself because in his opinion not only am I going to the dogs but I'm also a bad influence on my sisters and brother—he didn't even use their *names*. 'Your sisters and brother,' he wrote. Geez! Then he went on to say that, if I wasn't going to mend my ways, he didn't think it was a good idea for me to be around them just now. I could hardly *believe it!*" His voice was trembling now. "I mean, *me,* Aunt Honey, *a bad influence,* when twice now the cops have brought Gardner home drunk as a skunk, and the kid's only fifteen. You and I both know where Gardner got the idea drinking was the sophisticated man's pastime."

"Indeed, I do," she confirmed.

"Right." He took a steadying breath and said, "So I phoned home last night, ready to have it out with my father once and for all. But he was at the Harvard Club for dinner, so I talked to Lizzie, who at least has half a brain. And she said it'd be a good idea for me to lay low for a while because Dad's been ranting and raving nonstop for at least a week about what a no account I've turned out to be, how I'm on the road to hell."

What a fool Stevenson was; a puffed-up, pompous fool. "That is utterly ridiculous!" she said hotly, wanting to wrap her hands around Stevenson's throat and choke him.

"*He's* ridiculous, for crying out loud. I'm fed up to the teeth with him. It doesn't matter *what* I do, he never has a good word to say about me, so why

111

should I bother *ever* going home?"

You shouldn't, she thought, furious, but didn't dare say it. For more than twenty years Chip's father had been trying to turn her simplest, most innocuous remark or gesture into ammunition he might use against her. Initially it had been an ongoing, insidious effort to break up her friendship with Van. Then it had become a quest to discredit her in whatever way possible. He'd never succeeded on any front, but that hadn't stopped him from trying. There were few people she truly disliked, and he was the only one she'd ever come close to hating. "You're staying here over the break, Charlie, and I won't take no for an answer."

He exhaled tremulously and said, "Gee, thanks, Aunt Honey. I was hoping you'd say that. A couple of the fellas invited me to go home with them, but I'm not in the mood for being a bystander at a big family gathering. You know? It'd kill me to have to pretend to be enjoying myself. I'm still awfully torn up about DeeDee. So I was thinking, if you didn't ask I might just spend the time in some hole in the wall and hit the books until it's time to come back up here. All I knew for sure was that I absolutely, positively was not going home."

"Your room will be waiting for you, sweetheart, and if you want to spend your time studying, that's up to you."

"Why d'you think he's got it in for me?" Chip asked forlornly, sounding very much as he had at eight and ten, at twelve and fourteen—periodically asking that same question, in that same wounded fashion. "He's always hated me and I can't figure out why. You'd think at a time like this, when my girl's . . . when such an awful thing's happened . . . You think he'd bend a bit, offer a little sympathy. But, no. Not him."

It's never going to stop, not after so many years. Why did I think it would? The boy has a right to know, finally, what this is all about. "I think the time has come, Charlie my love, for you and I to have a little heart-to-heart about your dad."

"For all the good it'll do."

"I think it actually will help. When you get here we'll make the time to have a long talk, and I'll do my best to clarify matters for you. For now, finish your paper and sleep as much as you can, even though I know for you that's easier said than done. But try, sweetheart. You'll fall apart if you don't get some rest."

"I'll try."

"That's my boy. Get the paper out of the way, then throw your stuff into Clementine and bring your sweet self back here. Okay?"

"Okay."

"And Charlie?"

"Unh-hunh?"

"If you're feeling blue and need to talk in the next couple of days, pick up the phone and call me, and never mind what time it happens to be. Okay?"

"Okay, Aunt Honey."

"Don't let the man get you down. The plain fact

is he's just not worth it. I know that's a pretty tough line to take, but it's the truth. And remember this: No matter how black it all seems right now, things *will* work out."

"I hope so," he said, choked, and hung up.

The food had been keeping warm in the oven and when Honoria came back to the kitchen, Ruth brought the plate to the table, saying, just like a mother, "Sit right down now and eat that before somebody else decides to phone."

She was no longer hungry, but Honoria picked up her knife and fork and started in, eating mechanically while she scripted half a dozen ways to wipe that miserable sonofabitch Charles Stevenson off the face of the earth. The pancakes lumping in her throat, she thought of her beloved Van at the last, a skeletal figure with a grip of steel and sunken eyes glittering with feverish intent.

Look after Charlie, Honor. Don't let Charles destroy him.

I will you know I will. Rest now, rest.

"I stopped at the Ansonia on my way here this morning and had a little chat with one of the building's janitors, who just happens to live downstairs from Gussy Washington and her family on West 122nd Street—which, incidentally, is how Gussy happened to hear that one of the new tenants needed a maid. I have here"—Maybelle triumphantly waved a piece of paper—"the address of said Miss Washington, formerly in the employ of one DeeDee Carlson."

"Well, aren't you the crafty one! I would never have thought of talking to the building staff."

"I'm sure you would have," Maybelle disagreed. "Anyhow, I wrote a note which he's going to give Gussy tonight when he gets home, asking her to meet me at ten tomorrow morning at the Tree of Hope at 131st and Seventh Avenue."

"Did I just hear you say *me*, not *we?*" Honoria's carefully shaped, arching eyebrows lifted higher as her eyes widened.

"When the local folks without jobs and the families on relief come by to touch the tree for luck, you'd stand out just a bit, Honoria."

"*You* don't exactly look down on your luck. That's a *very* smart suit, by the way."

"Thank you. But I'll look the part tomorrow morning, when I go to meet Gussy. "

"Sorry to interrupt. Just wondered if you'd like some coffee, May," Ruth said from the office doorway.

"You're a life saver, Ruth. I'd love some. Walking over from the subway I thought my face was going to freeze and fall right off."

"A refill for you, dearie?" the housekeeper asked Honoria.

"Not for me, thank you. I'm swimming in it." Hearing May talk about her face freezing reminded her of Mick's verbal extravaganzas when he described the ferocious Russian winters, and she had to smile. After Ruth had gone, she leaned back in her chair and swung her feet up onto the corner of her desk, saying, "I would like to remind you that I am the same person who often goes to church with you and your grandmother."

"Because you like the music," Maybelle said.

"I do. And I like the *people* who *make* that music. Has it ever occurred to you," Honoria asked mildly, "that God might not be a bearded old man in white robes but a big colored lady singing gospel songs?"

"I'm sorry," Maybelle said softly. "I shouldn't have said that."

"It's okay, May. I understand."

"I know you do, which makes my saying what I did even worse."

"Forget it. I'll meet you by the tree at nine forty-five tomorrow morning. And let's hope Gussy shows up."

Chastened, Maybelle said, "Okay."

"By the way, I spoke to Chip this morning and he's going to try to track down Mrs. Carlson. If he connects, he'll get her to call me. In the meantime, let's see if we can set up appointments with some of the other girls in DeeDee's gang." Referring to the notes she'd made the previous evening, she read off the names. "Fluff Connors, Minnie Morgan, and Bitsy Sayers."

"What about DeeDee's boyfriends, and Dick Whiting in particular?" Maybelle asked. "I'm sure Dick will have an interesting tale to tell."

"I'm sure," Honoria echoed.

"I could call the personnel department at Sak's

and spin them some yarn."

"Or," Honoria improvised, "better still, we could make a trip to the store and take our chances on catching him in. If he isn't, I'll be able to do some Christmas shopping."

"I suppose," Maybelle said, not convinced.

"Look, May. I'm not wild about the idea of traipsing all over town, chasing down DeeDee's buddies, but I sincerely doubt that the personnel department of a store like Sak's would give us this fellow's address or phone number . . ."

"They would if I said I was with the IRS, or some other government agency."

"It's probably a federal offense to impersonate a tax collector."

Maybelle laughed. "It ought to be a federal offense to *be* a tax collector. But you're the boss. We'll do it your way. So now that that's settled, the question is: When do you want to head downtown to Sak's? And the next question is: Which of these girls d'you want me to try first?"

"Let's get some work done, then try the store around four. After that, I'd like to call on Minnie Morgan, if she's available. Then either of the other two. And of course I'll buy you dinner tonight."

"You don't have to do that."

Honoria grinned and said, "You should know by now I never do anything I don't want to do."

Maybelle grinned back at her as she reached for the telephone. "I guess I should."

Ruth returned a couple of minutes later to place

a cup of coffee on the desk beside Maybelle's typewriter. Now in the middle of a conversation, Maybelle gestured her thanks and Ruth went on her way.

Tuning out Maybelle's end of the telephone call, Honoria swallowed a yawn and looked at the stack of papers on her desk, fatigued by the very sight of the unfinished rewrites.

Where does he go for two or three days at a time? Is he some kind of criminal? And who are these men he entertains over dinner at the Players or the Friar's Club?

She thought of Paris, of dancing that first time with Mick; the best dancer she'd ever met, a man who could actually lead. The orchestra had played "You're Getting To Be A Habit With Me," and she'd had to smile, because in only a matter of hours, that was precisely what had happened with the ardently attentive Russian.

The last time they'd gone out dancing at the El Morocco—with its zebra-striped banquettes and glittering dark blue ceiling—the band had played "The Very Thought Of You," and she got teary over the lyrics. *I see your face in every flower.* There were a number of faces, a number of flowers, the ache undiminished, as fresh as if those losses had been only days before.

Shifting, her eyes settled on the elegantly framed selection of quotes from the Production Code which hung on the wall behind her desk. The Code was a document that had alternately amused and horrified her since it had been put into strict effect on July first of that year, and she often studied it, wondering what the future of motion pictures was going to be as a result of this so-called self-regulatory code of ethics agreed to by the Motion Picture Producers and Distributors of America.

Revenge in modern times shall not be justifed.
Methods of crime shall not be explicitly presented.
The sanctity of the institution of marriage and the home shall be upheld. Pictures shall not infer that low forms of sex relationships are the accepted or common thing.
Scenes of passion should not be introduced when not essential to the plot.
Excessive and lustful kissing, lustful embracing, suggestive postures and gestures, are not to be shown.
Seduction or rape should be never more than suggested. They are never the proper subject for comedy.
Sex perversion or any inference to it is forbidden.
Children's sex organs are never to be exposed.
Miscegenation (sex relationships between the white and black races) is forbidden.
Pointed profanity (this includes the words God, Lord, Jesus, Christ—unless used reverently—Hell, S.O.B., damn, Gawd), or other profane or vulgar expressions,

however used is forbidden.
- Indecent or undue exposure is forbidden.
- Ministers of religion should not be used as comic characters or villains.
- Actual hangings or electrocutions, brutality and possibly gruesomeness shall be treated within the careful limits of good taste.

No naked babies, no people who cared about each other making love, but it was okay to show in fairly graphic detail a rabid white mob lynching a black man. What a sorry state of affairs!

Turning back to her desk she frowned at her notes, trying to get back into the rewrite. Interruptions—of any kind—caused her to lose track of both the pacing and the story line. The more interruptions, the more difficult she found it to pick up where she'd left off; she started losing interest, started having doubts about the salvageability of the material. The only way to regenerate her faith in the basic narrative was by going right back to the beginning to read what the latest big yes-and-no-man from the coast had sent her. After that she would review however much had already been dictated and typed. At last, with a re-newed grasp on the line she wanted to follow, and a quick look through her notes, she could go ahead. With two scripts currently underway, not only was she unable to decide which one to attack first but she also found herself thoroughly disliking both of them. One was a hackneyed weepie about a pair of stereo-typical heroines. The other was a turgid creepie, written especially for Karloff and Lugosi. But it, too, had stereotypical lead roles. Both scripts had potential or she wouldn't have taken them on, and, of the two, she preferred the creepie. So, she decided, that was the one she'd focus on. Lifting her feet off the desk, she gathered up the finished pages of the script, grabbed her notes, and went to the living room.

She put "Georgia On My Mind" on the phonograph, then stood by the window, gazing out at the Hooverville in the park across the way as she listened to one of her all-time favorite recordings, with some of her all-time favorite musicians: Hoagy Carmichael singing his own composition in that good-natured, slightly twangy voice; Bix Beiderbecke on cornet, Tommy Dorsey on trombone, Benny Goodman playing clarinet, Eddie Lang on guitar, Irv Brodsky on piano, Gene Krupa on the drums, and a swell little Joe Venuti violin solo in the repeat. An amazing assembly.

She played the record a second time. Then, when it ended, she put on Bessie Smith's recording from the year before of "Gimme A Pigfoot" with Frankie Newton on trumpet, Jack Teagarden on trombone, Benny Goodman playing piano for a change, Bobby Johnson on guitar and Billy Taylor on bass. Pretty Bessie with her lovely smile and that rich full voice, the rasp applied judiciously to some of the bottom notes; one of, if not the best blues singers ever.

Finally, with a sigh, she sat down, folded open the original script, picked up her pencil, and got to work.

NINE

"**Y**ou're out for dinner again tonight?" Ruth asked as Honoria and Maybelle were donning their coats.

"Afraid so," Honoria replied, dropping Chip's keys to the apartment at the Ansonia into her handbag. "You'll just have to go see another movie."

"Not tonight. It's too miserable out. I'll stay in where it's nice and warm, get on with the cardy I'm knitting young Chip, and listen to the radio."

"If Mick gets back, tell him I shouldn't be too late."

"Right-O. And don't forget your bumbershoot, dearie," Ruth said, heading back to the kitchen. "You'll be needing it."

Both Honoria and Maybelle were smiling as Honoria made a show of removing her umbrella from the coat stand.

"*Bumbershoot, cardy,*" Maybelle repeated. "I love her expressions."

The telephone began to ring and Ruth called out, "I'll get it."

The two women waited to see if the housekeeper would call out again. When she didn't, Honoria opened the front door.

"We'll never get a cab in this weather," Maybelle said as they emerged from the elevator and started across the lobby.

"Sure we will," Honoria said, bestowing a bright smile on Cully.

"Afternoon, Miss Honoria, Miss Maybelle." The young man greeted them with his usual affability.

"How's the family, Cully?" Honoria asked. "And the new baby?"

"Everyone's just great, thanks for asking. Will you be needing a cab?"

"We will," Honoria told him.

"Okey-dokey." He gave the doorman the high sign, and in no time flat a taxi zipped over to the curb.

The two women thanked both Cully and Lou, the doorman, then dashed from the warmth of the lobby across the sidewalk and into the back seat of the cab. Honoria told the driver their destination, and they were off.

"The temperature drops a couple more degrees," the cabby grumbled, "and the city's gonna be one big skating rink. Roads're pretty slick as it is. My advice to you ladies," he offered, "is get back home soon's you can. Another hour or two, there won't be a cab on the streets."

"We'll bear that in mind," Maybelle said, noticing that Honoria was gazing fixedly out the window and seemed distracted. She wondered if it had anything to do with the fact that Mikhail had gone off, yet again, on one of his trips. At the beginning, when they were newly married and he'd gone off, Honoria had scarcely seemed to notice. But the last six months or so she tended to get into a distracted state, even though she insisted she enjoyed having the apartment, and—with typical candor—the bed, to herself for a change. Privately, Maybelle thought Mikhail was making a big mistake, handling things the way he was. It wasn't Honoria's style to question people about every little thing they did, but she did like to be kept involved. And that sure wasn't happening where Mikhail and these trips were concerned. She wished she were in a position to drop a word to the wise, let the man know he was running the risk of having his wife shut him out one day, both literally and figuratively. Over the years she'd seen Honoria go cold on someone—usually with cause—but it was still a pretty scary thing to see, because, without a word of warning, she stopped making eye contact. She simply walked away, and that was that. The friendship or romance was over, and Honoria removed the person from her address book, and from her mind.

Turning to look out her window, Maybelle thought how much she'd hate ever to have that happen to her. And recalling the—what could you call it, a tiff? a disagreement?—*difference of opinion* she'd had with her employer that morning, she felt bad about it all over again. Sometimes, from a lifetime's pure ingrained defensiveness, she said things that might have applied to a big percentage of the white people in the world but very definitely did not apply to Honoria. When these things came out of Maybelle's mouth before she stopped to think about what she was saying, Honoria challenged her every time, reminding her that there were exceptions to every rule. And Honoria was the exception to just about all of them. Maybelle had never known anyone remotely like her and loved her so fiercely that she'd had to wonder a time or two if there wasn't something just a bit unnatural about it. Certainly if she hadn't been as fond of men as she was, she'd have suspected she was a she-he. Fortunately, she'd had the wits to discuss it with her grandma, who said, "Ain't no sin to lovin' a good person, May. You wouldn't be makin' so much of it if she wasn't a white woman. It's the regard that's important, not the color of her skin. She cain't help bein' white, any more'n you can help bein' black."

The first time Honoria had come uptown to go to church with Maybelle and her grandmother, some five months after their initial meeting, Maybelle had been nervous and defensive in an entirely new way. Instead of feeling a need to be a part of, and to protect, the collective whole so that, as her grandmother had always taught her, they would have strength in their numbers, she'd been ready to defy anyone who so much as looked questioningly at the white woman with them. But she'd neglected to consider Honoria's habit of looking beyond skin color to see the person inside, and to remember how readily people took to the woman. Her looks, her energy, and her devilish smile were difficult to resist, and for the most part the congregation of the Abyssinian Baptist Church accepted Honoria into its midst with scarcely a blink. She was so visibly in thrall to the music of the choir and of the tremendous sixty-seven-rank organ; she listened so attentively to pastor Adam Clayton Powell's powerful sermons that now, almost six years later, if Honoria didn't show up at least one Sunday a month, friends and members of the congregation would approach Maybelle to ask why and to say they hoped Honoria was in good health. "You tell her we've been missing her," they said. And Maybelle felt a small flush of pride in her friend and employer every time, because Honoria cared about people and, in turn, they cared about her.

"I really am sorry about what I said this morning," Maybelle said now, quietly. "It was uncalled for. I forget sometimes. You know?"

Honoria reached over, took hold of Maybelle's hand, and gave it a squeeze. "I told you I understand, and I do. Put it out of your mind, May. I certainly have." She released Maybelle's hand and went back to gazing out the rain- and dirt-smeared window, trying not to think about Mick and his possible whereabouts.

It was a small cluttered office, with a rack crammed full of men's clothing samples pushed tight against one wall and an overloaded desk against the other. Maybelle and Honoria sat on the only two chairs available. Dick Whiting, one of the most handsome men either woman had ever seen, perched on the corner of his desk, with one foot on the floor, the other dangling over the side of the desk. He was in his late twenties and had dark, side-parted hair with just enough brilliantine to keep it in place. His large brown eyes were deep-set, very clear. His face was a pleasing, slightly squared oval; his features were perfectly sculpted, perfectly placed; he had a warm olive caste to his complexion, and a tidy mustache sat above beautifully delineated lips. His charcoal gray suit was the latest fashion, his white shirt was crisp and clean, with silver and onyx cufflinks. Black highly polished wingtips graced smallish feet that seemed almost dainty on a man just shy of six feet tall. He was well built, and charming, with a low resonant voice.

"I heard you were talking to friends of the late, unlamented DeeDee, so I knew it was only a matter of time before you got to me."

"Unlamented?" Honoria repeated, aware that he'd had some sort of reaction to the sight of Maybelle but unable to determine just what it was.

"I'm sure you've heard she threw me over. I'm hardly about to shed tears because she decided to take the big jump."

"It didn't surprise you to hear she'd done that?"

"As a matter of fact," he said, abandoning the tough-guy attitude, "it did. She was the last person I ever thought would kill herself."

"Why?"

"Because if I had to use one word to define DeeDee it would be 'tenacious.' When she got her hooks into something she wanted, nothing on earth could've induced her to let go. And there was plenty she wanted. So why would she take a header off her balcony?"

"What did she want?" Honoria inquired.

"The apartment at the Ansonia, for one. Have you *seen* that place?" Honoria shook her head, and he gave a small, dramatic shiver. "It's impressive, but spooky, like an elegant rabbit warren. Not that the rooms are small. But there are so *many* of them, and the hallways go on forever. I never did see the whole place, but I took a wrong turn a time or two and actually got lost. I felt like Hansel, finding my way back." He gave them a self-deprecating smile. "Why one girl would want a place that big is beyond me. But she wanted it and, by God, she got it. And her *clothes!* Let me run it down for you. Okay?

"Last year," he recited from memory, "for day-wear it was the V shape, wide shoulders, small waist, flared skirt; bolero jackets, puff sleeves, short fitted sweaters, and buttons everywhere; large-brimmed hats. Evening wear was high necklines, bare backs—Harlow stuff, bias cuts. So, we're talking about Chanel's satin suit, Schiaparelli's buttons, Lanvin's shell-pink satin blouse wrapped and tied around a high-waisted black satin skirt. With me so far?"

"Keeping right up." Honoria smiled, starting to warm to him.

"Good. This year it was ugly hats that looked like dinner plates or fancy funnels, worn at a jaunty angle, if such a thing is possible; Chanel's ready-to-wear collection—easy skirts and jersey jackets for her 'understated elegance.'" His wry smile said what he thought of designer patter. "Daytime color combinations that would make any sensible female sick at her stomach: brown and pink, or prune and turquoise. Just plain ugly, if you ask me. But nobody asked me."

Maybelle couldn't stop staring at him. He stared intently back at her for a second or two. Meanwhile, Honoria made a face, and he laughed. "Exactly. Schiaparelli goes 'hard-edged chic' with fantasy prints designed by Dali and Cocteau, with *more* buttons. But not just *any* buttons. Big ones, of fish, circus horses, stars. Wide padded shoulders covered in gold embroidery. The 'little black dress' for evening, and the long dinner suit in 'shocking' colors: Patou's citron yellow, Schiaparelli's 'shocking' blue and pink.

"DeeDee cleans out last year's *entire* wardrobe— scarcely worn, you understand—and just *gives* it to whoever wants it and, natch, everybody wants it. Then, with her closets nice and empty, she buys her *little black dress*, her *embroidered padded shoulders*, her *citron* yellow, her *shocking* blue. She's got the latest Mainbocher, the newest Lily Daché and Hattie Carnegie hats. The girl forked out an absolute *fortune* on clothes. Now I'm a fellow who has to dress for the job. Luckily, I can paddle my own canoe and the store gives me a good discount. But, frankly, I couldn't have afforded to pay for her *gloves*, never mind one of her little black dresses."

"But you were upset that she threw you over."

"Sure I was," he admitted, his eyes on Maybelle again. Then, with an effort, he looked back at Honoria. "We were going hot and heavy there for close to seven months. Then, boom! Out of the blue she calls me on the phone"—he glanced at the one on his desk—"to say sorry but she can't see me any-more. Could've knocked me over with a feather. I mean, we'd just spent the night together; we hadn't been apart more than an hour, and she's phoning to give me the kiss-off. Not a word of explanation. Just, 'Awfully sorry, Dickie. You know how these things are.' " Hurt and angry now, arms folded tightly across his chest, he said, "As a matter of fact, I *don't* know *how these things are*. I certainly had no illusions about marrying the girl. She was *way* out of my fi-nancial league. But we were having a grand old time, there wasn't a hint of a problem, and the next thing I know, I've been given the bum's rush, and when I try to get her on the phone the maid tells me she's out, or she's busy and can't talk."

"When did this happen?" Honoria asked, fasci-nated by the way his eyes couldn't stay away from Maybelle.

"When? About three weeks before she died," he answered distractedly.

What this meant was that DeeDee was seeing two men at the same time, sleeping with both of them. Honoria was thinking about that while, yet again, Dick's eyes went back to Maybelle. Then, as if un-able to contain himself a moment longer, he ad-dressed himself to Maybelle, saying, "I just have to tell you you're the most beautiful girl I've ever seen. I don't suppose you'd consider having dinner with me one night?"

Maybelle didn't react for a few seconds; too many thoughts were suddenly running simultaneously through her mind. No man, black or white, had ever looked at her the way this man had. And while quite a number had ogled her on the street or in the subway—one even made a big show of licking his lips, as if she were a pork chop he was just dying to eat—no white man had ever expressed any interest whatsoever in her as a person. She was flattered by the invitation, and a bit scared, but somehow couldn't dismiss him out of hand, because even though he was incredibly handsome he didn't seem vain and he obviously wasn't afraid to show his feelings. Thrown, she smiled, saying, "I don't know."

"You might?"

"I'd have to think about it."

"How about tonight?" he asked. "Would you be free this evening?"

Not sure how to handle this, Maybelle now turned to Honoria, seeking help.

"If that's what you'd like to do, May, by all means go ahead."

"But what about the interview with Miss Morgan?"

"I'll go on my own, and maybe have a look at DeeDee's rabbit warren before I head home."

Dick was following this exchange anxiously, as if his future depended on its outcome.

Maybelle wanted to have dinner with the man, but a voice in her head was telling her it would be a mistake, maybe even dangerous. All her life she'd heard horror stories about the kinds of experiences mixed-race couples had. Still, there was something

131

about this fellow, something about the openness of his interest in her that made her want to know—even if only for a single evening—what it was like to be in the company of such a singular man.

"Well, if you're sure you wouldn't mind," she said to Honoria before looking back at Dick Whiting, "I guess I could have dinner with you."

"Terrific!" He checked the time, saying, "I'll be finished here in less than half an hour. We could have a drink, then go on to dinner."

"All right," Maybelle agreed.

"A couple more questions," Honoria said, "and I'll get out of your hair, Mr. Whiting."

"Dick, please."

"Dick. Given that you can't see her as a suicide, do you have any thoughts on who might have wanted to get rid of DeeDee?"

"Only about half the people who ever met her," Dick answered seriously. "I could never see what had so many people so griped until the morning I got that phone call. After that I'd have happily thrown her off the balcony myself. I mean, okay. It wasn't the love-match of the century. But she made me feel like such a damned patsy. One night we're out on the town having a high time that ends up in her bed"—he cast an apologetic glance at Maybelle—"and the next morning it's the old heave-ho. I thought I deserved a little better than that."

Maybelle nodded, knowing how it felt to be thrown over.

"I'm sure you did," Honoria concurred. "Can you

132

think of anyone specifically?"

"Not really. Most of her crowd are people who make a beeline for the door at the first hint of trouble. They're not the type who'd go for someone's throat."

"Were you aware," Honoria asked carefully, "that she was involved with someone else at the same time she was intimate with you?"

"Is that true?" he asked, shocked.

"I'm afraid it is."

"Well, if that doesn't beat all." As the implications of this sank in, he exclaimed, "That's *sickening!* I had no idea, none. I thought we were intimate because she had some feelings for me, that it was mutual, even if it had no future." His eyes focused on the far wall and he thought a few seconds before looking again at Honoria, saying coldly, "If she was involved with two of us that you know of, maybe there were three, or four, or even five. I only saw her a couple of times a week, sometimes only once. That left five or six nights of the week when she could've been seeing other men. And obviously she was."

"But you wouldn't know who?"

He shook his head. "Not the foggiest. I know she hated to spend an evening at home alone, but I thought she was going out with her gang, or over to see her mother."

"Have you met Chip Stevenson?"

Dick broke into a smile. "Sure I have. He's a good kid, one of the few people in DeeDee's crowd who isn't a complete chowderhead. Minnie Morgan's another one. If that's the Miss Morgan you're planning to see this evening, give her my best. Minnie's a great gal."

"Was Chip often out with the gang?"

"Not that often. He's still at school, as far as I know."

"That's right," Honoria confirmed. "He is. So you had no idea that he and DeeDee were planning to get engaged at Christmas?"

Dick's mouth fell open and he gaped at Honoria. At last, he said, "You're joking."

"Afraid not."

"Are you telling me she threw me over for Chip, that he was the one she was seeing at the same time?"

"I am."

"Well, that poor kid." Dick shook his head. "Did *he* know he was sharing her with me?"

"Categorically not."

"So he probably didn't know about her fondness for Doctor White, either."

"Doctor White?" Honoria frowned. "Another boyfriend?"

"Cocaine," Maybelle translated, then asked, "She was a dope fiend?"

Dick laughed. "Not quite. She just liked a bit of, shall we say, *stimulation* now and then. *Expensive* stimulation. She persuaded me to try it once. The initial sensation was very nice. A wave of peacefulness and well-being that lasted ten or fifteen minutes. Then I was suddenly completely dehydrated and my heart started pounding so hard I thought I was having a heart attack. I got all jumpy and nervous. My hands started to shake and my eyes felt as if they were shrinking. It was *hours* before I felt halfway human again, and that was it for me, as far as Doctor White was concerned. But DeeDee liked the stuff. She always had some in a little silver box from Tiffany's that she kept in the drawer of the bedside table. She was forever offering it to me, then laughed at me for refusing, and called me a sissy. Which was fine. I didn't like the drug, and the idea of the two of us getting caught with that stuff scared the daylights out of me. This may not be the greatest job, but it's more than a lot of fellows have right now. I wasn't about to risk ending up out on my ear or in Osining because of DeeDee's fondness for the Doctor."

"Did everyone know about her 'fondness'?"

"I doubt it. It was her little secret and I think only maybe one or two of the crowd knew. She was a lot of things, but she wasn't stupid. She knew she'd be in big trouble if she got caught."

"Do you happen to know how she got it, or who she got it from?"

"I didn't *want* to know. That's the kind of information that can get you killed." The instant these words left his mouth, all three of them began to wonder if cocaine wasn't somehow connected to her death.

Honoria stood. Maybelle followed suit and Dick at once got to his feet.

"I'm going to run along now and see Minnie Morgan," Honoria said, offering the young man her hand. He clasped it warmly, saying, "It's been a pleasure meeting you. I like your style, by the way. The dress is French, isn't it?"

"Ten out of ten." Honoria rewarded him with a smile as she tucked her bag under her arm. "Enjoy yourselves, you two. I'll see you in the morning, May."

As Honoria left the office, she overheard Dick saying to Maybelle, "I hope you don't mind waiting while I finish a couple of things. It won't take long," and she replied, "I don't mind at all."

As she made her way through the men's wear department toward the escalator, Honoria was anticipating the tale Maybelle would have to tell the next day.

TEN

Minnie Morgan's address was a newish brownstone on the south side of 15th Street near Seventh Avenue. The door to the ground-floor apartment was opened by a sturdy young woman of about five foot four wearing a nurse's uniform, who on first impression, was unfortunately homely, with bright blue eyes slightly too close together under heavy eyebrows, a longish nose, and a wide face. Her skin was milky behind a splash of freckles, and her hair was extraordinary—a spectacular glossy mane of orange-red. Her smile was lovely, at once redeeming her homeliness, and her handshake was solid, confident.

"Good timing," Minnie said, holding open the door. "I got in from work twenty minutes ago and lit the fire first thing. It's going really well now."

After placing Honoria's coat and umbrella in the hall closet, she said, "Come sit down and get warm," and led the way along the hall past a small bedroom into a cozy living room about twelve by sixteen, with a fireplace in the wall opposite the doorway. On the far wall at the end of the room were a pair of high narrow windows, in front of which stood a round oak table and four chairs. Beyond the windows was a door leading out to a garden hidden beneath a rain-pocked layer of grayish snow. The furniture was well worn but comfortable, and had probably, Honoria surmised, been given to Minnie by her parents.

"I've got a bottle of good French wine," Minnie said. "Would you like a glass? Or maybe you'd prefer something hot, tea or coffee."

"A glass of wine would be swell," Honoria said, seating herself in one of a pair of easy chairs positioned either side of the fireplace.

"Make yourself comfy. I'll be right back." Minnie went off to the kitchen for the wine, and Honoria warmed her hands at the fire, looking around.

On one side of the mantel were a number of photographs in fine old sterling silver frames—Minnie at twelve or so and a boy who could only have been her younger brother, given the strong resemblance, grinned into the camera; a group shot of the family from that same era posed in front of a hot dog stand at Coney Island; an unsmiling elderly couple who were probably the grandparents posed stiffly in a studio portrait; a formal photo taken at Roberta's wedding with Minnie in a most becoming gown standing next to the bride; Minnie's graduation picture from nursing school; a photograph of a group in evening dress taken at some nightclub, with Minnie and Dick Whiting smiling, not into the camera but at each other. Obviously he'd been the boyfriend DeeDee had expropriated. Interesting. At the other side of the mantel stood a handsome pair of brass candlesticks. Centered over the fireplace hung a nicely executed watercolor still life of a bowl of green apples on a rough wood table. There were a couple of mismatched lamps, a low bookcase packed with classics and fairly recent novels, a needlepoint-covered footstool, and polished brass fireplace tools. No knick-knacks, satin souvenir pillows, or frills. Minnie was a no-nonsense girl with good taste.

She returned, gave a glass of deep-red wine to Honoria, and settled with her own glass in the other easy chair, saying, "I just want to say I think what you did for Robbie was wonderful. She called last night to tell me how helpful and kind you were, what good advice you gave her, and she sounded like someone who'd just been let out of prison. She's been pretty low the past few months and to hear her so bubbly was a real treat."

"She's a sweet girl," Honoria said. "All I did was make a few suggestions."

"You took an interest," Minnie said incisively. "Most people are too busy thinking about themselves to give a hoot about anyone else."

"As I said, she's a sweet girl," Honoria repeated, and took a sip of the wine. "This is very good. Just what the doctor ordered."

Minnie nodded. "My parents came for dinner last weekend and brought me two bottles as a housewarming present. I've only been living here three weeks."

"It's a charming place."

"I was lucky to get it. The rent's only fifty-three dollars a month, which is all I can afford. I came to look at it first thing the day the listing ran, and it was already rented. I was so disappointed I could've cried, but I asked the landlord to take my number in case anything else came vacant. He called that same evening to say the deal had fallen through, and did I still want it. I rushed right over to give him the deposit and sign the lease. I love my family, but I've been wanting a place of my own for ages. Oh, you don't want to hear about that," she said, impatient with herself for digressing. "You want to talk about DeeDee." Mention of her appeared to put a bad taste in Minnie's mouth. "You might as well know there was no love lost between us."

"I had heard that," Honoria said.

Putting her glass down on the table beside her chair, Minnie picked up a pack of Old Golds and lit one, then tossed the match into the fireplace before taking a good, hard drag. She watched the fire for a moment or two before looking back at Honoria, saying, "I don't want us to get off on the wrong foot, so I think it's only fair to tell you I know who you are. I mean, I know you're not a staff writer for the *Mirror*. I happened to mention your name to my dad last night after I spoke to Robbie, and it turns out he knows your accountant, Sidney Cohen. Mr. Cohen's one of the regulars, along with my dad, in a floating poker game every Wednesday night. Anyway, Sidney's mentioned you once or twice, and Dad said he was pretty sure you write for the movies, not the papers. That's fine with me. I hope you're not going to be miffed with Sidney for speaking out of turn. I'd hate to get him in the wrong with you."

"My being one of his clients is no secret," Honoria said. "It's an interesting coincidence."

"It really is. Anyway, I can't help wondering why you're doing this, going around talking to everyone."

"It's a favor to Chip Stevenson."

"You know him?" Minnie asked, brightening.

"I've known him all his life. His mother was my closest friend," Honoria explained. "And Chip is very dear to me. He asked me to see if I could learn anything about DeeDee's death. To make a long story short, I said I would."

"I see." Minnie drank some more of her wine, took another drag on her cigarette, then said flatly, "I didn't kill her. I thought about it often enough, but I didn't."

With a smile, Honoria said, "I didn't think for a

moment that you had."

"I don't strike you as the type, huh?" Minnie smiled back at her.

"Nope."

"In the end, I hated her," Minnie admitted. "The only reason I was ever part of that gang was to protect Robbie. The others, Taffy, Fluff, and Bitsy, were just followers. Did Robbie give you the rundown on us?"

"I'm not sure I follow."

"You know, how Taffy was the prettiest, Bitsy had the best taste, et cetera."

"Oh. Yes, she did."

"They called me the most ambitious, and it was true. I'd always planned to go to medical school, but then the money wasn't there any more. So I had to make do with nursing. But Margaret Sanger started as a nurse, and look what she's done."

"It's a most honorable profession," Honoria said.

"This Depression can't last forever," Minnie said, "and when it ends I might still get to medical school."

"You want to do something worthwhile," Honoria guessed.

"I'd like to make a difference."

"You probably will."

Minnie stared at her for a moment, then said, "You really are very kind. So, where were we? Right, the group. Right from the very beginning back in the first grade, they'd do whatever DeeDee wanted. Which is why, I'm sure, she picked them. Robbie would have gone along too, because she was such a shy, lonely kid, and they'd have taken advantage of her in a blink if I hadn't been around. Robbie," she explained, "inherited a fortune when her mother died. She's far and away the wealthiest one of the entire crowd, except for Bri who's a close second. Fluff is a distant third, then Bitsy and Taffy. And I'm not talking merely well off, but millions. Anyway, for as long as I can remember, DeeDee was forever hinting around, dropping unsubtle remarks about how she was a bit short that day or week or month, trying to get Robbie to give her money. And Robbie's such a good soul, she'd have given it to her if I hadn't warned her off. It infuriated me, the way DeeDee kept trying to get her hands on Robbie's dough. Of course when I did run interference and thwart her plans, DeeDee accused me of wanting Robbie's money myself. She couldn't conceive of my wanting to protect a friend simply because I cared about her. I had to have ulterior motives, because DeeDee always did and that's all she understood."

"But I thought DeeDee had money of her own."

"To hear DeeDee tell it, back when we were eight or nine, her father was rolling in it. She was forever bragging about her new this or her new that. But it never stopped her wanting Robbie's money, too. DeeDee was always after whatever anyone else had, whether it was cash or boyfriends or whatever. She did her damnedest, you know, to get Bri away from Robbie."

"That's rotten," Honoria said.

"It sure was. She was positively *blatant* about it, did everything but take her clothes off in public and rub up against him. When her best efforts didn't work, because the only girl Bri had eyes for was Robbie, DeeDee started a campaign to undermine Robbie's confidence; telling her Bri was only after her money or that he was just dating her out of pity. She was *such* a bitch! If you can imagine it, she actually tried making a play for Bri at the *wedding reception!* Can you beat that? Bri couldn't get away from her, and Robbie was on the dance floor with her father, watching with tears in her eyes. I marched over, said, 'Excuse us, Bri,' got hold of one of DeeDee's scrawny arms, and dragged her off into a corner, where I told her if she didn't behave I'd break her goddam arm. And just to show I meant it, I squeezed as hard as I could. Which is hard, believe me. I've developed quite the set of muscles working the wards, lifting people all day long, for one reason or another. Anyway, that shook her for, oh, at least ten seconds. I swear she was *impervious*. Then she said I was just jealous because she could have any man she wanted, but I was so ugly that the best I'd ever do was to snag some poor boob with a white cane. I laughed right in her face, which took the wind out of her sails but good, because very few people ever dared to cross her. So I won that round. Big deal. She was mean as a snake, and had no qualms about going for the jugular. I'm no beauty and I know it, but I have my fair share of boyfriends. That crack was downright cruel, and I don't mind admitting it hurt."

"I'm sure it did. It sounds to me as if she might have been jealous of *you*."

"Really?" This intrigued Minnie and she asked why.

"Well, you were close to Roberta, for one thing. And, for another, she couldn't push you around the way she did the others."

"You may have a point." Minnie smiled, liking this line of thinking.

"And, by the way, Dick Whiting sends his best regards."

"Oh, thanks. He's a decent guy, Dick. I guess he told you about how DeeDee threw him over without a word of warning."

"He did."

"But I'm sure he *didn't* tell you he and I were an item before DeeDee decided she deserved him more than I did."

"He didn't," Honoria confirmed. "It's obvious, though, that he thinks very highly of you."

"I still think highly of him. He couldn't help falling into the trap she set for him. When she wanted to, she knew how to be very persuasive, if you catch my meaning. He had the grace to tell me he'd started seeing her, and I appreciated that. Which is why we've managed to stay friends. But she had so many guys going at the same time I don't know how she kept track of them. Anyway, I steered clear of her after Robbie's wedding, except if it was an evening when the whole crowd was going out.

Safety in numbers, you know. We talked maybe twice this past year. And then, out of the blue, she called up a few weeks ago to announce she was getting engaged to Chip at Christmas. If she'd intended to knock me for a loop, she succeeded. All I could say was, "You've sunk to a new low, robbing the cradle. Does he know how old you are?'"

"How old *was* she?" Honoria interrupted.

"Almost twenty-six. How old did she tell Chip she was?"

"Twenty-four."

"She lied about her age because she was two years older than the rest of us. She had scarlet fever, or maybe it was diphtheria, when she was four or five, so she was late starting school. Anyway, to go back to that conversation, when I asked her if Chip knew about Dick, she said very quickly that they'd broken up—which I already knew because Dick had come over to cry on my shoulder after work the day she gave him the gate—and suddenly she was in a big hurry to get off the line. The next thing I heard was that she'd committed suicide."

"How long was that after her call?"

"Hmn. A couple of weeks, maybe three."

"And were you surprised to hear she'd killed herself?"

"To say the least. People like DeeDee tend to live forever, leaving decades of destruction behind when they finally do kick the bucket. And I didn't believe for a minute it was suicide. I figured someone had probably tossed her off the balcony."

"That seems to be the general consensus. No one I've spoken to so far believes she jumped. Do you have any thoughts, Minnie, on who might have tossed her off the balcony?"

The young woman took a final drag on her cigarette and threw it into the fire. "Not really. I do know that at one point a few months back she had three men on the string. And I'm not talking about casual dating. She was having affairs with all of them. I found out kind of circuitously. You see, Bitsy's father has an in with Arthur Schleiffer, the manager of the Tavern on the Green, so a bunch of us got to go to the opening back in October. I remarked that DeeDee was conspicuously absent—it was the sort of swanky shindig she'd never usually miss—and Taffy blurted out something to the effect that DeeDee had made a serious boo-boo and triple-booked herself for that evening. I was encouraging Taffy to elaborate when Bitsy very obviously gave her a kick under the table, which shut her up at once."

"When exactly was that, do you recall?"

"Let me think." Minnie took another sip of wine, then said, "My brother's birthday was the next day, so it had to be the twentieth."

"That eliminates Chip as one of her dates for that night. According to him they met at a Halloween party."

"That can't be right," Minnie said, frowning. "I'm almost positive they were dating before that. I mean, I was at the party he was talking about. Half of New York was there. It was a costume bash Fluff threw at

146

the Pierre, and I was under the impression Chip was supposed to be DeeDee's date that night. But she was fit to be tied because he'd driven down from New Haven and hadn't had time to rent a costume, so he borrowed a dress from one of his sisters, put on some high heels and makeup, and came as a girl." Minnie chuckled. "He made a better-looking girl than half the ones there. Anyway, DeeDee pitched one of her smaller fits and gave him the cold shoulder all evening, so he and I wound up together. That's a role I play pretty often," she elaborated, "the sturdy, unthreatening shoulder the boys cry on."

"Maybe," Honoria suggested, "they find you sympathetic, intelligent, and warm."

"Maybe." Minnie clearly didn't share this view of herself. "Whatever the reason, they're forever turning up to cry on my shoulder. I didn't have a date that night, so Chip and I stuck together for the rest of that party. We wound up having a pretty good time, all things considered. Afterwards, he ran me home in Clementine." Again she chuckled. "I've never known another boy who named his car and talked to it, too."

"Chip's a true original."

"That's exactly what he is!" Minnie agreed with energy. "I gave him my number and I was hoping he'd get in touch, but he didn't. Then, when I heard about the engagement I wanted badly to have a chat with him, because I knew he had no idea what he was getting into. I tried his home number and left a message, but I don't think he ever got it or he'd have called me back. He's not the type who doesn't return calls." Minnie picked up her pack of Old Golds, her eyes drawn back to the fire.

"No, he isn't," Honoria confirmed. "Were you aware that DeeDee dabbled with drugs?"

Minnie's eyes snapped back to Honoria's. "No. Who told you that?"

Seeing no harm in telling the truth, Honoria replied, "Dick did."

Minnie nodded and said, "Well, then, it must be true. Dick's a pretty straightforward guy. What kind of drugs?"

"Cocaine."

"Was there *anything*," Minnie wondered aloud, "that girl *wouldn't* do?" She got a fresh cigarette at last from the pack and lit it, again throwing the spent match into the fire.

"Have you any idea who the third man could have been?" Honoria asked.

"Not really. D'you suppose Chip knew about the cocaine?"

"I doubt it. I think it would've scared him."

"I think it would have, too," Minnie said. "He's very sensitive." She finished her wine and asked if Honoria would like more. She declined, and Minnie returned her glass to the table, taking a thoughtful drag on her cigarette. "I don't think it was any of the regulars—Jonathan or Cubby, definitely not Roger or Teddy. Roger's been seeing a Vassar girl for almost two years. And Teddy's got a secret pash for Bitsy. Besides, DeeDee was too rich for his blood. I honestly don't know who it could've been. But I'd say the other two were definitely Dick and Chip. I'm sorry I can't be more helpful."

"No, no. You've been very helpful. I'm getting a clearer picture of DeeDee."

"Not pretty, is it?"

"No, it isn't," Honoria said, considering the notion of this sensible, caring girl and Chip as a couple. It appealed to her. "I should be going," she said, dreading the walk to Seventh Avenue in the icy rain.

"You're welcome to stay and have pot luck for dinner with me. You're really easy to talk to."

"So are you, and it's very sweet of you to offer, Minnie, but I've got one more stop to make. Then I'm heading home to a long soak in a hot tub. But, listen. Chip's going to be staying with me during the Christmas break. Perhaps you'd like to come for dinner one evening."

Minnie at once said, "Sure. I'd love it."

"Good. I've got your number. I'll give you a call and we'll make a date. I'm sure Chip would enjoy seeing you again."

The temperature had dropped, making the sidewalks perilously slick, and the rain had turned to wind-driven sleet. Honoria made her way to the corner, hoping luck would be on her side and she'd be able to get a cab. But the few she saw had fares, or were off-duty and heading home. The wind was vicious and the sleet stung her face as she kept an eye peeled for either an oncoming uptown bus or a taxi. After ten minutes she decided to give up and walk to the subway station at 14th Street. She'd go take a look at DeeDee's apartment some other time. Just as she was stepping back onto the curb, she spotted an off-duty cab and tried to wave it down. To her surprise, it stopped. She got in, saying, "Thank you. I was getting drenched there."

"I noticed," the cabby said. "I figured I'd play the good guy and rescue you."

"You did, and I'll always be grateful."

"So where to, gorgeous?"

She debated for a moment, then thought what the hell, and said, "The Ansonia."

He put the flag down, checked the traffic, and pulled out.

When they were almost to their destination, Honoria said, "I don't suppose you'd be willing to wait for me, would you? I just want to run in and have a quick look at an apartment, then head home to the Kenilworth."

"Now, I don't know," the driver said, eyeing her in the rearview mirror. "You don't look like the kind of lady who'd pull a stunt, leaving me stuck for the fare."

"Tell you what," Honoria said, opening her bag. "I'll give you five dollars right now, if you'll wait. I'll never get another cab, and even though it's not that far, I'm not in the mood to walk home from here."

"Sister," he said, "you got yourself a deal. Just, please, don't turn into my wife, who knows from nothing when it comes to time, and make a few

150

minutes into half an hour. I'm hungry, my supper's waiting, and I've still got to drive to Queens."

"I promise you I'll be ten minutes tops. If I'm any longer than that, I'll give you another five."

He pulled up in front of the building and said, "Aw, what the heck. Go on and look at the apartment. I'll be here," as he reached for a folded newspaper on the seat beside him.

"You're an angel," she said, and climbed out of the cab.

ELEVEN

As Chip had said it would, the mention of his name and the fact that she had his keys got her into the building. She rode the elevator to the fifteenth floor, then, following the directions she'd been given at the desk, made her way down the hallway to the left of the bank of elevators and turned right into the upper part of the H configuration of the building's main corridors. DeeDee's apartment was at the end on the left.

Honoria opened the front door and was confronted by a long, dark hallway. Running her hand over the wall, she found the switch and turned on the light, then proceeded forward, feeling strangely nervous as she paused at the first doorway on her right. A quick look inside confirmed that this was the entry to the master bedroom, with an en suite bath. Continuing along, she came to an oval reception hall that had a fair-sized, unoccupied semi-circular sculpture niche. Off this charming hall, from right to left, were the entries she discovered to a living room in an ellipsoid shape, a perfectly round parlor, and, to balance the design, an ellipsoidal bedroom.

Smiling at the architectural whimsy of the place, she went out the far end of the reception hall, following the hallway there past a bathroom on the left to another, secondary hallway—Dick Whiting hadn't misrepresented—which branched off in two directions. Nervous again for no reason she could pinpoint, except that there was indeed something spooky about this vast eccentric apartment, she went to the right to find two more bedrooms, both empty; back again and going now to the left, she walked past an impressive paneled dining room containing nothing but a carpet on the floor. Going on, the hall took a jog which brought her to a big, well-equipped kitchen. The light switch was right where it was supposed to be, on the wall outside the door. With the overhead fixture on, she moved to the middle of the kitchen, where she saw at the far end a door opening into a further hallway that undoubtedly led to the servants' quarters. Very aware of the cabby waiting downstairs, she decided she'd have a look at these additional rooms some other time.

Retracing her steps, turning off lights along the way, she went to have a look at the master suite, which was the only room in the apartment with a full complement of furniture. Given what Honoria had learned about DeeDee's extracurricular activitics, it seemed perfectly logical that she'd have furnished her bedroom first.

It was a generously proportioned space, with the entire length of the exterior wall concealed by heavy draperies. A peek behind them showed a window and a door leading out to the narrow balcony that ran to the corner of the building and on around. Letting the drapes fall back into place, she turned to survey the room. The bed was a beautiful antique four-poster, fully made-up with a cover matching the draperies. On either side of the bed were night tables, each adorned with an exquisite Art Nouveau lamp: nude brass maidens in different poses, each holding a large seashell, inside of which was a small light bulb. She took a quick look in the drawer of each table. No little Tiffany box of cocaine. The vanity and the chest of drawers would have to be inspected on her next visit, when there was no one waiting for her. As she was about to leave, she thought to look beyond the curving wall against which the bed was set and discovered two doors. One opened onto the main corridor outside—a handy escape route, if somebody didn't want to be seen leaving—the other led into a dressing room, at the end of which was still one more door, this one to the bathroom.

Cutting through to the far door of the bathroom—an elegant rabbit warren, indeed—she turned off the lights to the suite and went past the echoey, untouched living room into the delightful round parlor. Unable to find a switch, she had to be

153

satisfied with the weak spill of light from the reception hall. It was enough to show her that here, too, the entire outside perimeter, which extended across more than half the room, was concealed by heavy draperies. To either side of the entry were arches leading into the ellipsoidal rooms that bracketed this one. And just to one side of each arch was another, smaller sculpture niche. DeeDee, or more likely her decorator, had managed to find two adorable marble cherubs, which stood, smiling happily, in each little alcove. The few pieces of furniture—a settee, a low round marble table, and a pair of Chippendale chairs—had been grouped like an island in the center of the room, atop pale yellow wall-to-wall carpeting. The walls had been painted a rich blue-green that was almost turquoise. The ceilings and moldings were done in creamy white. It was an unusual but strikingly effective use of color. Someone had very good taste, Honoria thought, heading silently through the dark room, her footsteps cushioned and muffled by the carpet, over to a point directly opposite the entry. She assumed from the symmetry of the overall design that there was bound to be a door here that opened out to the balcony.

She couldn't have said why, but her guess was that DeeDee had gone off the balcony outside this room. The newspaper stories hadn't been specific, probably either because no one knew precisely where she'd gone over or because the police hadn't disclosed that fact. Feeling along the draperies, she found a parting and pushed the heavy curtains aside just as there was a sudden rushing sound   someone or something hurrying over the dense carpeting—from behind her in the room. Fear sending a jolt of adrenaline shooting through her chest and making the hair on her arms stand on end, she started to turn just as something smashed into the side of her head. Stunned, for a moment, disbelieving, all she could think was, *For God's sake! This kind of stuff only happens in grade-B dick-flicks.* She wanted both to see what had hit her and also to touch her head. But her brain short-circuited, holding her frozen in place. And then, aware of a terrible pain just above and behind her right ear, she dropped like a rock, as the rushing sound receded.

Jake Matucci finished the paper and checked the time. Twenty minutes! Go believe a woman and see what it gets you! Ten minutes, my eye. He sat glowering at the entrance to the Ansonia, his stomach rumbling and a layer of ice forming on the windshield. Five more minutes, then to hell with her. She could walk to the Kenilworth. So she'd get wet. It wouldn't kill her. He started the wipers again and sat chewing on the side of his thumb, watching the entrance.

Ten minutes later, he climbed out of the cab and asked the doorman to keep an eye on it. "Listen," he told the guy on the desk. "That woman, the good-looking tall one, with dark hair. I'm waiting. She's supposed to be ten minutes. It's half an hour already."

"What's up? She stiff you for the fare, buddy?"

"Nah. But I'm waiting to take her home. She's gone so long, I figure maybe something happened. This lady ain't the type to do a disappearing act. Besides which, she paid me to wait. So what'd be the point of skipping out on me?"

The desk man thought it over, then said, "None I can figure. Let's go see." He got the keys to the apartment, told the doorman he'd be five minutes, then said to Jake, "Come on. We'll go have a look."

Figuring the worst that could happen would be he'd get an inside look at this ritzy place, something to tell Rita about when he got home, Jake went along, saying, "Some hell of a fancy joint, this is."

"It's that, all right. Craziest building I ever saw. Turrets and carvings, round rooms, funny-shaped rooms. Some apartments run to ten rooms. Others got two. All kindsa famous tenants. Caruso lived here back when the place first opened. Ziegfeld's got a permanent suite. The Bambino, too."

"*Babe Ruth?*" Jake was mightily impressed. He was riding in an elevator the world's greatest ballplayer probably rode in. Surreptitiously, he placed the flat of one hand on the wall, saying, "Whaddya know about that!"

"Yeah. A lotta famous folks. Course a lot of the tenants lost their shirts and had to let the servants go, then they moved into the smaller apartments. Some of them had to move out altogether. Used to have a crew of elevator boys, but the management hadda lct 'cm go a coupla years back. Tough times. But nobody's complaining. We got nice people here." They left the elevator at the fifteenth floor and started along the hallway. "Sure hope your lady isn't up to nothing funny in here. She had the keys, but you never know with people."

"Hey!" Jake said. "This is a *classy lady* we're talking about here, not some business girl. Watch your mouth, okay?"

"What, you know her personally?"

"Yeah, I do. So watch what you say about a friend of mine."

"Okay, okay. Don't get your shorts in a twist."

The door was standing ajar. The two men entered, and Jake called out, "Miss? Miss?"

The deskman said, "I thought you said you knew her."

"Be quiet, and help me look, willya."

"Boy, you're some touchy guy."

"That's right, I am. Jeez! Look at this place! Miss? Miss?"

Honoria opened her eyes, trying to think where she was. Then she became aware of the yellow carpet and remembered what had happened. Someone had actually hit her on the head with the proverbial blunt object. She could feel cold air creeping in under the door to the terrace, which she could see was directly in front of her, hidden behind the curtains. She had, in fact, an extremely good view of the inch or two of space between the bottom of the curtains and the floor. From the clean look of the wood at the base, it was apparent that the bottom of the door had been trimmed to allow it to clear the recently installed carpet. The result was a space perhaps half an inch deep between where the carpet ended and the door began. And in that space, under the door next to the wall, she could make out something small and round. Moving her hand forward, she pushed the object with the tip of her little finger and it rolled into the clear. A good-sized pearl. She managed to get hold of it as she heard someone call out, "Miss?" The pearl was cold in the palm of her hand.

The voices of two men got nearer as she thought about getting up from the floor. But it seemed like too much trouble. The cold air felt good on her face, and she had no great desire to move but thought it would probably be smart to try. So she took a deep breath, then told herself to sit up. Her body obeyed and moved her halfway to a sitting position, but her head didn't like it. Immediately nauseated, she had to remain propped on one elbow on the floor with her eyes closed.

The lights went on and Jake came hurrying over, saying, "Hey, you were gone so long I started getting worried. What's the matter, gorgeous? You sick or something? You don't look so hot."

"Believe it or not," she murmured, wishing they'd shut off the glaring light, "someone actually conked me on the noggin." Gingerly she ran her fingers over the side of her head, wincing when she made contact with a tender and sizable lump just behind her ear.

"You're kidding me!" Jake said, bending over her solicitously.

"Who could've conked you?" the deskman asked, looking around. "There's nobody here."

"No idea," Honoria whispered, as the driver hoisted her to her feet.

"You gonna be okay?" Jake asked, concerned, keeping an arm around her as Honoria stood, taking stock of her condition.

"Eventually."

"You want I should take you to the hospital?" Jake asked. "Maybe I should do that. You really don't look so hot."

"I don't *feel* so hot. But no, thank you. I just want to go home."

"Then that's where you'll go. The Kenilworth, right?"

"Right."

The deskman leading the way, they left the apartment and went slowly down the hall to the elevator, Jake's steadying arm keeping her upright. Movement seemed to activate the injury to her head, setting it to throbbing in heated waves that washed over her and heightened the nausea. Opening her hand, she dropped the pearl into her coat pocket, on top of Chip's keys, and concentrated on swallowing the bitter fluid that kept filling the floor of her mouth.

The deskman stayed quiet on the ride down to the main floor, eyeing her suspiciously. And the cabby, with touching consideration, kept his arm firmly around her, asking several times, "You okay?"

She replied with a whispered yes each time, determined not to be sick in the elevator, and very glad when they arrived back in the lobby.

"If you're sure everything's gonna be all right," the deskman said, returning to the safety of his position by the front door.

"Yeah, thanks," Jake said, guiding Honoria out of the building and into the back of the cab. "Just relax, sister. I'll have you home in no time flat."

She rolled down the window a bit, then leaned back and took deep breaths of the icy air.

"So what happened back there?" he asked, twisted around from the front seat to look at her.

"No idea," she said, not daring to open her eyes. "I heard a sound behind me, then *wham*. Didn't even have time to turn around."

"Imagine!" Jake said. "In a hoity-toity building like that. They take anything or anything?"

"I don't think so," she answered.

"Okay. Enough with the chit-chat. I'll get you home." He faced front again, and throughout the short ride home she kept her eyes closed. By the time Jake pulled the taxi over to the curb in front of the Kenilworth, the worst of her nausea had passed.

"You gonna be okay, or d'you need help getting inside?"

"I'll be okay." She fumbled her bag open, found a five-dollar bill and pushed it at him.

"Hey!" he protested. "Forget it! You don't owe me."

"I promised. And I always keep my promises.

160

Take it, please. What's your name?"

"Jake Matucci. What's yours."

"Honoria. Jake, you're a sweetheart," she said, as Lou came to open the passenger door. "It was my lucky night, flagging you down."

"Hey! You know Caruso used to live there, in the Ansonia?"

"Really?"

"Yeah. And The Bambino. Buncha famous people. Dufus, the desk guy, told me. So, listen. Take care of yourself, gorgeous. Okay?"

"You, too. Thanks a million, Jake."

He stayed until he saw her get into the elevator, then he drove on, thinking what a hell of a day this had been. Wait till he told Rita.

Ruth heard the front door open and came out of the kitchen to see if Mr. Mick had finally come home, but instead saw Honoria drop her umbrella and handbag and go flying past her, a hand over her mouth. She ran directly to the bathroom of the master suite to be sick in the basin. Trembling, eyes and nose streaming, head throbbing violently, she held on to the rim of the sink with one hand while, with the other, she turned on the cold water. After rinsing the basin, she drank from her cupped hand, then splashed water on her face and neck.

"Are you ill, dearie?" Ruth asked anxiously from the doorway.

"No. I got hit on the head." She drank some more water, sweating now.

161

"*Hit? Who* hit you?"

"No idea."

"And this happened where?"

"The Ansonia."

"Shocking! Here, let me take your coat. Then we'll have a look at you." Ruth got the coat off Honoria and hung it over Mikhail's robe on the back of the door, asking, "Where on the head?"

Honoria pointed to her right ear. "Back there. God! Don't touch it!" she warned, glancing at her reflection in the mirror. What a sight! Mascara had run in tiny rivulets on indirect courses down her face. She looked away, lacking the energy to clean herself up.

"Sit on the stool here and let me have a look. I won't touch," Ruth said in her most motherly fashion.

Honoria obeyed, folding her arm on the side of the sink and letting her forehead rest on it.

"It's a nasty great knob," Ruth said, cautiously shifting the hair in order to see. "Didn't break the skin, though. Maybe we should ring the doctor."

"There's no need," Honoria said tiredly.

"Hmn. I'm not so sure about that."

"I am."

"Well then, let me fetch you an icepack and a nice hot cup of tea."

"Just an icepack."

"Tea'll do you good. Don't argue."

"I need to lie down."

"Here, I'll help you."

Very wobbly on her pins, Honoria leaned gratefully on the smaller woman.

Ruth one-handedly threw aside the coverlet and folded back the bedclothes, then guided Honoria down onto the side of the bed. "We'll get you out of these boots, then you'll lie down while I fetch the icepack and the tea."

"I need about sixty aspirins," Honoria said, lowering her throbbing head to the soft cool pillow. Where the hell was Mick?

Ruth snorted and said, "Three'll do you. Rest now while I fetch your tea." She settled the blankets over Honoria, then bustled off to the kitchen.

It seemed only a minute later that she was back, setting a tray down on the bedside table. "In all the excitement, I forgot to tell you. Mr. Mick called."

Honoria wet her lips, then asked, "And?"

"Said to tell you he'll be home late tonight."

"Don't suppose he mentioned where he was?"

"Nope. Just said he'd be home late. Sit up a bit now and take these pills, then drink your tea." Ruth held out a glass of water in one hand, and on the palm of other sat the promised three white tablets.

Shakily, Honoria managed to sit up a little. The housekeeper tipped the pills into her hand, then gave her the glass and stood watching as Honoria swallowed the aspirin with a mouthful of water. "Now the icepack," Ruth said. "I'll let you do it." She passed this over, and Honoria cautiously placed it over the bump, swearing under her breath. So much for those guys getting bopped on the noggin, then coming to a few minutes later and going about their business! Complete bunk! Next time she had to doctor one of those scenes, she'd go for realism and show the guy having the wee-waws, heaving his heart out into the nearest sink or toilet.

The cold started to penetrate the rubber of the pack, attacking the heated swelling behind her ear. "That's better." She sighed, and finally accepted the cup of tea—Ruth's cure for all ailments—took a sip, and made a face. "Too much sugar," she complained.

"Just drink it, there's a good girl. The sugar'll give you back some energy. I don't suppose you've eaten anything? And where's May?" She looked around as if she might have failed to notice the young woman.

"On a date."

"A date? I thought you two were eating out after you finished playing Holmes and Dr. Watson."

"Change of plans." Honoria drank some more of the tea. "A very attractive fellow invited her out. I encouraged her to accept, and played Holmes on my own."

"Right. And look where it got you! Well, as luck would have it, I've got a nice pot of vegetable soup on the stove. We'll get some of that into you in a while. Now drink that up while I put your things away." Carrying Honoria's coat and boots, she went off.

With the ice beginning to numb the pain and the tea pooling warmly in her stomach, Honoria was starting to feel better. A bowl of soup sounded about right. She couldn't imagine trying to chew anything just then. But soup would be perfect. And, wonder of wonders, Mick was coming home.

TWELVE

When she awakened, the other half of the bed was empty; there was no sign that Mick had been there. She looked at the alarm clock, saw it was almost ten, and swore quietly. She'd missed the meeting with Gussy Washington in Harlem. And Mick hadn't come home. She was angry—with herself and with him—and, perhaps because of her present sense of physical vulnerability, very hurt. Which made her even angrier, because she hated giving in to what she thought of as weak-sister emotions.

The instant she sat up, her head started throbbing, bringing back very clearly the eerie moment the night before when she'd heard that ghostly rushing sound behind her just before something slammed into her head. With her fingertips she cautiously examined the lump above her ear. The icepack had kept it from getting any bigger, but it was exceedingly tender, and very hot, as though a small fire was blazing just beneath her skin. Moving slowly, as if her skull were a fragile glass bowl, she got up and made her way to the bathroom to cream off the residue of the previous day's makeup before taking three more aspirin tablets. Brushing her teeth, she decided, would have to wait until later, when she felt better.

"Ah, here you are!" Ruth said with relief when Honoria appeared bleary-eyed and barefoot in the kitchen doorway, belting her robe with hands that

165

lacked their usual co-ordination. "Feeling better, luv?"

"Marginally, thank you."

"Good, good. I thought the extra sleep would do you good."

"It did." She was nowhere near as sick and dizzy as she'd been the night before. But with the miserable rhythmic thumping in her head, she'd have been useless at the meeting with Gussy Washington, and less than useless with Mick, who invariably returned from his trips with a heightened sexual appetite—as if he'd suffered some rare and intense form of deprivation during these two- or three-day separations. Accepting the facts, she felt her anger dissipate, although the hurt remained. As a result of that damnable sense of fragility, the old sadness seemed to be hovering close by, as if waiting for a chance to overwhelm and disable her—the way it had once upon a time many years before. She wasn't about to succumb, and refused even to acknowledge its existence. She'd always found it difficult to sympathize with people who felt sorry for themselves, and the last thing on earth she wanted was to join their ranks. It was a point of honor to accept what came her way, good or bad, without complaint and without gloating.

"Sit yourself down, and I'll make you some breakfast," Ruth said. "I'll wager you're hungry."

Honoria thought about that, then said, "As a matter of fact, I am."

Ruth studied her critically for a moment, taking

note of the way Honoria was trying to hide the fact that she was still feeling poorly. Not once in ten years had Honoria taken to her bed for so much as a single day. She was a woman blessed with excellent health, which was a good thing considering she had no patience when it came to being sick. Not that she wasn't kindness itself if someone else wasn't well; she just couldn't tolerate weakness in herself. "You need the icepack again," Ruth decided, watching Honoria grimace as she lowered herself into a chair.

Ruth got the pack, dumped in some ice, screwed the top on, and brought it to Honoria. "There you go, pet. That'll help, I'm sure. Some coffee?"

"Yes, please." Honoria applied the pack to her head and looked longingly at the morning's *Times* sitting on the opposite side of the table, knowing her daily dose of news would have to wait, too. She was having trouble focusing on her surroundings. Newsprint, she knew, was beyond her capabilities at the moment.

Ruth set a cup of coffee in front of her. Honoria thanked her, then drank some, closing her eyes for a moment as the cold of the pack and the hot coffee both seemed to offer immediate comfort. Opening her eyes, she drank some more coffee before saying, "I see Mick didn't make it home after all."

"Oh, he did, dearie," Ruth corrected her. "He got in just past eleven. I was listening to the late news on WOR when I heard him come in, so I came out to see if he fancied a bite to eat, and naturally he did.

167

When is that man ever *not* hungry?" she asked with amused affection. "So, while I was heating up the soup, I told him how you got coshed on the bean and came home in a frightful state. He was ever so upset, went straight away to have a look at you, then came back, saying he'd sleep in the guest room so's not to disturb you. Right considerate of him, that was, don't you think? Then this morning he was up early, off to one of his meetings right after breakfast. Said to be sure to tell you he'll be back after lunch. He left and, not five minutes later, May telephoned, wanting to know why you weren't there to meet her by some tree or other. So I told *her* about your getting coshed, and *she* got very upset. Said she'd come to see you after *her* meeting, and on a Saturday morning, no less." Shaking her head, Ruth finished slicing two pieces of bread from the loaf, deftly cracked two eggs into a bowl, added a splash of cream and some ground pepper, then began vigorously stirring the mixture with a wire whisk.

Honoria leaned against the icepack propped in her hand and finished the coffee as she watched the housekeeper put the meal together with a speed and dexterity that told of her long-ago stint as a short-order cook.

Ruth had come to New York in 1919 at the age of thirty-six to be reunited with the army sergeant she had met and married in the autumn of 1917. Her first husband had died early on in the 1914 Battle of the Marne, and she had thought it most unlikely that she'd ever remarry. But she struck up a conversation with Sergeant Henry Wallace one afternoon in the Lyon's Corner House at Marble Arch. He seemed a pleasant-enough chap, and she was quite taken with his American accent. They spent the rest of that day together, strolling through Hyde Park, and later having a meal in a small Italian restaurant in Soho. The following morning his infantry unit departed. She doubted she'd hear from him again, but within a fortnight she received a long letter in which he described the horrible conditions at the front.

She at once penned a sympathetic reply and they corresponded for the next four months, their letters growing increasingly more personal. On his first leave he came directly to London to see her. That same day he proposed. She accepted—picturing an exciting new life in America. They were married a week later and he returned to the front two days after that. At the war's end they had a total of two weeks together in her flat off the Fulham Road in Worlds End before Henry Wallace was shipped home. Again, she doubted she'd hear from him. But seven months later he sent for her. She gave up the flat, sold the furniture, packed the bits and pieces she wanted to keep, and made her way to Liverpool, where she spent a night before boarding the ship.

Henry was there waiting quay-side when her ship docked, and the moment her eyes settled on the mid-sized, plain-featured thirty-three-year-old man in a fedora and a gray suit, with spit-polished brown oxfords, and a tired smile on his face, she knew she'd made a frightful mistake. It had happened to a fair number of women she knew who'd fallen for Yanks in the military. They married the chaps and later discovered the attraction had been the novelty of the accent and of the uniform, not the actual man. A few of her friends got left with buns in the oven, and a few others simply got left. But Henry did send for her—which gave her hope for their future—but the sight of his forced smile as he waited for her to disembark made her wish he hadn't, or that she'd sent him back the ticket and travel money. What had seemed meaningful between them at the height of the war seemed in peacetime almost trivial. She was already there, though. It was too late to go back. There was nothing to go back to, in any case. She was an only child, a late-in-life "surprise" to the soft-spoken solicitor and his shy wife who had died within a year of each other when Ruth was in her late teens. The gentle pair left her a small inheritance, and an abiding fondness for the elderly, which she put to good use at a home for the aged where she worked for five years before marrying Alfie Parker. Alf was a young copper who came to the home at least twice a week to look in on his gran, and after his evening visits he took to waiting to walk Ruth home. Within six months they were married, and they had three very happy years together before he went off to the war and got himself killed.

So she married Henry Wallace and for the next three years she tolerated his dark moods and lengthy silences, his occasional need for quick, impersonal sexual intercourse—it could scarcely have been called lovemaking, given that it lacked anything resembling foreplay or affection—that left her embarrassed for both of them; she tried to comprehend his lack of interest in almost everything except crossword puzzles—which he could do by the hour, while a cigarette burned in the ashtray sending a spiral of gray-blue smoke into the air—and his complete blindness to everything around him. He could have been up to his neck in rubbish and he'd never have noticed. Henry Wallace was oblivious to his surroundings, and that included her. She might as well have been wallpaper, and for the life of her she couldn't understand why he'd bothered sending for her. Some misguided sense of honor or obligation, she supposed.

She laundered his clothes, prepared his meals, cleaned the three cramped rooms of their West Side midtown flat, and spent her free daytime hours gazing out the kitchen window at the slice of sky visible above the building's airshaft—the irredeemably dreary flat's only source of light—remembering Alf and her parents, the life she'd once had which seemed idyllic, in comparison with the one she had now. Then one morning after Henry had left for his job as an actuary with an insurance company downtown, without ever having planned it, she quickly packed every last thing she'd brought with her from England, helped herself to half the cash Henry kept in his old kit bag (four hundred and eighteen dollars for each of them, which seemed fair pay for services rendered), and escaped. She left behind a note that said: "You don't really like me and I really don't like you. Let's pretend it didn't happen. Good luck to both of us, Ruth. PS: I feel I earned half the money. No hard feelings, I hope. R."

That same day she rented a sunny, second-floor room facing the street in a Murray Hill boarding house and took a job as cook in a small restaurant on Lexington Avenue. The boarding house turned out to be depressing, filled with silent single people well past youth and suffering from a gradual yet touchingly dignified decay as they traveled to their office jobs in the morning and returned to their rooms in the evening; their only social interaction occurring during breakfast or dinner in the communal dining room when they would say please, or thank you, or could you pass the bread or the salt. The only good thing about her job was that she was so busy from six in the morning until three in the afternoon—the restaurant catered only to the breakfast and lunch trade—that she had little time to think about her circumstances. Whatever free time she had she spent—as she had all her life in London—seeing films or plays or concerts. And for a special treat, she'd dress up and go to the opera at least once a month.

After almost two years of this rather lonely existence, she was, from habit, reading the help wanted ads in the *Times* on a Saturday morning and found herself circling one that tickled her fancy. It read: "Live-in cook/housekeeper wanted. Must have good sense of humor, common sense, and initiative.

Those without imagination and good grammar need not apply."

Ruth went directly out to the nearest pay telephone and got through to the Endicott exchange number given in the ad. When a woman answered, Ruth asked, "Are you the one placed the advert for a cook/housekeeper?"

When the woman said, "I am," Ruth said, "Good. My name's Ruth Parker, and if I had any common sense I'd never have married Henry Wallace and come to America. But I did, so I put up with the poor bloke for as long as humanly possible. Sorry to say, a drearier fellow I never have met. Finally, I took the initiative and moved out one morning a couple of years ago—into a boarding house because I thought it'd be a good way to meet new people. I've met them and they're a bloody depressing lot, I can tell you. Now, common sense tells me no ordinary or depressing person placed this advert. It appealed to my imagination, and what you're hearing is as good as my grammar gets. My sense of humor is well ready for a workout, I can tell you."

The woman laughed merrily, then asked, "Can you cook?"

"I'm fast and I'm good."

"Do you like movies?"

"I do. And the theater, and opera too."

"Ruth, I love you already. My name's Barlow. I'm at the Kenilworth on Central Park West between 75th and 76th. Come see me right now. Take a taxi. I'll reimburse you."

Smiling at the recollection of that ten-year-old memory, Honoria held out her cup, asking, "Any more coffee left, Ruth?"

"Of course, dearie. Something funny?"

"I was remembering what you said when you phoned about my ad. You were such a breath of fresh air. I knew you were exactly the person I was looking for."

Bringing the pot to the table, Ruth studied Honoria's face and said, "You were the one I was looking for, too, luv. You've got a bit of color back this morning. I was right to let you sleep."

"You're usually right."

"How you ever managed before I came along, I'll never know." The pot back on the stove, Ruth got the two pieces of bread ready for toasting.

"I didn't manage," Honoria said. "Before I moved into this apartment I never set foot in a kitchen except to make the occasional pot of coffee. And I never have figured out how to turn on an oven."

"A miracle you didn't starve to death."

Honoria laughed. "There's always been someone willing to buy me dinner, as you very well know."

"That's true." A pause, and then Ruth said, "I do miss Mr. Rosen, you know. Such a lovely chap. I thought you'd marry him one day."

"Evidently he thought so too. Unfortunately he neglected to ask me."

"Men are such silly buggers, aren't they? They're forever assuming things're 'understood,' so there's no need to say anything. Henry Wallace was guilty

174

of that. But my first husband, he wasn't. A lovely, thoughtful lad, was Alf. We had three happy years together before the war took him." Ruth sighed, gazing into space for a moment, then briskly got the eggs scrambled and the toast buttered, slid both onto a warm plate, and brought it to the table. "Get that into you, dearie, and you'll feel better still."

The food and the aspirin did the trick, and by the time she'd had a third cup of coffee Honoria was ready to try reading the newspaper.

"Looks as if we're due for more snow today," Honoria said as Ruth settled at the table with her own cup of coffee. "Rochester, Minnesota, was the coldest place in the country yesterday. Twenty-four below zero."

"Brrr." Ruth shuddered. "Felt near that last night here. Had to get up and shut my window. And you know how I feel about sleeping in a closed room. But it was bitter cold."

Honoria scanned the columns for a minute or two, then read aloud, " 'Less than a fortnight after Prince Paul, the Regent of Yugoslavia, departed from Buckingham Palace, where he was one of King George's guests at the royal wedding as the brother-in-law of the Duke of Kent's bride, the expulsion of Hungarians from his country has aroused indignation in the British press.' They say if Yugoslavia deserves sympathy on account of the murder of King Alexander, her government has already done much to alienate it by its treatment of Hungarian residents. The Yugoslav foreign office excuses the measures on account of the prevalence of unemployment in Yugoslavia."

"Beasts," Ruth declared. "Pushing people out of their homes."

"Unh-hunh. Now, listen to this. Yesterday customs agents seized 33,450 gallons of high-proof alcohol worth about $330,000 on the domestic market. They arrested thirteen men and seized a rum boat, a Canadian schooner, and a tug that was attempting to tow the boats through the turbulent waters of Hell Gate in the East River. Talk about idiotic! The Coast Guard was on a routine run when it saw the tow struggling with the two boats, so they went alongside to offer help. When they got on board the schooner, they smelled the alcohol, and that was that. It's the first big liquor seizure since Repeal. I thought all that smuggling business was finally over." Honoria shook her head and went on to scan the Books of the Times column, noting with interest brief reviews of four new mysteries. " '*House of the Damned* by Anthony Rud,' " she quoted with a smile, " 'is recommended to all folks anxious to get heart trouble, nervous prostration or St. Vitus' dance.' "

"Sounds right up your alley," Ruth said dryly. "Anything good on the radio this afternoon?"

"Have a look," Honoria said, passing her that page. "The print's too small for me today. I'm going to take a bath. I feel greasy." She started out of the kitchen, then stopped. "Do me a favor would you, sweetheart? Call Gloria and cancel my hair appointment for this afternoon. Explain I'm under the weather and tell her I'll come next week."

"Right you are, dearie."

While she was soaking in water as hot as she could stand it, Honoria thought of poor May standing out in the bitter cold, waiting to meet Gussy Washington, and hoped the woman had shown up. And why, now that she thought of it, hadn't Mrs. Carlson phoned? Closing her eyes, she slid lower into the water, feeling again Lucinda's tiny body in her arms, the infant's face instinctively pushing into her breast.

She awakened with a jolt. The water had gone cold. Shivering, she pulled the plug, stood up, and reached for a towel, wondering how long she'd been in the tub. At least half an hour, possibly longer. And she was so sleepy she had to fight to keep her eyes open and maintain her balance as she dried herself. She'd been intending to dress and put on some makeup before May came, but decided to lie down for a while. Plenty of time, she told herself, pulling on her robe.

Ruth had made the bed but left the spread off, and the blankets on Honoria's side were neatly, invitingly, folded back. She slipped beneath them and was asleep again within moments.

When she next awakened it was to find Mick sitting on the side of the bed, looking down at her with an expression of concern. She looked back at him, finding him remarkably attractive with his soulful eyes; high, smooth forehead; and thick, dark hair.

"I am worried about you," he said somberly, taking hold of her hand. "I never know you to sleep in the day. Is not good."

"Don't be silly, Mick. I was feeling dozy, that's all. It happens to the best of us. I'm getting old. Pretty soon I'll be falling asleep in my soup."

"You make joke," he persisted. "But is not funny to get hit on head. I told you is bad idea to do this thing for Chip."

"Yes, you did." She smiled at him, lacing her fingers through his.

"So now you stop, eh?"

"Soon, but not yet."

"*I* don't like it that you get hurt." He pulled his hand free in a gesture plainly meant to underscore his displeasure.

"I don't like it that I don't even get a hello kiss."

His somber expression held a moment or two longer, then he sighed and bent to kiss her lightly, as if fearful of hurting her. She looped an arm around his neck as he moved to straighten, and looked into his eyes at very close range before tightening her arm on his neck to bring him back to kiss him harder, longer, before finally releasing him. His left hand braced on the headboard, he remained leaning over her, examining her eyes as his right hand pushed aside the robe and began stroking her breast.

"Tell me when you will stop this investigating," he asked, watching his hand move over her.

"Soon, a few more days."

"This is a promise?" His eyes returned to hers.

"No, Mick. I can't promise because I don't know. But I think by the end of the week I'll be able to tell Chip I tried and came up empty. I said I'd do this and I've never broken a promise to him."

He withdrew his hand, pulled her robe closed, and sat away. "Is a big mistake to make this promise to him, Honor. But I say no more." He nodded in the direction of the door. "May is here, waiting to talk with you."

"Why are you so angry, Mick?" she asked, never having known him in a mood quite like this.

"Because what you are doing is *dangerous*. Already you get hurt but because you make promise to the boy you will go on, maybe get hurt more, get hurt worse. It makes me afraid for you. Is not so hard to understand."

"No," she agreed quietly, "it isn't. I'll be careful."

"Maybe," he said with a startling show of displeasure, "it is *no matter* if you are *careful*, Honor. Maybe you get hurt anyway because you are searching for someone who *kills*. Maybe this someone kills *you*. Then, what . . . ?" Eyes brimming, he broke off and turned away. Regaining his control, he stood up saying, "May waits. You want I should tell her to wait more?"

"Tell her I'll be out in five minutes."

"Okay." His shoulders stiff with anger he made his way to the door.

"Mick."

He halted and looked over.

"There's no need for you to be angry, to take this

179

personally."

Eyes going wide, he slapped his forehead, exclaiming hotly, "I take it personally because when you are *hurt* it is personal to *me!* Don't play like a stupid woman. You *know* this is *personal,* Honor." He pounded his right fist against his heart, glaring at her. "I *love* you! Perhaps you can say such stupid things because for you is not about love."

Shocked, she sat up saying, "That's not true."

"No? I think maybe is absolutely true." A hand on the doorknob he stood poised either to go or to hear her deny this.

She stared at him, an anxious palpitation in her chest as she tried to come up with an appropriate response. But she was unprepared for this confrontation and took too long. He sighed again, his shoulders dropped, and he left the room, shutting the door softly behind him.

"Damn!" she whispered, completely thrown. After a minute she got up to put on some clothes. Her hands were shaking and she wished she had time to analyze what had just happened. But May was waiting. Later this evening, she promised herself, they'd talk about this. Surely he couldn't believe she didn't care.

THIRTEEN

"**W**hy didn't anyone wake me?" Honoria asked Ruth and Maybelle, who were at the kitchen table, just finishing lunch.

Ruth got up at once, saying firmly, "You're not feeling well and you needed to sleep. Now sit yourself right down. I've been keeping your food warm."

"Are you all right?" Maybelle asked, rising to put her arms around Honoria in an embrace so tender and caring that Honoria felt a sudden inner tremor that was the certain prelude to tears. Appalled at the prospect, she gave a little laugh and eased away, saying, "You're sweet to be so concerned, May, but I'm fine."

Maybelle wasn't about to be put off so easily. She took hold of Honoria's hand while she studied her employer anxiously, thinking her eyes looked bigger, set deeper in their sockets, and overall she seemed smaller, as if in less than twenty-four hours she'd actually lost a substantial amount of weight. For the first time ever, Honoria failed to exude her customary aura of strength and confidence. And Maybelle found this particularly alarming because, from their very first meeting, Honoria had managed to convey the impression that she was immune to the periodic spells of self-doubt and uncertainty that most women experienced. Now, all at once, Maybelle could see the irrefutable signs of uncertainty, and it appeared that Honoria was susceptible, after all, to the fears both vague and specific that plagued other women. Yet seeing this confirmed Maybelle's long-held belief that Honoria was essentially a deeply emotional woman who hid behind a barrier composed of equal parts intelligence and humor. "Is that the truth?" she asked finally.

"I'm *fine*, May," Honoria repeated, giving the younger woman's hand a squeeze before taking a seat at the table. "Isn't Mick eating?" she asked, looking over at the doorway as she tried to quell the awful, almost ungovernable, desire to cry. That knock on the head seemed to have undermined her self-control. It also was having quite a profound effect on everyone around her.

"He went out," Maybelle said as she sat back down, unable to take her eyes off Honoria. Her view of the woman was shifting, altering like some trick mirror at a fun fair. And it was an occurrence of such significance that it seemed as if her very understanding of reality was being changed as a result. "He didn't say where he was going. Didn't say *anything*, as a matter of fact; just went charging out. Did you two have words or something?" If they were having trouble it might explain why Honoria seemed so diminished, as if in the throes of a fairly catastrophic metamorphosis.

"Or something," Honoria hedged as Ruth set a plate of Welsh rarebit in front of her, saying, "Careful now, dearie. The plate's hot. How about a nice cup of tea to go with it?" Ruth had a hand poised over the large, cozy-covered pot sitting on a wrought-iron trivet in the center of the table.

"Yes, please. Did Gussy Washington turn up, May?" Honoria picked up her knife and fork and started to eat. Until Ruth had come to work for her she'd never tasted Welsh rarebit, but over the years she'd developed a passion for the tangy concoction whose ingredients, aside from crumbly aged cheddar, Ruth kept a strict secret.

"No, she did not," Maybelle said with irritation. "I waited in the snow, freezing my face off, until half-past ten. Then I went over to her place to see if anyone was home, but no such luck. So on my way here I stopped by the Ansonia to see if my contact, Benjamin, might have any idea why she didn't show. But he was out doing some errand and nobody seemed to know when he'd be back. So I guess I'll have to start over from square one with Gussy, maybe drop in again on my way home and leave another note."

"I wonder why she didn't show up," Honoria mused, the heat of the kitchen turning her sleepy again and making it hard to pay attention.

"Beats me. But you'll be happy to know that while you were sleeping I typed up the last of the rewrites and got them off. Which means when the big boys out on the coast start ringing the phone off the hook Monday, we'll be able to say truthfully that the scripts are on the way. Your desk is now officially clear."

"Thank you. You're a treasure, May."

"Yes, I know," Maybelle said wryly. "Chip called, by the way. He said to tell you he'll be here in time for dinner on Monday. And of course he wanted to know how things are going. I filled him in a bit on who we've talked to and what they had to say, but I figured you wouldn't want me to mention your getting hit on the head, so I didn't. And speaking of that, what the hell *happened,* Honoria?" she erupted, unable to hold back a moment longer.

The other two women had to wait while Honoria swallowed a mouthful of food, followed by some tea. "Okay," she said, knowing they'd keep at her until they got all the details. She gave them a quick run-down of everything that had happened after she and Maybelle parted company at Sak's, up to her being whacked on the head in DeeDee's unlit living room. She fell silent as she relived that moment, thinking it was as if she'd been soaring blithely through space and had suddenly, shockingly, collided at great speed with an invisible wall—mashed like an airborne in-sect on the windshield of a fast-moving car. She gave a small involuntary shiver and tried to cover it by cutting another piece of the rarebit. After a few mo-ments, she picked up where she'd left off. "I guess I must have been out cold for fifteen or twenty min-utes. My cab driver got worried when I was gone for so long, and came looking for me. I was just coming to when he and the concierge arrived. Jake helped me downstairs and brought me home."

"That's very scary, Honoria," Maybelle said soberly. "Maybe we should forget about this whole thing, drop it right now."

All at once everyone seemed to want her to quit digging into DeeDee's death. "Have you been dis-cussing this with Mick?" she asked suspiciously.

"No, I have not," Maybelle declared indignantly. As if she'd *do* such a thing! That crack on the head had really shaken some of Honoria's screws loose.

"But if folks're starting to get physical, it might be smart to quit while we're still standing."

"Have to say I agree with May, dearie," Ruth put in. "It's one thing to go round visiting the dead girl's friends, chatting over a cup of tea or what-have-you. It's quite another to come home in the condition you did last night."

"I'm *fine* now," Honoria insisted stubbornly.

Ruth was prepared to argue but could see from Honoria's expression that it would be useless, so she shrugged and picked up her teacup. She knew better than to put her oar in when Honoria had her mind made up. She'd hammer away at this until she was satisfied, and nothing and no one would stop her.

"You don't *look* fine," Maybelle kept on, wondering why Honoria was so bent on pursuing what had now turned into a dangerous pastime. "Getting hit on the head's no laughing matter."

"I couldn't agree more. But I'm not prepared to throw in the towel yet. Not until I've had a chance to meet Mrs. Carlson. I'm very curious to see what kind of woman produced a child like DeeDee. Aren't you?"

"Sure I am," Maybelle allowed. "But not to the point where I'm willing to get hurt, or to see *you* get hurt a second time."

"I got a bump on the head. It's not the end of the world."

"Where do we draw the line, Honoria?" Maybelle asked. "After you get yourself killed?" Instantly, she wished she hadn't put the thought into words. Her grandma regularly accused her of being overly superstitious. "Just cuz you spoke out loud about somethin' that scares you," her grandma would say, "puttin' it in words ain't gonna make it happen. That's plain foolishness, May." Maybe, and maybe not, but she wanted her feelings on the record. "Getting bashed on the head's a pretty strong statement about how somebody feels about our 'investigating,' Honoria. Who's to say that next time that person won't be prepared to go even further? After all, if DeeDee *was* murdered, the killer would have no qualms about engaging in a repeat performance. You can only get the death sentence once, regardless of how many people you've killed."

Ruth drew in her breath and waited to see how Honoria took this.

Honoria popped the last of the Welsh rarebit into her mouth, considering how to answer. Why didn't she just admit defeat and walk away from this? Partly it had to do with curiosity, but primarily she was pushing ahead from habit. From her earliest days at the Asylum, she'd bridled when told not to do something, or when there was even the slightest suggestion that she was incapable of performing some act. Her response back then had inevitably been to go right ahead regardless, and it was the same now. When she left the Asylum she'd promised herself that no one would ever again have the power over her to dictate what she could or could not do. But no one was telling her she couldn't do it. They were all expressing concern for the risk she'd be taking if she continued. And it probably would be risky, so maybe the smart thing would be to call it quits. Chip would be disappointed, but it wouldn't be his first time, or his last. At length, she replied, "I won't know where the line gets drawn until the time comes to draw it. You don't have to come along, May, if you don't want to. I'll certainly understand if you'd rather not."

"Oh, sure! I'll just sit home and listen to the radio while you take off on your own. Look what happens when I leave you to go it alone for *one* evening!"

Honoria smiled. "So if you'd been with me it wouldn't have happened?"

"I sincerely doubt it. There's safety in numbers, you know. Whoever it was could hardly have hit both of us."

"You have a point."

"Of course I do." Maybelle sighed, then said, "Well, I guess I might as well tell you. Chip wasn't the only one who called earlier. The elusive Mrs. Carlson finally phoned."

"Well, wonder of wonders! I was about ready to give up on her."

"You don't know the meaning of giving up on things. Anyway, she said she's willing to talk to you, for Chip's sake—whatever *that* means. However, she's going to Palm Beach for Christmas, and the only free time she has is this afternoon."

"Tell me you made an appointment."

"Naturally! You think I don't know who I'm dealing with here? She's expecting you at three-thirty at 4 East 66th."

187

"Good. How did she sound?"

"Kind of angry, as if this was a big inconvenience. The only time her tone warmed up at all was when she mentioned Chip. Otherwise, she was very frosty. Oh, and she has a foreign accent, sort of English, but not."

"Interesting. And she's at 4 East 66th. Now, *that's* an address and a half."

"Why?" Maybelle and Ruth both asked.

Honoria finished the cup of tea, poured herself more, then said, "Aside from the fact that every apartment in the building has eighteen rooms, what would you like to know?"

"*Eighteen rooms?*" the other two chorused.

"I dated a banker years ago who lived there. Do you remember Scott Camberwell, Ruth? Incredibly tall, with red hair and freckles, and an odd fondness for spats?"

"Hmn. Can't say that I do. You'd think I'd recall a chap in spats in this day and age."

"He was a silly guy. The co-op was a lot more interesting than he was, which is probably why I saw him more than once. It's one of the best-designed buildings in town. The outside is misleadingly plain. But *inside!* I've never seen anything quite like it. Eleven suites, one to a floor. Two enormous main rooms side by side overlooking the park; six huge bedrooms and five bathrooms, twelve-foot-high ceilings, five fireplaces, a gallery maybe forty feet long leading to the dining room; immense closets, and tons of storage space. Picture an upside-down reversed L with seven servants' rooms, each with its own wash basin, plus two full staff bathrooms, and a big servants' dining room all in their own wing off the main corridor. There was a kitchen you'd have loved, Ruth, at least fifteen by thirty, with a pantry about half that size off it. A *fabulous* place, with exquisite detailing. Scott kept a full retinue of servants just to look after his every need."

"Cleaning his spats and what-have-you," Ruth put in.

"Obviously Mr. Carlson left his family very well off," Honoria thought aloud.

"Obviously," Maybelle said. "After that description, I can hardly wait to see the place."

"I would like you to come with me, May," Honoria admitted. "You're right about there being safety in numbers."

"Fine," she said rather sharply. "I'll go with you. But I don't feel good about keeping on with this."

"So noted. Let's make a deal. If my talk with Mrs. Carlson doesn't lead anywhere, I'll drop the whole thing."

"But if it does, you'll keep going?"

"Not for much longer. I might talk to Fluff Connors and Bitsy what's-her-name, but I doubt they'd have anything new to add."

"If you do drop it, what'll you tell Chip?"

"The truth—that I didn't make any headway. The girl's dead and that's the end of it. From what we've heard, he's damned lucky."

"He'll never believe that," Maybelle said. "But

189

you'll really give up on it?"

"Depending on what we get from Mrs. Carlson."

"Why don't I believe you?" Maybelle asked.

"Because you're a natural-born skeptic. Now, let's change the subject. Tell me about your dinner with the divine Mr. Whiting."

"That's right," Ruth remembered. "You had a date last evening, didn't you, love?"

"It was pleasant," Maybelle said primly. "He's very nice."

"He's a *knockout*, Ruth," Honoria said. "And not shy about saying he thinks May's the most beautiful woman he's ever seen."

"Well, she is, isn't she?" Ruth said, regarding Maybelle with a bemused expression, as if dismayed to learn that she was unaware of her attributes. "Of course you are, dearie," she told the young woman. "Prettiest girl I've ever seen, and that's a fact."

"The two of you are prejudiced," a discomfited Maybelle accused.

"Of course we are," Honoria said. "But that doesn't mean we're wrong. Now come on. Tell us about it. What did you do? Where did you go?"

"It was very nice. *He's* very nice. We had a drink, then we went to a French restaurant for dinner. But it's not going to happen again."

"Whyever not?" Ruth asked disappointedly.

Maybelle turned in her chair, resting one arm on the back and crossing her legs. "People stared and whispered," she said flatly. "I didn't *feel* pretty. I felt as if they were burning me alive with their eyes;

190

everyone looking at us. It was torture. I'd never put myself through that again. All I could think the whole evening was that everything I've ever heard about mixed-race couples was true. It wouldn't matter how much you might care about each other because those glaring eyes, and the whispering, and people who don't know you hating you because you're not white would kill the caring in the end."

"Are you sure you weren't misinterpreting?" Honoria asked.

"Not a chance," Maybelle declared. "You'll never know how it feels to have people hate you that way, as if you're less than human—just because of what you look like, because your skin's a different color."

"No," Honoria said gently. "You're quite right, May, I wouldn't know." *She could still recall so vividly that cluster of grubby boys playing stickball or sitting on the front stoop, pausing in their game or their conversation to razz her every morning as she went by clutching her typing and shorthand manuals, cracking wise about her telltale clothes, calling her an orphan bastard and other, worse things. And when she got a bit older, they'd see her coming and move to form a circle around her, taunting, threatening. Hemmed in by their scrawny arms she'd keep her silence, glaring at each of them in turn until they gave up and let her go on her way. Until the next time. A bit bolder, a bit more menacing as the months, then years, went by. Then one October morning three of the older boys dragged her into an alley. Refusing to show her fear, she'd dropped her books and took the three off guard, kicking the biggest in the balls, then jab-*

bing her fingers into the eyes of the smallest. The third and meanest member of the trio backhanded her across the face, then shoved her up against the wall, prepared to work her over but good. Still, she refused to show any fear. "You don't scare me," she'd said, her voice thick and wobbly as the narrow-eyed boy drew back his fist. "Some tough guy, beating up on a girl, afraid to take on someone your own size."

The arrival of Rooney, the beat cop, sent the boys running off down the alley. "Why d'you want to go mixing it up with these hooligans?" Rooney had asked, as if believing she derived some sort of satisfaction from these encounters. "Get along with you now and try to stay out of trouble." Humiliated and angry, but proud that she'd given as good as she'd got, she'd picked up her schoolbooks and hair ribbon, and hurried away, half her hair still neatly braided, the other half hanging in a wild mess. All that day she thought about what had happened, and what Rooney had said, at last deciding that the old cop had a point. She didn't have to go down that block every morning when she knew that gang would be waiting for her. But she'd been trying to prove—to them and to herself—that she was just as good as they were, had just as much right to walk the streets as they did. It was stupid, trying to prove points to boys who were too dumb to understand. She was wasting her time and energy, suffering abuse for no good reason. Thereafter, she'd set out half an hour earlier each morning, to take a longer, safer route to school.

What did the woman see when her eyes turned inward that way? Maybelle wondered, suspecting she'd probably made another stupid assumption. It was more than possible that Honoria knew how the heat simmered just beneath the surface of your skin, shame and anger gripping your insides, making you want to strike out, to kill, to disappear, or even die—all for something utterly beyond your control. She may even have known how it felt to loathe your skin because it was like a banner you had to carry around, setting you apart, forcing you to hurry back uptown to your own people where there was at least the comfort of sameness. But you couldn't stay uptown forever. Daily you had to travel into the white world, where, at best, you were ignored and, at worst, you were despised. Nothing she could ever say or do would change what was unchangeable.

Honoria looked at the time—it was twenty past two—and said, "Well, I'd better get dressed and fix my face before we go see Mrs. Carlson." In passing, she let her hand rest on Maybelle's shoulder for a moment. "I'm sorry it didn't work out," she said softly.

At a loss, Maybelle shrugged.

"Shall I read your tea-leaves, love; see what's in your future?" Ruth was asking Maybelle as Honoria left the kitchen.

FOURTEEN

The elevator doors opened into a foyer, where Mrs. Carlson stood waiting for them. A trim, strikingly beautiful woman, she either wore no makeup at all or applied it so skillfully that it was impossible to detect. She had on an exquisitely cut black broadcloth suit with hand-stitched detailing and a white silk blouse whose collar and cuffs were folded out over those of the jacket. She was at first glance a more refined, infinitely more elegant version of DeeDee, with the same pretty features and purity of complexion; the same blonde hair and pale, almost colorless, blue eyes. But unlike the flat coldness of her daughter's eyes, hers revealed many things—curiosity, sadness, and a profound weariness. Honoria was immediately predisposed to like the woman, finding her visible vulnerability touching.

Offering a firm hand to Honoria, she said, "Hello. I'm Karen"—she pronounced it "Car-in"—"It's good of you to come on such short notice."

"It's good of you to see us," Honoria said and introduced Maybelle.

Karen Carlson turned to offer her hand to Maybelle, saying, "Ah, yes. We spoke earlier on the telephone, didn't we? Thank you for coming. You may leave your coats just here." She showed them to the cloakroom to the left of the foyer, then led the way through the gallery to the drawing room, where everything, even the chandelier, was covered by dust sheets, and heavy draperies concealed the windows on either side of the fireplace. After switching on a table lamp, she lifted aside the sheet on a long white sofa and invited the two women to sit down. "I could give you tea or coffee if you would care for some, but I'm afraid there's no milk or cream," she said while uncovering an exquisite Queen Anne armchair upholstered in a deep red silk velvet.

Both Maybelle and Honoria thanked her but declined, and Karen said, "I've been longing for a cigarette. If you'll excuse me for a moment, I'll just fetch an ashtray from the kitchen."

"You weren't kidding. This place is astonishing," Maybelle said quietly, looking at the magnificent pure white marble fireplace and the portrait above it of two young Victorian girls in white cotton frocks seated on a grassy promontory in the late-afternoon sun, looking down at a stretch of deserted beach. "I love the painting."

"It's wonderful," Honoria agreed.

Karen Carlson returned and placed a small glass ashtray on the pie-crust table adjacent to the Queen Anne chair.

"We were just admiring the room," Honoria explained. "And the painting over the mantel in particular."

"Yes, it is lovely, isn't it." For a second or two she, too, admired the painting. Then she said, "Obviously, the apartment is not at its best just now." She indicated the shrouded furniture with her left hand—adorned by the plain gold wedding band that was, Honoria noted with interest, the only jewelry she wore—before seating herself and opening a monogrammed silver cigarette case. "The staff has already gone ahead to open the Florida house, you see. I was supposed to be leaving here this morning, but something came up so I won't go now until Monday. And that is why there's no milk or cream, or anything else to speak of in the kitchen." She lit a cigarette with a silver lighter, set both case and lighter next to the ashtray on the table, then took a long hungry drag on the cigarette.

Honoria watched, appreciating the woman's fluidity of movement as she rested the hand with the cigarette on an arm of the chair and crossed her legs. She had the extravagant length of neck, the slight torso, long slender limbs, and perfectly erect bearing of a classically trained dancer. "I'm sorry about your daughter," Honoria said by way of an opening.

"Thank you. It's still very hard for me to believe she's gone." The large, pale eyes looked off into space as she exhaled a plume of smoke on a slow sigh. She drew again on the cigarette, eyes still distant, then seemed to return reluctantly, running the fingers of her left hand through the chin-length wavy hair she wore brushed straight back and tucked behind her ears. It was an extreme hairstyle that suited her well, calling attention to her high, smooth forehead and admirable profile. Perhaps, too, Honoria mused, the absence of jewelry was meant to call attention to the fragility of her wrists and the lineless column of her neck. If so, Karen had succeeded. For a woman who had to be in her mid to late forties, she was, Honoria thought, remarkably well preserved. Only a slight softening of the flesh at her jaw and the telltale prominent veins on the backs of her hands gave any hint of her actual age. "Forgive me, please," she said with an apologetic little grimace. "I've been very distracted lately—as you can imagine. I lose track, sometimes in the middle of a thought. Where were we?"

"Nowhere in particular," Honoria said indulgently. "I'm sure it's been terribly difficult for you."

The woman shrugged as if to say difficult was nowhere near an adequate description. "I know Chip doesn't want to believe it any more than I do, but my daughter took her own life, Miss Barlow."

"You believe that's what happened?" Honoria asked, concealing her surprise at the bluntness of the statement. But perhaps going directly to the heart of the matter was the woman's way of dealing with a subject she'd have preferred not to discuss at all.

"I'm as sure of it as I can be of anything right now," Karen Carlson said with some bitterness, then took another long drag on her cigarette. "You see, Cordelia never really came to terms with her father's death. It haunted her. She was unable to accept the facts of the matter. Whenever we were together she inevitably talked about it, asking me again and again if I thought her father had always been suicidal or if he'd really done it because of his losses in the stock market. Again and again I had to go over it all for her."

"And what did you tell her?"

Karen gazed thoughtfully at Honoria for a moment before answering. "The truth: that it was because of his losses, which were enormous. Arne had invested all his assets and—without my knowledge—most of mine. He'd thought he'd make us fabulously wealthy, as if what we had wasn't enough. Of course it was; it was more than enough. But men seem to need to keep on. Have you ever noticed that? Like small children, they've got to acquire more and more and more. It's as if they lack the ability to be satisfied. Or perhaps it becomes a game of sorts, like playing roulette or baccarat over and over again, to prove they can defy the odds and win more times than they lose." She shrugged a second time, then put out the just-lit cigarette in the ashtray. "What made it so shocking was that Arne was by nature a conservative man, cautious even; certainly he was never a gambler. But he caught the fever, and once he started buying he couldn't stop. He explained everything in the letter he left . . ." She faltered briefly, chewing on her lower lip, then went on. "Luckily there were certain assets, insurance policies, trusts and so forth, that remained intact after his death. Otherwise . . ." Again she faltered.

"You must have been very angry when you discovered what he'd done," Maybelle suggested.

Karen looked over at her with interest. "I was astonished. But in truth I was more angry about his preferring to end his life rather than confess to me what he'd done. He needn't have killed himself. I understood how it was. After all, only a very few of the people we knew weren't buying like mad, on the telephone to their brokers half a dozen times a day. Arne was simply doing what most of his friends and business associates were doing. But to take his own life, to leave Cordelia and I alone, with our finances in such a frightful mess . . . No, no. I'm making it sound as if it mattered about the money, but it didn't. It *was* a mess, no question. What hurt so deeply was his leaving us that way, with no opportunity to discuss matters, or to say good-bye." Eyes brimming, her voice going thick, she said, "Arne was the love of my life, the most important person in the world to me. From the day we met, back home in Copenhagen, I knew he was the only man I could ever care for deeply. And for him, it was the same."

"How did you meet?" Honoria asked.

"At a reception."

"You were a dancer."

"How do you know that?" Karen Carlson asked warily.

"An educated guess. You have the carriage of a dancer."

With a slight incline of her head, the woman said, "I was with the company from the age of eight. For ten years life was class in the morning, class in the afternoon, rehearsals, performances. Strains and bruises, pulled ligaments, damaged tendons; soaking in hot baths, knitting leg warmers, stitching the toes of endless pairs of point shoes; rivalries, competition, small successes. At the end of ten years, when I'd become a principal soloist and got to dance the good roles, I didn't care anymore. I was longing for an ordinary life. No more hours at the barre, no more drafty rehearsal rooms with walls of mirrors to reflect your every flaw. I had no ambition left but to leave the company. And then, at the opening-night reception of that tenth season, there was Arne. I loved him at first sight." She paused, savoring the recollection.

"We married the following spring, when I was nineteen and he was twenty-five. Four years later, when Cordelia was almost three, we came to America. And for eighteen years we were so very happy. Arne had great success in business. We had a lovely home, many friends, a good life for the three of us." Her eyes again on distant vistas, she smiled at the recollection of that good life. Then the smile slowly disappeared. She blinked away the past and a tear ran down her cheek. "Such a foolish—such a *male* thing to do," she railed, wiping her face with the back of one hand. "Why did he feel the only solution was to end his life? It was no solution at all. Things would have been different, but we'd have managed. To take such a final, such a drastic step, it left me with no choice . . ." She sniffed, pulled a lace-edged handkerchief from her jacket pocket and blew her nose, then got another cigarette from the case. "I am sorry," she said hoarsely. "The world is too much with me today."

" 'The world is too much with us; late and soon, /Getting and spending, / We lay waste our powers,' " Honoria quoted softly from memory.

"You know this poem," Karen said, gratified. "That is *exactly* how it seemed to me—the stock market, the frantic buying, buying. And then Arne in his office, holding a gun to his heart, finishing everything we had." She shook her head sorrowfully, then lit the fresh cigarette and studied Honoria through the haze of smoke with slightly narrowed eyes, as if revising her first impression of her.

"I've often thought how appropriate Wordsworth's poem was to the Crash," Honoria said.

"And to many other things, as well," Karen said.

"And other things, too," Honoria concurred soberly. "About DeeDee . . . Cordelia," she eased the conversation back on track. "I get the impression you weren't altogether surprised by her death."

"Oh, you mustn't think that! I was horribly surprised, shattered, stunned. It's one thing to imagine that a child, a daughter you adore, is capable of harming herself, to recognize that she has a self-destructive aspect to her nature. But it's quite another thing when it actually happens, when that child does away with herself. I *never* wanted to believe she would do it—especially not when she hadn't ever recovered from the horror of her father's suicide. I never *dreamed* she would take her life."

"No, of course you didn't," Honoria said. "Yet when she did, there was a part of you, wasn't there, that had been anticipating such an eventuality?"

Karen nodded, smoke streaming from her nostrils. "You're very perceptive. It is true. And I felt very ashamed for having thought such a thing."

"It's awful to have one's darkest fears confirmed."

At this, Karen nodded a second time, searching Honoria's eyes, as if for any sign that she was perhaps being manipulated. Seeing none, she looked away and took a hard drag on the cigarette, tears again sitting in the rims of her eyes.

"And what's even worse," Honoria went on, "is that you've been deprived of the personal exit, so to speak, that you'd been keeping in reserve."

Karen's expressive eyes, widening with surprise, returned to Honoria. "How do you know this?" she asked in a hushed tone.

"Most of us consider suicide, when life seems too unfair or just too impossible."

"You yourself have thought of it?"

"I have," Honoria admitted. "I think we use suicide as a kind of yardstick for measuring our alternatives. Are things so bad that it would be better to die? Or are they not so bad that they're worth dying for?"

Maybelle looked first at one woman then the other, astounded by the turn the conversation had taken. Had Honoria truly considered suicide? And if so, when? And why? Or was she merely making statements calculated to draw responses from Mrs. Carlson? Maybelle had no idea what to think.

"Obviously you decided they were not so bad," Karen said. "For here you are."

"Here I am indeed," Honoria said. "I think we've got to have something to use for the sake of comparison. Suicide happens to be the measure a lot of us choose to help us decide whether or not life is still worth living. But you're going to have to live now, Karen, aren't you? Because your husband and child have robbed you of your secret option."

Her face wet, eyes fixed on Honoria as if to a lifeline, Karen Carlson's head bobbed up and down in agreement with what Honoria was saying. "It's how I feel and I am amazed that you know it. I can't speak of this to my friends," she said, choked. "They don't understand—or don't wish to. The few times I've started to confide my feelings to them, they've grown embarrassed—for me, not for themselves— as if I'd suddenly removed my clothes in a public place, or performed some lewd act. They've stopped me from speaking further by trying to cheer me up or divert me with platitudes. It takes time to get over such losses, they tell me. You've had a dreadful shock and you aren't thinking clearly. These things are true. But I have been needing to make the comparison, to take measurements on the yardstick, as you call it; I've needed to hear myself say the words, asking the ultimate question: Have things become so bad that I choose to die, or am I able to keep on living?"

"Death is too alarming, too possibly contagious," Honoria said. "People don't want to talk about it, to get too close to it for fear they'll somehow be inviting it into their lives. It's superstition. May's superstitious, aren't you?" Honoria turned to her assistant.

Caught off guard, Maybelle hedged, saying, "I guess I am."

"*Very* superstitious," Honoria said with a fond smile before directing her words back to Karen Carlson. "And there's nothing wrong with that, except that as a result any number of things don't get said—especially when it comes to death. In many ways, we're still a fairly primitive society."

"Primitive," Karen repeated thoughtfully, then took a last drag on the cigarette and stubbed it out. "It's the first time I've heard anyone say that, but I think it's true. Beneath the outer layer of sophistication, beyond the shield of protection that money can buy, there is a fear of death, a fear even of the very word, so people say 'passed away' or that someone is 'lost.' And you are quite right, Miss Barlow, that is primitive. When we are young, we never think of death. We are immortal; we cannot die; nothing can kill us. But when we are past youth and begin to encounter death, then we become afraid, and we grow greedy about our lives. There is so much we have yet to do; we are too young; death is for the aged, the ill, not for people still in their prime. This is why my friends have no wish to hear my thoughts. It is obvious to me now that you've said what you have. It explains a great deal."

"Sometimes we need to hear what others have to say before we can form our own opinions," Honoria said. "It's just unfortunate that the subject of death is not considered acceptable as polite dinner-table conversation."

There was a pause and then, with a surprised light in her eyes, Karen laughed as she got out the handkerchief again to dry her face. "I'm so very glad now that the delay in my departure meant I could get to talk with you. You're— What is the word? Irreverent. Yes. You are irreverent, and I admire that very much."

"Oh, I'm exceedingly irreverent," Honoria said with a measure of pride. "I've never been able to accept the notion that there are subjects unsuitable for discussion, that there are certain avenues open only to men and not to women. I've always believed that, given the opportunity, most of us *want* to talk about all the supposedly unsuitable subjects. When the situation presents itself—now, for example—I like to offer that opportunity to others. Nothing surprises me anymore and very little shocks me. But that doesn't preclude the need for discussion."

"You speak as if you've lived a very long time," Karen observed, "as if you are elderly. But you're still a young woman."

"So are you," Honoria said. "But inside my head I'm as old as the hills. And that has to do with what I've experienced and absorbed, not with age. I have known, as I'm sure you have, some incredibly banal and insipid old folks who've skimmed along on the surface of life and whose insights are on a par with the average eight-year-old's. And I've known some—like Maybelle's grandmother, and Ruth, my housekeeper, to name a couple—who have exceptional wisdom because they've watched and listened and thought hard about what they've seen and heard, then formed opinions that are rooted in reality. I think what you need, Karen, is someone to talk to who won't get upset and try to boot you out the door if the conversation turns to darker topics."

"You're right. I do need that." Karen sighed again and looked down at her hands as they twisted the lace-edged handkerchief. "Aside from this foolish business with the stocks, Arne and I always talked. At the end of each day we discussed everything. The best part of an evening out was when we returned home and could do what Arne called the post mortem—dissecting the event and examining all its aspects. When he died, that was lost, too."

"What about DeeDee? Did the two of you talk?"

Karen shook her head. "Not really. I would have liked to." She raised her eyes, saying, "More than just the man was lost when Arne held that gun to his chest. A husband and father puts an end to his life, and when he does this frightful, *selfish* thing, he also puts an end to the family. Not only is he gone, but the manner of his death makes real conversation between the surviving daughter and the wife impossible." Looking over at Maybelle, she said, "You asked earlier was I angry with Arne for what he did, and I was rather evasive. The truth is I was furious with him, absolutely livid, because he took so much away—far more than he left behind. Cordelia was never the same afterward. And neither was I. What he did was unspeakably selfish, *monstrously* selfish!" She stopped abruptly, as if embarrassed, and reached for her cigarette case but didn't open it. She simply sat holding it, again looking at her hands.

"I hope you're not going to regret anything you've said," Honoria spoke after a moment.

"No." Karen squared her shoulders, returned the cigarette case to the table, and once more ran a hand through her hair. "I was merely thinking of how very odd I feel now. It's if I'm a child again and at long last I've been allowed to run wild in Aunt Alicia's parlor." She found a smile for the two women on the sofa. "It was a room filled with many, many breakable objects and massive dusty pieces of uncomfortable furniture Aunt Alicia called antiques. We were forbidden to set a foot over the threshold, so naturally my brother and I wanted nothing more than to get inside and examine every last item in there."

"Telling the truth does feel dangerous, doesn't it?" Honoria said with one of her wonderfully devilish smiles. "But rewarding, too."

"How did you feel about your daughter getting engaged to Chip?" Maybelle asked.

"Cordelia was so excited. She was making plans, although they had not yet decided on when the wedding would be." Karen's eyes once more drifted away and her hand lifted, fingers raking through her hair. Then the hand settled on the arm of the chair and the eyes made what seemed to be a reluctant journey back to Honoria.

Maybelle's question hadn't been answered, but Honoria sensed it would be best not to push the matter.

"In the spring, when I return," Karen ventured, "perhaps we could meet again, for lunch or dinner; to talk more."

"Let's do that," Honoria said, admiring the adroitness with which the woman signaled that the interview was at its end. "We'll be on our way now, let you get on with your last-minute packing and what-have-you."

"Please give Chip my warmest regards," Karen said earnestly. "And tell him it would be best if he accepts Cordelia's death for what it was."

"Yes, he must do that," Honoria agreed with equal seriousness.

"Perhaps you could persuade him to try to put this tragedy behind him. He's still so very young. I'm sure in time he will find someone else."

"I'm sure he will," Honoria echoed, wanting that for him with all her heart and wishing she could tell him how lucky he was to have escaped the hell on earth DeeDee would probably have made of his life.

"He's a dear young man. I am so very fond of him." Karen again seemed on the verge of getting lost in the distant reaches of the past, but she caught herself and said, "I'm sorry I couldn't give the two of you anything to drink." She rose fluidly from the chair, ready to lead them back to the cloakroom.

"Don't give it a thought," Honoria said as Maybelle went ahead to get their coats. "We'll make up for it next time."

"Yes, next time." Karen offered her hand to each woman in turn, then rang for the elevator, which came very quickly.

"Take care of yourself," Honoria said.

Karen said, "And you must do the same. Thank you again for coming. I have profited greatly from our conversation." As the elevator doors began to close, she waved, smiled fleetingly, and then turned away.

FIFTEEN

"**W**as that true, what you told her, about considering suicide?"

"One hundred percent. But please don't ask me about it, May. I'm not up to rehashing ancient history just now."

They had to stop at the corner of 66th Street and Fifth while Honoria searched her pockets. "Damn! I must've dropped my gloves in the cloakroom. They're my new ones, too."

"I could run back for them," Maybelle offered.

Honoria considered it for a moment, then said, "No, don't bother. Karen's not leaving until Monday. I'll phone when I get home and ask her to leave them with the concierge. At some point over the weekend I can pick them up." Jamming both hands into her coat pockets, she looked up and down the avenue, saying, "We'll never get a cab in this." It was bitingly cold, and beneath a substantial layer of still-falling snow the sidewalks were treacherously icy.

"We could cut through the park. It'd be easier walking than this and wouldn't take us all that long."

"I couldn't bear to go past those shacks and think of the poor people huddled inside, trying to keep warm." Honoria could too easily picture the low row of makeshift dwellings she so often looked down upon from the apartment windows—layers of salvaged old shingles nailed to pieces of lumber canted at arbitrary angles to create roofs; discarded windows of random sizes retrieved from dump sites and fitted haphazardly into warped wood frames recovered from the same source; scavenged bricks or tin for chimneys that vented whatever the residents had found to serve as stoves which provided both a means of cooking and of precious heat. "I've got a better idea," she said. "The Pierre's only a few blocks from here. Let's go have a drink. Then, with any luck, we'll be able to pick up a cab afterwards outside the hotel. If we can't, we'll grab the cross-town bus and I'll walk you to the subway on my way home."

"You don't have to do that, Honoria."

"I know I don't. Look, sweetheart, it's too damned cold to stand here arguing about it. Come have a drink."

"Are you feeling all right?"

"I won't be if we don't get moving, and soon."

"Okay," Maybelle gave in. "Here." She removed the glove from her right hand. "Put that on," she told Honoria. "Then give me your left hand."

Honoria did as directed, and Maybelle's warm hand closed around hers, guiding it into the depths of her pocket. "That's better," Maybelle said as they started off, heads lowered against the driving hard-edged snow crystals that cut into any areas of exposed skin like tiny knives. "It's only December and I'm already fed up with winter, all this lousy snow."

"Tell me what you thought of Karen," Honoria

invited as they picked their way across 65th Street.

"I think she's either the world's greatest actress or she's lost the ability to dissemble."

"Really? You suspect she was faking?"

"I suspect something," Maybelle said. "I'm just not sure what. How about you? What's your take on her?"

"I want to hear your thoughts first."

"Okay. There were a few things that bothered me." Maybelle blinked snow out of her eyes. "One was how suspicious she got when you guessed that she'd been a dancer."

"She did jump on that, didn't she?"

"And how! It was as if she was scared you knew things about her you weren't supposed to."

"You've got a point. What else?"

"Mostly the way she kept insisting that the financial mess Arne left her and DeeDee in didn't matter, as if she wanted us to believe she was above such trivial considerations."

"Well, she's obviously not hurting for cash, so maybe that's the point she was trying to make."

"Maybe," Maybelle said doubtfully.

"And?"

"You'll think I'm petty, but the way she let us know it was time to go was too slick and sudden to suit me. I asked how she felt about DeeDee's engagement to Chip, and wham! Show's over, folks. Time to go, please. To be fair, it could be my reverse snobbism working, but I hate being given the bum's rush, no matter how swelegantly it's done. And *Car-*

in's a mighty classy act. I just don't know, Honoria. There's nothing I can put my finger on but I had a lot of trouble buying what she was selling."

"Do tell." Honoria was intrigued by the things Maybelle had picked up on, and the reasons why.

"For one thing, her philosophical stance didn't quite fit with the desperate way she smoked those cigarettes and kept running a hand through her hair; the way she'd trail off mid-sentence and her eyes would go all vague. I just couldn't believe some of the things she said. I can't be specific; it's more a *feeling* I had. You know?"

"I trust your feelings," Honoria said, then fell silent, thinking. She might as well have been nude for all the protection her outerwear offered. The cold was finding its way under her clothes, making her shiver so hard her bones ached, and turning her legs numb so that it became increasingly difficult to walk. As well, her cheeks were stinging, as if from being burned. This was not one of those occasions when snow turned the city beautiful, but rather one when the elements conspired to make being out of doors a complete nightmare.

Battling the wind and trying to avoid the icy patches on the sidewalk, they covered the remaining distance to 61st Street and didn't speak again until they were at a corner table of the hotel bar with drinks in front of them—a martini for Honoria and dry sherry for Maybelle.

"Are you ever going to tell me what you thought of her?" Maybelle asked.

"I agree that some of the things she said may or may not be true, but her grief was the real McCoy."

"You're sure of that, huh?"

"Come on, May," Honoria reminded her. "You know it was."

"Yeah, I know. She was too raw, too exposed. It made me so mad I wanted to spit."

Honoria reached over, picked up Maybelle's hand, and held it to her cheek. Maybelle's parents had died within weeks of each other in the Great Influenza Epidemic, leaving an eleven-year-old orphan whose only surviving family member was her grandmother. Even now Maybelle couldn't speak of them without getting choked up.

After a few moments Honoria set the young woman's hand back on the table, saying, "You can't be angry with Karen because of that, May. It's not her fault—any more than it was yours—that she lost the two people who meant the most to her."

Relenting, Maybelle said, "I was embarrassed for her, the way she said her friends were. I wanted her to have more—dignity, I guess."

"But that's exactly what convinced me it was real. It's damned hard to have any dignity when you've just been emotionally eviscerated."

"Okay, true. I admit that's true. But I *still* think she's as phony as a three-dollar bill. I'm really surprised you bought her act."

"I did indeed," Honoria said, popping the olive from the martini into her mouth and chewing it while she marshaled her thoughts. "I liked her and had nothing but sympathy for her—until she became yet one more person wanting me to drop the matter and forget about DeeDee's death. That purported message for Chip really got my goat. It was the one dishonest note in the entire conversation."

"It was only one of a whole *bunch* of them, as far as I'm concerned. In view of how hard I've been trying to get you to give this up, I wasn't going to mention it. But now that you've brought it up, I can't help wondering how she could be so sure it was suicide. I mean, even if DeeDee was obsessed by her father's taking his own life, that didn't mean the girl was a candidate to do it, too. And it definitely doesn't gibe with what everybody else has said about her."

"No, it doesn't," Honoria agreed. "Until an hour or so ago, I'd have bet good money DeeDee was the last girl in the world to take a flyer off a balcony. But you know, May, some mothers have frighteningly accurate insights into their children. Maybe Karen was one of those mothers. Maybe DeeDee was living so hard and fast because she was secretly scared of her own fascination with death. Maybe she really was obsessed with the idea of suicide."

"Unh-hunh. And in half an hour or so when we walk out of here, pigs in pajamas'll be flying down Fifth Avenue."

Honoria stared at her for a second or two then began laughing so hard that the bartender looked over, smiling automatically, and a couple on the opposite side of the room paused in their conversation, turning around to see what was so funny.

"You really are a tonic!" Honoria declared, blotting her eyes before taking another swallow of her drink.

"Glad you think so. Anyhow, I don't what to meddle, but d'you mind if I ask what's going on with Mick? Are you two on the outs?"

Honoria was unprepared for the question. In the aftermath of her laughter, her chest felt suddenly hollow, and her head ached slightly as she shook it. "I honestly don't know what we are. He's angry with me for refusing to give up the investigation and he's especially angry that I managed to get myself conked on the noodle."

"Well who *isn't?*" Maybelle said sardonically.

"Evidently no one."

"And that's *it?* That's why he went off in a big huff?"

"Apparently."

"Hmnn." Sipping her sherry, Maybelle looked around the near empty bar. "I know you're going to find this contrary of me," she said somewhat diffidently, "but now that we've met *Car-in,* I'd kind of like to keep poking around, see what we come up with."

"I find it *very* contrary of you, May," Honoria said, amused. "The fact is I just don't think we're about to come up with anything more. DeeDee's other friends are only going to give us variations on themes we've already heard. Some will be like Taffy, thinking the girl was simply divine. And the others'll be sensible, like Minnie, and have a realistic view of what a vicious little viper she was. Either way, they probably won't have anything new to say. Which means we're at a dead end."

"So you're going to quit?" Maybelle couldn't hide her disappointment.

"Where would you suggest we go with it?"

"You're joshing."

"No. I'm serious. Where should we go from here?" Honoria asked.

"It wouldn't hurt to talk to Fluff and Bitsy and some of the boys."

"It wouldn't get us anywhere, either."

Frowning, Maybelle looked into the depths of her glass.

Honoria smiled. "After trying everything under the sun to get me to give it up, now you're miffed because I've decided to throw in the towel."

"It's just that I'm not satisfied, Honoria. I've got this *feeling*, like I said. Something about that woman . . ." She was unable to put words to the sensation that had been like an electric current traveling up and down her spine throughout their meeting with Karen Carlson; a kind of primitive alarm system that didn't shut down until they were back out on the street. "Why, for example, wasn't a woman with her kind of money sporting any jewelry to speak of?"

"Maybe the Danes aren't as ostentatious as we are. The thing is, you disliked her, and that makes you suspicious. But disliking her doesn't point us in any particular direction. If it did, I'd pursue it. You

216

know how I hate giving up on things."

"I know." Maybelle drank some more of the sherry, then sighed and said, "So that's that, huh?"

"Afraid so."

"What'll we do now that we've cleared the decks, and you're giving up on this?"

"We'll go Christmas shopping, have fabulous lunches, take in some movies—this and that."

"Chip's coming Monday," Maybelle reminded her.

"We'll take him along. The kid could use some cheering up. And so could you. Don't look so down in the mouth, sweetheart. It's what you wanted. Remember?"

"Yeah," Maybelle said unhappily. "I remember."

She was soaking in the tub, getting some warmth back into her body after walking the four blocks from the subway station, when Mick knocked and peeked around the bathroom door.

"I come to ask how is your head."

"My head is fine," she said. "Don't stand there letting all the heat out. Come in and talk to me, Mick."

He slipped inside, closed the door, and leaned against it, still plainly peeved with her.

"Don't pout, Mick. It doesn't suit you. Where have you been all afternoon?"

"I have meetings," he said, not meeting her eyes, arms crossed over his chest: a living picture of righteous indignation.

"And I don't suppose you bothered to wear your overcoat?" she asked, knowing the answer. His face was red from the cold and his jacket was wet.

"I have no need."

"Of course not," she said, all fulsome indulgence. "Compared with winter in Siberia, this is a lovely spring day."

The corners of his mouth twitched, but he held back the smile, continuing to avoid looking at her.

"Why don't you get undressed and come in here? You look as if you need thawing out."

He didn't move but gave her a sidelong glance.

"You're being childish, Mick. I'm not going to beg you."

"Why do I love her?" he asked the ceiling.

"Beats me, sweetheart. Why *do* you?"

He smiled then and began taking off his clothes, saying, "You are impossible woman."

"That is correct. I am. And what are you?"

"Me? I am the poor man loving the impossible woman."

"Oh," she teased, making a mock sympathetic face, "poor, poor Mikhail."

"Be careful," he warned, waving a forefinger back and forth.

"Or what?" she asked, watching him pull off his tie and loop it over the doorknob before unbuttoning his shirt.

"Or I must teach to you a lesson."

"Unh-hunh." She smiled. "How would you do that, I wonder."

"Very soon you are finding out." He stepped out of his trousers, paused to return her smile, then finished undressing and climbed into the tub to sit facing her. "What do you do this afternoon?" he asked.

"I'm not going to tell you because it'll only make you mad."

"Good! Better you don't. You want we go out to eat?"

"Not a chance. It's nasty out there, and besides Ruth's making a roast with Yorkshire pudding."

"Ahh! I *love* this pudding. So we stay at home, make fire in living room, play music, maybe dance."

"Sounds heavenly."

"You like, uh?"

"Uh," she mimicked.

"Later, I teach you lesson," he growled.

"Oh, goodie." She grinned at him. "Nothing I like better than a good lesson."

His laugh echoed off the tiled walls, and she sank a bit lower in the water, grateful he'd been so easily cajoled out of his bad humor.

It was almost midnight. Ruth had gone to bed half an hour earlier. The radio was tuned to dance music on WJZ, and the only light came from the dwindling fire. "Stars Fell On Alabama" ended. They waited, not separating, and "Moonglow" began. Head on his shoulder, she followed the lead given by his hand at the base of her spine. His voice was a soft rumble as he hummed along to the music. The best dancer she'd ever known, she thought, as she did every time, very aware of the heat growing between their closely aligned bodies.

A kiss on the side of her neck made her shiver as the direction shifted and he danced her down the hall and into the bedroom. She reached out to close the door behind her as they moved into the room. Then, eyes locked in intent, they hastily removed each other's clothes; all the while Mick murmured his unintelligible endearments.

His skin—firm and resilient and warm—always gave her intense pleasure; she loved the feel of him, loved the broad expanse of his chest, the long muscles in his thighs. She loved the immediacy of his responses, his reciprocal instincts—a touch for a touch. And on this night she felt aggressive, taking herself on a tour of his flesh, investigating the gratifying symmetry of his construction, the smooth sweep of his back as it tapered to his hips. Giddily absorbing the varying textures and contours of his skin, she kissed the satiny bend of his elbow, the flat plane of his belly, elated to hear the breath catch in his throat. She lay over top of him, her hips beginning a slow undulation.

Holding his hands captive over his head, her lips next to his ear, she murmured endearments of her own as her hips now directed their dance, its slippery rhythm accelerating. The best dancer ever, she thought, smiling inwardly, before she put thinking aside.

Later, before gliding into sleep, her head throbbing slightly and her body cooling, she imagined how relieved he'd be when she told him she was dropping the investigation. Things would return to what passed for normal in their household—with Mick going off to his mysterious meetings and secret trips; and she and Maybelle trying to turn a fresh batch of sows' ears into something that, if nobody looked too closely, might pass for silk.

SIXTEEN

"We go to lunch at '21,'" Mick announced by way of a greeting the next morning.

"What time is it?" she asked, eyes still closed, reluctant to leave what had been a very deep sleep.

"Almost ten."

Opening her eyes, she saw that Mick—sitting atop the bedclothes, legs crossed, back resting against the headboard—was already dressed for the day in a shirt crisp and starch-fresh, the pure white cotton complimented by a clear red silk tie; gray flannel slacks. His navy cashmere blazer hung on the valet.

"If the weather's anything like it was yesterday, I'm not going anywhere."

"Is better," he told her. "Not snowing."

"You've been out already?" she asked. "No, let me guess. You had a meeting."

"Yes, I have meeting."

Frowning, she leaned on her elbow to look at him, wondering.

As if having heard the unspoken question, he said,

221

"Is important, Honor."

"Must be, to have you out and about before ten on a Sunday morning."

"Important," he repeated. "You are getting up now?"

"I believe I am."

"Okay. I tell Ruth. You want I bring you coffee?"

"No, thanks, Mick. I'll wash and be right out."

"How is the bump on the head?" he asked, turning back halfway to the door.

Automatically she reached behind her ear to examine the lump that was still tender but definitely somewhat smaller. "Getting better," she answered, sitting up.

"This is good. I am happy." He smiled at her and went out, closing the door quietly.

"This is good," she repeated to herself, running her fingers again over the fair-sized knob. Someday soon, if he didn't volunteer the information, she was going to have to ask what he was up to. But not today. Today she felt too contented to risk any fresh disagreements.

Pulling on a shower cap, she stood beneath the rush of hot water, feeling the ache in her thigh muscles, the not unpleasant soreness from the previous night's lovemaking. Thinking of it, happiness and immense sadness combined—collusive partners—to send her emotions into chaos. Closing her eyes, she leaned against the tiled wall, the hot water splashing percussively on the shower cap, thinking she should surrender to the happiness and dismiss the sadness, let it go at last. But she didn't know how. For too many years now she'd done so effective an acting job, playing the devil-may-care sort that, at moments, she almost succeeded in convincing herself as well as everyone else. Almost. *Take the next step*, she told herself over and over; *go past it, leave it behind.* She just couldn't. The French women she'd met during that memorable holiday had understood it; they accepted the sadness residing just beneath the surface of life as a matter of course. It was the flip side of pleasure, of happiness; a given. Perhaps if one grew up with that type of recognition and acceptance of the contrariness of a woman's emotional climate, it wouldn't weigh as heavily on her as it did. But, hell! At least there was the pleasure, the eminently satisfactory slaking of one's appetites.

Thinking, as always, that it was a shame to have to do it, she pushed away from the wall and began the task of erasing the scents and residues of the night's activities with an abundance of soap and hot water.

They had just left the restaurant and were turning the corner of West 52nd onto Fifth, when a man called out, "Mike! Hey, Mike!"

Mick glanced over, then, pretending he hadn't heard, made to continue on his way, his body sending an urgent message to Honoria, who was already stopping, despite the drag of his arm on hers.

"Someone's calling you," she said, puzzled by his

most atypical behavior.

"Mikey!" the man called, and, beaming, hurried up, saying, "This is some surprise! From one year to the next, I don't hear from you. Then I come down for a couple of days' business and look who I run into on the street! How're you doing, you son of a gun? What've you been up to? You living here now? God! It's great to see you!"

In his mid- to late-thirties, boyish features in an appealing round face, clear blue eyes, thinning light brown hair, he wore ear-muffs, sheepskin gloves, and a well-made black topcoat with an Astrakhan collar. A jolly man, he was grinning away with a mouthful of good, strong teeth. Immediately predisposed toward him, Honoria looked back at Mick, who was shaking his head, still dragging on her arm, saying, "You make mistake. Not Mike. Sorry."

The man laughed gleefully. "That imitation of your dad always did give me a laugh." Then he sobered, saying, "I still miss him, you know. He was a great man, Mikey." Recovering, his smile again flourished. "You haven't changed a bit! What is it, two years now, three?"

"Is mistake," Mick kept insisting stubbornly.

It was no mistake. Her recent meal turning to stone in her stomach, Honoria knew that everything was about to blow up in their faces. And Mick knew it, too. His expression was positively wretched as he watched her extend her hand to the man he claimed adamantly not to know, with a smile saying, "Hello, I'm Honoria Barlow."

The man pulled off a glove and wrapped a hand solidly around hers as he looked into her eyes with rare directness. She could feel the warmth of his hand right through her woolen glove. "Harold Rubin. A pleasure to meet you. What a pretty woman you are!" He smiled at her approvingly and she thanked him, feeling a strangely schoolgirlish compunction to be polite when she'd have preferred to unleash the crowd of questions that had started yammering away inside her head. But Harold Rubin looked away, hooked his bare hand over the back of Mick's neck, and towed him into an affectionate hug, exclaiming, "Mikey, I'm so damned happy to see you. Why the hell haven't I heard from you for so long, you skunk?" Releasing him, Harold kept smiling as he looked again at Honoria, then back at Mick. "Some hell of a friend this guy is," he complained with a fondness born in youth. "He takes off and doesn't tell a soul where he's going, or for how long."

As if paralyzed, Mick stood rooted to the spot, eyes wide with what looked like pure panic.

Desperate to escape from the scene of this reluctant reunion, her mouth gone dry, Honoria said, "I've got an errand to do, so I'm going to run along. Good to meet you, Harold. Mick, I'll meet you in an hour, give or take, at the coffee shop on the corner of 75th." She turned abruptly, saw that the light was green, and hurried across Fifth Avenue, deeply shaken by the realization that the door to the fool's paradise she'd been living in was about to be thrown open. The shadowy perimeters created by cautious mood-lighting were going to be starkly illuminated by a flood of harsh daylight. And she felt as fearful and bewildered as the five-year-old who'd first found her way to the morgue and discovered the cold blue babies, wrapped like small parcels awaiting shipment to some terrible place.

Almost at a run, she got to 57th Street, stopped abruptly, and stood at the corner, trying to think what to do. The wind whipped through the intersection and lifted open the bottom of her coat like the hand of some massive unseen deviant boldly reaching up under her clothes to touch her with chilling intimacy. She didn't want to go home yet. But where could she go? She thought of Harold Rubin's emphatic handclasp, the warmth of his grip, and remembered her gloves. She had tried, and failed, to reach Karen Carlson on the phone the night before, but had reasoned the woman had probably gone out to eat. She might well be home now, doing last-minute odds and ends before leaving for Florida. Glad of a destination, Honoria lowered her head and continued uptown.

Her eyes were streaming, her nose running, as she entered the building at 66th and Fifth. Near-frozen a moment before, the heat of the lobby made her feel woozy, and a dull throbbing started up at the base of her skull. Finding her handkerchief, she dried her eyes and nose before approaching the concierge—not the one who'd been on duty the day before. This one was older, with the kind of weary pale blue eyes that, having seen everything, were no longer capable of being surprised. He had a strictly-by-the-book demeanor and wore his hunter green, brass-buttoned uniform proudly, as if he belonged to an elite, little-known branch of the military. Nobody put anything over on this guy.

"Rotten out there, huh?" he observed pleasantly enough. "Papers say we're breaking all kindsa records for cold."

"I don't doubt it," she said, returning the handkerchief to her pocket. "My name is Barlow. By any chance did Mrs. Carlson leave a pair of gloves for me?"

"Carlson?"

"On eleven. Karen Carlson."

"Eleven is the Robertson family," he said, fair brows drawing together in a show of doubt touched with suspicion. For all he knew, she could be some kind of high-class grifter, trying to pull some scam. "And they're away, down in Florida, like always, for the winter."

At a loss, Honoria stared at the man, trying to make sense of what he was saying. Who were the Robertsons? Who was Mick Beliakof, for that matter? After a moment, she said, "My assistant and I visited Mrs. Carlson here yesterday afternoon in what you're saying is the Robertson apartment. The fellow on duty knew we were expected and sent us right up."

"That would've been John," he said, still suspicious.

227

"I'll take your word for that. Whoever he was, he certainly knew Mrs. Carlson. But you don't. And I have no idea who the Robertsons are. I was under the impression it was Mrs. Carlson's apartment, so you'll understand if I tell you I'm a tad confused."

"Brother, so'm I." It was his turn to stare at her, and he did, for a good fifteen seconds. Then, the proverbial light went on and, with a relieved little smile, he slapped himself on the forehead, saying, "Wait a minute! Now I got it. Good-looking lady, blonde, wears black all the time, moves like a dancer?"

"Right," she replied, impressed by his powers of observation. "That's the woman I mean."

The concierge smiled, all suspicion gone. "Couldn't think *who* you meant for a minute there. Forgot all about—what's-her-name, Mrs. Carlson. A friend of theirs—the Robertsons, I mean—she was staying the last couple of weeks. She wasn't in and out all that much. Only saw her a couple of times and she didn't have any visitors," he explained. "Which is why the name didn't ring any bells. Gloves, you're looking for?"

Honoria nodded.

"I don't think she left anything, but I'll have a look." He ducked down below the desk and popped right back up again, saying, "Nope, sorry. There's not a thing here except Mrs. Murphy's *Times* from this morning."

"Would you do me a favor," Honoria asked, "and call up, see if she's still there? I hate to walk away from a brand-new pair of leather gloves without at least trying."

"Sure. But I doubt she's there. John went off at midnight, and Frank, the night man, would've told me if she was. Always possible he could've forgotten, though." He dialed and held the receiver to his ear, then waited, giving it a good long time before he hung up, shaking his head. "Sorry. No answer. Far as I know, Mrs. Carlson was supposed to be leaving last Thursday. I haven't laid eyes on her in days, that's for sure."

"I see. Well, thank you."

"Too bad about those gloves," he commiserated. "Case they turn up, you want to leave me your number?"

"Good idea." She gave the man her card, thanked him again, and then left the building trying to comprehend why Karen Carlson had encouraged her and Maybelle to believe that she owned that fabulous apartment when in reality it belonged to friends. And if the place wasn't hers, where did the woman live, and why hadn't she invited them to visit her there? Confounded, Honoria walked to the corner to hail a taxi. Remembering Mick with an unpleasant jolt, she began priming herself to hear what kind of story he'd have to tell. As she scanned the oncoming traffic, she had to wonder if she wasn't turning gullible as she got older, accepting without question all sorts of lies. One thing for sure, May had been right in her suspicions. The Carlson woman definitely wasn't on the up-and-up. Her stomach clenching with dread, she tried to steel herself for the discovery that Mick wasn't either.

He was waiting for her, smoking a cigarette—something she'd only seen him do a few times before—an untouched cup of coffee and a pack of imported Player's in front of him. When he saw her he tried to jump to his feet but succeeded only in slamming both knees on the underside of the table. Wincing, he remained half-standing as she slid into the opposite side of the booth, then he sank back down and stubbed out the cigarette.

After shrugging off her coat and blotting her nose with her soggy handkerchief, she signaled the waitress to bring another coffee. Mick meanwhile was plainly trying to think of an opening, and she felt all at once horribly sorry for both of them. They'd been like children, playing with happy abandon. Now they were going to have to face the inevitable consequences of their actions. "You'd better start at the beginning and tell me everything, Mick," she said, her voice made husky by apprehension. "Or is it Mike?"

"It's Michael," he said quietly, with no trace of an accent.

She was mightily impressed, as if he'd done a fabulous trick—this foreigner speaking flawless English. But of course he wasn't a foreigner. It had been an act, a sham. What else had he pretended? She was starting to feel very, very foolish.

"My dad was Mikhail," he added, as if this fact in some way validated his long-term performance.

"I see. And he was a genuine Russian, was he?" She couldn't manage to keep a note of sarcasm out of her voice.

"*I* am a genuine Russian," he said, his tone still quiet. "I was born in St. Petersburg. Dad brought the family to Canada when I was four years old."

The waitress slid a cup of coffee in front of Honoria, turned and asked Mick, "Want me to hot that up for you, hon?"

Without looking up, he shook his head and murmured, "No, thanks."

Honoria listened, gazing at him, fascinated.

"Okey-dokey." Unfazed by the stilted behavior of this pair, the woman went back to the counter and her copy of the Sunday *Sun*.

"Why did you *do* it?" Honoria asked, still as cold as she'd been out on the street, and tried to warm her hands on the coffee cup. For a few seconds she looked at her hands curved around the cup, thinking they belonged to someone well past youth—thin-skinned and prominently veined, an older woman's hands. It was as if the aging process had begun to accelerate and she was acquiring additional years almost hourly. The throbbing in her head had become a full-fledged headache, and she couldn't help thinking that, if she ever tried to write such an absurdly improbable situation into a script, the big boys out in movieland would think she'd lost either her touch or her marbles. *Nobody* would buy this. But she had, and that made her some kind of mug. Absently, she fingered the knob behind her ear.

Mick pushed his cold coffee away, saying in a rush, "When I saw you in the hotel dining room that night in Paris, I *had* to meet you. But I thought if I came over and said so, or tried some line, you'd give me the brush-off, and I couldn't risk that. I didn't plan it, Honor. I walked over to your table and, when I opened my mouth, my dad's voice came out. I figured you'd catch on, but you took me for real, and then I didn't know *what* to do. After a while I thought if I dropped it and started talking normally, you'd think I was a jerk, or a con artist or something. *Jesus!*" he said despairingly. "The way that *sounds*." He shook his head, then bent it into his hand. After a few seconds he sat upright and tried again. "After we danced, I was ready to tell you, because you were someone I'd been looking for my entire adult life. But I couldn't, because I was so afraid to have it go wrong. I couldn't let that happen, couldn't let you get away. So I wound up trapped in something I'd never meant to start in the first place. Then, every single time I decided to come clean, it was the wrong moment. Finally, it was too late and I didn't know *how* to get out of it. Please believe me. I never intended to pretend I was someone else. It just happened, then it got out of hand to the point where stopping meant one or both of us would lose face. I admit I was an idiot. But I promise you it wasn't frivolous."

"No," she said. The headache had fastened itself to the rear of her skull like some sort of medieval torture device with screws that were slowly being turned tighter and tighter. "It was deadly serious."

"I love you, Honor. That's the truth and you *know* it."

"Do I?" She studied his wonderfully appealing face, the deep-set luminous dark eyes, and said thickly, "I have no idea anymore what I know or don't know, what's true and what isn't. You should've played it straight with me, Mick, taken your chances. This didn't have to happen. It would've been all right, because you were someone *I'd* been looking for."

He swallowed hard, then drank some of the cold coffee. "Do you believe I'm sorry?"

"Yes, I do."

"But I've wrecked it, haven't I?"

"I don't know," she answered truthfully. "I feel silly, ridiculous, like one of those foolish, lonely old women who gets taken in by a handsome gigolo who eventually makes off with her jewels and her money."

"*Don't!* That's not who we are. You're not old or foolish, and I'm no gigolo. This is exactly what I was afraid of. *Please* don't feel that way."

"It can't be helped. It's how I feel. *Think* about it, for God's sake! I don't even know who you *are*— Mick, Mike, Michael, Mikhail. I've been living for more than two years with a complete stranger. How do you *imagine* that would make me *feel?*"

"I'm sorry, profoundly sorry. What do you want to know?" he asked frantically. "Ask me anything. Just *ask* me!"

"You'd better tell me all of it," she said, far more upset with herself for her voluntary state of ignorance than she was with him for keeping her in it. Again, distractedly, she touched the swelling behind her ear.

The waitress returned with the coffee pot and, without being asked, topped up Mick's cup, saw that Honoria's was still full, and went back to the counter and her newspaper.

Gratefully, he drank some of the now lukewarm coffee and lit another cigarette, seeking a starting point. At last he opted for a capsulized version of the facts. "My father was a forty-two-year-old bachelor when he met Alla Ruskin. She was a twenty-eight-year-old spinster schoolteacher who'd always been more interested in books than in men. But she fell in love with Mikhail Beliakof, they got married two months after they met, and in the next seven years she gave birth to three children. Only the first one survived beyond infancy—me. My father was a diamond dealer, a highly respected, very successful man. He was also wise and intuitive. Becoming progressively more worried about the future of the country, he decided to take his family and get out. My mother not only spoke fluent English, French, and German as well as Russian, but also had a cousin who lived in Montreal. She wrote to her cousin to say they were considering a move, and the cousin wrote back encouraging us to come. So the house, the business, and the bulk of the family's possessions were sold; the trunks were packed, and we set off.

"During the trip, my mother began teaching us English. By the time the ship docked in Halifax on November fourth, 1902, Dad and I had mastered the rudiments of the language. Within six months of our arriving in Canada, we were living in a house in Outremont not far from my mother's cousin and her family, and Dad had set himself up in business. Our next-door neighbors were the Rubins. Harold, the one you met, is the youngest of the three sons and my oldest friend. Today, when I told him what I'd done, he cursed me up and down, said I was a schmuck, and advised me to crawl to you on my hands and knees if that's what it took to make things right." He paused and looked at her expectantly.

"I appreciate Harold's sentiments, but crawling wouldn't do it, Mick; it wouldn't even come close. Tell me the rest of it," she said, and at last drank some of her coffee.

He hesitated a few seconds, deciding where the rest of it actually began, then cleared his throat and went on. "I always wanted to go into business with Dad, but my mother insisted I go to university, have a degree in case at some point in the future I de-cided to pursue another career. So Harold and I went to McGill. He studied international law. I took modern English literature—there was nothing else that interested me. A week after graduation in the summer of '19, I went to work with my father. Three years later he died of a heart attack the day before his sixty-ninth birthday. He left the business to me, and the rest of the estate—which, by then, was substantial—went to my mother.

"For the next five years all I did was work. I expanded the business until there were twenty-two stores across Canada. And then one day, just like that, I'd had enough. I didn't care about the business anymore. My mother had been right; she'd guessed that in time I'd get bored. The problem was, I still wasn't interested in anything else. So I sold out, at a huge profit. Once the papers were signed and the money was in the bank, I didn't know what to do next. There I was, thirty-one years old, with more money than I could ever spend, with a big empty house, no life, nothing to do. People were always fixing me up with girls they knew would be perfect for me. They never were, and finally I said enough, no more of it. By this time my mother had met and married a very nice man, a retired clothing manufacturer whose wife had died a few years earlier. They agreed that the Montreal winters were getting to be too much for them, so they moved to Savannah, because on a trip they'd taken the year before, my mother had fallen in love with the city. And Simon would do anything for my mother. So they moved, and they're very happy there."

"And that's where you go every few weeks," Honoria guessed.

"Sometimes. Not always." He reached for the cigarettes and got one lit, then said, "If the smoking bothers you, I won't."

"It doesn't bother me. Is there anything more?"

"Not much. Thinking maybe I should, I got married back in '27. It lasted eleven months. In the divorce settlement, Monique got the big house, which I didn't like anyway, and alimony, which I only had to pay for about a year. She remarried, and that was the end of that. I started spending time here, connected with the people I'll tell you about in a minute, and eventually bought a co-op, moved more or less permanently to the city."

"You have an apartment here in town?" For some reason, this really shocked her.

He nodded. "At River House. I rarely set foot in it, though. Occasionally, if I'm very late getting back from a trip, I sleep there. But otherwise, from one month to the next, I don't go near the place. Are you very angry? Do you hate me now, Honor?"

"I'm not quite sure how I feel, but I could never hate you, Mick." Seeing the relief begin to spread over his features, she hurried to ask, "Why were you in Paris when we met?"

"There's a growing group of Jewish people working to get their friends and relatives out of Germany before it's too late. Things are very bad there."

"Yes, I know."

"Because I have a Canadian passport, it's easier for me to travel to some places than it is for Americans. So for the last three years I've been going over regularly, helping people to leave. On that particular trip, which my mother asked me to make, after a lot of persuading I finally convinced two of her second cousins and their families to get out, just take what they could carry and leave the rest behind. I saw them off on a ship sailing from LeHavre, en route to Montreal, where arrangements had already been made for them. Once they were gone, I wanted to relax for a few days before heading home, so I caught a train to Paris, checked into the Georges Cinq, got cleaned up, and went downstairs for dinner. I walked into the dining room, looked around, saw you alone at a table across the room, and felt as if something cracked wide open inside of me. It sounds corny, but it was as if, without my ever knowing it, I'd had this big egg in my chest, and a creature that was something like half-bird and half-mammal had been growing in it for years. At the sight of you, this *thing* broke through its shell and sat fluttering its wings until they were dry. Then it went about making a nest, using the fragments of shell and bits of whatever debris it could find lying around. Once I'd actually met you I promised myself, and the creature, that if you agreed to marry me, I'd drop the act and tell you the truth."

"You're not going to try to lay this at my doorstep, are you, Mick?" she asked warily.

He shook his head. "Never. I've got only myself to blame. I was stupid, making promises to an imaginary creature I'd started to believe was the better part of me. But you wouldn't agree to marry me, and I'd been counting on that. Somehow I got stuck on the fact that you wouldn't marry me, and I couldn't focus on anything else. Completely moronic! Especially since, so far as the rest of the world

238

was concerned, we *were* married. We had everything except the documentation." He crushed out the cigarette and waved away the smoke. "Once we came back and I moved into your place, as I became more and more afraid I'd lose you if I dropped the pretense, I grew more and more entrenched in being Mikhail." He shook his head in a show of self-disgust. "I'd have told you everything, Honor, if you'd expressed the least bit of curiosity. But you never asked me a single question about my life, not one. And I began to think maybe it was because you didn't want me to ask *you* any questions. It seemed as if we'd tacitly agreed to behave as if neither one of us had a past, that everything began the night we met, and nothing that had gone before had any relevance. If that was the way you wanted it, then that was the way it had to be. Because there wasn't anything I wouldn't have done if you'd wanted it. Because I wanted *you*. Does this make any sense? I feel so damned scared. Will you be able to forgive me? Will we be able to go on from here?"

For a few moments she sat considering the image of a creature, half-bird half-mammal, breaking free inside him. "I had no idea," she said sadly, "that you thought in such beautiful terms, Mick. A degree in English literature, and not once did you ever speak to me the way you are now."

"I did, Honor. All the time. But it was in Russian."

Those incomprehensible murmurings had indeed been endearments. What a lamentable waste!

239

"You'll never know how much I wish you hadn't pulled that stunt, Mick."

"Me, too. *Believe me!*"

"I'm going to need some time alone," she said. "I'll have Ruth pack up some of your things and have Cully send them by cab over to River House."

"You're throwing me out?" he asked, crestfallen.

"I'm asking you to stay away for a while, Mick. Until I figure out how I feel." Right then she actually felt sick, and said abruptly, "I've got to get out of here."

Crushed, he watched her struggle into her coat, saying, "Please don't leave yet. Let's talk this through."

"I can't talk right now. I've got to go."

"Don't let it end this way, Honor," he begged, sliding out of the booth and catching hold of her hand.

As always, contact with him weakened her. She stood looking up at him, torn. Part of her never wanted to see him again, and part wanted to close her eyes, rest her aching head against his chest for a time, then pick up with him and go on from here, discounting his absurd, needless charade. "It was a dumb and dangerous thing to do," she said, close to tears and determined not to break down in a crummy coffee shop with a gum-chewing, bored waitress watching. "I don't know if I could ever trust you again, Mick," she whispered. "Right now, I feel as if I couldn't. But I might feel differently later. I need time to think."

"Please don't end it," he pleaded. "*Please.* We love each other. We can work it out."

"We'll talk in a few days," she told him, then turned and hurried away.

SEVENTEEN

Throughout the short walk home, she couldn't help thinking Mick was right: She hadn't wanted him to ask her any questions because she had in fact wanted them to behave as if their lives had begun the night they'd met. That much was absolutely true. Still, his revelations assaulted her brain like a series of small, ongoing electric shocks: his accent-free speech, his degree in literature, his personal wealth, his trips in and out of Germany. She couldn't seem to assimilate these new facts, couldn't get them to mesh with her own imaginings of what he'd been up to. She'd thought he might have been involved somehow with that Canadian schooner and rumrunning, that his money came from some sort of illegal activity. For the past two years she'd gone along halfway believing she was involved with a criminal, but not really caring. As long as she didn't know, she didn't have to give the subject too much thought because, for the most part, being with him appeased the majority of her appetites. Now she kept thinking she should have refused to go out for lunch. None of this would have happened if they'd stayed in.

So distracted was she that, despite the lancing cold, she actually walked right past her building. It wasn't until she got to the corner of 76th Street that she realized she'd gone too far, and turned back.

Ruth knew the instant she saw Honoria that something dreadful had happened. She had a look to her eyes that put Ruth in mind of the soldiers she'd seen on leave in the London streets during the war—a starkness born of disbelief and shock. "What's happened, dearie?" she asked uneasily, as Honoria closed the front door, then sagged against it, the starch gone right out of her.

"Do me a favor, Ruth, and pack up a few of Mick's things, then ask Cully to send them over to River House in a cab."

"Mr. Mick's not coming home?"

"For the time being. I'll tell you about it later." Opening her purse, Honoria got out a ten-dollar bill and gave it to the housekeeper, saying, "This should cover the cab and a couple of dollars for Cully's trouble." Then, leaving her open purse on the hall table, she drifted away and sat down on the edge of the living-room sofa.

Following her into the room that was already full dark at just past four in the afternoon, Ruth said, "Why don't you give me your coat?" and held out her hands for it.

Once more in the grip of that schoolgirlish compunction to be polite and obedient, Honoria got her coat off and surrendered it.

"Head bad again, dearie?"

Honoria nodded, and Ruth said, "I'll fetch you something for it."

While she was gone, Honoria folded her arms over her chest and leaned forward, watching the slush melt off her galoshes and pool on the rug. Her head was pounding in syncopation with her heartbeat, and her mouth was bitter with the taste of stale coffee. She wanted to go to sleep and wake up in the morning to find that things were as they'd been only a week ago, before Chip's arrest. No DeeDee or her mysterious mother; no stranger named Michael with a jolly, likable friend named Harold Rubin whose hand she still seemed able to feel warmly closed around her own.

"Let's get those boots off you," Ruth said, handing Honoria two aspirin tablets and a glass of water before dropping down to pull the sodden galoshes off one at a time. Straightening, she said, "Take those pills now," and carried the boots out to the front hall. When she got back, Honoria had curled up on the sofa, her arms still wrapped tightly around herself, jaw clenched to keep her teeth from chattering. It seemed that the cold had penetrated right to her bone marrow.

"Lay yourself down properly," Ruth said, tucking a pillow under her head and draping the old afghan over her. "Rest awhile," she said. "It's the best remedy for whatever ails you."

"Don't forget to pack a bag . . ."

"I'll see to it. Close your eyes, and we'll talk in a bit."

While she was having a cup of tea in the kitchen a

couple of hours later, speculating on what could possibly have happened between the couple over lunch, the telephone rang and Ruth hurried to snatch the receiver off the hook before the ringing could disturb Honoria.

"Ruth," a familiar yet not familiar voice said, "it's Mick."

For a second or two she was so taken aback she couldn't get a word out. Then she said, "What's happened to your accent, Mr. Mick? You don't sound like yourself."

"Actually, I do. It's a long story."

"I'm sure it is. Did your valise get to you safely?"

"It did, thank you. Is Honor okay, Ruth?"

"Matter of fact, she was feeling poorly and fell asleep on the sofa. I didn't have the heart to wake her, so I've let her be. Look, I know I'm stepping out of place, Mr. Mick, but would you care to tell me what's going on?"

He sighed heavily before answering. "Let's just say that I did something very dumb and I'm going to regret it for a long, long time. Look after her, please, Ruth. That bump on the head worries me. I notice she keeps touching it, as if it's bothering her."

"Certainly I'll look after her. You needn't concern yourself on that score."

"You're a good soul, and I appreciate it."

"You don't sound as if you're doing too well yourself," Ruth observed.

"I've had better days. Let me give you the number here, in case you need me for anything."

"Right-O." She jotted down the information, then said, "Let me ask you one more thing, if I may."

"Sure."

"Did you mean to act the complete prat with the play-acting, Mr. Mick, or did it just happen accidental-like?"

"I didn't mean it, Ruth," he said unhappily. "You know how much Honor means to me."

"I do, and I'd never take you for a prankster. But you'll have your work cut out for you, fixing this, you know."

"You think it's fixable?" he asked, a note of hope lifting his voice.

"I think it might be. Take my advice and don't push, Mr. Mick. You're going to have to sit back and wait for her to come round. It could take some time."

"I don't care *how* long it takes."

"Didn't think you would. For what it's worth, dear, I believe you meant no harm."

"Thanks, Ruth. That means a lot to me," he said, his voice cracking, and hung up.

She put the receiver back on the hook and stood staring at the telephone, in a undertone saying, "Well, this is a right old cock-up, isn't it?" Whatever possessed the man, to go pretending he was Russian when, from the sound of it, he was North American born and bred?

Throughout the evening, she kept going in to check, but Honoria didn't stir. At last, deciding it best not to disturb her, Ruth went off to bed. She left her door ajar and, while she sat reading, she listened for the slightest indication that Honoria was up and about. Not a sound. At eleven-forty she took one last look before calling it a night and turning off the light.

When she got up as usual at six-thirty the next morning, she tiptoed to the front door, got the morning paper from the mat, then peeked into the living room. The sofa was empty. Leaving the paper on the kitchen table, she went down the hall to the master suite. The bed was still neatly made but Honoria had left her clothes on the closet floor and Ruth could hear the shower going. Satisfied, she returned to the kitchen to put on a pot of coffee.

Her wet hair wrapped in a towel, Honoria stood in front of the bathroom mirror taking topographical stock, repelled by her reflection. She was especially disturbed by the deep blue veins so clearly defined right beneath the surface of the pale, pale skin of her upper chest and shoulders—branching tributaries of rivers whose primary source lay centered beneath a pair of heavy breasts that were beginning very noticeably to fall. She was able to tolerate only half a minute of this visual inspection before grabbing her robe and pulling it on. Better, safer, not to look. The life of the mind had no proscribed dimensions, no age, just the gratifying freedom to wander from here to there, considering this, considering that, untethered by physical considerations. It struck her as ironic that she'd lived primarily in her mind until the age of thirteen or so. And then her body had captured her attention, keeping hold of it for the next twenty-odd years. Lately, though, as she'd witnessed the undeniable effects of age on her body, she'd begun going back for ever-longer periods of time to the more tolerable realm of the mind.

She opened the dressing-table drawer for the key, then got down on her knees at the back of the closet to open the steel lockbox. She removed the envelopes of money Mick had given her and dumped them on the bed. A lot of envelopes of various sizes, some thicker, some thinner; none containing less than five hundred dollars. Had she suspected something all along? Was that why she'd left the envelopes intact? Turning away, she went to the window. Still dark outside, all she saw in the glass was her own reflection and that of the room behind her. For a moment she had the bizarre notion that she was a be-robed ghost hovering outside the window, looking in at the distraught woman inside. A moment. Then it passed, and she turned to look over at the spill of envelopes on the bedspread, a great deal of money she couldn't possibly keep. Something had prevented her from spending the money, had prompted her to put the envelopes, intact, in the box. It was awfully convenient, facile even, to think it might have been intuition. She had no idea why she hadn't touched the money.

God, what a fool! She really did feel like one those seamed but still-elegant, chiffon-clad females she used to see at tea dances back in the great, giddy years before the Crash. She could see them even now: haughtily proud, being swept around the dance-floor by sleek young men with pomaded hair and an overweening, posturing style bred of self-confidence and youthful arrogance.

Watching the stately, deluded dowagers years ago, she'd thought cynically of the gifts from doting late husbands that would go missing in the near-distant future, along with substantial sums of money that had been given willingly to the prancing young men, in the belief that the attention being so scrupulously paid was genuine. Those old women had made her sad, angry, and contemptuous. Now, although she'd suffered no monetary losses, she felt herself to be among their number, as needy and intentionally blind as any of them, driven by disproportionate desire to accept questionable displays of affection. And she was in retrospect conscience-stricken over the particular brand of youthful arrogance that she had displayed toward those women—some of whom had probably not been very much older than she was today. They'd deserved her sympathy, but one's salad days were a time of unparalleled intolerance and self-importance, so she'd felt only anger and contempt. The prickling shame that had overcome her the previous afternoon remained undiminished by her retreat into a lengthy sleep and the sight of the money on the bed sickened her. She was simply going to have to get rid of it.

"You look better," Ruth declared diplomatically after giving her employer a quick once-over and deciding she looked haggard. "Hungry, dearie?"

"A little."

"A little," Ruth repeated. "That would be one egg and a piece of toast, would it?"

Honoria opened her mouth to answer but, to her complete horror, instead erupted into noisy tears. Startled by this extraordinary display, Ruth crossed the room and gathered Honoria close, stroking her damp hair, saying, "There, there. We all need a good cry now and then. You just go ahead and get it out of your system."

Honoria wanted to protest that what she was doing was undignified and childish, but the upset was determined to vent itself, couldn't be stopped. So she sobbed into the housekeeper's apron as the clock on the wall ticked the time away until the worst of it had passed. Then she eased away, accepted the handkerchief Ruth offered, and hiccupped a "Thank you," before mopping her face and blowing her nose.

Ruth poured two cups of coffee and brought them over to the table, opting instead of her usual seat at the opposite end to sit in the chair next to Honoria's. "Drink some of that," she advised, interested to note that, unlike a lot of women who were at their worst when they wept, Honoria actually looked young and rather fetching. It was one surprise after another lately, Ruth thought, having just seen an entirely new aspect to someone she'd believed she knew inside out. "I'd like to help," she said, "but it's hard to do, without knowing what's going on."

Resting her forehead on her upheld palm, Honoria said, "I can't right now, Ruth. All I can say is that it's about more than just Mick."

"It's not always easy to talk about the things that bother us most."

"No, it isn't," Honoria agreed.

"But talking does help, and I'm always willing to listen."

"Thank you," Honoria murmured.

"Now I know I'm changing the subject, but, in case you've forgotten, Chip's arriving this afternoon."

"Oh, God! I completely forgot." Her head still resting in her hand, Honoria closed her eyes, wishing she could go off somewhere and hide for a week or two.

"Not to worry. Everything's under control. The guest room's ready and I've got a lovely chicken for dinner. We'll have roast spuds and some nice veg a bit undercooked, just the way you like them. So"— Ruth gave her an encouraging smile—"what about your breakfast?"

Honoria offered her a watery smile in return, saying, "I really do love you, you know. You're such a brick. I think of you and May as family."

Getting to her feet, Ruth said, "I love you, too, dearie. And so far as family goes, I think of you as mine. Drink some of that coffee before it goes cold. Food'll be ready in two ticks."

Honoria was pouring a third cup of coffee and had

just picked up the newspaper when she heard the sound of the front door being unlocked. She forced herself not to turn to look, thinking if that was Mick letting himself in she was going to be very angry.

After pausing only long enough to kick off her boots, Maybelle came flying in, asking excitedly, "Have you seen this morning's paper yet?"

"Not yet," Honoria answered, amazed by the contrariness of her emotions. She'd been all set to be furious with Mick, but here she was, disappointed that he hadn't come after all. Was this, she wondered, how those poor old girls had felt, knowing they were purchasing affection, yet trying to persuade themselves that some small spart of it was real?

Ruth glanced over at the clock. It wasn't yet eight. "You're bright and early, May," she observed. "Some coffee?"

"Love some, thanks. Look at this!" Maybelle said, slapping a copy of the *Daily News* down on the table, pointing to a small item in the lower corner of the page.

COLD OF 19° HERE
HOMELESS GIRL DIES

Bitter weather nipped New York's ears yesterday for the third successive day and sent the mercury down to 19 degrees in a cold wave that covered a large section of the country between the Mississippi and the Atlantic seaboard and from Maine to Florida. Deaths from motoring mishaps, exposure and other conditions traceable to the cold were reported in various parts of the country.

In this city the mercury was well below the freezing point when the body of Augusta Washington, 22, was found inside a large cardboard box in an alley off 74th Street. According to a family friend, Miss Washington was seeking work at the time of her death. It has been determined that the girl had been dead for at least two days before she was discovered.

"She wasn't homeless," Maybelle said hotly the moment she saw Honoria's eyes leave the printed page. "Benjamin, the janitor at the Ansonia gave me her address. They lived in the same building. He'd have *known* if she'd left. He wouldn't have told me to look for her there."

"You think she was murdered," Honoria guessed.

"You bet I do! It's just too coincidental for my liking. The one person who might have been able to give us, or the police, the inside scoop on DeeDee just happens to wind up dead in an alley? Sorry, I don't buy it, not for a minute!"

"Poor girl," Honoria said, looking again at the small item. "Obviously they did a post mortem and concluded she froze to death."

"Come *on*, Honoria! First they thought DeeDee was a suicide. Then they decided Chip was good for the murder. Then they went back to thinking it was a suicide. I *know* Gussy was murdered. We're just going to have to prove it."

"We are?" Honoria watched Maybelle pace back and forth, still in her coat, grinding her hands together, radiating angry energy. "Why don't you take off your coat and sit down, May, so we can talk about this?"

"What? Oh!" Maybelle did as Honoria suggested, then came back and sat down.

"I had kind of an interesting experience yesterday afternoon," Honoria said, and proceeded to tell about her trip to East 66th Street to retrieve her gloves.

"She was only a *guest* in that apartment? She sure didn't *act* like one. She behaved as if the place was hers—all that guff about how we weren't seeing it at its best because the staff had gone ahead to get the Palm Beach house ready."

"It seems as if your hunch about her was right."

"I *knew* there was something fishy about that woman."

"Didn't care for her, I take it, dear," Ruth said with a smile.

Maybelle looked over at the housekeeper, then at Honoria, who seemed preoccupied, as if she'd lost interest in the matter of DeeDee's death. "What do we do next?" Maybelle asked her.

It took a moment or two for the question to register. "About what?" Honoria responded.

"About this whole thing—DeeDee and Karen and Gussy. Two people dead and this peculiar woman pretending she lives in somebody else's swanky apartment. Where did she go, if she's not at East 66th anymore? Someone must know. And maybe you could make a couple of calls, see if we can get any more information about Gussy."

"I wonder why she didn't want us to know where she lives," Honoria mused, leaning chin in hand and gazing off into space much in the way, Maybelle noted, that Karen Carlson frequently had during their visit with her. What was going on here?

Maybelle looked around and said, "Where's Mick?" then saw Ruth give an almost imperceptible shake of her head, so she quickly added, "Off at another meeting?"

"Probably," Honoria answered, pushing back from the table. "I'm going to get dressed." At the door she paused to say, "I could give Len a call. He's got an in with the coroner's office. He might be able to get us a bit more information."

"Good idea," Maybelle said. "And Chip has to know where Karen lives. We can ask him when he gets here later, then pay a call on the lady and find out what her game is."

Honoria nodded, then continued on her way. Irony on top of irony. After she'd persisted with it when everyone wanted her to drop the matter, now that she'd lost interest in it, May was all hot to trot. At this point she didn't give a damn about DeeDee or her mother. But, still, it was something to do, something to keep her mind off the fact that she'd made a complete ass of herself. And, just to ice the cake, she'd broken down in front of Ruth. Being a little superstitious herself—although she'd never have admitted it to Maybelle—she had to wonder what was next. After all, disasters always came in threes.

EIGHTEEN

"**W**hat's going on?" May asked in a whisper the moment Honoria was out of earshot.

"I don't actually know, dear."

"I'm worried."

"So am I," Ruth admitted.

"I've never *seen* her look so—I don't know *what*," Maybelle said. "But why the signal not to ask about Mick, if you don't know?"

"Oh, *something's* going on right enough. I'm just not aware of the details."

"At least tell me what's been happening."

"Well, yesterday the two of them, happy as can be, went off to lunch at '21.' At fourish she came home alone in a frightful state, agitated as can be and with a sick headache, to boot. Within twenty minutes she was curled up, sound asleep on the sofa. And I had instructions to pack a suitcase of Mr. Mick's things and get Cully to send it over to River House in a taxi."

"River House?"

"That's right. More coffee, dear?"

"Love some, thanks. Are you saying they've split up?"

"Only temporarily, I'd say. It wouldn't surprise me to see him home again within the week." Ruth poured coffee into Maybelle's cup, topped up her own, then returned the pot to the burner.

"Why wouldn't it surprise you? Come on, Ruth. Tell me everything."

Ruth sat down at the table, leaned in close and, in a low voice, said, "He rang last evening at about seven, and for a moment I couldn't think who it was."

"Why not?" Having to drag the information out of Ruth was starting to get on Maybelle's nerves. Sure, she understood the housekeeper's reluctance to tell tales out of school, but it wasn't as if they were indulging in idle gossip. This was important, concerning, as it did, someone they both loved.

"Because," Ruth lowered her voice even further, "he'd completely lost his accent."

"I don't follow."

"He didn't have any," Ruth elaborated. "Not a trace of one."

"Oh, my God!" May clapped a hand over her mouth, eyes gone round. "He was *faking* it? That whole big-brawny-Russian routine was an *act?*"

"Apparently so."

"How could he do that to her? I'll *kill* the bastard! I swear if I get my hands on that louse I will *pulverize* him!"

"He feels very bad, May. He told me he'd done something dumb that he was going to regret for a long time to come. He also said he hadn't intended it; it simply happened. And I have to say I believe him."

"It simply *happened?* Oh, come *on*, Ruth! Things like that don't just *happen*. The rotten son of a bitch! I *knew* from the get-go there was something fishy about him."

"I can't agree with you on that, May. I think most likely he did it as a lark and later found himself stuck with it."

"Why the *hell* would he *do* such a crummy thing?" Maybelle was getting angrier by the moment.

"Knowing the way most men operate, I expect he did it simply to get her attention. Men can be such silly sods." Ruth shook her head. "But I'll tell you this: The man adores her. He would never intentionally hurt her. No, I think he was indulging in a bit of make-believe and ended up having to live with it."

Maybelle was prepared to argue the point when Honoria's footsteps could be heard in the hall. Falling silent, the two listened to her go into the office. A minute or so later she went back to the master suite.

"What is she doing?" May wondered.

"Why don't you go ask her, dear?"

"Bad idea. She'll bite my head off."

"Under normal circumstances she might. But as you pointed out, she's not herself."

"No," Maybelle agreed, "she definitely is not. Maybe I'll do that."

"One thing, May," Ruth cautioned. "I haven't told her about my chat with Mr. Mick. It seemed wiser not to."

"I won't let on I know anything."

"I strongly recommend that."

Maybelle got up and went along the hall in her stocking feet. The door to the master suite was ajar and she stopped dead, floored by the sight of a great deal of money strewn over the bedspread. Honoria, still in her dressing gown, sat counting out sums and putting them into envelopes.

Just as Maybelle decided it might be smart to back off and pretend she hadn't seen anything, Honoria glanced over and said, "I haven't gone crazy, although it probably looks that way. Come on in, May."

"What're you doing, Honoria?"

"I'm not going to tell you because you might try to talk me out of it. And my mind's made up."

Maybelle sat down on the side of the bed and watched Honoria fill the last of the envelopes. Then she gathered the remainder of the cash and stuffed it and the stack of envelopes into her handbag. "There. That takes care of that." She glanced at the time and said, "Do me a favor?"

"Sure."

"Be a darling and bring me a fresh cup of coffee."

"Okay, sure."

Fretful and puzzled, Maybelle went back to the kitchen. When she returned with the coffee, Honoria was in the bathroom, smoothing skin cream over her face.

Accepting the coffee, Honoria took a sip, then sighed and said, "Thank you, sweetheart. Grab a seat and keep me company while I try to make myself resemble something human. I look like the wrath of God this morning." She parked the cup on the rim of the sink, stared hard at her reflection for several seconds, then reached for the familiar pink-labeled can of Supreme Liquid Whitener.

Perched on the edge of the tub, Maybelle watched her put on her makeup, always intrigued by the process. First dabs of the whitener went below each eye and were smoothed out with the tip of Honoria's forefinger. Then came an all-over dusting of powder. The residue got whisked away with what looked like a hairbrush but had long, soft white bristles. Next the dark gray eye shadow was applied with a narrow, flat-edged brush. After that came the mascara, and finally the clear red lipstick. Less than ten minutes and she looked her familiar self again.

No chance of tears now that the mascara was on. She'd strangle on her emotions before she allowed anyone to see her weeping snail trails of black across her cheeks. Tears were a sign of weakness, a sign of one's inability to handle whatever came along. "Thank god for Max Factor, huh?" She smiled into the mirror at Maybelle before gulping down some more coffee. As she brushed her hair, she asked, "How's the weather today?"

"Three guesses." Maybelle made a face. "My place is like an ice-box. I had the oven on all evening trying to get warm. Finally, I gave up and went over to Grandma's for the night. I'm really going to have to think about moving. This is the third winter with on-again, off-again heat. I think the landlord's behind with the fuel bill, because half the tenants owe him back rent and he doesn't have the heart to evict them. So he's running the building out of his own pocket. He's a decent man and I hate the idea of bailing out on him, but I can't live this way, even though I do love the apartment. I'll probably never get another place that's as nice."

"Why don't we go buy you some kind of heater? I'm sure I saw an ad recently for an electric radiator or something like that. Why don't you give Macy's a call, see what they've got. They're bound to have *something*."

"What a great idea! I'll do that as soon as they open. You are such a smart cookie."

"That's me, all right." Honoria finished the coffee and handed Maybelle the cup, saying, "Give me five minutes to put some clothes on, then we'll make a few phone calls."

"Are you going to tell me what's going on?" Maybelle asked at the door.

"No, sweetheart, I'm not," Honoria said quietly.

"You know I'll help if I can."

"I know that, May. Go on now, please, and let me get dressed."

Somewhat reluctantly, Maybelle left. Honoria drew in a long, slow breath, then went into the dressing room.

She gave the secretary her name, and Leonard came on the line right away. "Honoria, girl of my dreams. Weren't we supposed to talk last week about making a date for lunch?"

"Yes, we were. I just didn't get a chance. How are you, Len?"

"Hunky-dory. You?"

"Oh, the same as ever. I've got a couple of favors to ask."

"Fire away."

"I need some information about a young woman who was found dead a few blocks from here."

"The one who froze to death?"

"That's right. Augusta Washington. I was wondering if you could check with your pal at the coroner's office and find out whatever you can about her death, see if there was anything they kept out of the papers, anything odd or unusual."

"I'll give it a try, but you know I can't guarantee results. What's the second thing?"

"Would you happen to have the time to see me this afternoon, Len?"

"I've always got time to see you. How about letting me buy you that lunch we talked about."

"I'd love it, but not today. Could I have a rain check?"

"Of course."

"You're an angel. How's two-thirty for you?"

"Hold on and let me check the book. Better make it three. I've got a two o'clock deposition that shouldn't take more than half an hour."

"Perfect. See you at three."

"I'll look forward to it."

Honoria hung up, turned to Maybelle and said,

"Okay. If Len manages to find out anything about Gussy, he'll tell me when I see him at three. Now there's something I've got to do. You're welcome to come along, if you want."

"Come along where?"

"To the park."

"The *park?*"

"Don't look at me that way, May. I know you think I've lost my marbles, but I haven't and it's important. If you decide to come, I'll buy you lunch before we go look at those room heaters at Macy's. Then you can head uptown to try to talk to Benjamin or to Gussy's family, and I'll head downtown for my appointment with Len. All things being equal, I should be back here in time to greet Chip when he rolls in from New Haven."

"What about Mick?"

"What about him?" Honoria's eyes narrowed slightly.

At once realizing Ruth had been right, she played innocent, asking, "How was his trip?"

Dropping her guard, Honoria said, "Fine, I suppose. You know he never tells me what he's up to. So, are you coming with me or not?"

"Oh, I'm definitely coming."

"Good. I was hoping you would."

The frozen ground crunched beneath their feet as they entered the park; the wind whistled in the bare, brittle branches of the trees. As they emerged into the open, beyond the scant shelter of the trees, the cold seemed to intensify and the wind pushed as if trying to throw them off course.

"Where are we going?" Maybelle asked, pulling her hat lower over her ears.

"Just over there." Honoria indicated the shanty-town in the distance on the Great Lawn. The clutch of dwellings looked shockingly small, mean, and dark compared with the tidy row of buildings lining the far side of the avenue beyond the park, rising above the skeletal trees along the perimeter.

"You mean Hoover Valley?"

"Unh-hunh."

All at once Maybelle knew what Honoria planned to do. How typical of her, she thought, to take her upset and use it to do good. "I don't think you've lost your marbles," Maybelle said, linking arms with the older woman. "And I wouldn't dream of trying to talk you out of it."

In response Honoria smiled and touched her gloved hand to Maybelle's cheek. "Why did I think you wouldn't understand?"

"Temporary amnesia probably." As they continued to walk north into the wind, Maybelle said, "I always wonder what they do for water. Where do they get it? How do they bathe? What do they do with their waste?"

"I've wondered that, too. It must be hell, especially in this weather."

"Look at those shacks. They're like something I'd have imagined seeing out on the plains a hundred years ago, not here, today, smack in the middle of the park, or down at 9th Street by the East River."

"D'you remember that incident a few years ago, when the good citizens of Fifth Avenue complained about the hobos sleeping in the park?" Honoria asked.

"I don't think so."

"Twenty-two men were arrested. When they came before the judge, he suspended their sentences, gave each man two dollars out of his own pocket, and sent them back to the park."

"Good for him!" Maybelle said, touched.

"A decent man with a functioning heart. There are seventeen shacks over there. I've counted them so many times the past few years. And the people who live here aren't bums, May. One of the places belongs to a performer named Ralph Redfield I remember from the vaudeville days. In decent weather he puts up a tightrope from one end of the town to the other and charges a nickel to anyone who wants to watch him walk it. His act actually inspired a pretty decent novel by Robert Nathan called *One More Spring*. I heard through the grapevine one of the studios has taken an option on it."

As they drew nearer, they saw a quartet of children playing tag behind the houses, laughing as they zig-zagged away from the one who was "it." No matter what, Honoria thought, children would always find some game to play, some energetic diversion. Once upon a time she and the other orphans had played under the watchful eyes of the Sisters. No shrill cries of delight, noise was discouraged, but they played none the less; fairy-tale games about knights and damsels; fabulous pirate adventures that derived in large part from stories by Robert Louis Stevenson. But the absolute favorite, the one they played most often, was the family game. Mother, father, and children. They took turns acting out each role, giving it their all. Mama was busy getting the great big house clean, taking care of the children, fixing the supper before Papa got home from his important job to give everyone happy hugs. Then they all sat down at the table to eat the best meal in the world—a wide variety of menus that depended on whose turn it was to be the mother.

One of the children caught sight of Honoria and Maybelle approaching and signaled to the others. And the four flew off like starlings, probably to warn their parents.

"They're frightened," Honoria said sadly. "They think we're here to make trouble."

"They'll find out soon enough they're wrong."

"But, May, what a life for them."

"Yeah. People think they've got it bad. They should come have a look at what bad really is."

At the first place no one responded to Honoria's knock. After a moment, she bent down and pushed one of the envelopes under the door. At the next shack the door opened before she even had a chance to knock, and a thin, pallid man of thirty or so, in several layers of clothing, with a curious tow-headed toddler clinging to his leg, asked, "What d'you want?"

"To give you this." Honoria held one of the sealed envelopes out to him.

"What is it?" he asked, eyeing it suspiciously as the child decided to indulge in some peek-a-boo with Honoria and pushed his face into the back of his father's leg.

"It's a Christmas present." The child peeked out and Honoria grinned, saying, "I see you." At once the child again hid his face.

"Who from?" the father asked.

"From me." The little face slid into view again, and this time Honoria covered her eyes with her hand, then whipped it away, and the boy laughed.

"Who're you?" he asked, softening as she indulged the child, again concealing her eyes behind her hand until she knew the child was looking out from behind his father's leg. "Gotcha!" she exclaimed, pointing a finger at the startled toddler, who gulped a mouthful of air and then chortled merrily.

"No one in particular," she said. "Take it, please."

Finally he accepted the envelope. "You some kind of do-gooder, one of them charity people?"

"No. I'm just a neighbor, and this is my friend." Maybelle said, "There are no hooks attached."

"Well, gee. Thanks. Thanks a lot."

"You're most welcome."

"You calling on everyone here?" he asked.

"Yes I am. Is that all right?"

"I guess so. Only you won't find too many around. Most're out trying to make a buck or two for the holidays."

266

"That's okay. We'll leave the envelopes under their doors. Have a happy Christmas," Honoria said. Maybelle echoed the sentiment and the two of them started toward the next place.

"God bless, lady!" he called after her. "God bless both of you!"

"And you, too!" she and Maybelle called back.

"This is wonderful," Maybelle said, hugging Honoria's arm. "*You* are wonderful."

"No, I'm not. The truth is, this is as much for me as it is for them."

"I know, but so what?" Maybelle said. "It *feels* like Christmas, and I'm glad you invited me along. I'm always going to remember this."

Not bothered now by the cold, they proceeded from one dwelling to the next until all the envelopes were gone. When they were on their way out of the park, the quartet of children materialized, waving and calling good-bye, before picking up their zig-zagging game of tag.

NINETEEN

Leonard came out from behind his desk to embrace her with such a show of affection that for the second time that day she found herself ready to break into tears. Instead she kissed his cheek and said, "Get back on the other side of that desk and behave yourself."

"Yes, ma'am." He did just that as she dropped into the chair facing him and unbuttoned her coat. "How is everything?" he asked, noting with some

267

alarm that she appeared to have lost weight and was decidedly paler than usual.

A quip readied itself, but she didn't have the heart to deliver it. "Everything's in a muddle," she replied truthfully. "A great big muddle. But I'm sure it'll sort itself out in time."

"The Russki giving you problems?" he asked perceptively.

"Actually, he's giving *himself* problems."

"Oh?" Leonard leaned forward, folding his arms on the desk. "Care to elaborate?"

"Not really, Len. As I said, the likelihood is it'll sort itself out." She opened her handbag, removed the wad of bills, and placed it on his blotter.

"What's this?" He sat back, regarding the money with raised eyebrows.

"It's about fourteen thousand dollars. Could you put it in escrow for me?"

"I could. May I ask why?"

"Because after giving the matter considerable thought I've decided I'd like it to be part of my estate, which means I want to make a couple of changes to my will."

"What aren't you telling me?" he asked, becoming even more alarmed.

"Oh, plenty." She tried for a high-voltage smile but couldn't manage more than one of fairly low wattage. Shamming today seemed to require more energy than she could muster and, abandoning the effort in favor of more of the truth, she said, "It turns out the Russki's not a Russki but a Canuck,

268

and the cash is some of what he's contributed to the household the past couple of years. For some reason I hung onto it. Don't ask me why, because I haven't a clue. I just did. Aside from that, I got conked on the head a few days ago, so I'm not feeling up to snuff. The weather's getting me down, which is neither here nor there. And I've been doing a lot of thinking, about a lot of things." She paused for a few seconds, then said, "This comes under the heading of attorney-client stuff, Len."

"If that's the way you want it, fine. Who hit you on the head? And what d'you mean he's a Canuck?"

"A Russian-born Canadian who grew up in Montreal. He hung himself out to dry on a line of his own devising, and yesterday the fates conspired to snap the line on him but good. The truth came out courtesy of an accidental encounter with a childhood friend of his on Fifth Avenue. For the moment he's living at his place—another little item that came out yesterday. He's had an apartment at River House for a number of years but claims he's scarcely used it since we met. I suppose I believe him. Of course he deeply regrets the pretense and its present repercussions."

"I'll just bet he does," he said caustically. "A Canadian, for chrissake! If that doesn't take the cake." He shook his head, thinking it was no wonder she looked worn out. "You still haven't told me who hit you."

"I have no idea who it was. As for Mick, I care for him." She heard the words, almost like an echo, and

269

asked herself why she had started out being truthful and then, mid-stream, taken to dealing in euphemisms. "I love him," she said, hoping she didn't sound too much like a soap opera. "It doesn't, however, stop me from feeling like an idiot right now."

"So what will you do?"

"In the long run there's every chance I'll take him back."

"Why, for God's sake, Honoria?"

"That's one of the things I've been thinking hard about, and the answer is because I'm less miserable with him than I am without him. It doesn't sound like much but it is, because after all these years, and everything that happened then—and now, for that matter—I trust him. You of all people should know how monumental a declaration that is. I *know* he loves me, Len. He's shown it in more ways than I can enumerate. So in the last analysis, even though what he did was childish and stupid, it's not completely unforgivable. I'm not the appalling innocent I was twenty-odd years ago. I've learned some tough lessons over the years and, at this point in history, I'm not prepared to walk away from something that's the genuine article."

Leonard sank back in his chair, his melancholy eyes fixed on hers.

Seeing his disappointment, she said, "You've always meant the world to me, Leonard. And if you hadn't known as much about me as you did it would, without a doubt, have come to something. But your knowing's been a significant stumbling block, because, regardless of what you or anyone said, I believed what happened was my fault. Every day, month after month, for years, I kept turning it this way and that, trying to pinpoint precisely where I'd made my mistake, what I'd done wrong. I never could find it, but that didn't stop me from trying."

"But you *didn't* do anything wrong!" he argued. "We've been over this a thousand times. I thought you'd long ago come to terms with that fact."

She shook her head. "We could've gone over it *ten* thousand times and I'd still have felt that way. It's decades later, and sometimes I'll remember and the guilt's so total, so piercing, it stops my breath. The difference now is that, for long periods, months at a stretch, I forget to remember, so there's no pain anymore, only a massive emptiness—and the guilt."

"Honoria," he said softly, "it was a terrible, terrible thing. But it was *not* your fault. How can you possibly feel guilty so long after the fact?"

"Probably because I'm a woman. We are supremely gifted when it comes to guilt. I wouldn't be surprised to find out it's genetic." This time she managed a halfway decent smile. "If not for you, though, Len, I'd never have survived. And I'll always love you for that."

"You'd have survived it," he disagreed. "You're the strongest person I've ever known—male or female."

"You really think so?" she asked, intrigued by his perception of her.

"Yes, I really do."

"That's very kind, perhaps too kind."

"Don't be silly. It isn't *kind*. It's the unvarnished truth. What that family, that *woman,* did to you was despicable, evil. But you fought her right to the bitter end, and I was so proud of you, Honoria. I still am. And *I* will always love *you*—for that in particular, and any number of other things, too."

For several seconds they sat gazing at each other. Then she said, "I think we'd better drop this now, or we'll both end up in tears."

"Okay," he capitulated, not without a measure of relief. He did not possess anything like her emotional resources and too often was confounded by the depth of his feelings for her. It was safer these days—at least since she'd taken up with Mick—to keep a lid on those feelings, because there was always the unattractive possibility that they'd take him over and have him behaving in a fashion that would make it hard for him to live with himself. "Let's deal with those changes to your will." He reached for his fountain pen and pulled over a ruled legal pad.

After they'd covered the areas she wished to amend, he said, "I'll have Evelyn type up a codicil and get it to you for signature by the end of the week."

"Would you do me a favor and have her type it now? I'd like to sign and get it out of the way."

Once again he wondered if there was more she hadn't told him, but he didn't have the heart to pursue it. He'd absorbed as many revelations as he could handle for one day. "Fine. Sit tight for a minute. I'll give this to Evelyn and be right back."

While he was gone, she got up and walked over to the window to look down at the people going in and out of City Hall, at the traffic flowing along lower Broadway.

"It'll be ready in ten or fifteen minutes," Leonard said, coming back in and closing the office door.

"Oh, good." Turning, she leaned against the window sill, asking, "Did you manage to get anything on the Washington girl?"

He tilted back in his chair and propped his well-shod feet on a corner of the desk. "A couple of things. Let me find my notes." He pushed some papers around, found the one he wanted, and quickly refreshed his memory. "Okay. Number one, the autopsy revealed she was high as a kite, so high that it's unlikely she knew where she was or what she was doing."

"High on booze?"

"Nope. She had a good-sized package of cocaine in her bag. She'd obviously taken some of it."

"Taken how?"

"Orally and by inhalation. Her nostrils in particular had a lot of residue."

"Interesting. What else?"

"It turns out she wasn't homeless after all."

"No, that I knew."

Reading from the page, he said, "Along with the cocaine she had twelve dollars and thirty-six cents in her change purse, a hefty ring of keys, a handkerchief, a lipstick, and five loose pearls."

"*Pearls?*" Startled, she stared at him for a long moment, then went back to the chair in front of the desk.

"Yup. Real ones," he elaborated, "of a decent size and luster. Worth plenty if someone had a whole string of them, according to my source. You find this significant, don't you?"

"I found a pearl in DeeDee Carlson's apartment the evening I got hit on the head. I completely forgot about it until now. There has to be a connection." Just as the newspaper article in that morning's paper had galvanized Maybelle into action, Honoria found herself being powerfully pulled back into the puzzle of DeeDee's death—and now Gussy's.

"Honoria, what does it matter? The Carlson case is closed. And there's no question the Washington girl died of exposure. What she was doing in that box in the alley is anyone's guess, but there's no mystery to how she died. She froze. End of story."

"When do they think she died?"

"Sometime between Friday afternoon and Saturday morning. They can't be any more precise than that because of the extreme cold."

"It's definitely connected," she said, thinking aloud.

"What is?"

"Augusta Washington was DeeDee Carlson's maid. DeeDee liked to spice up her active and very varied sex life with regular snorts of cocaine. When I checked her bedroom there was no sign of her supply. And there was some question as to where

274

she got it. It's possible Gussy was her source. What I need to find out is who owned the pearls."

"I'm lost," Leonard said, lifting his feet off the desk. "Why do you need to find out anything?"

"Because I promised Chip I would." She looked at her wristwatch. Almost three-thirty. Chip would probably be there by the time she got home. Anticipation bloomed inside her at the prospect.

"Well, that certainly tells me all I need to know."

"I realize it doesn't, but, speaking of needing to know, I've decided to tell Chip everything. Stevenson's been treating him like garbage and it's time the boy finally knew why. I was hoping I'd never have to tell anyone what happened, but I don't see that I have a choice."

"He's a decent kid, Honoria, and I agree with you."

"Do you?"

"Any other woman would've told the *world* by now. I often wish I had even half your restraint."

"No you don't, Len. My kind of restraint doesn't do any good. I'd have been far better off if I had told the whole world. But hindsight's always twenty-twenty. I can't go back and undo promises I made to myself so long ago."

"I understand."

"I know you do. It's what I count on you for. You're my oldest and dearest friend, Leonard. Lovers come and go, but friends are forever."

"You know I feel the same way about you."

"Yes, I do." She smiled at him, this time without

effort.

"Keep me posted on how things go, will you? And if there's anything I can do, on any score—"

"We'll talk in a day or two. And I'm expecting you to join us for Christmas dinner."

"You think that's such a good idea, with what's going on?"

"It's the best idea I've had in an age. Write it down in your book right now. It'll be something we can both look forward to. Or not, as the case may be. Whatever happens, it won't be dull."

With a laugh, he picked up his pen and did as she asked. "I never could say no to you."

"You're such a sweet sap."

"That's me. Just remember, if it starts flying thick and fast, I'm only a phone call away."

It was after eleven. Ruth had gone to her room and Honoria put another piece of wood on the fire before sitting down beside Chip on the living-room sofa. Taking hold of his hand, she said, "I promised we'd talk when you got back."

"If you're tired, it can wait. We've got a couple of weeks before I have to go back to school."

"No. I think it's waited long enough."

His stomach lurched and he was suddenly apprehensive of what she might be about to say. Nervously, he blurted, "Are you my mother? Is that what you're going to tell me?"

"No, sweetheart. I am not your mother. But your father has always thought that I am."

"*What?*" His face screwed up as he tried to process this piece of information. "I don't get it. You and my father. . . ?"

"*Never!*" She shook her head so fiercely that her hair flew into her eyes, strands catching on her eyelashes. Lifting the hair aside, she said, "I'm sorry, but I wouldn't touch that man with a barge pole. He's pompous, self-important, and boring. I tried every way I knew how to talk Van out of marrying him, but she'd already accepted his proposal and, being a woman of her word, she insisted on going through with it."

"I never could understand why she married him," Chip confessed. "So Van really was my mother?"

"Absolutely. And she loved you more than anyone or anything else, ever. You know that."

"I know she did, but I thought——"

"You were wrong, Charlie." She gave his hand a squeeze. For a time she stared at the fire, while Chip stared at her. It was silly, but she was scared, as if time had rewound like the film on a projector, and she was caught again in the nightmare. Then she thought of Leonard saying he was proud of her. It helped her get to the threshold. She wet her lips and began. "It's a long story, sweetheart. But here's the condensed version.

"One spring evening a long long time ago, when I was seventeen, I met a twenty-one-year-old Princeton senior named Parker Albright at a club up in Harlem. It was, in short, a case of the fabled love at first sight. Three months later, after spending every possible free moment together, we got married downtown at City Hall. Then, until he finished school, Parker spent five days a week in Princeton. On Friday afternoons he'd hop on the train to come spend the weekends with me. By the time he graduated I was pregnant. He used some of his inheritance to buy an apartment, which he insisted on putting in my name so that, in case anything happened to him, the baby and I would have some security. He landed a good job with a shipping company and I was working as a script girl in Astoria. We were unspeakably happy." She broke off and again looked into the fire, battling the surge of memories and emotions. To speak of the past after keeping silent for so long was to relive it, and the image of Adelaide Albright unspooled, large and forbidding, on her mind's screen.

Open-mouthed, Chip could only stare at her profile, shaken to learn that the one person he'd thought he truly knew was unknown to him after all. *A previous husband and a child.* He was grateful she'd broken off, because his brain felt bruised, as if the facts she was relating were high-velocity pellets being fired into his ears. "I didn't know you'd been married before," he said stupidly.

"I've only been married once."

"You mean you and Mick aren't—?"

"No, we're not, Charlie. It was just simpler to tell everyone we were."

"Oh! Okay. It doesn't matter."

Giving his hand another squeeze, she picked up

where she'd left off. "As I told you, we were very happy—except for one thing: Parker's mother. She was furious with her only child for getting married without telling her, and that upset him terribly. He was devoted to his mother, you see." She turned to look briefly at Chip, then turned back to the fire. "He was also very afraid of her. Most people were, and with cause. She was the single most heartless being I have ever encountered; she was also the most ruthless. After her husband died, when Parker was eight years old, she had the money to buy any-thing—including people. What Abigail wanted, Abi-gail got. Except this one time, when her son got married and didn't tell her until some months after the fact, very likely because he knew she would never have allowed the marriage to take place had she known." The panic was beginning, squeezing her lungs and causing her heartbeat to accelerate.

"So, finally he told her and she went into a rage. The next evening, having cooled down a degree or two, she came into the city to inspect her new daughter-in-law." Her voice going husky, she said, "It was a horror show. She came through the door, looked me up and down, and declared I was nothing but a low-class gold-digger. If he didn't consent to it, and get me to agree to an annulment, Abigail was going to disinherit him. Parker held my hand and told her to go to hell. We didn't need her approval or her money. We had each other, and our friends. We'd get along just fine. She stormed off in a red-faced fury, and within twenty-four hours she

279

started her campaign to break up the marriage. Letters, telegrams, half a dozen telephone calls a day to Parker's office, half a dozen more each evening at home. If I happened to answer, she refused to speak to me. She'd say 'Put him on!' and wait for me to obey. If I didn't, she'd call again and again until either he came on the line or we took the phone off the hook. She was relentless, determined to separate us at any price—and her offers to me, via a battery of lawyers, escalated into the stratosphere—so that her son could find someone more suitable.

"The last time she telephoned, which was one evening in May, two months before the baby was born, Parker delivered his ultimatum. Either she accepted our marriage or she could go ahead and disinherit him, cut herself off from her only grandchild. 'It's *my* life,' he told her. 'This is *my* family. If you don't want to be a part of it, that's your choice. But leave us alone. Stop trying to bribe my wife, and stop this endless harassment!'

"He was trembling when he hung up, so distressed he couldn't speak, just sat with his head in his hands for a time. While I was glad he'd stood up to her at last, I felt terribly sorry for him. After all, regardless of her hatefulness, the woman was his mother. I thought it best to leave him be, and over the next few days he pulled himself together. Miraculously, the calls and letters stopped, and gradually we relaxed, relieved that it was over, that she was out of our lives." She fell silent, her eyes drawn back to the fire. "What *children* we were," she said hoarsely, loathing the reconstructed image of Abigail Albright and her own remembered powerlessness. "This is very difficult," she whispered.

Unable to think of what else to do, he said, "Let me get you a drink, Aunt Honey."

"Thanks, sweetheart. Scotch, neat, no ice." His hand slipped from hers and she continued to watch the fire, mesmerized by the flashes of color, the occasional sparks; glad of the heat that seemed to ease some of the interior ice. *You're the strongest person I've ever known.* What choice had there been? Either you were strong, or you died.

TWENTY

Her headache was back, sharp little claws digging into the base of her skull as it began its ascent. She couldn't remember ever feeling so punk for so long. Her appetite had dwindled and she'd hardly done justice to Ruth's lovely dinner. If this went on much longer she was going to have to pay a visit to the doctor—something she avoided assiduously. Seeing doctors meant you were sick, and being sick had no place, ever, on her agenda. Good health had a lot to do with state of mind. Once you got into the habit of relying on doctors, your health went to pot because you started believing what they had to say. And doctors usually only had opinions, not facts. *I've got opinions of my own,* she'd been saying for years. *I don't need to pay for somebody else's.*

"You okay, Aunt Honey?"

"I'm okay, Charlie. Just playing an old game of mine that hinges on avoiding things that tend to be upsetting. How it works, sweetheart, is you settle on a subject and then let your brain go off on tangents. For example, let's say you're worried about a paper you've got to write at school. You start there and focus on, say, paper. How, you wonder, does a great big, gorgeous tree end up as a ream of paper or a notebook on somebody's desk? And what happens to all the newspapers at the end of the day? Why aren't the streets filled side to side, three feet deep with leftover newspapers?"

He smiled. "Gosh. Why aren't they?"

"See." She smiled back at him. "Before you know it, you're miles off topic. It works every time. Don't you want anything to drink, sweetheart?"

"No, thanks."

"Well, if you change your mind, help yourself. Okay?"

"Okay."

She took a swallow of her scotch, shuddered as it seared its way down her throat, then said, "The baby was due in four weeks and I'd arranged to take six weeks off work, so I was home the morning Parker left for the office and came back two hours later, in a state of shock. He'd been summoned into the boss's office and told apologetically that his services were no longer required. He was to clear out his desk and leave at once. The boss wouldn't say why, but I knew in my bones that Abigail had been responsible. She was going to make Parker rue the day he'd dared to defy her. I think he knew it too, but we didn't discuss it because neither one of us wanted to believe she'd go that far.

"I greatly underestimated her. Somehow, she made it impossible for him to get another job. He lined up one appointment after another and was politely turned down everywhere. We were all right for money at that point. Parker still had a good part of his inheritance left. But he wasn't capable of sitting idle. When the last of the companies regretfully turned him down, he applied for a job at B. Altman's and was hired, just like that.

"He came home with flowers, all smiles. We celebrated over dinner at our favorite Italian restaurant. The next morning he went off to start his new job in the shoe department, and by noon he was back. He'd been called to the personnel office and told there'd been a mistake. They were sorry but the position wasn't available after all." She stopped and took another swallow of the scotch.

"His mother was doing this?" Chip wanted to know. Honoria nodded, and he asked, "How?"

"Parker and I couldn't figure that out either. A long time later I found out she'd had a private detective following Parker wherever he went. Then all she had to do was have one of her lawyers make a phone call and that was the end of any possibility of a job. But Parker didn't know that. He kept trying day after day, until Zoe was born." Shocked at hearing her daughter's name—spoken aloud for the first time in more than fifteen years—she stopped and tossed down the last of her drink.

"Would you like another one?" Chip asked quietly.

"Yes, please."

He took the glass from her hand, poured her another, and brought it to her.

"Thank you," she said, trying not to look at the new reel being projected on that interior screen. But she couldn't help herself. She focused and there was her baby girl, with her surprising mass of black hair, her tiny fists curling reflexively as she yawned, then settled into herself, asleep. Noticing the glass in her hand, she automatically drank from it. "We agreed that I'd go back to work and Parker would stay home and take care of the baby. He was mad about her and happy to do it. Looking after her made him feel useful, he said. He'd been so despondent, I was quick to agree to something that gave him such a lift. So when Zoe was two weeks old, I went back to the Famous Players Film Company on West 26th Street."

For five weeks Parker stayed home with Zoe while Honoria worked. And although he made a heroic effort to conceal it, each day of those five weeks he became a little quieter, a little sadder. She tried every way possible to raise his spirits—complimenting him on his manifest skill with the baby, on the way he'd stood his ground and refused to give in to his mother, on anything and everything she could think of. Parker responded with typical charm and courtesy, but he was becoming, she thought, something like an electric fireplace. It looked good enough but gave off no warmth and couldn't possibly fool anyone into believing that it housed real flames.

While Zoe napped he sat at Honoria's typewriter and composed dozens of letters, applying for jobs, not just in the city but in New Jersey and Connecticut, too. Swallowing his pride, he pursued connections with former classmates and with his father's two brothers-in-law. Each day's mail brought a few more rejections. He joked about his lack of desirability and kept on trying. In the meantime he bought some cookbooks and began preparing simple dinners. "Maybe I'll become a chef," he quipped as he served up stews and casseroles. "I'm getting pretty good at this."

She joked with him, but her heart was starting to feel like a piece of badly glazed pottery; its surface was gradually becoming crazed by ever-spreading, overlapping cracks. She wanted to go over to Beekman Place and kill Abigail, just wrap her hands around the woman's thick throat and squeeze all the life out of her. But there wasn't a thing either she or Parker could do.

Their one source of pure happiness was Zoe—a fat, sunny baby given to sudden huge grins of recognition or of amusement; a wonderfully easy infant who was sleeping through the night after four weeks and who cried, it seemed, only when absolutely necessary. She nursed greedily when Honoria was home but was perfectly content to accept the bottles

Parker gave her during the day. She loved being bathed and waved her tiny, dimpled hands, squirming and grinning the instant she was immersed in water. Having her diaper changed seemed to amuse her, and she was drawn to anything within reach, clutching an offered finger, or a handful of hair, or Parker's tie, and holding on tight. She also seemed to love the sight of new faces and gazed thoughtfully at each new one for a second or two before breaking into one of those irresistible, chubby-cheeked grins.

Sarah Applebaum, the widow across the hall, was crazy about the baby and offered to baby-sit any time. Honoria jumped at the opportunity, and she and Parker had their first evening out when Zoe was seven weeks old. They went up to Harlem to hear some music, then came home and made love with all the heat and inventive intensity that had been missing for many months. Eased and considerably more optimistic about the future, Honoria was in no way prepared for what took place only three days later.

She was on the set—luckily during a lighting break—when one of the secretaries came to tell her she had a telephone call. Thinking it was probably Parker, she hurried to the office and picked up the receiver. It was Sarah Applebaum.

"I'm a nosy parker and it's probably nothing, but something funny just happened and I wondered if you knew."

"Knew what?" Honoria asked, fearing there'd been some mishap with the baby.

"I got into the elevator about fifteen minutes ago with a uniformed chauffeur who got off at our floor and knocked at your door. I was curious, so I kept my door open a crack to see what was going on. It looked as if Parker had been expecting him because he was in his topcoat and started passing over suitcases."

"Suitcases?"

"That's right. Then Parker went inside for a minute. He came back carrying Zoe, locked up, and left. It didn't feel right to me, so I thought I'd give you a call."

"He left with Zoe?" Honoria had to put a hand on the desk to brace herself. Her legs had gone weak.

"You didn't know about this, did you?" Sarah Applebaum guessed.

"No. How long ago did they leave?"

"Five minutes maybe. I called you the minute they got into the elevator."

"I'll be right home!" Honoria hung up and stood trying to decide on the fastest way uptown. The subway. "I've got to leave," she told the secretary. "Family emergency. Let them know on the set, will you, Mary?"

"Sure. The baby okay?" Mary asked.

"I don't know!"

She ran. All the way to the Seventh Avenue station at 28th Street, she told herself Parker would never take Zoe away from her. But Abigail would. The uniformed chauffeur could only be hers. No one else they knew had one. But maybe it was a job out of town. Some company was so impressed by

287

Parker's grades that they wanted him to start work right away, hence the chauffeur. And of course he'd have to take the baby with him. He couldn't just leave her. That was it. It was good news, not bad. Good news, not bad. She kept repeating this to herself as she flew down the stairs at the subway station, nearly tripping. She had to grab hold of the handrail to keep herself from falling, and wrenched her shoulder instead. A moment's pause to try to catch her breath, then she ran on.

It seemed to take forever for a train to come. But she was in luck. When one finally did arrive, it was a local. She darted inside and stood right by the doors so she'd be able to get off as soon as they got to 59th Street.

But the train sat at Penn Station for an eternity while Honoria's foot tapped impatiently, sweat collected beneath the weight of hair gathered at the nape of her neck, and her hand grew slick on the strap. What was taking so long? What were they waiting for? Her stomach was rising. She was going to be sick. If the doors didn't close in another thirty seconds, she'd get off the train, run up to street level and get a cab. *Why didn't the doors close?* At last, at last, they did, and the train gathered speed as it traveled through the underground darkness to 42nd Street.

This time the wait was a short one before the doors again closed. Perspiration trickled down her sides and between her breasts, as she pictured Parker carrying Zoe off in the wake of Ronald, Abigail's chauffeur. Who else could it possibly have been but Ronald? Squeezing her eyes shut for a moment, she offered up a prayer to the God she hadn't believed in for years. *Just let me have Zoe and I'll never ask for anything again; just let me keep my baby.*

After a ride that seemed to have taken hours, the train pulled into the 59th Street station. She bolted through the doors the instant they opened and ran along the platform toward the stairs that would take her to the street. Holding her skirt up with one hand, the other moving on the handrail, she took the steps two at a time, turned smartly at the top, and started to run the last three and a half blocks to West 62nd Street.

The stitch in her side started at 60th and slowed her down to a quick walk, which allowed time for her fear to expand so that it occupied all the space inside her skull. *Don't do this to me, Parker. Please. Don't let that evil woman make you do something you know will destroy you and me, and our child. Parker, be home with the baby when I get there. Please, please.*

Sarah Applebaum had been waiting. The instant Honoria emerged from the elevator, Sarah's door opened and she stood wringing her hands while trying to look as if nothing was wrong. Honoria couldn't speak, but Sarah seemed to understand that and waited while Honoria got the key into the lock and stepped into the apartment. The emptiness rushed at her; not a sound inside, only street noise muted by the curtains.

Everything of Zoe's was gone except for the receiving blanket Van had crocheted and, beneath it, the mother-of-pearl and silver Tiffany teething ring Mr. Zukor, Mr. Porter, and Mr. Frohman of Famous Players had sent when the baby was born. Honoria ran into the master bedroom and threw open the closet. Parker's clothes were gone; the dresser drawers had been cleared.

"Oh, please!" she whispered, her knees clamped tightly together as she looked around the room for some hint of where they might have gone.

"Here's something," Sarah said, bending to pick up a small piece of paper from the bed.

"What is it?" Honoria looked down at the paper in the woman's hand. In her husband's familiar assertive script was written:

Mauritania, Pier 60
Departs 3 p.m.
I'm truly sorry. Parker

"It's two twenty-five. Pier Sixty is where?" Honoria asked frantically, unable to think.

"20th or 21st. He doesn't want to do this. He wants you to stop him. That's why he left the note."

"He's not the one. It's his mother, she's behind this."

"Never mind that! Go, darling!" Sarah ordered. "You could still make it." Giving Honoria a push, the woman said, "*Go! Run!*"

Honoria went clattering down six flights of stairs rather than wait for the elevator, and turned right, toward Ninth Avenue, praying for a cab. Just as she arrived at the corner, a hansom cab was crossing the intersection. She shouted and ran into the road. The bowler-hatted driver yanked hard on the reins, but before he'd managed to stop the cab she was climbing in, saying, "I've got to get to Pier Sixty before three o'clock. Please, can you get me there in time?"

He looked over his shoulder at the overwrought, pretty young girl, and said, "We'll give it our all, darlin'," then snapped the reins and the horse leaped forward.

At 61st Street he directed the horse right and urged it to pick up speed. "There'll be less traffic on Eleventh Avenue and it's the most direct route," the driver explained, half-turning his head toward her as he let the horse have free rein except to shift to the right or left. "Sailing at three, are you?" he asked, never taking his attention from the road.

"My *husband's* taken my *baby!*" she shouted over the noise of the cab and the pounding of the horse's hooves. She wanted to, but she couldn't say more than that. Her throat hurt. Her mouth was too dry. Her eyes were stinging. And her body was melting beneath her layers of clothing, itching and wet.

"The rotten scoundrel!" the driver said feelingly, caught up in her urgency. "Gidjyup, Samson! Gidjyup!"

As the cab took a wild left turn onto the avenue and the horse began to gallop, Honoria opened her coat to look at the watch pinned to her bodice. Two

thirty-seven. Twenty-three minutes remaining before the ship left the pier. But they had another forty
blocks to travel. Hanging on hard as the cab rattled
along, she shut her eyes and offered up another
prayer. *Please get me there in time. If you do this one
thing, I promise I will never again doubt you. I will lead
an exemplary life and teach my child to believe in you. I
will honor the houses where you live, light candles to the
Virgin, attend Mass faithfully until the day I die. Please
get me there in time so that my little girl won't have to
lose her glorious smile, her easy nature, and grow up in
fear, the way her father did.*

When next she opened her eyes, the cab was
bumping through the intersection at 57th Street
and another minute had been lost. Twenty-two left
now. They'd never make it.

*Blessed Mary, intercede on my behalf. Please, I want
my baby back. She's not yet two months old, not yet
weaned. What kind of god would allow an infant to be
stolen from her mother? You're a mother, you understand.
Please don't let them take her from me.*

55th Street. "Gidjyup, Samson!" Turning his head
slightly to the side, he said, "I don't like the whip,
you know, darlin'. And Samson, grand old fella, he
has no need of it. He hears in my voice that he's to
imagine himself a colt again, racing through the
meadow. See how he runs!"

The wind pulled her hair from its moorings,
sending strands flying like streamers around her
head as the lovingly tended cab—brass fittings well
polished, paint gleaming, the interior spotlessly

clean—careened past automobiles and other horse-drawn vehicles; drivers looking over, startled, as the hansom rocketed past them and crossed 54th Street.

Twenty minutes. Holding the watch on the palm of one hand, clutching the side of cab with the other, she prayed soundlessly, her lips moving. *I will go down on my knees to you in gratitude every day from here on in if you'll get me there in time; I will be faithful, devout, I'll believe again most sincerely. God, the father, will you permit this? God, the father, you gave your only begotten son. I beg you to allow me to keep my only begotten. I want to believe; I will believe. Please, please.*

At 42nd Street a traffic-control officer in the middle of the intersection saw them approaching, took in in an instant that the cab wasn't going to stop, and threw up his hands while blowing on his whistle to stop the oncoming traffic on 42nd.

"Bless you, brother!" the driver called out as they flew past. And the officer's eyes connected with those of the stark-eyed, wild-haired passenger, the whistle silenced as her fear made itself felt like a stunning blow that drove the air from his lungs. Then they'd gone past, her image still in his eyes as the cab flew off, on down the avenue. After a moment, remembering his job and the ever-present whistle, he blew it hard, angry but not clear why, as his hands reversed position and summoned the 42nd Street traffic forward.

"Gidjyup, Samson! Gidjyup, old darlin'!"

37th Street. A pair of pedestrians midway across

the road looked up, paused, then scurried back to the safety of the sidewalk. Eleven minutes. The air filled with the sound, deep and unmistakable, of ships' horns—oddly animal sounds, leviathans capable today of unintentional cruelty. Unencumbered tugs chugged cheerfully up the Hudson, other tugs guided all manner of vessels toward Ellis Island and Liberty and Governors Islands in the distance. Ships at almost every pier were being loaded with cargo, with passengers, with vast quantities of provisions for lengthy sea voyages. Men crowding the dock-side toiled, while up on the decks the captains watched, conferring with their mates.

Please don't take my Zoe, my beautiful baby, away. She's my heart, my life. I'll die without her. Could a god, if there was one, be so cruel? And if you do exist, what did I do to offend you? What have I done to deserve this? But if I have sinned, I throw myself upon your mercy now. Please don't let this happen, please, please. I implore you, I beseech you . . .

32nd Street. Six and a half minutes. Eleven more blocks. It was possible. But the poor horse was in a lather, froth falling from its lips, its broad sides heaving as it gallantly galloped on. And now, eyes wide open, she was praying for herself, and her baby, and the horse. She wanted the aging beast to survive this valiant run.

Let us get there in time, please. It's such a small thing to ask, something minuscule in the mountain of requests being made every moment of every day. If I had the money I would, like Carlotta, poor mad Empress of

Mexico, promise to construct a font of finest alabaster for the little church on the corner. I will give you my heart for all eternity if you will grant this one wish. And, please, keep Samson's heart strong—for this kind, kind man who is trying so hard to reunite me with my Zoe.

Ocean-going liners came into view now as they passed Pier Sixty-four, Sixty-three, Sixty-two. One minute left. Ahead, with a terrible pang and a bitter taste in her mouth, she could all at once see the great ship moving away down the river. A few passengers could still be seen on the decks, leaning elbows on the rails as they took in the skyline.

The hansom was slowing and she jumped from the cab, fell to one knee, got up, and ran onto the pier as the last of the crowd on land dispersed. So hard that the blood vessels in her head felt as if they'd burst, she screamed, "THERE IS NO GOD!"

Nothing happened. The scream reverberated off the inner walls of her skull, diminishing in volume. Then it was gone. The ship continued on its way, growing steadily smaller, clouds of smoke billowing from its great stacks, the passengers no longer visible. In no time at all the pier was deserted and she could hear the slap of waves smacking against the pilings, could feel the wind whipping her hair and the stinging in her palms as her fingernails dug into the flesh, could taste salt mixing with the bitter liquid in her mouth.

The ship's prow was aimed at those islands it would pass very soon, on its way through the harbor to the ocean. How could something so immense move so quickly? Her helpless hands clenched and unclenched, her breathing grew louder in her ears, as the *Mauritania* glided out of sight. Too late, too late. Gone, they were gone—her husband, her baby, her future. What a fool she was, never for an instant to have considered the possibility that her watch might be winding down, running slow. Why, why, *why* hadn't she thought to ask someone else the time?

She felt a touch on her shoulder and turned to look into the sympathetic Irish blue of the middle-aged man's eyes.

"I'm that sorry, I am, darlin'."

Her chest heaved as she considered the blue of those eyes—a rare cerulean, clear and pure—as they gazed back at her, unflinchingly, immensely sympathetic. Then she dropped her head to his shoulder and wept, broken, inside the circle of the cab driver's awkward, brawny embrace.

TWENTY-ONE

Sitting with her elbows on her knees, she looked down into her empty glass, tears dripping from the tip of her nose. A gentle touch on her shoulder returned her to the present.

"Aunt Honey, I'm so sorry," Chip said in a cracked voice, then realized, to his horror, that he was echoing the words of the note. Insensitive jerk, he berated himself. But she didn't react and he kept silent, patting her back consolingly.

After a time, she said, "Get me another, will you, sweetheart." She handed him the glass, then roughly wiped her face on her sleeve before getting to her feet. "I'll be back in a minute."

Halfway to drunkenness, she walked stiffly out of the room and down the hall. Leaving the master suite dark, she got out of her clothes and went into the bathroom, where she hung over the sink, a hand resting either side of the basin. She felt rusty and soiled, like garden furniture left too long out in the rain. Yet, there was a degree of relief mixed in among the excavated emotions. And that was a surprise.

She cleaned off the makeup she knew without having to look was a streaked mess on her face. Then, slightly dizzy from the booze that seemed to have put a muffler on the headache, she pulled on her dressing gown and in bare feet walked back to the living room, determined to tell the rest of the story and never, ever, again speak of this as long as she lived.

"Are you okay?" Chip asked as she returned to the sofa. He thought, as he always did, how much younger and more accessible she seemed without her makeup. Her complexion was so pure, her features so attractive, that he always enjoyed looking at her.

She picked up the fresh drink from the coffee table, saying, "More or less. How about you, sweetheart?" She turned at last to look at him.

"The same as you, I guess. I'd like to hear the rest of it, but if talking about it upsets you, let's forget it."

"You have such a good heart, Charlie. It's one of the reasons I love you as much as I do."

"You have a good heart, too."

She gave a low laugh. "Mine is cast-iron, with a few soft spots for certain special people. But I'm fair. I am definitely that. Funny thing, but while I was washing my face it occurred to me that I need to hear me tell about this as much as you do—maybe so I can be done with it once and for all."

"I can understand that," he said.

"Can you?" She studied him with narrowed eyes, then said, "Yes, of course you can. Poor Charlie. You've had a rough row to hoe."

"So have you."

She shrugged and looked into the depths of her new as yet untouched drink. "The only people who have it easy are the ones who're too dumb to know things stink or the half-dozen who have families who genuinely love them. The rest of us slog through the mire somehow, learn to put a pleasant face on it, and grab a good time when it happens by."

"But you didn't always feel that way," Charlie offered.

She sighed. "Nope. You're right. For about seventeen months a long, long time ago, I believed in happily-ever-after." A sip of her drink, then she said, "I never went back to the apartment. I couldn't. That first night I stayed with Sarah. I needed help, in her opinion, and it so happened she had a nephew who was a lawyer. Which is how I met Leonard—one of the youngest graduates ever of the Columbia Law School. He hadn't yet passed the bar exams, but he'd already been hired by one of the most prestigious firms in the city. Sarah got in touch with him and he came over that same evening. You should've seen him, Charlie." She smiled. "He was such a kid—like you in some ways. He was almost twenty-two but looked about sixteen. And even then he wore three-piece suits, which only made him look younger. Of course the instant he opened his mouth you knew this was no kid. He was fiercely bright and passionate about justice for all. Anyway, he agreed to take on the case and do whatever he could.

"The next day, not knowing what else to do, I went back to work. I spoke to your mother that afternoon and she insisted I come stay with her. Your father was in Paris on business—he was working his way up through the family firm then, overseeing some of the foreign pulp and paper sales—and her mother was at the Newport house for the summer. Van was in her eighth month and had been sick all the way through the pregnancy. At that point she was seeing her doctor every few days and spending a lot of time in bed, and she didn't like being alone in the Park Avenue apartment with just the maid, hence the move to her grandmother's place." She paused for another sip of her drink. "So I went to stay. Like a robot, I dragged myself to work each morning and went back to Van at the 71st Street house in the evening. And every evening she talked about how I'd get Zoe back, that I wasn't to lose heart." Choking up, she said, "Your mother was the kindest girl who ever lived, Charlie."

"I know," Chip said softly.

Honoria cleared her throat before going on. "I got back to the apartment on the third evening of my stay, and the staff were in a panic. Van had taken a bad spill on the just-washed bathroom floor and had been rushed by ambulance to Lenox Hill Hospital. I hurried over there to be told by Granny Kelly that not only had Van broken her arm but the fall had also sent her into premature labor, so the doctor was performing an emergency cesarean section. I waited, terrified I was going to lose her, too. Granny Kelly and I sat for hours holding hands, both of us afraid to speak. She was devoted to Van, you know."

"I know."

"The doctor finally came in near midnight to tell us everything had gone well and Van was asking for me. I hesitated, and Granny Kelly, in that impatient way she had, said, 'Go along now!' and I ran down the hall to see Van.

"She looked like a child, small and tired, with one arm in a cast and the baby in the other. She was so happy, Charlie. And you were the most perfectly beautiful infant. I stood there speechless, afraid if I tried to say anything I'd start to cry, because all I could think of, seeing you, was my own baby. Van said, 'Will you nurse him for me, share him with me?' And then I did start crying, because she was, in the only way she could, giving me a child to re-place the one I'd lost. Naturally, I agreed to do it."

With a thrill of embarrassment, heat flooding his face, Chip automatically looked at the swell of her breasts beneath the dressing gown. They had been intimate in a fashion he'd never dreamed of.

"War had broken out in late July, but the actual fighting didn't start until early August, when the Germans invaded France through Belgium. Your father managed to get out of Paris and over to England just before the invasion. Once in London, though, he couldn't get passage back home for quite some time, despite strings being pulled on both sides of the Atlantic by his father. In the meantime Van brought you home from the hospital, and the routine we worked out was much like the one Parker and I had with Zoe. I fed you in the morning before I went to the studio, and then again in the evening when I returned. During the day, while I was gone, the nurse would put you into Van's arm and she'd give you a bottle.

"It was a remarkable and generous thing your mother did, Charlie. No one has ever understood or accepted me as she did. She, and you, kept me from losing my mind—especially when it turned out that Abigail had Parker take all the documentation with him when he left: our marriage license, Zoe's birth certificate, every single photograph that showed the baby or Parker or the three of us together. It was as if she wanted to erase me. But her money couldn't buy everyone, it turned out. In particular, a clerk at the records office refused to remove those records from the register. So when Leonard personally went there for copies, he was able to get them. We also got affidavits from any number of people, including Ronald the chauffeur,

301

who were willing to testify to Abigail's actions in arranging the kidnapping of the baby. But there were two primary obstacles standing between us and Zoe's return. One was the fact that she'd been taken to England, and the other was the war.

"Communication was slow to impossible. Leonard arranged to hire a British solicitor to act on my behalf, but the man could do very little because Abigail simply ignored his letters and the case had no real standing in the British courts. So the wheels turned very very slowly. But because of you, holding you, nursing you, I could pretend—sometimes for hours—that my husband hadn't betrayed me and that I hadn't lost my child.

"Then everything blew sky-high. By mid-October I'd sold the apartment, banked the proceeds, and was using the money only to pay the legal fees. When the cast came off Van's arm, she moved back to the Park Avenue apartment and I moved in with her. So there we were, the baby, his two mothers, and the domestic staff. It was a very serene time. In the evenings, after you'd been put down for the night, Van and I would have dinner and talk for hours. I think she was hoping your father never would come back. Many times she came as close as damn it to admitting the marriage had been a mistake. She really didn't like Charles Stevenson and had been persuaded to accept his proposal as much by the fact of his wealth as by his ardent pursuit. The boys had always been after Van, but so many of them had been drawn primarily to her money that she'd grown very wary. And because of that she'd chosen the wrong man."

"Was there a right one?" Chip asked.

"Oh, very definitely yes. She realized that once she'd already committed to your father. And no matter what anyone said, she couldn't be persuaded to break off the engagement because not only had she given her word, as I've already told you, but she also couldn't bear the idea of hurting anyone. Which is laughable, given your father's narcissism and profound indifference to everyone's feelings but his own."

"Who was the right one?"

"No one you've ever heard of, sweetheart. He was a darling, shy boy from a fine Boston family who'd been at St. Paul's School with Charles. He fell head over heels for Van, but by the time he got his nerve up to ask her for a date she'd started seeing your father, so he bowed out, even though I've always believed that if he'd persevered she'd have realized much sooner what a mistake she was making with Charles. But he didn't, so she went ahead, and the rest is history." She stopped to look at the dying fire while she swallowed another mouthful of scotch.

"Shall I put another piece of wood on the fire?" Chip asked.

"Don't bother, my love. It's late and we'll be off to bed shortly."

"But you're cold."

"It doesn't matter. Where was I?" she wondered aloud.

"Mid-October," Chip reminded her.

"Ah, yes. That's right. So we come to a Saturday afternoon in late November when you were fifteen weeks old. Van had gone out to do an errand and I was sitting in the rocker in the nursery, feeding you, when the door flew open and your father came striding in."

Chip winced, picturing the scene.

"What was I doing there? he wanted to know straight off. And where was his baby? 'This is your baby,' I told him, trying to cover myself up, when Van arrived back. It certainly *wasn't* his baby, he insisted, rounding on Van in a fury. What was going on here? Why was *that girl* here, half naked in *his* nursery? And where was *his* son? 'That's your son,' Van told him, but he wasn't having any of it. After moving heaven and earth to get home, he arrives back to have his wife and her awful girlfriend try to persuade him that somebody else's baby was his.

"It was an appalling scene. You were screaming, still hungry, and upset by the raised voices; Van was attempting to reason calmly with the man who would *not* stop shouting; and I was trying to cover myself so I could put you back in your crib. But he wouldn't allow me to put *my* baby in *his* baby's crib. Nothing would convince him he was mistaken—not your birth certificate; not Granny Kelly, who came at once to tell him to stop behaving like such a fool; not his parents or hers. Nothing. He was adamant, immovable. Van and I were in collusion, trying to dupe him into accepting a child that was not his.

Where was his *baby? What had we done with it?* It went on for hours, until Van was in tears and Granny Kelly put an abrupt stop to his tirade by hitting him across the side of his head with her walking stick. That shut him up. In fact, he dropped like a rock and lay on the floor moaning, while Granny said, 'I am taking Vanessa, the baby, and Honoria home with me. When you come to your senses, you may call upon us. Until then, you will not be welcome in my home.' She told the servants to pack bags for us and see that they were brought to the house, then she shepherded the three of us down to her car. During the short ride home, she said, 'The man is a complete ass!' Those were the strongest words I ever heard your great-grandmother speak, Charlie. I'd never seen her so angry. And devout as she was, she said to Van, 'I were you, my girl, I'd get shut of that fellow. He's as nasty a piece of work as I've ever seen. I think a dispensation could be arranged, under the circumstances.'"

"So why didn't Van *do* it?" Chip asked impatiently, maddened by what he was hearing. "How could she have stayed with him and had two more children? I don't *understand*."

"I suppose his parents managed to talk some sense into him. After all, they'd been to the hospital; they knew you were their grandson. *Everyone did,* except him. In any case, a few days later, most subdued, he came to the house to talk to Van. Whatever he said to her, it worked. The next day she took you and went home. Granny Kelly said I was welcome to stay, but Sarah Applebaum wanted me to move in with her, and I was very fond of her, so I did. And that was that."

"But what happened to Zoe, and to Parker and his horrible mother?"

She wrapped an arm around herself, finished her drink in a gulp, then set the glass down, saying, "Parker enlisted in the British army early in 1915. He wrote to me saying he'd never forgive himself for what he and his mother had done. He said he hoped I'd believe that he regretted it with all his heart and that he'd pleaded with his mother to return Zoe to me. Her response to that was to deny *him* access to his daughter. So she lost both her parents. Parker was killed in the Battle of the Somme in 1916. I knew because, as his wife, I was notified by the British government. They sent me his medals, his papers, and his kit bag. Which is how I got a few of the photographs back. Parker had them with him at the front."

She drew a long, slow breath, and exhaled tremulously. "Abigail didn't give a damn about the baby. Zoe was merely an instrument she used to push her son into line. And after Parker enlisted, Abigail left Zoe entirely to the care of the housekeeper and her husband. They were good people, I know. We corresponded briefly—after. But for the entire five and a half years of her life, Zoe was an isolated, lonely, and neglected little girl, cut off from other children, cut off altogether, on the estate Abigail bought in the Midlands, near Worcester. While she spent most of her time in London at her flat in Mayfair, Zoe was left in that enormous, drafty stone house in the country."

"That's awful," Chip said.

"Yes, it is," Honoria agreed. "By the time the British lawyer located the estate it was too late. Zoe had died of pneumonia several months earlier in the housekeeper's cottage—the only part of the estate the couple had been given permission to heat. Abigail, you see, considered it a waste of money to provide a supply of coal for one small child. Appalled, the housekeeper moved Zoe in with them. But it was too late. She was already ill. Her lungs slowly filled, and within a week she was dead. *God!*" She shook her head despairingly and tightened the arm wound around her midriff. "Abigail died of a stroke in 1924 in London at the age of fifty-seven. Unfortunately, she went quickly. I'd have liked her to suffer a long, wasting illness. But she died within hours. On my trip to Europe a couple of years ago, I went to England, hired a driver, and drove up to Worcester to see Zoe's grave with the marker I had bought. Abigail hadn't cared to spend the money. I went to see my daughter in the little cemetery beneath the shade of a massive old oak, with a pink-granite stone that says 'Zoe Albright, cherished daughter of Honoria and Parker, born July lst 1914 died December 16th 1920.' " She coughed, swallowed, then continued, determined not to break down again.

"I never did find out where Parker was buried, or even if Abigail had bothered. As for Stevenson, whatever promises he might have made to Van he didn't keep them. He never accepted that you were his child and to this day believes I substituted my baby for his. He's so stupid it wearies me just talking about him. Write him off and get on with your life because he's never going to have an epiphany and realize he behaved badly toward his natural-born son."

"No, I agree."

"Wise of you. So, Charlie my dearest, my darling, we come to the end of the story. Do me one last favor now and go to bed, sweetheart. I'm all talked out and I'd like a couple of minutes alone before I go to bed, too."

Not knowing what else to say or do, he pressed a kiss on her shoulder, touched his hand to her hair, then got up and went along the hall to the guest room, where he flopped on the bed and lay staring at the ceiling, blinking away tears as he pictured the little girl's grave and a soldier lying for eternity on the field of battle where he'd fallen.

Still not as drunk as she wanted to be, Honoria was debating whether or not to have another scotch and get completely plastered, when the telephone rang. She looked over, knowing it was Mick and asked herself if she wanted to talk to him. She did. She unhooked the receiver and said hello.

"I know it's late but I wanted to hear your voice."

"It's okay," she said, slurring a bit. "When the phone rang I decided I wanted to hear yours. Although, by rights, I should tell you to go straight to hell. You've made me feel like such a goddam dodo."

"I know, and I'm sorrier than I can say."

"If I didn't believe that I'd've spit in your eye and that would've been the end of you."

"I'm a lucky man," he said without so much as a hint of sarcasm. "How are you, Honor?"

"Tired, and fairly drunk—if you hadn't already figured that out. How're you, Mick, Mike, Michael?"

His deep laugh rumbled pleasantly in her ear. "Sober and lonely. I miss you."

"How did you know I wasn't already sleeping?"

"Because the lights are still on."

"How do you know that?"

"I'm at the pay phone in the coffee shop on 75th. I've been walking up and down outside the building for a couple of hours, getting up the nerve to call. I was afraid you'd hang up on me."

"Your timing's pretty good. I'm drunk enough to think making love to you right now would be a damned fine idea."

"You mean that?"

"I do. But you have to leave after. You can't come home yet. It's too soon and I wouldn't want people thinking I'm a patsy."

"No one would *ever* think that. I'll be there in five minutes."

"Come up the service elevator. And try not to make a lot of noise."

"I'll be quiet as a mouse," he promised.

After hanging up, she put the screen in front of the fireplace, turned out the lights, and made her way unsteadily to the bedroom.

Still staring at the ceiling, Chip heard her go past and waited for the sound of the bedroom door closing. But it didn't come. Ten minutes later, as he was pulling on his pajamas, he thought he heard footsteps in the kitchen, but when he went to look no one was there.

You're cracking up, fella, he told himself, going through the dressing room into the guest bathroom to wash and to brush his teeth.

Mick stood in the bedroom doorway until his eyes had adjusted to the dark, knowing from the sound of her breathing that she was asleep. It didn't matter. He tiptoed across the room and sat down carefully on the side of the bed, enveloped at once in her scent as he listened to the slow, deep rhythm of her breathing. It was probably just as well she'd fallen asleep, because, if they had made love, she'd have been furious about it in the morning. As it stood she might not even remember that they'd spoken on the telephone, but at least he'd been invited back for a brief visit. It was more than he'd hoped for, sooner than he'd dared hope for it. Better not to push his luck. After a couple of minutes he tiptoed out, quietly closing the door behind him.

The light was on in the kitchen and Chip was sitting at the table, a robe on over his pajamas, waiting. "I thought it was you," he said. "Then I thought I must be cracking up because, when I looked, nobody was here. How come you're creeping around in the middle of the night? I thought you were away

310

on one of your trips."

"Is that what Honor told you?"

Chip's eyebrows drew together, his entire face screwing up so that he looked like a little kid. "You don't sound like you, Mick. *Am* I cracking up?"

"No, you're not. Hungry, Chip?"

"Kind of. There's leftover roast chicken. What's going *on?*"

"Let's have a sandwich and we'll talk." Mick opened the ice-box to get the chicken, while Chip, still frowning, went to slice some bread.

Mick had taken off his jacket and was removing his cufflinks when Ruth came out of her room and made a show of closing the hall door as she said, "Quiet you're not. Sit down the two of you. I'll fix the sandwiches and a nice pot of tea, and then the *three of us* will have a talk."

TWENTY-TWO

The telephone rang. Automatically she reached to lift the receiver and croaked out a hello.

"I have to tell you that next to making love to you, what I like best is watching you sleep."

With a groan, she said, "Thank you. What time is it?"

"Ten past eight. Early, I know—"

"But you've got a meeting."

"I do. I just wanted to hear your voice before I leave."

"Another trip?" She shoved the pillows against

the headboard and sat up.

"No, just another meeting."

"Oh, hell!" she said, remembering. "I just meant to close my eyes for a minute while I was waiting."

"It doesn't matter. Do you forgive me, Honor?"

"I'm getting there. So you arrived and I was out like a light."

"You certainly were. I only stayed a minute, and I tried to be very quiet. But Chip heard me and was waiting in the kitchen, wanting to know what was going on. Then Ruth came out and fixed some sandwiches. So I told them what a mug I'd been, explained everything. I mean, I got myself into this mess. It seemed only fair that I should square things with them rather than leave it in your lap."

"Very mature of you. I appreciate it."

"Are you mad?"

"No."

"You're sure?"

"Quite sure. I really do appreciate it. I was dreading trying to tell them."

"Well, now you don't have to. They know I'm a schmuck but they're working on forgiving me, too."

"Ruth's pet elephant," she murmured.

"What?"

"Nothing."

"You think of me as an elephant?"

"No, I don't."

"So, when will I see you, Honor?"

"Phone me later, when I'm awake, and we'll discuss it."

"Okay. I love you."

"I know you do. We'll talk later. Bye, Mick." She put the receiver down and turned to look at the sliver of light showing at the intersection of the curtains. Mercifully, in spite of three glasses of scotch on an empty stomach, she had no hangover. And revealing at long last all that ancient history to Chip proved to have been an emotional emetic. She felt wonderfully purged, thoroughly cleansed. Now if she could just keep that persistent damned headache at bay, everything would be peachy. Taking her eyes off that warm looking slash of light, she got up and went into the bathroom.

"When did you actually start seeing DeeDee, Chip?"

"Well, I consider the beginning her phoning me at school to ask if I'd be her date to the Halloween party. I mean, we'd met a few times here and there, but I think of that as the 'official' start. Why?"

"Merely a point I wanted to clarify," Honoria replied, mentally checking this item off her list as another dead end. "Would you happen to know how to get in touch with Karen Carlson?"

"DeeDee's mom? Sure."

"If it's the number you gave me, May and I had no luck with it."

"I've got a couple of others."

"Maybe you could try reaching her after breakfast," she suggested, doubting he'd have any success.

"Okay, sure."

"If you do get hold of her, I'd like to have another talk with the woman."

"More points to clarify?"

"Unh-hunh."

"Have you managed to find out anything yet?" he asked with endearingly feigned casualness. The boy really was the most guileless soul she'd ever known.

"A few things that don't yet add up to a whole picture," she hedged, reluctant to hurt him but equally reluctant to have him canonize his late girl-friend. "By the way, did DeeDee have a string of pearls?"

Chip finished chewing a bite of toast before answering. "Mrs. C. had beautiful ones, with a platinum and diamond clasp. DeeDee had her eye on them."

I'll bet she did, Honoria thought. "Meaning?"

"She was always asking if she could borrow them, but Mrs. C. wouldn't hear of it. She wore them all the time. They'd belonged to her mother and had a lot of sentimental value—which I could certainly understand, feeling the way I do about the watch Van got me when I turned thirteen. I've worn it every single day since, except for one week a couple of years ago when it had to have the mainspring replaced. For the entire week I felt as if an actual part of my body was missing. Anyhow, DeeDee didn't understand how her mother felt. She wanted those pearls so badly that I finally offered to buy her some instead of an engagement ring."

"But she wanted the ring *and* the pearls, right? And not just any old string but one with a platinum and diamond clasp, exactly like her mother's."

"How did you know?"

"Lucky guess." Honoria poured herself more coffee. "What was the compromise?"

"We agreed she'd get the ring right away and the pearls later on."

"How much later?"

Chip flushed. "Christmas."

"So she'd already picked them out."

"Unh-hunh. I left a deposit."

"What about the ring?"

"It was being sized at Tiffany's. Gosh! It's probably still there. I should do something about that."

"Yes, you should. What did you know about DeeDee's maid?"

"Gussy? Not much. Why?"

"She was found dead on Saturday morning in an alley off 74th Street."

"*What?*" Staring at her, Chip slowly put down his half-eaten piece of toast. "That's horrible! How did she die?" All at once his stomach was aching.

"She froze to death inside a big cardboard box in the alley. I heard through a connection that she'd taken so much cocaine she'd have been oblivious to her surroundings."

"Could she have been murdered? Is it possible her death has something to do with DeeDee's?"

"May's convinced it has everything to do with it."

"But you're not?" he asked.

"As it happens, I tend to agree with May—for a couple of reasons. Go ahead and eat, my love. You look as if you haven't had a square meal in days."

"I haven't. I hardly left my room. I just wanted to finish the papers and get out of there."

"So have some breakfast, Charlie."

"What about you? Are you going to sit there and watch me eat while all you have is coffee?"

"Indeed," Ruth put in. "*Is* that all you're planning to have, Miss Honor?"

"Not if the two of you are going to gang up on me."

"How about a nice poached egg on toast?" Ruth proposed.

Wrinkling her nose, Honoria said, "How about a nice piece of your fried bread?"

"All right. Would you like some, too, Chip?"

"No, thank you, Ruth."

"This may sound like a strange question," Honoria picked up where she'd left off, "but were you aware of a silver box DeeDee kept in the drawer of her bedside table?"

"I don't remember anything like that. Why?"

"One of her friends mentioned it."

"What was so special about this box?" he asked, retrieving his toast.

Here goes nothing, Honoria thought. "Apparently, that's where DeeDee kept her cocaine. When I looked through the apartment it was gone."

"Are you trying to tell me that people, that her so-called *friends*, said she used *drugs?*"

"Afraid so, sweetheart."

"It's a rotten *lie!* She would *never* have touched

stuff like that."

"She would have and she did. She was no angel, Charlie."

"Maybe not. But she was no dope addict either!"

"I doubt she was an addict. It was more that she liked to spice up her encounters."

"What encounters?"

"I'm sorry to have to tell you this, but she was seeing other boys."

"Well, sure she was—before we got engaged."

"Before, during, and after, sweetheart. I've talked to someone she ditched just three weeks before she died. And there were others."

"Three weeks? That can't be. He was mistaken."

"He wasn't, Chip, and he had no reason to lie. According to most of the people May and I interviewed, DeeDee was very bad news. Much as I hate to say it, she was using you."

"No, she wasn't," he argued, despite the doubt that instantly took root inside him and began sending up shoots. In a fragment of time so minute it couldn't have been measured, too many incidents suddenly took on an entirely new slant.

"Why were you paying half the rent on her apartment?"

"She got in a little over her head with the decorating, so I was helping out. I mean, she deserved a nice place to live."

"You were paying more than half, weren't you?"

"All right," he admitted. "I was. I was paying all of it. But once we were married we were going to be living there anyway, so what difference did it make if I paid the rent?"

"None, I suppose."

"It's not as if I couldn't afford it," he said defiantly.

"No, it's not," she agreed calmly. "And I'm sure she was well aware of that."

"That's not fair!" he railed. "Neither is people saying these nasty things about her when she's not here to defend herself."

"Even if she were here, Chip, people—I—would still be saying these things. Because they happen to be true."

"How do you know that?" he challenged, wounded.

Reaching across the table to cover his hand with hers, she said, "Do you think I'd pass on idle gossip just for the hell of it, knowing how much it would hurt you?"

"No. You'd never do that."

"Then why do you think I'm telling you?"

Childishly, he said, "I don't know."

"It wasn't DeeDee who was in over her head, sweetheart."

"We loved each other," he insisted, despite his exponentially proliferating doubts.

From the stove, Ruth said, "You wouldn't believe the way otherwise intelligent people can be turned around by sex, dear boy. Men and women both."

"Now the two of *you* are ganging up on *me*," he accused.

"I know it looks that way," Honoria said. "But that's not how it is."

"No? How is it, then?"

"I knew when I saw the photos of the girl that she wasn't what she'd led you to believe she was. For one thing she was almost twenty-six, not twenty-four. Did you know that?"

Shocked, he shook his head.

"I thought not. She was also *intimately* involved with several boys, even though she was engaged to you at the time. Not very nice, would you agree?"

"I guess so."

"Then there was her fondness for cocaine; her meanness to people she saw as of no use to her—dear Minnie Morgan, for example; and her ruth-lessness—making a play for Brian at Robin Apple-gate's wedding reception, to cite one case. Any way you want to cut it, she was no sweet young innocent. Charlie, my darling, facts are facts. And DeeDee was a cool, calculating little number who got what she wanted no matter how she had to go about it."

"So I'm a dumb sucker, is that it?" he demanded, eyes filling.

"Not at all. She took advantage of your youth and inexperience."

"If she thought I was such a sucker, why was she going to marry me?" he put up one last argument.

"How much do you stand to inherit when you turn twenty-one next August?"

"Whatever's accumulated in the trust."

"You don't know?" Honoria asked.

"It's about a million, I guess."

"You'd better start paying closer attention to your financial affairs, sweetheart. It's got to be a good three or four million by now."

"How could that be?"

"It's simple. Because her mother died first, Van inherited Granny Kelly's entire estate. Plus she got half her mother's estate. And as you well know the Kellys were not impoverished. You are going to be very, very rich, my love, as are your sisters and brother. And between now and your birthday you're going to have to start toughening yourself up, because girls are going to be coming out of the woodwork, trying to get their hooks into you. DeeDee was merely the first."

"I refuse to believe that!"

"Why, because she took you to bed and you interpreted that as a sign of love? Charlie, Charlie, Charlie. Sex very often has nothing whatever to do with love. You'd better be sure that you and the next girl you fall for have something to talk about once the heat dies down. Because lust, my sweet, can turn to contempt in the blink of an eye if that's all there is between two people."

"Truer words never have been spoken," Ruth said, bringing a plate with two slices of golden fried bread to the table. "Pay attention to what your auntie's telling you, dear. It's the God's honest truth and you're a lucky lad to have someone who cares enough to tell you. Most of us have to blunder through it and find out for ourselves the hard way."

"So, in your opinion DeeDee was taking me for a ride?"

"In a word, yes."

Mortified, he pushed the plate of cold toast away, crossed both arms on the table and laid his head down atop them.

Stopping to put a hand on his shoulder, Ruth said, "Don't be blue, dearie. From what I've heard of this girl, you're well out of it. Next time round you'll be more careful."

"I feel stupid," he muttered. "Stupid, stupid."

"It happens to the best of us, believe you me," Honoria said, picking up her knife and fork. "No one thinks any the worse of you for having made a mistake." Interesting, she thought. Barlow's rules had application to everyone but her. That *was* stupid. No one would think the worse of *her* for having bought Mick's highly convincing act. What did it matter in the long run, so long as the underlying affection was genuine? And what harm had actually been done—except the questionable damage to her pride? None, really.

"*I* think worse of me."

"Well, don't! We're allowed a small ration of mistakes in judgment when we're young. With any luck, we learn from them."

At the sound of the front door opening, the three of them went quiet. Chip sat up and looked over at the doorway.

"It's only me!" Maybelle sang out. "Be right there."

She came in carrying a large box of flowers. "These're for you," she told Honoria. "Cully asked if I'd mind bringing them up."

Honoria opened the box to reveal a dozen long-stemmed red roses. Maybelle and Ruth sighed appreciatively over their moist, just-unfurling perfection as Honoria read the card, which said, "We adore you. Mick, Mike, and Michael." She laughed and tucked the card into the pocket of her robe.

"Aren't they splendid!" Ruth said, bringing a cup of coffee to the table for Maybelle. "Shall I put them in water?"

"Please," Honoria answered.

"How're you?" Maybelle asked Chip, wondering why he looked so down in the mouth.

"He's upset with me," Honoria explained, giving his hand a quick squeeze. "I've been giving him the lowdown on DeeDee."

"Not a nice girl, Chip," Maybelle said, sitting down next to him. "Not nice at all."

"Neither of you knew her." It sounded puerile. Why was he still trying to protect her when the truth was starting to stack up, holding solid like a newly erected brick wall?

"No, but the people we talked to did," Maybelle said, wrapping one long slim hand around her cup. "And she wasn't going to win any popularity contests. Oh, I finally caught up with Benjamin this morning," she told Honoria. "He never managed to give Gussy my note. Which explains why she was a no-show at the Tree of Hope—aside from the salient

322

fact that she was already dead. But he did have an interesting story he was willing to tell me for the price of breakfast at the diner."

"Do tell," Honoria said, going back to the now lukewarm fried bread.

Maybelle looked at Chip, not sure about adding to his misery. But he said, "Go ahead, May. I might as well get all the bad news in one dose."

She put an arm around him and kissed his cheek, then sat back saying, "You deserve better than DeeDee, Chip. The perfect girl's out there waiting for you."

"Oh, sure," he scoffed.

"She is," Maybelle said emphatically. "And she's going to be wild about you because you're one of the dearest, sweetest boys who ever came down the pike."

He flushed again and lowered his eyes as he pulled the plate of toast back over.

"That's gone cold," Ruth said, swooping in to whip the plate away. "I'll make more. Fancy some toast, May?"

"I couldn't, thanks." Maybelle patted her stomach. "I just ate my way through the greasy-spoon special."

"So, tell all," Honoria said, washing down the last of the fried bread with a gulp of coffee.

"What about Leonard? Did he find out any-thing?"

"He did." Honoria quickly ran down for them what Leonard had told her and finished by reaching into her pocket, saying, "Gussy also had five of these in her possession." She opened her hand to reveal the pearl resting on her palm.

"Is that one of them?" Maybelle asked.

"Nope. This I found the other evening at DeeDee's apartment. It was under the balcony door in the living room."

"You think Gussy found hers in the apartment, too?" Chip asked.

"Seems logical to think so," Maybelle said.

"Somebody broke a string of pearls," Honoria said. "And so far as you know," she addressed Chip, "the ones you intended to buy Gussy are still at Tiffany's."

Chip swallowed nervously and said, "I'd better make a trip down to 37th Street this morning and see what's what."

"We're talking about a lot of money, aren't we?" Honoria guessed.

"Two thousand for the ring and a thousand dollar deposit on the pearls." Chip's stomach was now aching in earnest. "Most of what I'd saved from my allowance for the past few years."

Everyone was silent for several moments. Then Honoria said, "If necessary, I'll make good on the money, sweetheart."

"I couldn't let you do that."

"Yes you could, and you will. I won't take no for an answer. Now, May. What did Benjamin have to say?"

Maybelle didn't respond right away. She was too upset by the idea of DeeDee's having taken such advantage of the poor kid.

"May?"

Reining in her anger, Maybelle said, "One morning about six or seven weeks ago Benjamin was on his way to work and noticed Gussy up the street, heading toward the subway station. He put some speed on, thinking he'd catch up and ride down with her, when she stepped into a doorway. As he got near he glanced over and saw Gussy talking to an uptown hoodlum named Leroy Perkins, who gave her a package she stuck in her purse. The next afternoon Benjamin was in the service elevator on his way down to the basement with some trash from one of the penthouses when the doors opened on fifteen, and there was Gussy handing a wad of money to Leroy. Then, cool as can be, he got into the elevator and rode down with Benjamin. When they got to the ground floor, Leroy turned, aimed his fingers like a gun at Benjamin, and said, 'You didn't see me yesterday and you didn't see me today. You got that?' Benjamin said he did and Leroy sauntered off.

"He saw Leroy two more times after that. But he thought it was Gussy buying whatever he was selling. And I didn't tell him otherwise."

"Smart girl," Honoria said. "So, now we know where DeeDee got her cocaine. We'll let that rest for the moment. What I want to work on next is how those pearls came into Gussy's possession and whose they were. Maybe you and Chip could try tracking down Karen Carlson while I get dressed.

Okay, Chip?"

Dispirited but game, Chip said, "Okay, Aunt Honey."

"If you like, May and I will go with you to Tiffany's for moral support. Afterwards, provided you two manage to find her, let's pay a call on Mrs. Carlson. And at some point today, I want to take another look at DeeDee's apartment. Of course if you don't find Mrs. Carlson we'll have to shift directions."

"All right," Maybelle agreed. "What d'you say, Chipper? Wanna hit the phone?"

"Sure. Why the heck not."

TWENTY-THREE

She suddenly became so dizzy that she had to grab onto the bathroom door to steady herself. Everything seemed a little distorted too, which made the dizziness worse. Closing her eyes, she hung on to the door, concentrating on the slow, heavy rhythm of her heart. After a minute or two she risked opening her eyes. The vertigo had passed. But to be on the safe side, she kept holding onto the door while with her free hand she examined the area behind her ear. It was puffy and swollen, still tender, no smaller—taking its time healing. After another minute she went ahead into the bathroom.

As she was about to apply her mascara, she paused, studying her reflection. She looked odd somehow, but couldn't determine why. According to the mirror, everything—eyes, nose, mouth—was right where it was supposed to be. You're going nuts, she told herself finally, and wet the mascara brush. But she wished she felt like her old self again.

"The doorman there told me the Carlson apartment was sold more than two months ago, which came as a big surprise to me," Chip told Honoria while Maybelle sat listening at her desk, twirling a pencil between her fingers.

"She never said a word about moving," he went on. "Anyhow, I've tried all the places and every last person I can think of, but nobody seems to know where Mrs. C. is. As far as I can make out, you and May are the last people to have seen her recently. It's strange," he said, badly bothered. The morning so far had been one upset after another. "If she was moving, or going south for the winter, why wouldn't she tell anybody? It makes no sense. Something's going on, and I sure wish I knew what."

"Where was she when you last spoke to her?" Honoria asked.

"I'm not honestly sure. Back when DeeDee and I first started dating, Mrs. C. said if I ever needed to contact her but wasn't having any luck I was to call her lawyer's office. When I couldn't track her down last week, I left a message there. She called me back inside an hour. We talked for a couple of minutes and I asked her if she'd talk to you. She said she would, and that was that. I have no idea where she was calling from. Then, this morning when I phoned, her lawyer's secretary told me Mrs. C. has been checking in for messages every day for a couple of months now—from about the time, according to the doorman, when the apartment was sold. At that point, being fresh out of ideas, I left my name and asked her to get in touch with me here. I don't know what else to do."

"It sounds as if there's nothing more you *can* do," Honoria said, feeling all at once that she was missing something. It was staring her right in the face but she just couldn't see it.

"We could go by her old place and ask if she left a forwarding address with the doorman," Maybelle suggested.

"I already asked him," Chip told her. "She left word she could be reached at East 66th Street until last Thursday."

"But no mention of going to Florida?" Honoria asked, gazing out at the park across the way. The trees shivered in the wind, sending sprays of accumulated snow drifting across the frozen ground. Thin strands of smoke rose from a few of the chimneys in the Hooverville.

"Nope. So what do we do now?"

Moving away from the window, Honoria thought a moment before saying, "Now I think we should head down to Tiffany's and see if the jewelry's still there."

"How many will there be for dinner?" Ruth asked from the doorway.

"The three of us and you, sweetheart," Honoria

replied, on her way out of the office.

"But what about Mick?" Chip asked, then comically clapped a hand over his mouth.

Honoria gave him one of her devilish smiles and patted his cheek as she passed, saying, "Mick told me all about the confab you three had last night. It's okay, my darling. You haven't spilled the beans."

"In that case, why isn't he coming?"

"If you want him to, phone up and invite him." Honoria opened the closet to get her raccoon coat.

Chip looked questioningly over at Ruth.

With a shrug Ruth indicated, Why not?

"Okay, then. I'll do it." Chip went off to the telephone in the living room.

"Fine." Honoria sat down to pull her galoshes on over her shoes. She did it quickly because lowering her head caused it to start aching. When she stood upright, the ache at once stopped.

"Would somebody mind telling me what's going on?" Maybelle looked first at Ruth, then at Honoria, then back at Ruth.

"You'll find out over dinner" was all Honoria would say on the subject. "By the way, I've been meaning to ask. Have you heard from Dick Whiting again?"

"How did you know?" Maybelle asked guiltily.

"I didn't. I was just wondering. So he's been calling?"

"Every evening, regular as clockwork."

"And?"

"I don't know," Maybelle hedged. "I like talking

to him. He's a nice guy."

"He's a delicious guy. Think you'll go out with him again?"

"I've already told you how I feel about that."

"You'll get over it," Honoria said blithely. "The two of you are a good match. And, besides, I think you like more than just talking to him."

Nonplussed, Maybelle couldn't think of a thing to say.

Chip spotted the salesman from whom he'd bought DeeDee's ring and, his stomach in knots, he approached the man.

Recognizing him, the tall, foppish fellow with a well-made suit and brilliantined, center-parted hair offered a welcoming smile. "Mr. Stevenson, so good to see you again. How are you, sir?"

"I'm fine, thank you."

"You're here for the ring, I assume."

"It's still here?"

"It is. I'll go get it for you."

Relief flooding his system, Chip smiled at Maybelle but she didn't notice. Brows drawn together, she was watching Honoria at the counter opposite, being shown a selection of men's jewelry by another smartly turned-out salesman. "What's the matter?" Chip asked in a low voice.

"Have you noticed the way she keeps turning her head to the right, as if she's developed a tic?"

"No." He, too, now looked across at Honoria.

"You watch. She's done it half a dozen times since

I got to the apartment this morning."

The two of them kept their eyes on Honoria as she examined a handsome pair of burnished-gold cufflinks. And, sure enough, her head turned, seemingly of its own accord.

"Maybe she's got a stiff neck," Chip said. "I turn that way sometimes when I've been sitting for hours over a textbook."

"Maybe," Maybelle allowed, convinced this was completely different.

"I'm sure it's nothing," Chip said as the salesman returned.

Maybelle continued to watch Honoria, worried.

"Here you go, Mr. Stevenson." The salesman opened a satin-lined box to reveal the simple platinum band with its half-carat brilliant-cut solitaire.

At the sight of it, Maybelle let out a low whistle. "That's a beauty, Chip."

"It surely is, Miss," the salesman agreed proudly. "VVSI quality, a fine stone."

"I can't believe DeeDee didn't come pick it up," Chip commented to Maybelle.

"Forgive me for eavesdropping, but the young lady did indeed pick it up, sir, when she came in to ask for a refund of the deposit on the pearls."

"And you gave it to her?" Chip asked, his stomach knotting again. He'd been hoping to use that money to buy Christmas presents, among other things.

"No, sir. We didn't. The young lady was *not* pleased. I had to explain that, since it wasn't she who'd paid the deposit, Tiffany's couldn't refund the money without your approval. She got very angry and demanded to see the manager."

"Oh, boy!" Chip said under his breath.

"The manager told her the same thing and offered to let her use the telephone to call you, but she made a rather offensive remark, grabbed the ring, and stormed off. We were sorry but . . . Well, I'm sure you can understand Tiffany's position in a case like that."

"I certainly can," Chip said, almost giddy now with relief. "And if it's not a problem I actually would like my deposit back."

"Certainly, sir. I'll see to it at once."

"One question," Maybelle put in.

"Yes, Miss?" the man responded pleasantly.

"If Miss Carlson took the ring with her, how did it get back here?"

"Oh, her mother returned it and said Mr. Stevenson would be by to pick it up."

"I don't suppose you remember when that was, do you?" Maybelle asked.

"Let me think." The dapper fellow posed, one arm folded across his chest, the other elbow resting on it as he tapped a manicured forefinger against his graying temple. "It was several weeks, possibly a month ago. I'd like to be more specific, but I just don't remember. I do remember her, though. Such a gracious woman." It was clear that he was wondering how she could have given birth to so ungracious a daughter. "I do recall her saying the engagement had been broken, and asking if we'd hold the ring until you came in for it, Mr. Stevenson."

"Thank you for clearing that up," Maybelle said, intrigued. Mrs. Carlson had returned the ring before DeeDee died.

"Happy to oblige, Miss. Now if you'll excuse me for a minute or two, I'll arrange for the return of your deposit. Oh, it'll be a bank draft," he said apologetically. "I hope that's all right, Mr. Stevenson."

"That'll be fine," Chip told him. "Thank you very much."

"Very good, sir." The man smiled and went off.

"Well, what d'you make of that?" Maybelle said. "Mrs. C. brought the ring back, saying the engagement was off. What d'you suppose prompted her to do that?"

"Beats me. But I sure am glad she did." It was true, Chip realized. With every passing hour he was feeling less stricken by DeeDee's death. Imagine creating a scene in Tiffany's! The awful thing was he could easily picture DeeDee in one of her snits. When she didn't get her way she could be very unpleasant.

"Are you, Chip?"

"Yeah, I am. If I'd heard last week about what Mrs. C. had done I'd've been pretty miffed. I mean, as far as DeeDee and I were concerned, the engagement was definitely *on*. And I thought Mrs. C. liked me."

"Oh, I think she does."

"But she didn't want me to marry her daughter."

"Maybe she was doing you a favor, Chipper." Maybelle put a hand on his arm. "Maybe she was trying to save you from making a big mistake."

"So you think we were wrong for each other, too?"

"Afraid so."

They fell silent, watching as Honoria paid in cash for the cufflinks.

"She's buying them for Mick," Chip murmured, tickled by the prospect of their reconciliation. He'd always liked Mick and, after their talk the night before, he liked the man even more. So what if he'd put on an accent? No harm had been done. He wasn't any different than before. And it was kind of a relief not to have to puzzle out some of the more peculiar bits of syntax he'd used. *Please bring to me from the newsman a paper, Chip.* Chip smiled to himself and shook his head.

"Maybe she's buying them for Leonard Rosen," Maybelle said.

"Nope," Chip said confidently. "They're for Mick. Bet you five bucks on it."

"No bet," Maybelle said. "So, what's the story on this confab last night?"

"Mick explained to me and Ruth what had happened."

"And that was?"

Honoria was coming around the counter toward them. "I'll fill you in later," Chip promised.

"All set?" Honoria asked.

"I'm just waiting while they write up a refund

check for my deposit," he said happily.

"Well, well, well. A break for a change. That's just swell, Chip." Honoria looked at the time, then opened her handbag, pulled out a ten-dollar bill, and gave it to him, saying, "I want to run across town for an hour or so. Take May to lunch, then go do some Christmas shopping or admire the decorations on Fifth Avenue. I'll meet you both at two o'clock in the lobby at the Ansonia and we'll take another look around the apartment."

"Run across town to do what?" Maybelle asked, eyes narrowing.

Honoria chucked her under the chin, saying, "Don't be so suspicious, May. It's nothing sinister, just an errand I've got to do."

"Okay," Maybelle gave in, but with misgivings. "Seems as if you and I have a date for lunch, Chip," she said as Honoria moved briskly through the store and out to the street, where a cab immediately pulled up to the curb. She climbed in, spoke to the driver, and the cab moved on.

"Fine by me," he said, his mood now much improved. "I'm going to enjoy being seen around town with a beautiful girl. It'll enhance my image no end."

She laughed and punched him on the arm. "You're way too young for me, kiddo."

"Word is Dick Whiting's giving you the rush."

"Where did you hear that?" she asked, shocked.

"Minnie Morgan happened to mention it when we spoke on the phone over the weekend. Am I out of line, May? I'm sorry if I am."

"No, it's okay. You just caught me off guard."

"He's awfully decent," Chip said seriously.

"I think so, too. Let's go eat. I'm starved." *Going to have to watch your step, girl. Gossip travels fast in these circles.*

Mick came to the door in his shirtsleeves and broke into a grin at the sight of her. "Have I won the Irish Sweepstakes?"

"Nope, only my curiosity. And, before I forget, thank you for the flowers."

He stepped back, swinging the door open wide. "You're welcome. Come in," he invited. Enormously pleased, he watched her push off her galoshes, shoes and all, then walk in her stockinged feet into the living room to take a slow look around.

"Nice," she said of the uncluttered, white-painted space with its modern, streamlined furniture. A pair of long, pale gray sofas faced each other, separated by a low, glass-topped coffee table. All were positioned upon an exquisite predominantly blue, old Persian carpet. Gray and blue figured drapes were gathered at either end of the windows. A large, splendidly rendered impressionistic oil painting of a young woman bathing a small child was the only piece of art. "*Very* nice. But then, why wouldn't it be? You've got impeccable taste."

"Especially in women."

"You flatter me."

"No, I tell the truth. Care for a tour?"

"Absolutely. Mind if I shed my coat?"

"Allow me." He moved behind her to help her off with it, but she leaned back against him, asking with a wave of her hand that took in the entire place, "Is this who you are, Mick?"

Putting his arms around her, he answered, "I guess so. But if necessary I could change."

"No one would want you to do that."

"No?"

"You know what occurred to me about twenty minutes or so ago in Tiffany's?" she asked, relishing the solidity of his embrace, the comfort it always offered.

"What?"

"You've taken a hell of a lot on faith, Mick. Not once have you asked about my life before we met."

"I figured if there were things you wanted me to know you'd tell me. Maybe that's faith, or acceptance, or both. The fact is I don't *care* about *before*, Honor. I only care about you and me and now."

She didn't speak for several seconds, then shifted inside his arms to look into the depths of eyes that never failed to meet hers straight on. "That's faith and acceptance, by my sights. Which is why, a short while ago when that occurred to me, I stopped feeling like a fool."

"Really?"

"Unh-hunh."

"Well, that's wonderful, because you're not a fool. *I* am."

"You're not, either. Tell me this. Have you ever

lied to me, Mick?"

"Not if you don't count my putting on the accent, no. I never would."

"What about those fantastic stories about the cold in Siberia?"

He laughed and smoothed her cheek with the back of his hand. "All right, that was a stretch. But you've obviously never been to Montreal in the winter."

"It's that cold, huh?"

"They've got a patent on it. If you don't believe me, I'll take you for a visit, let you find out for yourself."

"That won't be necessary. I believe you."

"Am I forgiven, Honor?"

"Not quite, but we're getting there."

"That's good, since I'm coming to dinner tonight. It could've been awkward."

"It still might be. Nobody's filled Maybelle in yet and she's sniffing the wind."

"You're making her sound like a basset hound. I doubt May would appreciate that."

"You've got to be the one to tell her," she warned. "I refuse to start feeling foolish again, and if I have to explain all this to her I will."

"Fair enough. I'll tell her what a schmuck I was, and apologize. May I come home now, please?"

"I haven't made up my mind yet."

"Okay." He kissed her cheek, then the tip of her nose. "I thought you were going to take your coat off. Aren't you kind of warm in that thing?"

"A tad."

"So, let's take it off." He undid the buttons, lifted the heavy coat off her shoulders, dropped it over the back of the nearest sofa, then looped his arms around her again. "My favorite dress," he observed.

"Not surprising, since you picked it out."

"I *do* have good taste. So what would you like to do now?" He kissed the side of her neck, breathing in her perfume.

"The tour?" She wanted to slow things down, get answers to her questions before he succeeded in distracting her.

"Okay. One tour coming up." Unwinding his arms from around her, he took hold of her hand. "That's the foyer," he said quickly. "This, as you can see, is the living room. Over there"—he pointed off to the right—"are the dining room and kitchen, staff quarters. And over this way"—he towed her along the hall to the left off the foyer—"are the bedrooms."

"Not so fast! I want a chance to see everything. How many bedrooms?"

"Four. Ridiculously big place for only one person, but I got it for a song."

Glancing into spacious, empty rooms as he hurried her past, she asked, "Two bathrooms?"

"Three." At the end of the hall was the master suite. They paused at the door and stood looking in. "Thirty-two-hundred square feet," he said. "I like to have plenty of room to move around, hate feeling cramped."

"I know that. I don't like it myself." Against the far wall was the biggest bed she'd ever seen, with half a dozen oversized thick pillows stacked against the oblong, upholstered headboard. Three of them on one side were dented and the bedspread was folded back. An open book lay face down on the slightly mussed bedclothes.

"I was reading," he said.

Squinting, she tried to make out the title, but it was in French and upside down, to boot.

"Baudelaire, *Les Fleurs du Mal,*" he told her.

She nodded, gratified.

Beside the bed was a large marble-topped table bearing a squat, round lamp with an umbrella-like paper shade, several more books in French and English, an alarm clock, and a silver-framed photograph of the two of them, taken by an impossibly beautiful young woman the night they'd gone to see Josephine Baker at the Casino de Paris.

"I forgot all about that photograph," she said.

"It's the only one I've got of the two of us in Paris."

Why, she wondered, had she never realized how sentimental he was? Perhaps because he'd made concessions on a scale that had never occurred to her: moving in to her apartment and adapting himself to her lifestyle rather than insisting—as the majority of men would have done—that she be the one to make the concessions.

"We could knock down a wall or two," he said, lacing his fingers through hers, "and Ruth could have her own apartment, completely private. You could use the bedroom next to the living room as your office. Chip's things would be here for whenever he's in town, and there'd still be one bedroom left for guests, or for when May spends the night."

"You've got it all figured out, huh?"

"Just thinking how best to put the space to use, that's all."

"I have another question," she said, leaning against him again, her eyes on the immense bed as a churning started up low in her belly. "Why have you consistently interrupted us when May and I are working?"

"What time of day is it usually when I do my interrupting?"

"Afternoon."

"*Late* afternoon, more like early evening. By which point the two of you have been hard at it for eight or nine hours."

"That's what my work's all about, Mick."

"I know what your work's about, Honor."

"Oh?" She looked back at him. "Meaning?"

"I think it's what kept you going for a long, long time. Now it's become a habit."

"What is it you think you know about me, Mick?" she asked, daunted by his acuity.

He sighed and once more looped his arms around her waist. "I know about working until you're ready to drop because the rest of your life's a washout; I know how when you go out for an evening it's with someone you like well enough but don't particularly want to see a second time. I know about feeling separated from people because you're different, because you never feel a hundred percent yourself with more than a couple of people; because even when you're speaking the same language, half the time the majority of the population doesn't get your humor, or even know what the hell you're talking about because you're so much brighter, so much more aware than they are. That's what I know about you. Sound right?" he asked softly.

She nodded.

"I'm greedy about you, Honor. I want more time to watch you eat; more time so we can talk and dance, or go uptown to hear some music. I want more time just to look at you, or to spend making love, because every minute I spend with you is a full sixty seconds, not fifteen or twenty because my attention's wandering. Maybe in a few years I'll get less greedy—but don't count on it. You're the only person, ever, I'm always happy to see. I can't wait to find out what you're going to say or do next because you're the most completely unpredictable woman I've ever known. So," he wound down, "I come and interrupt for two reasons. One is to remind you that you don't have to hide behind a barricade of scripts anymore. That part of your life's over now. And the other reason is because it's been too many hours since I've had you all to myself."

"Well," she began, then had to stop.

He drew her closer.

"I'm not accustomed to being understood," she

342

said at last.

"I know that," he said quietly.

"Why me, Mick?"

He pressed his lips to her temple. "It's your turn to answer a question. Why *me*, Honor?"

She thought back to finding that grave in a country churchyard, and afterward the train trip down to Kent through countryside greener than anything she'd ever seen—painfully, piercingly green; then the channel crossing to Calais, where she boarded the train to Paris. Late in the day she'd arrived at the hotel feeling numb, and had gone down to the dining room because she couldn't bear to stay in her room with only sorrow for company. So she'd freshened her makeup, changed clothes, and made the effort. Once there, she wished she'd stayed in her room after all. She wasn't hungry and she'd have liked to get very, very drunk.

"I was in a mood far beyond blue, almost into black," she said. "Nursing a gin and tonic when what I really wanted was to drink gin straight from the bottle until I was beyond caring; ordering food when the smell of other people's dinners was making me queasy. I looked up and there you were, asking me in that thick accent if I'd like to dance. You were so, I don't know . . . so *tangible*. Big and very, very present; all faculties visibly intact. I decided instantly I was going to make love to you. I wanted to take little bites out of you, to chew on your fingers, close my teeth on your wrist, taste you from head to toe, and then bite you some more. But that's not all it was, Mick. I liked everything about you on sight—your eyes, the shape of your mouth, the sound of your voice, the size of your hands, the cut of your clothes; everything. It was as if the god I'd stopped believing in a long long time before had decided to prove he existed after all and show me he could create perfection when the mood suited him. You were precisely, specifically, what I wanted and needed. And by the end of our first dance, to 'Little White Lies'—which seems terrifically appropriate now—I was irredeemably in love with you."

"That's very flattering," he echoed her earlier remark.

"It's the truth, Mick. Now you tell me why."

"I looked across that dimly lit, rococo dining room, and you were so lovely and ripe, so visibly, proudly intelligent. I simply couldn't *believe* you were alone. Half the men in that room were looking at you, but they were intimidated. I was, too, a bit. But I *had* to find out if you were everything you seemed to be. So I walked over—a journey of what felt like several hundred miles—to ask you to dance. Why? Because I knew you were as lonely and alone as I was, and just as sick and tired of trying to figure out why you bothered leaving your bed every morning. I wanted a lush, world-weary, all-grown-up woman to be my lover and friend; someone who already knew the facts of life and didn't need to be taught, because I'd long-since lost interest in teaching anybody anything. You gave me back the enthusiasm and excitement I'd thought was gone forever. I knew you on sight. And when you looked up at me and smiled that smile of yours, I was a goner. I loved you."

"It's the stuff of a truly bad script," she said, smiling.

"Or of an epic novel. It would depend on who's doing the writing. How's the forgiveness coming?" he asked, his hands on her hips easing her closer.

"Progressing nicely. Where on earth did you get that astonishing bed?"

"I had it made. It's *very* comfortable. Care to try it out?"

"I would *love* to."

TWENTY-FOUR

She slept deeply, sprawled on her stomach, face turned toward him, limbs splayed as if she'd been dropped from a great height. For a time he sat admiring the rich black of her hair against the pale, flawless complexion; the strong aristocratic nose; the perfect balance of forehead and chin; the generous sculpting of mouth; the bare, vulnerable stem of her neck. He studied the shapely lines of her body—the smooth arms, small wrists, and capable, long-fingered hands; the pronounced tapering of back into trim waist, the curving flare of her hips, the length of rounded thighs, delicately delineated ankles, arching insteps, well-formed feet. He wished he had a talent for drawing and painting, or for photography. He'd have been happy to spend this time trying to capture her image, to place it on paper of one sort or another so that he could look at it whenever the desire took him. But lacking those special skills, he had to be content with simply absorbing details: the bluish sheen to her hair; the perfect ovals of her fingernails; the thin white scar near her right elbow where, most likely as a child, she'd injured herself.

Now that the lengthy charade was over and their feelings for each other were going to survive his stupidity, it was a relief to be able to communicate openly with her. He no longer had to mangle his English, and could express himself with a fullness that seemed to satisfy them both. For a long time he'd been waiting for just the right moment to confess. Yet, if Harold hadn't happened along, the pretense might have continued indefinitely because Mick couldn't bring himself to risk having her turn away from him. Now the truth was out and Honoria had all but forgiven him. She was a singularly magnanimous woman, not given to placing blame. And he was very fortunate that, ultimately, she'd chosen to see the humor in what he'd done.

At last, his senses temporarily sated with the sight of her, he pulled on his robe and went to the kitchen to fix a pot of coffee and something for them to eat. He could tell she hadn't been eating much lately. Her pelvic bones seemed closer to the surface of her skin, as did those of her hips and shoulders, and her face was growing more angular. The area where she'd been hit was still tender and painful, as he'd discovered to his upset when he'd touched it accidentally during their lovemaking and she'd been jolted as if from a massive electrical charge. But when he suggested she have a doctor look at it, she'd insisted there was no need. It was healing; she'd be fine. He could scarcely argue with her; his position was still far too tenuous.

While the soup was warming, he sliced bread and got the leftover chicken, mayonnaise, and lettuce from the ice-box. He made several sandwiches, sliced them, dished up the soup, poured the coffee, and placed everything on the kitchen table. Then, returning to the bedroom, he sat on the side of the bed, and, unable to resist, slowly stroked her until she stirred.

"I've fixed us something to eat," he said in a low voice.

She stretched lazily and turned onto her side, smiling at him. "You're hungry, of course."

"Always."

"Got something I could throw on while we eat?"

"Sure." He picked up his shirt from the floor and passed it to her.

She put out her hand to accept the shirt, saw what he'd done while she was asleep and, amazed, sat up saying, "Mick, what's this?"

"An eternity band."

"My God! It's . . ." Lost for words, she looked at the circle of large, square-cut diamonds set in engraved platinum on the third finger of her right hand, fracturing reflected light from the lamp in dazzling flashes. As she gazed at it, all at once what she'd been missing with regard to Karen Carlson came clear. And quickly reviewing her meeting with the woman in that beshrouded apartment on 66th Street, she couldn't believe she hadn't picked up on it sooner. She and May had even talked about it, but it was only now that she realized the assumptions they'd made, based in large part upon the setting rather than what they'd actually seen.

"You like it?" he asked, watching as her head turned slowly to the right and then back again, as if her neck were stiff.

"Pardon?" Distracted, she looked at him blankly.

"Do you like it, Honor?"

"Oh, I do. Very, very much. It's the loveliest gift I've ever received. But why? We've never given each other lavish presents."

"Not because I haven't wanted to. But that's another story. It's by way of apology, and to say I love you, and that it's forever. Forever being a synonym for eternity, it makes a complete circle, hence an eternity band."

"Thank you, Mick, Mike, Michael. I'll always wear it." She kissed him, then sat back to admire the ring, deciding to make another trip to Tiffany's. "If I bought you a ring, would you wear it?"

"I would wear anything you gave me, except perhaps hip waders or a hair shirt."

She laughed. "All right, then. I'm going to get you one."

"I'll wear it proudly, show it off to my friends."

"Are your friends under the impression you're married?"

"I've allowed them to form that impression," he admitted.

"And does your mother know about me?"

"I told her the day after we got back from Paris. She keeps asking to meet you, telling me to bring you to Savannah to meet her and Simon."

"What excuses have you given her for our not doing that?"

"Not very clever lines about how busy we both are."

"Does she believe you?"

"Nope. She thinks I'm hiding something."

"Smart woman. I'd like to meet your mother, Mick."

"Then you will. We'll drive down to Georgia for a visit, make it a holiday. All you have to do is say when."

She thought for a moment, her head again slowly turning to the right and then back again, before saying, "After the first of the year."

"I'll arrange it. Come eat something now."

She slipped on the shirt, fastened a few of the buttons, and climbed off the bed, only, frighteningly, to find herself falling. If Mick hadn't caught her, she'd have tumbled to the floor. It scared her, but she didn't want him to know that, so with a laugh she busied herself fastening another button. "Getting kind of clumsy in my old age," she murmured.

"Have you eaten today?" he asked, not buying her display of unconcern. He was getting more worried by the minute.

"I had breakfast. Look, I'm fine, Mick. I just lost my balance. It's nothing earth-shattering."

"Breakfast," he pointed out, "was a good six or seven hours ago, Honor."

"*What?*" She looked at the alarm clock, saw the time, and said, "Oh, damn it all to hell! I was supposed to meet May and Chip at two and it's almost five. I don't have time to eat now, Mick. I've got to get back across town and it's rush hour. I'll be lucky to get a cab."

"Wait a minute!" He took hold of her arm as she bent to pick up her step-ins from the floor. "What's your hurry? They won't still be waiting for you."

"I know, but I really have to go, Mick. It's important."

"So important that it can't wait until you eat a sandwich or have some soup?"

"I'm sorry, but it is." She had to know if she was right and that meant going back to the Ansonia.

Knowing it was useless to try to talk her out of anything once she was set on it, he released her arm. She gathered up the rest of her clothes and hurried into the bathroom. A few moments later the water started running in the sink. Deflated, he sank down on the side of the bed to wait.

When she emerged dressed about five minutes later, he tried one last time to persuade her to stay, but she said, "Mick, it's not as if we're never going to see each other again. We'll be having dinner together in a couple of hours. And right now there's something I really have to do."

"Why?"

"Don't ask me, please. We've had such a wonderful afternoon. I don't want to spoil it by arguing."

She stood for a moment searching his eyes, and, against his better judgment, he backed down. "Okay. I'll drop it."

"I'll explain later, Mick, I promise," she said over her shoulder as she flew to the living room to retrieve her coat. While he watched from a few feet away, she got on her galoshes then moved to the door.

"Lately, you're not taking proper care of yourself, Honor. It's not like you."

She smiled, put her hands on his face, pressed several quick kisses on his mouth, and said, "Don't be such a worrywart. I'll eat like a horse at dinner to make up for missing lunch." Then she opened the front door and went on her way, turning once to smile and wave good-bye.

What was so damned important? he wondered as he closed the door and headed to the kitchen. Undoubtedly it had something to do with the late DeeDee and Chip's quest for the truth. Maybe he'd have a quiet talk with him this evening, get the boy to persuade Honor to drop the whole thing.

Disturbed, he tipped the soup back into the pot, wrapped the sandwiches in waxed paper, dumped both cups of coffee in the sink, poured a fresh cup from the percolator, and sat down with it at the kitchen table. After a couple of sips he got back up and went to the telephone to call his friend Reuben Goldblatt.

He was in luck, Reuben was actually in his office and came on the line right away, asking with typical bluntness, "Mike, what's up?"

"I'd like to describe a situation to you and get your opinion."

"What kind of situation?"

"Medical."

"It's personal?"

"Very."

"Okay. Fill me in and don't leave anything out, no matter how minor you might think it is."

Honoria arrived at the Ansonia at five-twenty.

"Say, how's your head, Miss?" the man on the desk asked at once. "Quite a knock that was you took a few nights back."

"It's improving, thanks. Nice of you to ask."

"Your friends were here, you know. They waited almost an hour. What happened, you get caught in traffic?"

"Something like that. Did they go up to the apartment?"

"They talked about it back and forth but said they'd wait for you. In the end, when you didn't show, Mr. Stevenson said they'd maybe come back tomorrow. He told me if you turned up I was to say they'd see you at home for supper."

"Okay, thanks. I'm going to take a look around upstairs. I might be a while, so don't worry if I'm not back in half an hour."

"Whatever you say, Miss. Help yourself."

Even though she'd been expecting, it she was still surprised to find that the apartment had been cleared. All the furniture was gone, including the carpets and curtains. What she wanted to see, though, wasn't in any of these rooms, so it didn't matter. But without furnishings the place seemed bigger, and even spookier; her footsteps echoed off the walls and ceiling. She paused at the entry to the living room, thinking she could hear the muted, distant ringing of a telephone, and nodded to herself knowingly when the ringing abruptly stopped.

As she put her hand out to the light switch for the kitchen, she stopped, turning to look through the window just beyond the doorway that she'd failed to notice on her first visit. She wouldn't have noticed it now except that the removal of the curtains on the far side of the light shaft provided a clear view of a section of the hallway leading to the front door. Moving close to the glass, she counted two further windows to the left, and three smaller ones to the right, in the servants' wing. Interesting. She put on the light and walked along the short hall to the kitchen proper.

The faint aroma of cooked food lingered in the air, and the heavy, scrubbed wood table and chairs she remembered from her previous visit still sat toward the far end of the room. Opening the cupboards she found a supply of staples—sugar, flour, salt and pepper, rice, a bag of ground coffee, a small canister of tea, a half-loaf of bread, a jar of mar-malade, a box of soda crackers, one of tea biscuits. A little more looking turned up some pots and pans, a few plates, several mismatched cups, and a cheap set of cutlery. After closing the cupboards, she went over to the door leading to the servants' quarters. It was locked, but she'd expected that, too, and sorted through the keys on Chip's ring until she found the one that opened this door. As she turned the key in the lock, she distinctly heard the sound of another door quietly opening and closing. All as expected, but still she felt a quick frisson of alarm. What if she was wrong? No! She was *not* wrong.

For such an enormous apartment, precious little space had been allocated for servants. The first bed-room was no more than ten by ten, and it contained only a metal single bed with a bare mattress that re-minded her, with a pang, of the Asylum. She'd slept in a cot just like it for the first dozen years of her life. If she closed her eyes, she could smell the harsh bleach in the sheets, feel their stiffness and the weight of the rough gray wool blanket; she could hear the night sounds of the other children— coughing, slow even breathing, random words spoken aloud from the depths of sleep, quiet crying, and now and then the snoring of a nurse, asleep over her corner desk with its dim light.

Next door to this first bedroom was a utilitarian bathroom with sink, toilet, and shower stall. But its plainness was relieved by a pair of thick white Turkish towels folded neatly on the rail and a bar of fragrant, imported soap on the rim of the sink. In the medicine cabinet were containers of Ardena Skin Tonic and Venetian Cleansing Cream, another bar of soap still in its wrapper, as well as sundry other toiletries and over-the-counter remedies. On the back of the door hung a handsome white silk robe and, beneath it on the hook, was a cosmetic bag.

The second bedroom was larger, perhaps eleven by fourteen, and fully furnished with a sleigh bed invitingly made up with crisp white monogrammed linen sheets and a thick down comforter with a pale yellow cover, also monogrammed. An oriental rug, about four by six was centered on the floor. There was an elegant little Louis XV desk below the window. On the desk top was a zippered leather writing case. A slipper chair was tucked into the far corner next to a triangular table holding a radio, and atop a fine marquetry chest of drawers positioned midway along the wall opposite the bed sat an array of photographs in sterling silver frames, along with a telephone. She moved closer to look at the photographs but touched nothing. Then, backing up, she studied the small painting hung low on the wall near the head of the bed. In oils, perhaps nine or ten inches wide by a foot high, it was of two pale pink zinnias with deep green stems and leaves against a gray-white background. Only one person painted flowers like this. Honoria remembered going to see an exhibit of O'Keeffe's work ten or eleven years earlier. She'd been powerfully tempted to buy one of the pieces but, because of the fairly hefty prices, had talked herself out of it. A serious mistake. It would have been deeply satisfying to be able to look at a painting like this whenever she wanted. Next time there was an exhibition she'd buy one of O'Keeffe's flower renderings, and perhaps position it similarly by her own bed.

At last she turned reluctantly from the extraordinarily potent painting to see a small door at the near end of the opposite wall. It opened into the cloakroom, where a modest collection of clothes on quilted hangers was tucked away at the extreme rear; below it was a row of shoes and a pair of good-looking custom-made calf-high black leather boots.

The cloakroom, she noted, ran the complete length of the adjoining bedroom, and its primary door led out to the apartment's central hallway. Fully half the rooms in this place opened into other rooms. Remembering her gloves, she turned on the light and looked around. On an ornamental shelf on the wall to her right there they were. Pleased, she tucked them into her handbag.

Then, retracing her steps, she noted with a bemused shake of her head the door facing the first of the two servants' bedrooms. Having mastered the eccentric layout of the place, she knew that this door gave onto the main corridor, as did the rather well-hidden one she recalled finding in the master suite. The oddest apartment ever, she thought. She opened this door and, staying well back so that she could not be seen from the corridor, said quietly, "I know you're afraid, but don't run away, please.

Come inside and talk to me. If you don't talk to someone about this soon it'll eat you alive."

There was only silence for a moment and she wondered if she'd overplayed her hand.

Then, "How did you know I was here?" Karen Carlson asked, stepping into the doorway, her coat over one arm, handbag tucked under the other.

"Purely guesswork. Let's sit in the kitchen, shall we?"

"If you like."

"Would you be a dear and make some tea? I could use a hot drink. I can't seem to get warm lately."

"Of course. I would like something, too. It's drafty in that hallway." Draping her coat across a chair, Karen filled a kettle.

"I was hoping you wouldn't run away when the doorman told you I was on my way up."

"I am very wearied of running," Karen said. Once the kettle was on the burner with the flame turned high, she looked anxiously over at Honoria, asking, "Does anyone else know?"

Honoria shook her head. She shouldn't have. The motion brought the headache back with a vengeance. Maybe Mick was right about her seeing a doctor. The thing just wouldn't go away. Frowning, she touched her fingertips to her temples.

"Your head is hurting?" Karen asked sympathetically.

"You don't happen to have any aspirin, do you?"

"I do. I will get you some at once."

While she was gone, Honoria sat concentrating

357

on the pain, foolishly trying to will it away. Now and then when she missed a meal she'd get a headache. Maybe if she took the aspirin and ate something it would go away. Oh, sure! Who was she kidding? Like a tiresome house guest, this headache enjoyed her company. It was never going to go.

"I have been worried about you," Karen confessed, returning. She filled a glass with water and brought it to the table along with a bottle of aspirin.

"Well, that makes us even because I've been worrying about *you*."

"Have you?" The woman looked astounded. "Why? I am quite all right."

Honoria had to smile. "No, you're not," she said gently. "We've got a lot in common, Karen. Neither one of us likes to admit it when we need some help."

"How did you know you would find me here?" she asked again, watching Honoria tip three aspirin tablets into her hand and wash them down with the water.

"Let's have our tea and we'll talk about all of it."

"You are right," Karen said. "We must do this properly, in a civilized fashion, even if I have nothing left of my life that is civilized." She opened the cupboard, got the package of tea biscuits, and brought it to the table.

"Yes, you do, my dear," Honoria corrected her. "I know how difficult it is for you to see it just now, but you do."

TWENTY-FIVE

"**W**hy did you say you were you worried about me?" Honoria asked, discovering she needed both hands to pick up the cup of tea. What was happening? First she went to climb off the bed and her legs buckled. Now her hands seemed to have no strength. It was as if the ache in her head was drawing all her energy to itself, gradually growing more and more powerful.

"I saw what happened," Karen said ashamedly. "I was staying at Lillian and Scotty Robertson's apartment—where you came to see me. But I had stop by here to collect some things I'd forgotten. I was letting myself in at the door to the servants' quarters when I heard someone moving about in the kitchen. It frightened me because no one was supposed to be here. So I closed the door and came in again through the bedroom. I was very quiet, which is why you and that unpleasant girl didn't hear me."

"Gussy?"

"Yes. I walked into the bedroom just as she was taking the box from the bedside table. I stopped and hid behind the wall. Do you know of this box?"

Honoria indicated that she did.

"She put it in her bag and started to look for other things to take when we both heard you coming back along the hallway. Gussy ran into the living room. I tiptoed out into the corridor, and ran back again to the servants' entrance. It was rather like a child's game. This apartment, it is—*absurd*." Karen smiled tentatively.

Returning her smile, Honoria said, "That's the perfect word for it."

"My daughter was completely serious about it." Karen's smile faded. "To her it was—everything. It tells a great deal about her, don't you think?"

"A great deal," Honoria agreed.

"That evening I was afraid of what might happen if you encountered that girl, so I crept through the back hall to the bedroom next to the parlor. But when you came into the parlor, I couldn't see. The only thing I could think of was to go out to the balcony and watch through a gap in the curtains. It was my hope that Gussy would leave while she had the opportunity. All she had to do was go back through Cordelia's bedroom and out the door behind the bed. But she was under the impression you were from the police. You see, I had threatened to inform them of her carrying drugs. So, instead of leaving she was watching you from the dark beyond the living-room doorway. I'm sure she thought you were looking for the silver box, and it was in her purse. But if she left how could you find it? You couldn't. There was no sense to her actions. After a minute, she moved away and I thought everything would be all right. But then, before I could warn you or do anything to frighten her away, she ran in with one of the brass figurine lamps from the bedroom in her hand and struck you with it. She stood waiting for a few moments—to see if you would get up, perhaps—then she looked in your handbag, expecting possibly to find some police identification. When she found nothing like that, she swore loudly, took some of your money, and finally went away." Eyes lowered, Karen got a cigarette from her silver case, lit it, and drew deeply on it. Then, looking across at Honoria, she said, "She hit you so hard I was quite afraid she had killed you. I came inside but couldn't think of what to do. If I rang for a doctor, how would I explain? The same if I rang the police. People would think I had been the one to hit you. I was a terrible coward. You were not conscious but there wasn't any blood and I thought this must be a good sign. I stayed with you for several minutes and then I left by the service elevator. I am *very* sorry I didn't do more."

"Don't be. It's not as if you were the one who hit me."

"But I should have stopped her."

"I don't see how you could have. It all happened pretty quickly. And from the way you describe it, it was over before you had a chance to do anything."

"That's true. Still, I feel responsible. If I had not threatened her with the police she might not have struck you."

"Let's back up," Honoria said, "and start at the beginning. Could we do that?"

"Yes, of course."

"Begin with DeeDee. Fill me in on how she got you into this bind."

"Bind?"

361

"Predicament."

Karen shook her head, uncomprehending. "My English has left me," she apologized.

"A mess," Honoria suggested.

"Ah! Yes, a dreadful mess." Karen drank some of her tea before having another drag on her cigarette.

Keeping the cup close to her mouth, Honoria took sip after sip, feeling the heat pool in her stomach as she watched sad, beautiful Karen sorting through her thoughts and finding it difficult to latch onto a starting point. "It was the absence of jewelry that brought me back here today," Honoria said over the rim of the cup.

"Oh? How is this?"

"All you were wearing the afternoon we met was your wedding ring—no earrings, not even a wristwatch. May and I discussed it after we left here. It rang a false note with her, but I thought it was merely a matter of your personal style. Today I saw the error of my assumption, and I started adding things up: the absence of jewelry, your pretending the Robertson's place was yours, Chip's discovering that your apartment had been sold, your having returned his engagement ring to Tiffany's.

"With hindsight, so many of the things you'd done suddenly seemed logical. If you no longer have your own home but don't want anyone to know it, you simply 'borrow' an impressive apartment. If most of your jewelry is gone, wear none, and make it appear to be by choice. If there are questions you don't care to answer, hide yourself away where no one's likely to look for you. And where better to hide than here? The rent's paid up for several more months, and the sale of the furnishings would provide you with a little nestegg so that you don't have to spend any of your dwindling capital.

"It made sense, as I've said. But what if I was making more assumptions? The answer had to be in this apartment, so I came to have a second look and found just what I'd expected: you, hidden away here."

"You are very clever," Karen said in a near whisper.

"Will you tell me about it?" Honoria asked coaxingly.

The woman's hand trembled as she held the cigarette to her mouth, took a frantic puff, and put it out only half-smoked. Then she grabbed handfuls of her hair as if wishing she could pull it from her scalp. Her face made suddenly older by pain, she looked off into space as tears spilled from her eyes.

Honoria didn't move, didn't speak, gripped by the plain view of such naked suffering, remembering all too well the barren landscape of interior devastation. Only the passage of time could clear the rubble and dull the anguish. The random kindness one sometimes encountered had the effect of deepening the sense of loss and could not be appreciated, except at a distance. But kindness and sympathy were all anyone could offer. Nothing could restore what had been lost, and that knowledge was as unbearable as the loss itself. *I lost a daughter, too,* she wanted to say but thought it would be scant comfort. If women by the dozen had lined up to tell her, decades ago, that they too had lost children, she'd have wondered why such confessions were intended to be consoling. Her sorrow would merely have been multiplied by the number of others with tragic tales to tell. There were some experiences so horrific they defied consolation. To keep on living one had, with great diligence, to put those experiences in a dark room in the mind and then barricade the door.

At last Karen freed one hand to find a handkerchief, and dabbed at her face, saying, "She was very difficult to love, Cordelia. Not at first, of course. But by the age of six or seven already the signs were there of what she would become. Always I wondered how she came to be that way, but there was no answer. Arne and I did not spoil her in the way Americans often speak of spoiling children—with excesses of gifts and too few rules. We gave to her in moderation, and she was taught right and wrong, good and bad, but the teaching seemed of no consequence to her. What Cordelia wanted, Cordelia had to have. And she would do anything to obtain it. *Anything.*" She shook her head despairingly. "I would look at her and think, *Where have you come from? Who are you?* Never have I known anyone like her. In books I have discovered women characters like my daughter and I read those books with special care, seeking an answer, but it wasn't there, ever." She broke off and reached for the teapot, refilling both their cups, her every move innately graceful and fluid.

"I had a mother-in-law like that once upon a time," Honoria said. "Only *her* desires were authentic."

Eyes widening, Karen said, "So you know how it is."

Perhaps, Honoria thought, certain people—this woman, for one—could derive comfort from somebody else's tale of loss, after all. "I know exactly. My mother-in-law took back her son *and* our daughter; took them so far away I could never get them back."

"Oh, no!" The utterance was so heartfelt that Honoria felt her composure start to crumble. Karen's hand closed around hers and there was suddenly some question as to who was consoling whom.

"Tell me about DeeDee," Honoria urged, giving the woman's hand a gentle pat before sliding her own free in order to lift her cup. She wished the aspirin would kick in and provide some relief. As each minute passed she felt worse instead of better.

With an air of helplessness, Karen said, "After Arne died, little by little she took everything. I could not make her understand that she was taking away all I had. But my explanations, my begging her to stop, were no more to her than noise. She didn't wish to hear. She *had* to have new clothes, new shoes, and in the last year or two, she *had* to fill that silver box with the white powder. At first, if I wouldn't give her the money she demanded, she would find someone else who would—her girlfriends, or the men she dated. Soon, the girlfriends wouldn't give her any more, and the boy she was seeing at that time had very little. So she began to steal from me.

"I should explain. There was a good amount of insurance money after Arne died. The apartment had no mortgage and the accountant said that if I was careful I would be able to live—not so well as before, but not so very badly, either." She lit a fresh cigarette, delicately picked a shred of tobacco from her tongue, then cocked her head to one side, asking, "How is your headache?"

Honoria made a dismissing gesture with one hand. "It's all right," she lied.

"I am beginning to know you," Karen said with a show of fondness that softened her expression. "And I think you do not like to speak of how you feel. But your eyes . . . I have headache powders. Would you like to try this?"

"Thank you. Perhaps in a while, if the aspirin doesn't help."

"Please tell me if you would like it."

"I will," Honoria assured her.

Karen drank some of her tea, took another puff of her cigarette, then said tiredly, "At first my daughter took things she knew I wouldn't notice immediately—pieces of my wedding silver I used very rarely, and small decorative items: an antique paperweight, a very valuable little watercolor sketch by Watteau, a diamond ring that had belonged to Arne's mother, my father's ruby dress studs. She forged my name on several checks until I realized what was happening and closed that account, shifted my money.

"She was a complete hedonist, wanting constant pleasure—beautiful clothes, beautiful men, and, finally, what she thought was a beautiful home: this silly place with its too many doors and odd rooms." A shake of her head, another inhalation of smoke. "After three years, I refused to allow her into my home. By this time she had made away with so much of value I knew I must take steps to protect what I had left or I would find myself penniless, with nowhere to live. The lawyer and the accountant made arrangements so that she would have no access to my money until after my death, and, without informing Cordelia of it, I put the apartment up for sale. I would have liked to go back to Denmark, but everyone has been saying there will be another war in Europe, so I decided to rent a small place and stay. You will think me terrible, but I wasn't going to tell Cordelia where I lived. I wanted nothing more to do with her."

"It sounds sensible. Given half a chance, she would have bled you dry."

"You understand many things, Miss Barlow, that others would not."

"Maybe so. Please call me Honoria."

"Thank you. Will we be friends?" Karen asked.

"Oh, I think we already are."

"I liked you very much on our first meeting. I was so ashamed of my pretense about the Robertson's apartment, but I couldn't explain what was actually going on."

"You needn't feel that way. As far as pretenses go, it was fairly harmless. There are much worse things."

"Yes," Karen agreed gravely. "What Cordelia planned to do to Charles was far, far worse. She had known him casually for quite some time, but had given him no thought. He was far too young. But when she learned through one of his friends of the great wealth he will have in a few months' time she threw herself at his head."

"I suspected as much."

"When she got him to agree to pay for the rental of this place, I knew I must do something because once she persuaded him to start paying for the things she wanted it would never end. Even if eventually he saw through her, she would make him pay and pay and pay, for the rest of his life. That's how she was: she would drink from the well until the water was gone. And I had a great fondness for the boy from the outset. Such a dear boy, so very kind-hearted, but so naive."

"Something we have in common," Honoria said. "I've loved Charlie all this life."

"He spoke of you often—Aunt Honey said this, Aunt Honey did that. He thinks the world of you."

"And I of him. So," Honoria prompted, bent on keeping Karen on track, "instead of moving into a new, smaller apartment, you moved in here to keep an eye on things."

"Yes. I sold many of the larger pieces of furniture, put the rest into storage, and brought with me those things you've seen. Of course Cordelia wanted me to give everything to her but I said no. In fact, for the first time, I played one of my daughter's favorite tricks and lied to her, said that I had no money left. I let her believe she was doing me a favor by allowing me to live here—in the servants' quarters. All those unoccupied bedrooms, but I was not to be seen. It would be too embarrassing to have people know she lived with her impoverished mother. Actually, I didn't care to be seen, so the arrangement suited me." Karen stubbed out her cigarette and again shook her head. "Until she hired Gussy.

"You see, clever as she was in some ways, Cordelia was an appalling judge of character, and a frightful snob. The girl was recommended for the job by a man who works in the building. She was young and very attractive, but it was of no consequence, because she was colored. She wanted the job. That was all Cordelia needed to know. She hired her on the spot. Gussy was so much like my daughter in her selfish ways that I was uncomfortable with her. But the fact that she could obtain the white powder was an undreamed-of bonus and Cordelia required little more of her than that. Gussy took complete advantage of the situation, did not a lick of work. She wore the uniform—Cordelia insisted on that—and answered the telephone, or opened the door to guests. She would clear dishes from the table if Cordelia had food sent in. But

Gussy refused to live in, refused to clean, or to wash a dish. She had the position of her dreams. She came and went when she chose, and delivered the packages of powder. Then she passed the money Cordelia gave her to a man named Leroy who would come up in the service elevator to collect it. I saw this exchange take place several times, but since Leroy and Gussy believed I was the housekeeper, they—like Cordelia—paid no attention to me.

"I did the cooking and cleaning. It justified my presence and let me keep watch over what was going on. Cordelia," she said with her first display of bitterness, "was perfectly happy to treat me as the housekeeper. It seemed as if she completely forgot I was her mother, so cavalier was she toward me. It was a revelation, my living here. During that time I came to the realization that Cordelia was empty, completely without feeling. Yet once I saw this I was able to give up trying, to stop telling myself this was my daughter, I must love her regardless of the wicked things she did. For many years now I *didn't* love her; I couldn't. No one who knew her could love her. Even Arne, before he died, confided to me that he feared for her future because she was so *selfish*. Ah, yes, she fooled some of the girls at school, years ago. But the others feared her. The clever ones, like Minnie Morgan, and the gentle ones, like dear Robin Applegate, were frightened by her. Because this child I bore, this creature, was not *human*. Do I shock you?"

Honoria moved to shake her head, felt the pain

threaten to grow worse if she did, and said instead, "No. It's what I thought when Chip showed me her photograph. Her eyes were flat, cold, dead. I knew there was only one reason why she'd taken up with Chip—his money."

"You were quite right. And it was why I was determined to stop the marriage." Karen opened the cigarette case, then looked over at Honoria, asking, "Would you prefer I did not smoke?"

"I really don't mind."

"Thank you. Soon I will give up cigarettes. But not quite yet. For now I have a great anxiety and I need them." She got one lit, then said, "What I did was to play another of my daughter's tricks. One evening when she was out, I stole the ring from her room and the next morning returned it to the store. When she couldn't find it she went wild. I claimed to know nothing of it, which left, to her mind, only one other person who could have taken the ring: Gussy. When the girl came through the door late the next morning, Cordelia was waiting here, in the kitchen, to accuse her. I was also here, but, to them, I might not have been. I was merely the invisible housekeeper." She shook her head wonderingly. "I saw them both with absolute clarity that morning. My daughter was a vicious, self-centered virago, and she had met her match in Gussy, who defended herself—quite rightly—with formidable energy, but also with hatred. She had only contempt for Cordelia and called her many names. When Cordelia lashed out and hit the girl, Gussy did not hesitate to hit her right back—hard. I admit I enjoyed seeing that. Cordelia was rude so often to so many people it was surprising that no one had hit her sooner. But no one had. There was a shocked silence afterward. Cordelia was stunned. And Gussy was surprised at what she'd done. But I think she had been wanting to hit someone, someone white, all of her life. She was not sorry.

"Then my daughter recovered herself and screamed at the girl to get out, she was fired. Gussy laughed and called her a dumb floozy. She said Cordelia would have to go to Harlem and buy—what did she call it? Old lady white, that was it—herself. 'See how you like that!' Gussy said. 'Won't take but five minutes for Leroy to teach you some manners.' She said she'd be happy to go but not before she got her wages and what was owed to Leroy. Cordelia told her she'd see her in hell first and pushed the girl out the door. Gussy pounded at the door, shouting at first and then pleading for the money, saying Leroy would kill her if she showed up without it. I tried to tell Cordelia it was a mistake not to pay, but she wouldn't listen, just brushed me aside. After a time, crying by now, Gussy went away. I had a very bad feeling about this.

"That same night, while Cordelia was out, Leroy dragged Gussy back here and took some of Cordelia's jewelry to cover what he was owed. I'm sure he would have taken everything of value she possessed if I had not arrived back with a friend and interrupted him. As I've told you, he believed I was the housekeeper. He made a joke about the mice playing while the cat was away, because, you see, my friend and I had come through the front door. Out of his sight, Gussy shook her head, warning me not to say or do anything that might arouse his anger. I heeded her warning. However, accustomed to having many Negroes in her household staff, my friend began to question him sharply, asking what he thought he was doing here. His eyes seemed to turn red with rage and his mouth went very thin. He pointed his hand at her as if it was a gun and told her, 'You don't talk to *me* that way. Understand?' Moving very close to her, he held the make-believe gun between her eyes, saying in a soft voice, 'You didn't see or hear a thing tonight, did you?' Frightened, she kept still. 'That's more like it,' he said. Then he gave Gussy a shove so hard she nearly fell down, and the two of them left. I hurried to lock the door and I could hear them in the hallway—she was trying to explain, he was hitting her, calling her dreadful names. It was terrible, and I knew we hadn't seen the last of either one of them. By refusing to give the girl the white-powder money, I was certain Cordelia had put all of us—herself, Gussy, and me, as well—in danger."

TWENTY-SIX

Karen stopped speaking and stared at Honoria for several seconds, watching as her head turned to the right and then back again. It was perhaps the fifth or sixth time she'd seen Honoria do this. Karen put out her cigarette and got up, saying, "I will fetch you a headache powder."

Through the spreading pain and mounting nausea, Honoria whispered, "Thank you." While Karen was gone she held her head in her hands, eyes closed. The room was warm, stuffy. She sat up, unbuttoned her coat and shrugged it off. At once cooler, lighter, she watched Karen fill a glass with cold water and bring it over to the table, where she poured the contents of a folded paper into the water, stirred it, and said, "Drink this. It will help, I think."

Honoria drank the mixture down, ignoring the slightly bitter taste of the undissolved particles that remained on her tongue.

"More water?" Karen asked. "Sometimes it leaves an unpleasant taste."

"Please."

Half of the second glass of water washed down the residue of the powder, but the bitter taste still remained. "I'm going to have to go home shortly," she told Karen in a voice lacking volume, "but I really would like to hear what happened."

"After so much effort to find me, I think you *should* hear," Karen said. "But first, is there anything more I can get for you? A fresh cup of tea, something small to eat?"

"No, this is fine." She moved to pick up the water, but instead her hand sent the empty teacup to the floor with a crash. Her headache responded to the noise like a zoo animal made wild by a child dragging a stick back and forth across the bars of its cage—it roared, raging inside its confinement.

"It's all right," Karen said quickly, collecting the fragments and depositing them on the counter before Honoria could even think of apologizing. "Don't give it a thought. Just a dime-store cup, nothing to worry about." Resuming her seat at the table, she picked up the cigarette case and held it as, again, she stared at Honoria.

After his upsetting and very specific conversation with Reuben Goldblatt, Mick took a shower and tried to plan his approach to Honoria. But everything he came up with sounded contrived and silly. It was also a complete waste of everyone's time. *Just do it,* he told himself, getting a fresh shirt and slipping it on. *Just go get her, and do it!* They could not afford to waste time.

Knotting his tie in front of the mirror, he concentrated on trying to remember what she'd said. A missed meeting with May and Chip. Definitely not at home, at the Kenilworth. No, she'd fretted about getting back across town in the rush hour. So she had gone over to the West Side. Where? It was important, but something they'd argue about. That could mean only one thing: her looking into the death of Chip's late girlfriend. What was her name? DeeDee. Where was it she'd lived? It started with an A. The Apthorp? Alwyn Court? Come on, come on, *come on*. He couldn't think. *Slow down. Think.* The

Ambassador? The Algonquin? *The Ansonia!* That was it! She'd gone back to the damned Ansonia.

Grabbing his jacket and keys he ran out of the apartment.

"My daughter didn't believe me when I told her what had happened that evening," Karen said. "She refused to believe that this man had actually had the audacity to come into her bedroom and make off with some of her jewelry. 'He wouldn't dare come in here!' she kept insisting. I told her she was taking risks with someone very dangerous, but she laughed at this, saying he was nothing, a small-time hood from Harlem; Gussy's boyfriend. He was *something,* I told her, and very dangerous. He'd be back if she didn't give him the money. Why, she argued, should she give him the money if he'd stolen her jewelry? 'That's how I know none of this is true,' she declared, as pleased with herself as if she'd cleverly solved a complex riddle. 'If he's already got the jewelry, he's got far more than I owed him.'

"She could not, would not, comprehend that the issue had now gone beyond money. She had offended him, insulted his pride. He'd taken the jewelry only to hurt her, but he would keep coming back until he got the cash. 'We'll see about that,' she said. Had I at least got the keys back from Gussy? she wanted to know. I told her I had not. That set her off again.

"It did no good reminding her that it was she who had pushed the girl out the door so that there had been no opportunity to recover the keys. Cordelia carried on for several minutes about how useless I was, then said she'd take care of this entire business herself. One could never win an argument with her and I was sick of trying. Exhausted, I went to bed. But from that night on, I locked all the doors to the servants' quarters—including the one leading into the cloakroom—from the inside. I might have been the invisible housekeeper, but Leroy was not so foolish as to believe *I* was blind. When he came back—and I was certain that he would—I wanted to be safely behind locked doors.

"But he was even more clever than I had thought. He did not come back. He simply waited for her to run out of white powder, which she did a few weeks later. I am sure she tried to get it somewhere else, but in the end she had to get in touch with him— through Gussy. She knew of no other way to contact him.

"And so Gussy returned late one evening when both Cordelia and I—not together, of course—had been out to dinner with friends. Gussy brought a package. And she was to be paid on the spot or the package would not leave her hands. Infuriated, Cordelia nevertheless contained herself somehow, and gave the girl the money. Then, to my daughter's horror, after counting it, Gussy said it wasn't enough. The price had doubled. Cordelia didn't have the additional cash. Too bad, then. Gussy couldn't give her the powder. They argued. My daughter said to take the money and give her half what was in the package. Gussy said no. She had been told not to do that. Either Cordelia paid in full or she would get nothing. Gussy put the bills down on the table and started for the door. Cordelia said she would find the money. But she had none. All three of us knew that. Cordelia asked Gussy to wait, then beckoned me to come with her.

"I must explain that while I lived here as the housekeeper I dressed very simply and kept my jewelry hidden—something not difficult to do in this crazy apartment. But when I went out to visit with friends I liked to wear the few pieces I had left, particularly my pearls."

"Which DeeDee had been wanting you to give her for quite some time," Honoria interjected.

"How did you know of this?" Karen asked.

"Chip knew."

"Ah, I see. So then you also know they had been my mother's and were very valuable. But to me they had great sentimental value."

"He told me," Honoria acknowledged, the noise in her head like malfunctioning machinery, loud and grating, demanding her attention.

"It was a wet night but oppressive. My daughter wished to talk to me out on the balcony. I hesitated, more afraid of her right then than I was of Leroy. As I have told you, Cordelia would do *anything* to get what she wanted. I knew she wanted me to provide her with the means to have that white drug. And I also knew that if I refused . . ." Karen hesitated, leaving the thought unspoken. "I did not want to go

378

out onto that balcony, yet I couldn't help myself. I stepped through the door as if in a dream, my eyes on this woman who was my child but a stranger . . . not just to me but to everyone. I don't think there is anyone who knew her. All any of us knew was what she chose to show to us. And I was forever curious to learn what she would show me next. So I stepped through the door into the heavy wet night.

"I remember looking past her at the lights glinting in the rain . . . lit windows where I could see people in other buildings, unaware they were being seen; streetlights casting pale yellow reflections on the shiny pavement, and the headlights of passing automobiles cutting the darkness and catching the rain like needles falling to the ground. I was captivated by the splashes of light, the puddles of it, as if it, too, were liquid, like the rain. There was a wind rising and it carried the rain in drifts . . . quite refreshing, really, after the closeness inside. Then Cordelia said I must give her the pearls."

It had started to snow again, fouling the traffic. Mick sat behind the wheel of the Cadillac, cursing the traffic. Overheated, he rolled down the window on the driver's side, resisting the temptation to press the heel of his hand into the horn and make a lot of noise, get people going. Doing that would do nothing to clear the jammed intersection. But he wanted to do *something*, to start *moving*. He had to get across town to Broadway but he was stuck between Fifth and Sixth. And while he sat, his hands slick on the wheel, some of Reuben's more alarming words and phrases repeated themselves inside his head, over and over, gaining in volume as if Reuben himself were sitting next to him shouting, pummeling him.

He'd experienced most of the emotions life had to offer, but fear was something new, and he was discovering he had what might be construed as a positive gift for it—at least where Honoria was concerned. The longer he sat in the traffic, inching ahead as the minutes passed, he found his new gift blossoming into a full-scale talent. He was scared, and it was having a profound effect on his entire being. He was sweating, yet his insides felt as if they were being flushed with ice water. His heart was racing, drumming in his ears. His legs were shaky, and his right foot had started to bounce around, making it hard to keep the brake depressed. He wanted to abandon the car and take off running. He'd get to the Ansonia a lot faster on foot than he would in this traffic. But he needed the car, and he needed to get across this immobilized city.

In Montreal people knew how to drive in snow. Here, the moment it started falling, they went into a panic, started doing stupid things. In Montreal he could have got off the main streets, traveled quickly along laneways to his destination. But New York hadn't been built with anything as sensible as alleys that ran behind most streets, offering access to back doors and the garages situated behind the majority of houses.

Pedestrians, heads down against the gusting snow and accelerating wind, were moving at a good clip while the vehicular traffic hadn't gone more than half a block in ten minutes. He imagined having a car out of some science fiction tale that could project a ramp from under the hood, thus allowing him to drive across the roofs of other cars; or one that could fly. What the hell was holding everything up? He leaned out the window, craning to see ahead, but all he got was a blast of sharp-edged wind-driven snow in his face.

Shops were closing up for the day. Warmly lit restaurants looked appealing. But this was no time to be thinking of food. His stomach felt shriveled to the size of a walnut—another side-effect of his new-found talent. He was being garroted by his starched collar and undid the top button, at once able to breathe more easily. His fist pounded the steering wheel as he sat listening to the smooth hum of the engine, longing to be able to floor the accelerator and shoot across town.

As she had on the afternoon Honoria and Maybelle had called on her at the East 66th Street apartment, Karen drifted off, gazing into space. Looking at the woman through what seemed to be a red haze, Honoria wondered why she was persisting with this when all she wanted was to be at home in her bed, resting her head on a yielding feather pillow. She wanted something to stop the pain before it overwhelmed her like an avalanche. Ruth's icepack, perhaps, or a double shot of neat scotch, or an injection of some kind. She'd never experienced pain like this, not even giving birth. "Karen, tell me," she said in a whisper, desperate to get to the end of this and go home.

"I am sorry." Karen's eyes came back into focus. "It is not pleasant for me to speak of this."

"It'll be worse if you don't talk about it. Believe me, I know."

"I do believe you." Karen sighed, then squared her shoulders. "Cordelia wanted me to give her pearls worth many thousands of dollars to pay for fifty dollars' worth of *powder*. Can you imagine such a thing? I said it was out of the question. Then, her eyes on my throat, she insisted I must give her all the cash in my bag. I stood there, thinking this one last time I would give her the money. After that she would have to find some way to manage on her own—which, of course, I knew she couldn't do. Before I could begin to tell her this, she grabbed at the pearls, and all at once I had had enough. I was tired of having to hide what I owned; tired of playing housekeeper to this ungrateful, greedy stranger; tired of trying to love someone so undeserving of my affection. I pushed her away, saying I'd had quite enough of her. She would get nothing from me. The pearls broke in her grasp as she lost her balance. It seemed to happen like a film in slow motion. A look of surprise on her face, she fell back and went over the balcony. I couldn't believe what I was seeing. One moment she was there, the next she was not.

There wasn't a sound, except that of the traffic below. I hurried to the edge of the balcony and looked down to see her land—like a child's dropped doll—on the roof of an automobile."

Giving herself a shake, Karen said, "I couldn't absorb what I'd seen. It didn't seem real. I stood looking down, waiting for her to get up and come raging back into the building. But she didn't move and I knew she was dead. Common sense told me she couldn't have survived such a fall. And, I confess to you, one part of me was immensely relieved. It was over. Never again would I be subjected to her tempers and demands. Another part of me was filled with sadness because I had given a life that had been badly used, and now, inadvertently, I had taken it away. I didn't know what I should feel—my emotions going everywhere at once—and I don't know how long I remained there, looking down at what had been my daughter, but at last I thought I must leave. The police would come soon and were they to find me there they might not believe it had been an accident. In the dark I collected all the scattered pearls I could find, put them in my pocket, then went to the staff quarters to tell Gussy she must go. But she was already gone, the package of powder still on the table. Again, I was relieved.

"After I collected my things, I hurried to put the package in the silver box in Cordelia's bedroom. I couldn't think where else to put it, and there was no time to dispose of it. Then I locked up, took the service elevator down, and went, as had long been planned, to East 66th Street. Once there, though, I couldn't rest. I kept reliving that moment when Cordelia had grabbed for the pearls and I pushed her away. I thought about Chip and how he was free of her, saved from making a frightful mistake. That was good. I thought about the life my daughter might have had if she'd been a different sort of girl. That was sad. I thought also about what I should do now that I had no family left. I was alone; and a part of me felt optimistic, and another part despaired. It was as if I were riding a carousel of emotions, around and around, up and down, making me light-headed, confused.

"Through the night, while I waited for the police to ring me, I sat smoking, drinking many cups of coffee, staring at that exquisite painting, over the mantel, of those two pretty Victorian girls who so re-minded me of my cousin and myself. I wished I could disappear into that painting, that I could go to sleep and wake up young again on a summer's af-ternoon at the seaside with all my family—the grandparents, the aunts and uncles and cousins. I wished that my life in America had been nothing more than an awful dream." A tear slid down her cheek. Absently, she wiped it away with the back of one hand as she reached for her cigarette case but didn't open it.

"I'm sorry," Honoria said softly.

"Yes," Karen said. "I am, too. So much ugliness. And then, when I thought it was over at last and I might begin making some small plans for the future,

I returned that night to see Gussy steal the package of powder, then attack you. I am certain Leroy must have been very angry that she left it. So he sent her back here to retrieve it."

"I think she saw what happened, and that she was still in the apartment when you left here."

"The night of Cordelia's accident? Why do you think that?"

"Because when they found her body she had some loose pearls in her pocket."

"*Her body?*" Karen's face froze with shock. "She is *dead?* My God! How could. . . ?" She stopped, then said, "Leroy. He must have killed her. But why?"

"Maybe just for the hell of it," Honoria murmured, bending her head into her hands. "Or maybe he was angry because things had gone wrong. In any case, it appears he made her inhale the cocaine until she didn't know what she was doing. Then he left her outdoors in a cardboard box, on a bitterly cold night, to die."

Karen shook her head, eyes hollow now. "Perhaps he will come back to kill me, too."

"I doubt it. Did Gussy know you were living here?"

"No."

"Then you're safe."

"Safe," Karen repeated, frowning. "I am responsible for my child's death and perhaps for the death of that girl, too."

"No, you're not," Honoria disagreed. "And where Leroy's concerned, you don't figure into any of it.

You were just the housekeeper who's probably gone on to another job."

"The housekeeper," Karen echoed, watching Honoria massage her temples. "The headache is no better, is it?"

"No." Eyes closed, Honoria swallowed the fluid that kept collecting on the floor of her mouth—a certain prelude to vomiting.

"Perhaps if you lie down . . ."

Mick pulled up in front of the building, took the key from the ignition, and ran inside.

"Honoria Barlow," he said to the man on the desk. "What apartment did she go to?"

"Who?"

"Tall woman, black hair. She was supposed to meet a couple of kids here earlier."

"Oh, right, her. She's upstairs in the Carlson place. Lemme phone up."

"There's no time for that! Just tell me the apartment number!"

"Can't do that. Sorry. Give me your name and I'll phone up."

Mick reached across the desk and grabbed the man by the lapels, lifting him right out of his chair. *"Tell me the apartment number!"*

"Jeez! Okay, okay." The man told him the number and Mick let go of him.

Slapping a piece of paper down on the desk in front of him, Mick said, "Call that number! Tell them Mick's on his way. I'll be there inside twenty minutes. Got that?"

The man looked up at him, his face filled with questions.

"*Got that?*"

"Yeah, yeah. I got it."

"It's an *emergency!* There's no time to kid around. Make the call!"

"Okay." He unhooked the receiver as Mick raced to the elevators.

Thirty-five goddamned minutes to get across town and now he was in one of the slowest elevators in North America. His fingers digging into his palms, Mick watched the floor indicator as the elevator climbed, whispering, "Come on, come on, *come on!*" When it stopped and the doors slid open, he looked both ways up and down the corridors, trying to figure out how the numbers ran. A false start to the right, then he reversed and tore off in the other direction.

The pain had control of her, distorting her vision, turning her stomach. Lurching to her feet, she made it over to the sink just in time. Solicitously, Karen stroked her back as Honoria retched into the basin; tears streaming down her face. Then Karen wet a cloth in cold water and bathed Honoria's face, saying, "You must come lie down in my bed."

The smaller woman put an arm around Honoria's waist, saying, "Come," and Honoria turned blindly as the pain seemed to explode inside her head. Crying out, she pressed both hands to her head.

As he was running past the door, Mick heard the cry and stopped, backed up, and pounded on the door.

Afraid to let go of Honoria, Karen didn't know what to do.

"OPEN THE DOOR!" a man yelled. "OPEN IT NOW!"

Honoria was sliding away. Unable to hold on to her, Karen tried to ease her down. The pounding on the door grew harder, the man's voice louder. After a moment's indecision spent watching Honoria curl up on the floor, Karen ran to the door.

"Where is she?" Mick demanded, moving inside.

"Who are you?"

"Mick. Where *is* she?"

Responding to his urgent authority, Karen said, "Here. This way," and led him to the kitchen. "She's very ill. I don't know what to do."

Mick saw Honor on the floor and hurried to her. "Honor?"

"I think I'm dying, Mick."

He could scarcely hear her, and she looked terrible—deathly pale, eyes sunken. "You're not dying. Can you get up?"

"Sorry. I don't think so."

"Doesn't matter. I'll carry you." Bending, he got one arm under her knees, the other around her back, took a deep breath and rose to his feet.

"What can I do to help?" Karen asked frantically.

"Can you drive?"

"Yes."

"Can you drive in snow?"

"I am Danish. I can drive in *ice*."

"Good! Reach into my left pocket. The keys are in there. Now run ahead and get the elevator."

Karen fished out the keys, grabbed Honoria's handbag and her own, then ran. Honoria nearly a dead weight in his arms, Mick followed as quickly as he was able.

The elevator doors were opening just as he got there. Karen pressed the button, the doors closed, and they began their slow descent.

Honoria moaned, the pain eating through her brain like acid.

Terrified, but refusing to succumb to it, Mick held her to his chest, saying, "You'll be okay, Honor. I'm taking you to the hospital. You'll be okay." The slowest goddamned elevator in the entire Western Hemisphere. "You'll be fine, Honor. Just hang on. It won't be long."

TWENTY-SEVEN

Mick climbed into the back seat with Honoria on his lap, the left side of her head resting against his shoulder, while Karen slid behind the wheel, urgently asking, "Where are we going?"

"Mt. Sinai. Fifth and 100th. Can you figure out how to get there?"

"Yes. Tell me please how to bring the seat forward, also how to turn on the lights and the wipers."

He did. Then the engine roared to life, the lights

and windshield wipers went on, and, after a glance at the oncoming traffic, Karen spun the wheel, put her foot to the accelerator, and went fish-tailing into the road. Mick opened his mouth to comment, but the woman instantly corrected and got the heavy car headed uptown. She *could* drive in ice. Reassured, he turned his attention to Honoria, who was whispering something he couldn't quite hear.

Leaning closer, he was horrified by what she was saying.

" . . . pray for us sinners, now and at the hour of our deaths. Oh, my God, I am most heartily sorry . . ."

"Don't say that prayer, Honor! You're not going to die."

"I am, Mick. The pain, it's . . ."

"No! Don't think that! I won't *let* you die." Holding her closer, he said, "People are waiting to look after you at Mt. Sinai. You're going to be all right. I promise." With his handkerchief, he began gently to dry her eyes and clean the mascara from her cheeks. One eyelid seemed to be drooping and the sight of it set off a flare of panic in his chest. "I know it's bad," he crooned, "but it'll be over soon. My friend Reuben Goldblatt's waiting to help you, Honor. He's a fine doctor, the best. You'll be good as new once you're in his care."

Her body was taut, battling the pain, every muscle tensed. "I can't stand it, Mick. It's as if there's a razor slashing away inside my head."

"Hold my hand. Squeeze hard and try not to

think about the pain. We'll be there in a couple of minutes. Talk to me."

Her nails cutting into the fleshy part of his thumb, she looked up through the red haze, barely able to focus on his face. "I want to tell you something."

"Tell me anything," he said, giving her a smile. "I love the sound of your voice."

"For so many years I told myself I didn't want to care; I wouldn't be a mug and fall into that trap again. It wasn't true, but believing it got to be a habit I couldn't break. But next to Zoe and Charlie, I've loved you best, Mick—even with the bogus accent." She tried to return his smile but didn't quite make it, her eyes tearing uncontrollably. "You're never boring."

"Neither are you."

"And you're the best dancer ever."

"You're not bad yourself."

"I wish I'd spent more time with you, Mick."

"Your work's important. I wouldn't dream of trying to take you away from it."

"Ruth and May, you, me and Charlie, we were like a family. And that's made me very happy."

"Correction. We *are* a family, and we'll continue to be one. You're everything I care about, Honor. When you're well again, we'll take a holiday; drive down to Georgia to visit my mother and Simon, maybe spend a week in Palm Beach, or sail down to the islands."

"Somewhere warm would be nice, Mick. I'm so cold."

He looked up and met Karen's eyes in the rearview mirror. "Put the heat on, would you, please?" he asked. "The control knob is just to the right of you on the dashboard."

At once she did as he asked and a rush of warm air filled the car.

"We'll get you warmed up in no time," he said, as Honoria's grip on his hand eased, and she was suddenly heavy, limp. The panic threatening to overwhelm him, he pressed his hand to her chest and felt the reassuring surge of her heart beneath his palm. But she was no longer conscious—a bad sign.

"*Go faster!*" he called to Karen. "*We're running out of time!*"

"We are almost there," she replied, swerving out into the oncoming traffic to pass several cars before easing back into the right-hand lane. The car shimmied as the tires hit icy ruts, but, again, she corrected, maintaining her speed. "94th Street. Only a minute or two more."

Keeping hold of Honoria's hand, he started whispering, "I won't let you die, Honor. I won't. Just hang on. A few more minutes and we'll be at the hospital. You're strong. You can do it. Don't dissipate your energy praying to be forgiven for sins you didn't commit. Use that energy for your life, Honor. It is *not* the hour of your death. We've got twenty-five or thirty years ahead of us. Maybe more. And we're going to enjoy them. So don't give in and surrender. Fight this. You can *do* it. Do it for me, because I love you and I wouldn't be any good without you."

Traveling at better than forty miles an hour, Karen swung out again to pass several more cars, then cut hard directly in front of another car, whose driver slammed on the brakes and honked his horn indignantly, to pull up in front of the hospital. Without bothering to turn off the engine, she leaped out, threw open the rear passenger door, then got out of the way as Mick climbed from the car with Honoria. Shouting for help, he burst through the emergency-room doors to be met by two attendants and a medical resident hurrying toward him with a stretcher.

"Put her down!" they ordered. "We've got to get her right up to surgery. Dr. Goldblatt's standing by."

With the greatest care, he deposited Honoria on the stretcher. Then the trio of men went speeding away with it toward the elevators. Mick stood for a moment, lost, then ran after them, squeezing into the elevator just before the doors closed. During the ride up, while the resident lifted back her eyelids to shine a light into her pupils, Mick again held Honoria's hand, and remained bent close to her ear, whispering. *Live for me, for all of us. Don't let go, Honor. So many people love you.* Then the doors opened, the stretcher shot forward, and Mick ran alongside, all the way to the doors to the operating room, where one of the attendants stopped him, blocking his way.

"You can't come any further. There's a waiting room down the hall," he said, pointing. "Get yourself a cup of coffee. Try to relax, have a smoke. Someone'll be out to see you the minute there's any news."

Winded, crazed, Mick collapsed against the wall, bent nearly double as he tried to catch his breath, the litany ongoing inside his head. *I won't let you die don't you die you can't die. We all love you, need you, don't die.*

Twenty minutes later, he and Karen were sitting side by side in a drafty little waiting room down the hall from the operating room, sipping cups of stale coffee, staring at the puddles on the floor, the thick snow swirling beyond the window, the stack of tattered magazines on a small table.

"My name is Karen," she said at last, breaking the silence. "Would you like a cigarette?" She opened her case and offered it to him. He took one. She lit it, then her own.

"What were you doing there?" he asked, noticing that his hands had acquired a tremor. They fluttered without something to grip, and his shoulders, arms and back ached.

"I have been living in the apartment."

He turned to look at her—a beautiful woman, her fine features were drawn with concern. "How do you know Honor? Explain to me what was going on when I got there."

"I am Cordelia's mother." Seeing his confusion, she clarified, "DeeDee."

"Oh! Her mother." It explained nothing, but he was so preoccupied with what was going on down the hall he was unable to form sequential thoughts.

"And you are the husband of Honoria?"

"As good as," he answered.

"I like her very much," Karen said in the way of a shy child who's found a new friend. "She isn't like most of the women I have met in New York."

"She isn't like *anyone*. You're a hell of a driver, by the way. Thank you for getting us here so fast."

"You are most welcome. I have put the car on Fifth Avenue, very nearby."

"Good, good," he said absently, and took a drag on the cigarette. He pictured his friend Reuben cutting into Honoria's skull, shuddered, and blinked the picture away. The fear was, if anything, larger than before; the cold rushing through his bowels as sweat trickled down his sides. If only there were something he could do, anything. Having to sit there, waiting, was sheer torment.

When Ruth, Maybelle, and Chip arrived a few minutes later, he thought, *We are a family; we care deeply for one another,* and wondered why he hadn't realized it sooner. Jumping up, he threw his arms around all three, gathering them to him.

"Any news yet?" Maybelle asked.

"Not a word," Mick answered.

Karen had risen from her seat upon the arrival of the other three and now stood, thinking perhaps she should go. But Chip came over to give her a hug, saying, "Mrs. C. How are you? How come you're here?"

"She drove us," Mick explained. "Got us here in no time flat. This is Ruth," he introduced the housekeeper. "And I think you've already met May."

"I have, yes," Karen said, as she extended her hand to Ruth, then to May. "I am so sorry for all that has happened."

"It's going to be a while," Mick said. "We might as well sit down."

"I reckon we could all do with a bite to eat," Ruth said, thinking she'd never seen Mr. Mick look so wretched. "I'll just go see what I can do about that, shall I."

"I'll come with you," Chip volunteered.

The two of them went off, and Karen said, "Perhaps I should be going."

After seeing her display of affection toward Chip, Maybelle hastily revised her previous opinion of the woman, and said, "But you'd like to stay, wouldn't you?"

"I would, yes. If I may."

"Then stay by all means," Mick said.

Maybelle slid into a chair, saying, "I'm confused. How did the three of you come to be together?"

"She came to find me at the Ansonia," Karen told her.

"Why there?"

"That is where I have lived since Cordelia moved to that apartment."

"How come nobody knew that?" Maybelle asked.

"I didn't wish anyone to know."

"But Honoria figured it out," Maybelle said.

"Yes, she did. She is very clever. No one else guessed."

A number of rejoinders came to her mind, but

Maybelle chose not to give any of them voice. Somehow she knew Karen was not responsible for Honoria's getting hit on the head. That lay, one way or another, at DeeDee's feet.

Karen opened her cigarette case and once more offered it to Mick, who automatically took one. He leaned in as she lit his cigarette, then sat with his arms propped on his knees, head lowered, eyes focused on the floor as he smoked.

Maybelle took off her coat, then got up and went to stand by the window, watching the snow blowing this way and that, at some moments appearing to be flying upward. She could see very little beyond the snow, an instant of light, then darkness. When Mick had phoned earlier, she'd taken in the words, but their import had been delayed, perhaps by the gush of adrenaline that had sent her flying through the apartment to get Chip and Ruth and bring them here. Now, filled with dread, she thought she could smell sickness in the very air of this place. She hated the smell—like a gauze bandage left too long on a suppurating wound; below the heavy scent of disinfectant, it reeked.

If Honoria died . . . No. She couldn't die. But if she did. God! Maybelle felt her lungs being crushed. Honor was her mother, her sister, her best friend. Without her, what would May be? Where would she go? What her grandma had said about her feelings for Honoria was true. In the end it wasn't the color of the skin that mattered but the person who lived inside that skin. Honoria was everything—teacher, staunch ally, mentor. If she died . . . Unthinkable. Turning her eyes toward the invisible sky, she spoke silently—as she did every Sunday—to the God that lived near enough to keep an eye on the sparrow.

"She'll recover from this, mark my words," Ruth was telling Chip as they headed for the cafeteria. "You're not to worry, dear."

"I can't help it. They're operating on her *head*, Ruth. That's serious business."

"It is," she conceded. "But you've got to have faith."

"We should've *known*."

"Dearie, you were off at school. *I* should've known, perhaps. Or May. The truth is we had no way of knowing. Miss Honor kept insisting it was nothing. At the best of times it isn't easy to argue with her. But when it concerns her health, it's impossible. She's got no time for being unwell, won't acknowledge it. What's one supposed to do with a woman like that?"

"I don't know," he said.

"She claimed all she had was a rotten headache from getting coshed. Would you have challenged her, love? Because I wouldn't have dared. And Mr. Mick and May wouldn't have, either." Putting an arm around his shoulders as they walked along, she said, "It won't do any good to have you imagining the worst. For all we know, by the time we get back upstairs with the food she'll be out of surgery, on her way to being well again."

"I hope so. I really hope so. Ever since Van died, Aunt Honey's been the only one who's given a damn about me. And this whole thing's really my fault. If I hadn't begged her to look into DeeDee's death she wouldn't be in surgery right now."

"Listen, dear. Miss Honor wouldn't want to hear you talking this way. It was her decision to do what she did. You may have asked, but if she hadn't wanted to, she wouldn't have done it. Frankly, I think she and May were enjoying themselves, playing detective. Now, you come along and help me organize some food."

Mick sat thinking about what Reuben had told him over the telephone a couple of hours earlier. "It sounds like an epidural hematoma. These things can take days, even weeks, to develop. But you've described classic symptoms, Mick. You've got to get her in here right away so I can remove the clot before it's too late."

Before it's too late. Why had he bothered to stop and take a shower? Or to spend time trying to think how best to approach her on the matter? He'd squandered precious minutes. *Too late.* They'd been waiting almost ninety minutes now. He straightened and looked at his plate of untouched food. The sight of it turned his stomach. The others had all eaten a little, but he couldn't manage even a single bite. And if he sat one minute longer he thought he might start screaming. "I'm going to stretch my legs," he said, standing.

"Mind if I come with you?" Chip asked.

"I don't mind. We'll be just down the corridor," he told the three women.

Only Ruth responded, nodding. Maybelle was back by the window, hands on either side of the frame, fixedly staring out. And Karen sat smoking, sorrowfully gazing into space, her eyes glazed with unshed tears.

"Mick," Chip began, "I feel—"

Mick cut him off. "I think we all feel guilty. Let's not talk about it. Okay?"

"You, too?"

"In spades. Tell me something. Who's Zoe?"

"Zoe was Honoria's daughter."

"*Was?*"

"She died, a long, long time ago. I guess Aunt Honey didn't tell you."

"No," he said, choking. "She didn't."

"I didn't know either, until the other night. She said she'd never told anyone, but I didn't think that included you."

Stricken, Mick stopped and sagged against the wall, covering his face with his hand. Even without knowing the details, everything made sense now, as did her remarks in the car. Begging forgiveness for sins, real or imagined. Christ almighty, but life was sometimes very damned hard. A daughter lost long ago. No wonder she'd convinced herself it was dangerous to care.

"You okay, Mick?" Chip put a hand on the man's shoulder. "I could get you some water, if you like."

400

"I'm okay." Mick dragged a handkerchief from his pocket, dried his face, and blew his nose. Then, going with the impulse, he embraced Chip because he was Honoria's first remaining love and for that reason alone he'd have cherished the boy. Holding Chip away by the shoulders, he looked into the clear blue eyes and said, "No matter what happens, don't ever feel guilty. She did this for you because there's no one in the world she loves more. We do what we can for the people we love, Chip, because, when it comes right down to it, that's all there is. I wouldn't want it any other way. Whatever the outcome here, you and I and May and Ruth have to agree not to blame ourselves. Honor would hate it if we did. Right?"

As if mesmerized, Chip said, "Right."

"And one more thing. I'm here for you if there's anything you need."

"Thanks, Mick."

Releasing him, Mick saw the doors to the operating room open and Reuben coming through them. Breaking into a run, Mick flew down the corridor toward him, his nerve-endings popping like firecrackers; his coordination out of whack so that he seemed to be lurching from side to side, making slow progress—toward either the end of all he'd come to value or forward into those twenty-five or thirty years he'd promised Honoria they would have together.

His heartbeat like drums in his ears, he ran, filled with equal parts dread and hope. *Don't let her die she can't die.* The longest run of his life, more fraught with peril than convincing distant relatives and complete strangers to leave everything behind and flee their homes with him as their guide. It seemed to take hours to get from one end of that corridor to the other, and he was so frightened. He couldn't read Reuben's demeanor, couldn't read his expression. *Is this the beginning or the end? Don't let her die.* As in one of those dreadful dreams of trying to become airborne only to find oneself weighted down by invisible anchors, he moved, as if through congealing mucilage, toward his friend.

And then, as the gap closed to only a few feet, Reuben smiled.

EPILOGUE

DECEMBER 31ST. 1934

SCENE:
Interior Apartment at
the Kenilworth--Evening;
wide shot

It is New Year's eve and a party is well underway. The doors between the living and dining rooms have been opened to accommodate the guests, and the fireplaces in both rooms are alight with crackling, aromatic logs. The dining table has been shifted to the far end of the room for the occasion. Both dressed in their best, Ruth and Birdie Robinson, Maybelle's grandmother, are chatting away as they arrange platters of food on the table. A trio of jazz musicians—piano, bass, and drums—plays in the corner of the living room by the window.

The camera pans slowly across the room and we see Chip, clad in a new tuxedo, hair slicked back and eyes sparkling, dancing with Minnie Morgan, who looks particularly well this evening in a simple long black dress, her spectacular fiery hair flatteringly arranged in a Gibson-girl topknot. We see Leonard Rosen in an impeccably cut black suit, crisp dress shirt, and polka-dot silk bow-tie. He is sitting on the arm of the sofa near Karen Carlson, who has, for the occasion, abandoned her customary black garments and is lithely elegant in Grecian-style draped red chiffon; they are enjoying each other's company, and that of Reuben and Sarah Goldblatt.

Among the dozen or so pairs of dancers are a euphoric Roberta Applegate and her debonair husband, Brian; Pete Hennessy, the sports reporter from the *Daily Mirror*, with his wife, Lou; and Maybelle and Dick Whiting. Maybelle seems surprised to find herself in the arms of Mr. Whiting, yet is obviously not unhappy to be there. They are a remarkably handsome pair.

The camera moves on, finding Honoria and Mick.

Medium Shot

They are standing very close together in the corner of the room, beyond the fireplace. Honoria wears a bias-cut black satin evening dress with a slashed neckline that sits precisely on her shoulder blades. It has long tight sleeves and a plunging back. On her head is the beaded and sequined mesh evening hat from the twenties she has unearthed from the darker recesses of the dressing room. It fits snugly, rather like a bathing cap, and most flatteringly; it successfully conceals the shaved area of her scalp and the healing incision.

In the week and a half since she was released from the hospital, her days have been strictly regimented. In the aftermath of the surgical removal of the hematoma that was—on the verge of rupturing—pressing further and further into her brain, she has suffered from slight motor impairment and mild aphasia. Two hours each morning have been spent

406

working with Chip and Maybelle. To help restore her skills, the pair of fond disciplinarians have daily given her increasingly difficult spelling and grammar tests, both written and oral. And for ninety minutes every afternoon, Karen Carlson comes to demonstrate and assist Honoria in stretching and strengthening exercises. Throughout the day Ruth pushes food at her, anxious that she regain some of the fifteen pounds she has lost. In the evenings, she reads aloud from a series of novels to Mick, who listens with pleasure and corrects her when she makes the occasional error. He has also encouraged her to sing, in her husky contralto, all her favorite songs, and is quick to join in, providing both the music, by means of the upright piano he bought for the purpose, and the lyrics when she falters.

Her recovery, as a result of everyone's efforts, is--according to Reuben— nothing less than astonishing, and she is very nearly back to where she was. She still has a slight limp and, when she's tired, gets a little wobbly on her pins and tends to misspeak. But nobody minds, least of all her. Were it not for Mick she would not be here tonight, celebrating the arrival of a new year. She admits it's uncharacteristically mushy of her, but she feels that Mick has given her her life, in more ways than one. So, despite the frustration of not being in complete control either of her limbs or of the injured part of her brain that controls speech and perception, she is more content than she ever imagined it possible to be.

The trio finishes their rendition of "I Get A Kick

Out Of You," and everyone applauds enthusiastically.

Mick takes Honoria's hand, saying, "This is our dance."

Apprehensive, her balance still somewhat precarious, she says, "I don't think so."

"You have to. I made a special request." He smiles and tugs on her hand.

The trio begins "The Very Thought Of You," and, feeling a catch in her chest, she looks up at him and says, "You asked them to play that?"

"Unh-hunh. Come on."

They move into the center of the room and, as his arm slides firmly around her waist, he says, "It's just like riding a bike. You don't forget how."

She laughs, but he's right. Her body remembers this. And her brain remembers the lyrics.

The very thought of you and I forget to do the ordinary things that everyone ought to do . . . I see your face in every flower . . .

She closes her eyes and lets her head rest against his shoulder, confident that he will not let her fall.

Slow Fade out